MW00575778

THE ROACH

RHETT C BRUNO

www.aethonbooks.com

THE ROACH

Print and eBook formatting, and cover design by Steve Beaulieu. Artwork provided by Luciano Fleitas

Published by Aethon Books LLC.

CHAPTER ONE

I tossed a bottle into the river and watched it drift across polluted water. I couldn't see my reflection—nobody had seen anything but brown in the Horton River since the settlers bought this land for pennies, let alone now in the 1980s. But I knew how I looked—like a homeless, raving lunatic wandering Iron City in a costume, begging for change. I'd spent a lifetime lurking in the shadows, and now I could roam down the busy streets and go unnoticed.

The sludge lapped at the concrete pier of Horton Point beneath me, and I wondered what the papers would write after someone fished me out.

THE ROACH RESURFACES IN THE HORTON RIVER AFTER FIVE YEARS.

MISSING VIGILANTE FOUND, WASHED UP WITH TRASH.

Or maybe I would keep floating. The thing might have been dirty as shit, but it had a strong current. My bloated corpse could get dragged for miles, lost in the thick fog until some simple fisherman saw what he thought was driftwood. Man, would he be in for a surprise. Most likely, I'd never be found again, relegated to the action figures on local comic bookstore shelves alongside the far more famous, made-up superheroes. Forgotten.

I think I'd prefer that.

I rolled my wheelchair an inch closer until my legs dangled over the pier's edge. How far is too far? I'd been asking that question every second of every day for five years now. One last push, and I could finally know for sure.

Some people called me a monster for killing. Some, a hero for who I killed. Not one of them didn't have it coming, that's for damn sure.

Now, there was one last life to be taken. What do you think? Should I do it? End this before I'm too old and decrepit to wipe my own ass? More than halfway there already.

All the shipping workers helping to revive my city after its many factories fled overseas had already gone home to their families. An abandoned car factory to my right stood like a rusty temple to some capitalistic god of manufacturing. Its spire, a great iron chimney, was just one of the many across the skyline that had worked so hard to drown the city in an eternally drab haze.

There was a joke that blue skies never shined over Iron City. Jokes are only funny when they're excruciatingly real.

I sat alone at dusk. My only companion was the breeze, heavy with the familiar, fishy-dead-animal stench of polluted water mixed with roasted peanuts from a food stand around the corner.

Closing my eyes, I pictured the tears running down Laura Garrity's face. She was the last person I'd ever saved. I imagined the coked-up crotch stain who forced her into an alley lying bloody at my feet, and that rookie cop caught in the right place at the right time putting a bullet in my spine.

My fingers gripped my wheelchair's worn pushrims so tight my knuckles blanched. I rolled it another quarter of an inch. I was so close to being free... and then I heard it—the familiar squeal of someone in trouble.

"Fuck."

My eyelids snapped open.

I know, I know. So close, why stop now? But that kind of scream got me salivating like Pavlov's dog. It was instinct. Visceral.

Another cry rang out, followed by the distinct *thud* of a body hitting concrete. My chair whipped around before my brain could refuse. My devil of a foster dad always rattled on about how you can't teach an old dog new tricks. Bingo. The asshole was right about one thing.

I raced across Horton Point toward the alley, following the sounds of struggle. The shriveled husks I had for legs bounced as I crossed bumps and potholes. I ran over one of a dozen fliers for Mayor Garrity's re-election campaign littering my streets, then rounded the corner of an abandoned warehouse on Ferris Avenue so fast I almost tipped.

Two kids were beating up on another. He was no older than fifteen, mixed-race with dark skin, darker freckles, and a mop of curly hair that didn't quite fit. A pair of thick glasses magnified his dark eyes, and he wore a ratty, bright green Jansport backpack using both straps. He reminded me of the first person I'd ever saved—Steven Dixon—the one kid I was close with back in the foster home where I grew up. Not the way he looked exactly, but the way he cowered like an abused dog.

His bullies had to be seniors in high school, at least. Maybe even legal adults. Probably dropouts. Two future gangsters and wife-beaters from Harborside practicing their trade.

"Just fork it over, Isaac!" the taller of them shouted before kicking their flinching victim in the gut.

"Yeah, Isaac," snickered the other. "Is it really worth getting your ass kicked again?"

"Leave me alone!" Isaac cried out.

"Or what? You gonna go home and tell your mommy?"

"Maybe I'll pay her a visit," the taller one said. "She's hot for a ni—"

Isaac unleashed a pathetic grunt and charged. One bully grabbed his backpack and yanked it up over his head while the other tripped him. He fell hard, his glasses skidding across the pavement.

"Hey, why don't you two head on home!" I hollered, my voice gravely from a half-decade bender. The liquor on my breath was so pungent even I could smell it, and my vision was too blurry to even read the graffiti covering the brick walls.

They glanced up at me, and even after all this time, it surprised me when someone regarded me without trepidation. Iron City's underworld once feared me. I was the Reaper of Iron City. The Haunt of Horton River. The Roach. Fearless vigilante willing to do whatever needed to be done.

Someone stole a purse from an old lady, they lost some fingers.

Someone murdered, they lost their life, too.

Someone took a young woman or a child into a dark room and had their way with them... they lost the part of them they held most dear.

Instead, the two bullies looked like they'd just heard a good joke. They turned away from their groaning victim, nudging each other and sneering like two idiots.

"Go home, gramps," one said, obviously the leader. Taller, fitter, and wearing a tough-guy tank top under an open, black leather jacket despite the brisk weather, like he was already part of the local chapter of the Iron Riders Bike Club. He probably excelled at sports in school and little else.

"Yeah, this don't concern you," laughed his chubby sidekick. He looked like a little Hostess Cupcake ready to get the cream squeezed out of him.

Naturally, I rolled toward them. I knew how I looked. I couldn't quite remember putting it on before leaving my house, but I wore my old suit made of reinforced leather with a Kevlar weave and some light plating at weak spots like the kidneys. It had too many rips at too many seams to count. The Roach logo on the chest used to instill fear, but it, like me, had seen better days. Faded to a barely legible red splotch.

I must've looked like I'd been struck by a bus on my way home from a comic book convention. Like a joke. I didn't even have my mask on.

I guess I'd figured when I was fished out of the lake, the ungrateful city I guarded could finally know my face. Not that they deserved it. In fact, the very thought of them knowing churned my stomach. More likely, I'd just drunk too much and forgot the mask.

None of this was well-thought-out. My suit had been locked up for all these years, but some mornings you just wake up, toss back a few bottles of Jack, and it's clear what needs to be done.

"Back up, old-timer," the leader said. I'd like to believe I was still middle-aged, but I guess to him I was old as sin.

"Yeah," Chubster chimed in. "What do you think you're the Roach, wearing that?"

I stopped a few feet away. Close enough to smell the body odor of the pubescent punks. Close enough for them to whiff the whiskey on my breath.

"What happened to make you two like this?" I asked. "Mommy didn't give you enough milk?" My gaze fell toward their nether regions. "Or maybe you inherited something a bit too small from daddy."

"Bum's got a mouth on him, huh?" the leader said. "What, you think I won't hit you cause you're in a wheelchair?"

"Trust me," I said. "This chair is the only thing keeping you from being sent home crying. Now, leave the kid alone and beat it."

"Or you'll what?" He circled around behind me, cackling. "Run over my foot?" He shoved my wheelchair hard, and his sidekick caught it by the armrests on the other side.

"Yeah, what're you gonna run over our feet?" the chubby kid said.

"I just said that, moron."

"The next one of you who touches me is going to need a cast," I growled.

"Oh yeah?" the chubby one poked me in the side of the head. He beamed ear-to-ear afterward, like he'd just won a gold medal in being an asshole.

All I could muster was a sigh. I used to take down drug lords, pimps, mobsters, and murderers. I used to make front-page news in the *Iron City Bulletin.*

He tried to poke me again, emphasize his point. He never made contact. Before he knew what hit him, I'd snapped the finger and shoved him into the wall. I went easy on him, made it a clean break. He wouldn't need surgery or anything, but he'd damn sure learn a lesson.

"You crazy, old asshole!" he howled.

That was usually when things de-escalated these days. It took a special kind of dirtbag to strike a guy in a wheelchair, even in retaliation, but I'd apparently found them. The leader grabbed my chair's push bars and tipped me over. His foot zoomed toward my gut. I caught it and twisted, flipping him to the ground. But, of course, he flailed like a wounded wildebeest, and his Doc Marten boots cracked me in the jaw.

As the Roach, I was as familiar with getting hit in the head as an NFL linebacker. No longer. Chubby-chubs jumped in while I was dazed. I took a fist to the head. A foot in the ribs—and those Docs were definitely steel-toed. I felt the bruising even through my suit.

I used my forearms, blocking as much as I could, educated by a lifetime of absorbing blows. But fighting isn't like hopping back on a bike. It doesn't just come back to you—especially when you're drunk. The muscles I had that still worked were weak. Untrained.

When the assholes finally backed off, the one I'd injured said, "He ain't getting back up, man."

"Good. Old prick." The leader spat on me, then they ran off. They had something to say to the underclassman they'd beaten on their way by, but my ears rang too loud to hear. All I noticed was the chubby one crunch his glasses, cracking the lenses and bending the frame.

With effort, I rolled onto my back. A bit of blood coated my gums with that all-too-familiar tang of iron. My first instinct was to laugh. It made my sore ribs sting, but I couldn't help it.

"Thanks..." their victim, Isaac, muttered. His voice still hadn't dropped despite his height.

My head lolled over, and I saw him kneeling nearby, scrounging up his broken glasses. He winced, then pulled his thumb in and sucked at it. Instead of prostrating himself at my feet, he looked like he wanted to hit me.

"My pleasure," I replied.

"I was being *facetious*," he said, emphasizing the word that was probably on his latest vocab test. "They're gonna kick my ass even worse next time. Why couldn't you just stay out of it?"

"I'm wondering the same thing."

Isaac seemed fine in retrospect. Dog tags hung crookedly from the silver chain around his stringy neck. That was apparently what the bullies were trying to take from him: a memory of a father or someone else who'd died in a war that'd never affect us on this side of the pond. I couldn't even remember which one was being fought.

He put his hand on my arm to help me up.

"Hands off, kid," I said, slapping him away.

"You're hurt."

"I already got my ass kicked by two runts today. I don't need a third helping me up like I'm some sort of cripple."

"But... You are."

I glared at him, and the color drained from his cheeks. Now that was the reaction I expected when people came face-to-face with me. The one I longed for. Isaac stayed quiet while I crawled across the pavement toward my chair. My head still rang, but I was able to flip it upright and position myself before it.

Then came the hard part: raising my booze-filled body sculpted from withering muscle and worthless legs I wasn't sure why the doctors hadn't just cut off. I got about halfway, arms shaking from the strain before Isaac assisted me the rest of the way. I didn't notice until afterward since he'd grabbed my boots.

"I said not to touch me," I snarled, giving him a shove. Even as weak as I was, it sent him stumbling and me rolling backwards.

"Fine," Isaac groaned. "Whatever. I just couldn't watch that anymore."

"Yeah? Do me a favor, kid, so I don't need to swoop in and save you again. Next time those two racist pricks try to steal that thing around your neck, kick 'em in the nuts and run away. That's the beauty of having legs."

He stood tall, soft belly poking out from under a shirt one size too small. "My father told me never to back down."

I eyed his dog tags. "Yeah? And look where that got him."

I started to roll away just as Isaac's eyes got watery, and his cheeks flushed red. I wished I could take it back. Sometimes, I snap, either because I drank too much, or the world is shit or any other of the million reasons. The kid didn't deserve it, even if he was ungrateful for the help like everyone else in Iron City.

But good advice is good advice. Some people simply aren't meant to fight, and even though he wasn't the smallest kid for his age, he may as well have worn a note on his backpack that said BULLY ME. Others, well, I'm still kicking... figuratively speaking.

So much for that lucky reporter who might've found me washed up in the river.

CHAPTER TWO

An empty bottle clinked against concrete. My eyes blinked open to see my empty, scarred palm where it had been. I never had many friends, but Jim, Jack, and Johnnie never let me down. The next best thing to ending my miserable life was whiskey—scotch, bourbon, didn't matter. Getting lost in that amber hue...

I rubbed my face and went to swing my legs off my cot. They didn't move. It was nothing new, but you'd think after five years, I would be used to it. From time-to-time, my mind would play tricks on me like I could still feel something. Phantom limbs, they call it. Man, the human brain is a fucking cunt.

Rolling off my floor-cot instead, I grabbed a chain hanging from the ceiling and used it to lift myself into my chair. I had no clue what time it was. Somehow, my Roach suit was off and tossed haphazardly on the floor. Fresh, purple bruises covered my ribs, accompanying a smattering of age-old scars.

"Damn, kids," I grumbled, like the old hermit I'd become.

I put on a pair of pants in all the painstakingly long ways it took my broken body to do so. By the end of it, tugging on them left my arms so sore I didn't even bother buttoning my shirt. I just shoved my arms through, trying to ignore the pops and creaks of my bones.

My wheel caught on my old Roach suit as I turned. A multi-colored SuperBall rolled free. I vaguely recalled picking it up as a gift on my way home from Horton Point when I bought the bottle of Johnnie Walker to help dull the pain.

I strained my aching abdomen as far as I could, bending to pick it up. Laura's daughter Michelle would love it. She didn't talk much, but she loved anything colorful. Kids are easy when they aren't yours. It's no wonder so many parents fuck it up.

I stuffed the ball in my pocket, grabbed my suit, and rolled out along the grated catwalk encircling the *Roach's Lair*. The press would've called it that if they had any idea it existed. It was my control center in an old service node for a sewage line, abandoned along with the factories and football stadium that once made Harborside the most vital district and historic downtown in a city that was once important.

An array of big, bulky monitors, surveillance systems, police radio monitors, and a self-destruct button rested in the center, unused for years, covered in dust and cobwebs. Under it sat dozens of crates packed with empty folders once stuffed with pages of intel on criminals across the city. I had to give it all up after I got shot, though not entirely by choice. Thank you, Mister Mayor.

Against a nearby wall stood a lighted, upright display case with a naked mannequin inside. It usually wore my uniform when I wasn't taking it out for a suicidal spin. Presently, it only wore my mask—a painted gas mask with two tubes in the front like insect antennae.

The thing *actually* covered my face. Not like some flimsy domino mask heroes wear in the comics, their mouths, noses, and chins all exposed. How dumb do you have to be not to recognize that?

The red bulb flickered periodically, but otherwise illuminated my entire lair. Behind me, a hole broken through the concrete wall sealing this station remained black as the ace of spades and led into a seemingly endless tunnel offering access to Iron City's vast underground sewer-system. The stink of stale sewage seeped through, pleasant now after so long.

My display case remained open from when, in a drunken stupor, I'd apparently decided to don my old suit. What had I been thinking?

I considered redressing the mannequin, like usual, but I couldn't muster the energy. Instead, I tossed it over the thing's shoulder, closed the glass, and entered the code on the keypad to lock the case. Then, turning around, I ran my fingers along the desk of my control station. A layer of filth peeled away, so copious it turned my pale flesh a mustard shade of brown. I glanced up at the newspaper clippings arrayed on the empty stone wall above the desk. They were brown too, aged and worn. I couldn't help but chuckle. Here I was, the infamous Roach, living amid darkness and grime like a real insect.

All those headlines. If those reporters could only see me now. It was like the sad shrine to a high school scholar-athlete who'd never done a damn thing with the rest of his life. Going from "Blue, forty-two. Hike!" to, "You want small, medium, or large?", if they weren't out causing trouble and getting caught by me.

I'd kept every newspaper mention of my exploits for as long as I can remember. I'd even recorded news on VHS from the TV in the early years. The good and the bad.

They weren't trophies, however much it might have looked like that. Not to me. They were reminders of how people really are. Same as the news stories: the good, and the far more frequent bad.

THE ROACH BREAKS UP MAFIA GAMBLING RING ON BLEAK STREET.

That was a real old one.

SUSPECTED PEDOPHILE MINISTER FOUND CRUCIFIED OUTSIDE SAINT DONOVAN'S CATHEDRAL.

That one was a little too poetic. He'd died for his sins just like his idol, with all the pictures of his victims scattered at his feet. I always did have a romantic side.

HERO OR VILLAIN? CITY DEMANDS THE ROACH COME FORWARD AFTER SHOOTOUT AT HORTON POINT LEAVES THREE UNDERAGE GIRLS DEAD.

Yeah, at the same shipping yard in Horton Point I'd almost rolled off a few hours earlier. Romance. Poetry. That's just me.

Of all the stories pieced together by hacks without all the information, that last one was one of the few to ever bother me. Maybe the only one. That the sheeple I'd spent so long protecting could think I would purposely hurt, endanger, or *kill* young girls made my blood boil.

How was I to know that the Bratva 'soldiers' drugging up foreign girls and selling their bodies in backrooms would also use them as human shields as they unloaded on me with fully-automatics? How was I to know that after I ravaged and kicked nearly every other major gang out of Iron City, the worst would fill the void? How was I to know I'd made room for the Goddamned devil himself?

Did I go too far? Maybe. But the cops weren't going to do anything back then, and I tried my best to avoid collateral damage. I'm sure those few lost girls would have gladly given their lives if it meant no other kid would have to go through their hell—that the other girls would have a chance to escape slavery and go off to do great things.

Hell, Reagan had been the president. An actor known for hunky westerns, now leading America into conflicts like a gun-totting, trigger-happy cowboy. Anybody could be anything they wanted to be these days.

I knew Chuck Barnes, the author of that article, wrote the piece just to crawl under my skin like my moniker's namesake, but that didn't matter. I almost gave in. A decade protecting the city, and I had as much slack with the squawking hens as a mass-murderer on parole. It had me so distracted, the very next night I got shot saving Laura and was taken out of the game anyway.

That article became the last one ever written about the Roach that didn't include terms like MISSING or PRESUMED DEAD.

I dragged my hand across the page like I did every time I saw it. This time, the loose corner finally gave out, folding over and tearing away from the strip of Scotch tape in the bottom right corner. Next thing I knew, I'd ripped it off completely and crumpled it up in my fist.

"Ungrateful, sons of..." I seethed, flinging the paper ball. It bounced against a wall, then fell behind my control desk to join the spiders and the dust. My fingernails dug into my palms, drowning out the echoing memories of the gunfire and the screams.

After drawing a few raspy breaths to calm myself, I rolled onto the lift to my townhouse. The rusty, accordion-style metal door clattered shut behind me. The pulleys were in even worse shape, rusted, grinding with each movement. Every night I spent down in my lair, I wondered what would fall apart quicker: my body or the rickety elevator that sounded like a rat being strangled.

I held my breath, expecting it to give out and drop this time. I almost hoped it would. Instead, it jerked to a stop with a rumble and a loud screech. The grates folded open, and a switch signaled the hidden doorway built into a bookcase to slide open and reveal my first-floor study.

I know. How original. But it isn't my fault that sometimes movies have great ideas that any real person would never think to check in a million years.

But my bookcase wasn't like all those with big, priceless leather tomes.

"There you are," a voice called from the kitchen. I recognized it instantly as the only adult permitted inside my house. The sizzle and smell of cooking bacon practically pulled my chair across the room like a fish on a lure. Laura Garrity knew me too well.

She stood by the stove with a spatula, looking every bit as beautiful as the day I'd saved her. Her form-fitting pantsuit didn't fit the occasion, but she never looked out of sorts. The daughter of the city's long-time mayor, a burgeoning lawyer after graduating top of her class, single mother—the kind of woman that made being a hero worth it.

"You're letting yourself in now?" I said to her, then coughed. My throat burned from too much liquor and too little restful sleep.

"I knew you were downstairs," she answered.

I pulled up right next to her, accidentally ramming the counter. "I told you to never go looking down there."

"I didn't. *You* left the front door open. Again."

"I like the draft."

Laura rolled her eyes, then leaned over to observe my face. I hadn't passed by a mirror yet, but I'm sure it wasn't a pretty sight.

"Did you get into another bar fight?" she asked.

"Something like that," I said. "Where's Michelle? I got her something."

"In the living room, watching TV so low it's basically off. She didn't want to wake you."

"Now that's the smartest idea I've heard in weeks."

"And you wonder why she's scared of you," Laura remarked as she returned her attention to the pan. The bacon crackled, probably already burned. Considering how busy she was, learning how to cook well wasn't in the cards, no matter how hard she'd tried. But at least it smelled good.

"I never wonder."

I spun and rolled into my dreary living room, curtains drawn over the front windows to keep out prying eyes. Opium dens had better lighting. As expected, tiny Michelle sat on my couch, which probably wasn't sanitary enough for a child. She didn't make a peep, pulling a pillow close to her chest as I appeared. I joined her in silence.

I never was great with children. They reminded me too much of how I grew up. Even when Laura was in a pinch and she had me watch Michelle for a day here and there, we would just sit in silence. Like now. Judge me all you want, that's better than not being there at all.

What could I say to her anyway? "*Hey Michelle, I was there when you were conceived by a rapist in an alley having his way with your mother.*" Though, I suppose I did understand growing up without a father.

I checked what was on TV. *Good Morning, Iron City,* covered in grain thanks to a bent antenna. The prettied-up host and hostess were talking local politics with Election Day coming up. Mayor Garrity had a narrow lead in the polls, chasing his fourth consecutive term under his usual campaign slogan: A SAFE CITY, STRONG AS IRON. His competition, Darrell Washington, a city councilman from the Stacks, the city's poorest neighborhood, was actually putting up a decent fight this time. Especially now that the city wasn't a crime-infested nest.

Mayor Garrity liked to take responsibility for that after the Garrity Act bolstered the ICPD and gave them the tools necessary to fight organized crime. Stop and frisk, CCTV cameras all over downtown, higher precinct budgets, denying parole, lenience on warrants —the works. But really, the worst groups, like the Bratva, fled Iron City because the city was dying like all those along America's Rust Belt.

Too few jobs, too few industries... it wasn't worth the hassle for larger operations. That, and I'd hammered most of them beyond recovery.

The talking heads showed clips of marches in support of Darrell Washington's tax cuts on the lower-class causing traffic downtown, with the man himself making the rounds and supporting them. Was it that hard to figure out why he was losing? People are fickle. You mess with their routines, cause traffic, they'll hate you for it. You don't, they won't even know you exist. So simple.

Regardless, it seemed no matter who won, nothing ever really changed. It was a fucked town, run by fucked politicians, fucking people.

And poor Michelle. I'm sure watching the news in my grubby townhouse was the last thing she wanted to do before pre-school, but my busted antenna only got one clear channel.

"I have something for you," I said. I rustled through my pocket and found the SuperBall. Other than the dust from my lair, it was a fancy thing. Colorful, like a miniature version of the Earth with swirling green and blue.

Michelle stared at the toy. She looked up at me, then to her mom, who watched us from the kitchen. I saw Laura nod her daughter along in my peripherals.

"Thank you, Uncle Reese," Michelle said meekly, plucking the ball carefully with two fingers so as not to graze my calloused hand. Who could blame her?

I grunted in response, then watched as the girl gave it a few exploratory bounces. The ball glanced off the foot of the couch and rolled away, and Michelle went after it like an explorer in the Amazon.

"You know, you really don't have to keep dropping by," I said to Laura as I rolled back into the kitchen.

"Then who would make sure you eat?" she replied.

I stopped by the low cabinet, where I kept my booze. Down to my last bottle. There wasn't much of a pension for retired vigilantes. Mayor Garrity did what he could for me in the coverup of what really happened the night I met his daughter, but the payoff for an Iron City Sanitary Worker on an injury settlement was barely enough to scrape by.

I took a swig straight from the bottle. I didn't bother screwing the top back on.

"This early, Reese?" Laura scolded.

I drew my wheelchair up to my corner table and clanked it down hard. "I'm nocturnal, remember? My whole body is out of whack."

She set a plate down in front of me. Overcooked bacon, scrambled eggs, and liquor. The breakfast of champions.

"You haven't been nocturnal for... what is it... five years now?" she said, wearing a cheeky grin.

"Rub it in, why don't you."

"I'm just saying, you're going to kill yourself."

If she only knew...

I chuckled at the private joke in my head as Laura carried breakfast to Michelle in the living room, who was busy trying to reach her new ball under my cluttered coffee table. We'd given up trying to get her to sit down for a meal without things getting uncomfortable. Children that age have a sixth sense, I think. Like she could see through my shriveling shell and into my rotting core.

"Are you going to eat anything, or just stare at it?" Laura asked, returning to sit across from me.

I lifted a piece of the blackened bacon and stuck out my tongue. "Now I really regret not going through with it."

"Through with what?"

I took a bite and crunched. Nothing ruins bacon like overcooking it until it tastes like a mouthful of fresh ash. "I considered drowning myself last night," I said casually, as if announcing my plans to go grocery shopping. Laura was midway through a sip of water and nearly choked.

"What?" she asked.

"Yep. I was down by Horton Point, right near the edge. It was perfect, Laura. Gentle breeze. Quiet. It was the first time in so long, I felt like I could breathe."

"Why would you even think that?" she demanded.

"Do you really need to ask that question?"

I watched a hundred different responses, neurons firing in her brain, while her hazel eyes glinted from welling tears. It made the subtle flecks of gold and green shimmer.

"So, why didn't you?" she asked finally, returning to her eggs. I could tell she wasn't interested in them anymore, though. She just sort of shoved them around on her plate as a way of avoiding eye contact with me.

"Apparently, I'm too good at playing hero. It's not my time yet."

"I..." She exhaled. Her fork clattered on the table and she dropped her hands into her lap. Then, she looked at her daughter in the next room and said. "Maybe it's time you talk to somebody, Reese."

"I'm talking to you."

"I mean someone that can help you. With all the things I've given up asking you about because you never say anything."

I scoffed. "They'd run right out the door."

"There are people—"

"No," I said firmly. I knew all the questions. Where did I come from? Who was I before the Roach? Why did I do what I did? Blah, blah-fucking-blah. I was grateful she'd stopped pressing for answers to things she'd never want to know.

"Well, I... I don't know what to say," she said.

I reached across the table, and took her soft hand, gaining her full attention. "You've never had to say anything," I whispered. "You've never had to take care of me or keep checking in. You can stop wasting your time with a relic like me."

"You really think I'm wasting my time?" She yanked her hand free and pushed away from the table. "I come every week because, somehow, I care about you. I know who you are, even if you've forgotten."

All I could manage was a feeble laugh.

"It's not funny," she bristled.

"I know. I know."

"What then?"

"You," I said. "Still so stubborn."

"And you're not? You spend so much time locked in here wallowing that you've forgotten about all the people who'd be dead in an alley, if not for you. Sure, you made mistakes. But haven't we all?"

"So, you're telling me I shouldn't kill myself?"

She threw up her hands in exasperation. "You do whatever you think you need to, Reese. Go ahead. But I'm going to be here next week like I always am. I hope I see you."

I bit off another piece of charred bacon-ash. "Was it something I said?"

"Everything's a big joke to you."

"Laura, I'm not—"

She stormed out of the kitchen.

I turned, bumping the corner of the table, spilling more than a little of her water, then followed at a distance. Our visits ended this way more often than I'd probably care to admit. I really could be an insufferable wretch sometimes, but more than anything, in that moment, I wanted Laura to be mad at me. To not care when I returned to the river and finished what I already should have. With her around, I knew I'd never go through with it. I could blame poor Isaac and his bullies all I wanted, but I know me better than that.

No, she and her daughter kept me going. Laura couldn't realize how much better off her whole family would be with me out of the picture. She mostly only got to hear about all the people I'd *saved.* About the kids, beaten by their stepfathers or sold smack by gang-bangers wearing matching bandanas.

It was different being out there.

Eventually, after you wipe enough filth from the streets and it keeps bubbling back like a sickness, it's all you can see in people. A roll down the street and I wonder which man in a prim suit struck his wife last night or is screwing his secretary. Which woman is seducing a man to steal everything he's got? Which harmless, glasses-wearing civilian doubles as a serial killer or is cutting coke in his basement?

The dark side of humanity clings to you like wet sand from the beach.

"Come on, Michelle. It's time to go," Laura said, mustering her stern, lawyer-like tone. Her daughter was busy bouncing her Super-Ball rather than finishing her meal. Her mother grabbed her arm to stop her. The ball fell, but Laura snatched it out of midair and forced it back into Michelle's hand.

"Let's go," Laura tried again. "Say goodbye to Uncle Reese."

"Kay..." Michelle replied in her tiny voice. She glanced at me momentarily and offered the slightest wave. I hovered in the doorway, waving back with the bottle of Jack and putting on a goofy, crooked smile. She immediately averted her gaze and clung tight to her mother's hand with her free one.

They went for the door, but a hard knock stopped them in their tracks.

"Laura Garrity, I know you're in there!" someone shouted.

I raced over to my covered window and drew back the tattered drapes just enough to peek outside. A skinny fellow holding a notepad stood on my porch.

"Not this asshole again," I grumbled. "Laura, go to the back. I'll deal with him."

"He's harmless," she said.

"So am I. Now go."

She spent a few seconds considering it before finally listening, taking a confused little Michelle with her. I rolled up to the door and stretched my fingers around the handle. That article in my basement about the dead girls and me being to blame? The man outside wrote it.

Chuck Barnes used to write for the *Iron City Bulletin* but he'd had such a hard-on for revealing who the Roach was behind the mask, that he destroyed his credibility. Asking too many questions and stalking the Mayor's daughter will do that. He'd disappeared for a bit after getting fired, but he was recently back to chasing the truth like a dog after a mailman.

In my prime, I would've broken into his apartment to convince him to back off. More for his sake than mine. Chuck was ruining his life over an obsession with questions whose answers he'd never get. But he lived in a walk-up across town, and I couldn't very well get up that high in a wheelchair and manage to remain intimidating.

I tossed my bottle onto the couch and then swung the door open.

"I know she's in here, Roberts," he said and immediately tried to stick his head inside. He was literally the epitome of working himself to the bone. Skinny everywhere with a five-o-clock shadow that never seemed to go away or even grow longer. When I'd first encountered him, he had a thick head of hair. Now, he was bald as a Q ball.

I blocked him with my chair and said, "How many times do I have to tell you to keep off my damn property?"

"Until you tell me why you're hanging around a much younger woman who also happens to be our mayor's daughter."

I gave him a nudge with my chair, forcing him down the ramp a bit. "What can I tell you? We're in love." I stroked my ragged beard, straining out a few droplets of liquor and licking it off.

He jotted down a note. "Last time, you said you were her babysitter."

"And how sweet a romance that kindled."

Footsteps echoed from inside my townhouse.

"What was that?" Chuck leaned over me again, so close I could see the crumbs in his disgustingly thin mustache. I smacked the notepad out of his hand. It landed in a puddle adjacent to my front stoop, and he quickly jumped down to retrieve it. Ink bled through the wet pages, rendering his mad scrawling illegible.

"Oh, real nice," he pouted as he shook it off. "You know how much work was in there?"

"I did ask nicely, didn't I?"

He jabbed his finger out at me. "You know, one day, the truth is going to come out! All the people you've hurt. Taking the law into your own hands. Every time I find a new bread crumb about the Roach, it leads back to you, Reese Roberts. No hospital records of your 'incident.' Sanitation says it's *confidential*."

"I'm self-healing." I rolled backward and went to close the door.

He bolted back up my stoop and blocked it with his foot. "I don't know who you're paying off, but you'd have to be dense not to see all the pieces. The Roach used the sewers and water lines to move around unseen. *You* worked in them."

"Wow. Now that is rare to find in this city. At least come back with something interesting."

"Oh, trust me, I have it. I've been digging more around the time the Roach disappeared. Right after he got all those girls killed."

My grip on the door handle tightened. The wood whined as it threatened to snap off. "Yeah, I remember the article you wrote about that. Riddled with typos."

Chuck adjusted his glasses. "What about how Laura Garrity was sexually assaulted at the edge of Harborside, and how our honorable mayor used it as a springboard for cleaning up the city? A rookie cop on a beat supposedly saved her. A *rookie*. Now, he's already a lieutenant on track to be the next chief of police. Doesn't that sound convenient to you?"

"It sounds like politics."

"It took me a long time to get anyone there talking, but I went door-to-door. One old blind woman who lives above that alley remembers hearing a gunshot and arguing between men that night."

"A blind woman. Really?"

"Oh, yes. But she isn't alone, Reese. A couple of others mention a shadowy figure in a mask—a man screaming in agonized pain. Yet, the police report only mentions Laura's unknown attacker fleeing after officer Montalvo had arrived. October 21, 1980, in the district where nearly half the Roach's reported incidents occurred. Right around when the Roach vanished even, and the day before your supposed 'accident.'"

I bit my tongue.

In every comic, the hero has an arch-nemesis. Batman has the Joker, Superman has Lex Luthor. As usual, I got the shit end of the stick. Chuck Fucking Barnes—since all the other options were either dead or behind bars. I guess maybe he's a bit like my James Jonah Jameson. You know, the guy from Spider-Man, except Chuck was a pencil-necked, coke-bottle-glasses little twerp with pit-stains and Cheeto breath.

He was a man so hell-bent on uncovering the truth and redeeming his once-sterling reputation that he'd do anything. Go too far.

Except, every part of what he'd said was true. The only reason my identity hadn't come out was because of who I'd saved. Laura's dad got me the treatment I needed and kept everything quiet. From the Iron City Water and Sewage Authority head to the former police chief to José Montalvo, the officer who'd ended my vigilante career. Anything that could potentially place the Garrity Act in jeopardy.

For about a year, people asked what had happened to the Roach and why he stopped popping up. By the time the old chief retired, nobody even cared. I was a memory—a name in some old newspaper clippings that'd inspired some cheap action figures and a few knock-off graphic novels of solely local repute.

Only Chuck Barnes kept searching. I might've told him the truth just to shut him up if it weren't for Laura and her father's involvement. Okay, that's a lie. The very thought of him getting a win after all the things he'd written, and then a dozen reporters rolling up on my street and hounding me made my skin crawl.

All those eyes on me. All those eager fools stampeding to my door. Asking questions. Making accusations. Talking about things they didn't understand.

Biting my tongue wasn't working. "I suggest you walk away," I said.

Chuck smiled, his little mustache wriggling like the worm he was. "I've been doing my homework. You know what I think? I think—"

I grabbed his wrist and squeezed. I had it in mind to snap it, but I controlled my temper.

"I don't care what you think," I growled. "A tunnel collapsed downtown and nearly killed me. I met Laura when she led a fundraiser for her father to improve worker conditions. Pretty damn simple." I remembered that charade we put on. When I had to roll before the crowd and be applauded at for my phony story. I shuddered.

"Fine, fine," Chuck strained to say through the pain. "Just tell me one thing first." He jutted his chin into my house, toward Laura and Michelle. "Who's the father?"

"I said walk away!" I burst through the door and rammed him in the shins with the footplate of my chair. He stumbled back off the stoop, sliced his hand on the rusty railing, and landed hard on the sidewalk.

"Well, that's just great!" he shouted, staring at his bloody hand. "So, that's the kind of hero you are?"

"Exactly the kind."

"You may have everyone staying quiet, but I'm going to find out what really happened that night! I swear it."

"Have fun."

Chuck was pulling at threads without an end. The piece of trash who'd attempted to rob and rape Laura wouldn't be found. He was at the bottom of the Horton River, where I belong. Mayor Garrity made sure of that during the coverup, just like he'd taken care of the trigger-happy cop who'd shot me. My compensation for saving his daughter's life? I got to avoid being unmasked and going to jail. He got citywide support for cleaning up Iron City in a Roachless world.

Everyone won. Well, except Chuck Barnes and his pursuit of truth. And Laura, though she got Michelle out of it. And my legs. And the Harborside district for that matter, which slowly reverted to the vacancy-ridden shithole it'd been ever since the automobile industry moved on.

I rolled backward into my house just as a police cruiser turned the corner. Its driver blared the siren and flashed the lights once, then stopped in front of my townhouse. A scratched-up sedan followed close behind.

"You've got to be kidding me," I groaned, pushing my fingers up through my thinning hair.

"Is everything all right?" Laura asked from the kitchen.

"Fine!" I yelled back.

The officer stepped out of his car. His head was shaved like he was in the military, but his eyes were tired. I knew when a cop had seen it all, and this one was jaded. He'd put on a few too many L B's. chowing down on donuts and fast food tacos. Iron City has a way of grinding down a man.

Chuck crawled to his feet, leaving bloody handprints on my ramp.

"Did you see that?" he demanded of the officer.

The cop brushed right by him, and it took me all of two seconds to realize why. That chubby bully sidekick from the day before exited the sedan behind them, arm in a sling. A woman who could only be his mother accompanied him, hair in curlers, and wearing so much gaudy jewelry, it hurt my soul—West Harborside trash. And wouldn't you know it, but Isaac stepped out behind them.

The little assholes must have followed me back home, and I'd been too drunk to notice. Great. Kids do so love raising hell for their elders.

"Is that him?" the mother asked her son.

"Yeah," the sidekick replied. "That's the crazy asshole who assaulted me, right, Isaac?"

Isaac's eyes were magnified by an even thicker, uglier pair of new glasses. That made it easy to tell that he couldn't even bear to look at me. He just stared down at the street, right past his father's dog tags.

"You piece of shit. How dare you strike a child!" The mom stormed forward. The officer stuck out a hand to hold her back, but she was like a freight train.

"Calm down, ma'am," he said.

"I won't calm down! I don't care what he is, you don't hit a child. The boys even said they smelled alcohol on his breath!"

"Is that what the punk told you?" I chortled. Then, for the second time in as many minutes, I groaned, "You've got to be kidding me."

The bully sidekick didn't say a word, just wore a shit-eating grin.

"Oh, this is even better," Chuck said. He flipped to one of the few dry pages in the back of his notepad and approached the kid. "Would you mind telling me exactly what this man did to you? I'm a freelance journalist after the truth."

"Everyone, back," the officer ordered. Then he turned to me, and I got a good look at his badge. Officer Dennard.

"Sir, I'm going to have to take you down to the precinct and ask you some questions," he said. The way he addressed me made my skin itch. Like I was utterly useless. If I had my legs, I bet he would've arrested me right then and there, but who would believe me capable of doing anything to a healthy young man? They didn't even bother sending two cops.

"What if I say no?" I replied.

"I'm afraid that isn't an option. Now, please, let me help you down."

"You're going away for a long time, asshole!" the sidekick shouted at me.

If he was a legal adult and Isaac had told the truth, I would get a slap on the wrist. But I hadn't taken the time to vet them like I would have when I was the Roach, listening from shadows. And Isaac continued avoiding eye-contact, silently kicking the sidewalk near the back of the car.

If the sidekick was actually a minor and I'd broken a bone... the cops would hear the two bullies' stories, and they'd force Isaac to back them. Honest people didn't avoid looking at others. Why would he protect a stranger and earn himself more beatdowns, anyway? When had saving lives been enough? By the time cops got to my story, it wouldn't matter what I said.

Is this really what I'd turned away from death for? Is this the way the Roach goes down?

"You have some nerve, asshole," the mom spat.

"I see where your son gets it from," I replied. I looked to him. "By the way, anyone ever tell you what happens to rats in Iron City?"

A flicker of shame rippled across his features. His mother cursed something fierce.

Officer Dennard took my hand and guided my wheelchair down the narrow ramp tracks I'd had built onto half of my stoop. He did it slowly, like I was a delicate vase in an antique shop. He read me my Miranda rights. I have the right to remain silent, yada-yada, get an attorney. I eyed the holstered pistol on his hip the entire time. I could grab it and finally end things. Quicker than drowning. Probably less than what I deserved, but there wasn't time to be picky.

"What's going on, Officer?" Laura asked, interrupting the officer before he finished.

My hand was halfway toward stealing the gun when her voice made me freeze. I peered up at the doorway and saw her standing, arms around her daughter.

"What's going on, Mommy?" Michelle asked, still clutching her SuperBall.

"Leave it alone, Laura," I said. Of course, she ignored me.

"Someone is making a mistake." Laura left her daughter and rushed down the stoop to stop the officer. "Where are you taking him?"

"I'm just doing my job," the cop said.

"Well, I'm sure this is easily explainable. An accident. Let me make a call. I'm a lawyer. I can—"

"There they go," Chuck interrupted. "Protecting this scumbag again. When are people finally going to let him answer for his crimes?"

"When are you going to leave us alone and get back to your sorry life, Chuck!" Laura countered, making me exceedingly proud.

Officer Dennard released my chair. "Look, ma'am. I don't know what's going on here, but I have to take him in. If those young men are lying, we'll get to the bottom of it, but now, I have no choice. Assault of a minor is a serious accusation."

"I'll tell you what's going on, Officer," Chuck chimed in. "Do you know who she is? The Garritys have spent years protecting this man to hide the fact that he was the Roach."

Officer Dennard stopped and looked back at him like he was an alien zapped down from a UFO. What did Chuck expect, throwing out ludicrous accusations like that?

"That's what you think?" Laura scoffed. "That's insane."

I missed the rest of the argument. While everyone got riled up and the bully and his mother joined in with their foul mouths, Michelle had slipped away from her mother and chased after her SuperBall as it bounced into the street. Four years old, no sense of the world's many dangers—I saw it all unfolding. A mail Jeep sped a bit too fast, and when Michelle stepped beyond the line of parked cars, it would barrel right over her.

I launched my chair forward. Officer Dennard blurted something and tried to catch me, but was far too slow and reacting to the wrong danger. Laura saw where I was going and screamed her daughter's name.

Wind blew through my hair as I zipped off the sidewalk and onto the street. I felt like I was sprinting down tunnels and leaping across rooftops again. Michelle didn't turn around upon hearing her mother. The truck couldn't see her and, like I'd feared, wasn't stopping.

How far is too far?

I'd been asking that question every second of every day for five years until I was drunk enough to forget it, and it was finally time to find out. I went just far enough, grabbed Michelle, and threw her forward onto the other sidewalk. The truck driver hit the brakes when he saw me and tried to turn, but it was too late.

In the second before it plowed into me, my whole life flashed. All the fights. All the devils slain. I was the Roach, the bane of Iron City's criminal underworld, and I'd go out on my own terms...

CHAPTER

Sirens. The cathedral bells of the night in Iron City. Might as well have been its theme song.

I never ran to them. Sirens meant the police were already on their way. Sure, following them was tempting. That's why they were named after those seductive, mythical creatures luring ancient ships to their doom in the Mediterranean. Did you know that? Nah, you didn't.

Anyway, in the old stories, everyone knows the danger Sirens present, but they just can't look away. It's like rubbernecking on I-75 after a bad accident, or how people watch a fire from across the street or gather to 'not' cheer-on a suicide jumper. Or the god damn, twenty-four-hour news cycle.

So-and-so died today. Tear up. Feel sad. Rinse and repeat. Oh, and here's a cute cat or the world's biggest fucking cookie. That's right. Forget the pain of the last forty-five minutes with this fluff piece. Tomorrow, we'll start all over again.

No, following the sirens was for the men in blue, and I wore shit-brown. I lurked in the darkness, watching the drunks and the junkies file by. Ear to the streets, I listened for the kind of horrors nobody wanted to know about. Or the stuff cops were only fast enough to clean up after the fact. The stuff people hear about the next morning, and it makes them cringe because they wonder if, maybe, that depth of evil could possibly exist in them too.

I promise. With the right push, it does.

So, I trudged through the sewer lines, knee-deep in human excrement. If it wasn't for my gas mask, I'd have probably died a long time ago from inhaling the toxic fumes. It'd grown worse since the city's vacancy rose, and the homeless multiplied.

The way it clung to my body armor was how I got my name from the press. The Roach. Occasionally, somebody would snap a picture of me in the night. A blur racing by in a twin-tubed, custom gas mask, looking awfully like a giant cockroach before disappearing through a grate.

That night, I came up for air at the edge of Harborside and Downtown. After what had happened when I busted the Bratva sex trade and those girls got killed, I was on the prowl for someone to save. Or, if I'm being honest, somebody to beat to a pulp. Somebody who deserved it.

I remember the night—every excruciating detail—The way the constant smog blurred out an oversized full moon. I remember the 1972 Impala slamming on its horn when a drunkard darted in front of it on Harris Street.

And I remember the scream. Oh, do I remember it. Shrill for a second before being forcefully muffled. It was a flash in the pan. Nothing anyone out after dark might hear. Not in Iron City, where learning to sleep around car horns and belligerent shouts was a carefully groomed skill.

I was out from under the sewer cap so fast, I think I blew the cardboard box off a sleeping bum. The scream could've been nothing, but I'd been doing this long enough to trust my hunches.

My feet pounded on the pavement, through alleys, around trash. I used the side of a wall to skip up over a fence blocking a back street. That was when I heard the scream again, followed by a meaty *thump*.

I bolted around a corner and saw a man with a young woman bent over a dumpster in an alley between Dalton Street and 4th. Vinny Statman, that was his name. Nothing extraordinary. You'd expect something like Vinny Darkh, or some crazy moniker like Vinny the Vandal—but no. As normal sounding as could be. An architect from downtown Iron City, a far cry from the Big Apple. He was the type of scumbag that makes me wonder if humankind deserves to live at all. I knew right away he had a decent job downtown judging by his suit. Everything going for him. But he liked to get hopped up on coke and show young women how much power he deserved.

His victim's dress was hiked up, her purse spilled all over the pavement. He had one hand over her mouth, the other with an expensive, silver embellished pocket-knife to her throat.

In a city with every imaginable option for a man to get his rocks off, this hair-gelled crotch-stain chose rape. In *my* city. I didn't warn him to get off her. That wasn't my style. I wasn't some speedster like the Flash, racing up to a bad guy only to stop short and make sure *everyone* knew he was there. Those fucking prima donnas.

My steps were soft, silent, bringing me right up to them unnoticed. I stared straight at the side of the asshole's face while he bit his lip, eyes rolled back, enjoying every second of his perversion. Before he knew what hit him, I wrenched the knife out of his hand, breaking it, and yanked him away from his victim.

Vinny flew back against a brick wall, howling in pain as his suit jacket tore. His victim remained folded over the dumpster, crying, terrified, mascara running down her cheeks.

As I moved beside her, it was more like she stared straight through me. Like I was a ghost, and she was in hell.

Woman... she was still a girl. Couldn't have been far into her twenties. Whole life ahead of her. Probably was on her way to party with friends downtown, trying to be a normal youngster when she found herself in a spot no girl wants to imagine exists.

I took her by the shoulders. She shrank away, and I let her. Then, after a moment—when I felt like she might've realized I wasn't one of the bad guys—I tried again. This time, she allowed it, and I gently lowered her to the ground. I'm sure looking through the lenses of my mask didn't put her at ease. She shook, or I shook, I'm not sure. Maybe both of us. What happened with the Bratva and the dead girls the night before loomed heavy on my thoughts in a way my nightly activities rarely did. I kept picturing Chuck's headline, blaming me.

Murderers, gangbangers, corrupt... I could handle them all. But not this. Overpowering someone physically weaker than him simply because he could. He didn't deserve a second chance. Guys like Vinny couldn't change.

"Reese," she said, her voice soft and warm. I dropped her and staggered away, shocked that she knew me. I searched from side to side, only now there was blackness.

"Reese, can you hear me?"

I opened my mouth to answer, but my throat burned. It was dry. Impossibly dry. And the itch... I wanted to claw out my own trachea.

"Reese!"

My eyes blinked open slowly. White light blinded me from every direction. For a moment, it felt like I'd woken in heaven, but c'mon, I'm a realist. When I go, it'll be the devil that greets me with a pitchfork and a beer. Too much blood on these hands, deserved or not, and angels have their rules.

"Reese," a woman whispered. A pretty, heart-shaped face took shape above me. The same face of that helpless girl in the alley who I'd tried to save, all grown up now.

I wanted to answer, but I wore a different sort of mask than back then, one stuffed into my mouth and forcing oxygen down my throat.

More of my surroundings took shape behind Laura. White walls, white floor, white ceiling. Gizmos and gadgets galore, and me at their center hooked up to machines to be kept alive. For what?

"Oh my God," Laura said, her eyes going wide. "Nurse. Nurse!" she screamed, nearly slipping on the tile floor on her way to the door. "His eyes opened."

She ran back to me and gripped my hand. I had pins and needles all over, but I could feel her touch. The scars on her palms from scraping against that dumpster as her abuser took her had left them rough. Though, maybe that was my own imagination, pissed at me because I didn't get to her sooner before that filthy pile of shit could pull out his tiny little pecker.

"You're alive," she said, voice trembling.

My expression must have informed Laura that I wasn't quite sure. She squeezed harder and smiled. That ugly kind of smile, forced through tears, blowing spit bubbles. Doctors and nurses rushed in behind her. Heroes wearing white and masks of their own.

"I told them all," she whispered into my ear. "You can't kill a cockroach."

Laura paced nervously while a nurse poked and prodded me. Employees from all over whatever-the-hell-hospital I was in watched me like I was a carnival show, explaining little beyond the fact that I'd been out for a while.

I couldn't ask anything.

I could barely talk.

I just wished they'd leave me alone and stop staring.

It was a nightmare on repeat, and I could barely remember what put me in the bed. Only shouting, screeching tires, and a bouncing ball.

My heart started to race when I watched the nurse testing my feet for sensation. Stranger things have happened in comics than a paraplegic getting hit by a car and waking up able to walk again. But my origin story had come and gone a long time ago, and this was real life, not some funnybook.

As expected, I still didn't feel anything from the hips down to my big toes. And yeah, that means *everything* in between.

My energy dwindled after that. Whatever they had in my drip had me dozing in and out. Laura stood nearby, then sat by the window, then paced—but always with me. Years since I'd saved her, and still, she was there. No matter how often her father might've told her to keep away from me, she always showed.

Eventually, my consciousness winked out completely, and when my eyes opened again, I rasped for breath all on my own. I still had oxygen plugging my nostrils for that extra little boost, but now it wasn't enough to help me ignore how sore my every muscle was from the waist-up. The injuries I'd suffered from being hit by that mail truck were healed, or healing, judging by the sling they had my left arm in.

The truck! I realized.

My right hand shot out and at Laura. She'd fallen asleep reading some law book and startled awake. I could see the twitch of her muscles, ready to defend herself as if that asshole Vinny Statman had just shown up. I know that pain never went away. That fear. It's always there. Always gonna be. People who've gone through what she has... they never wake up easy. No matter how put-together they look on the outside, there's always one piece of the puzzle lost under the carpet.

"Mich..." I struggled to say, throat itching. The muscles of my larynx stung. "Michelle," I forced out. "Is she—"

"She's fine," Laura said. "Thanks to her guardian angel."

"Far from that, I'm afraid."

She smiled, ignoring me, and nodded toward the bedside table to my left. The SuperBall I'd given Michelle lay against a smudged glass of water.

"She had me bring it for you," Laura said.

I tried to reach with my slung arm to grab it and failed miserably.

Laura leaned across me to get it. Her arm brushed my cheek, and her shirt draped against my chest. I had to close my eyes. I hated seeing her stretched out like that. Exposed. All I could picture were her tears that awful night.

"Here," she said. She sat back down, placed the ball in my hand, and folded hers around mine with it in the center.

"Great," I said. "A memento from my slayer. Car bumper."

Laura rolled her eyes and let go of me. I rolled the SuperBall along my palm.

"You give a kid one gift," I said.

"It's the thought that counts," she replied.

"Says every shit gift-giver who's ever lived." I placed the toy back on the table.

"I think her life is a good trade-off, no?" Laura's playful façade faded, and tears welled in her eyes. I didn't become the most infamous vigilante anyone's ever heard of by not being perceptive. It clearly took all the meager energy she had to keep herself composed.

"Reese, what you did—I can't—"

I raised a finger to my lips. "A hell of time you had bringing Michelle into the world," I said. "Her life wasn't going to end because of me."

Laura sniveled and wiped her face. Her lips parted to speak, but nothing came out. All she could manage was a timid nod. This time, I took her hand and clasped it in my own.

"I'd do it the same every time," I said. "You never need to thank me."

She cleared her throat. "The doctors say that your chair absorbed the brunt of the crash. Without it, you'd have been killed instantly."

"Saved by the prison I can't escape. Lucky me." I looked around. "Where the hell am I?"

"Downtown at Iron City General."

"You know I hate it downtown. All the suit-wearing, shoe-kissing—"

"It's the best hospital in the city," she interrupted, avoiding eye-contact now. I'd known her long enough to know that meant something bad. Especially after she stood and started pacing again. She always did that when she was nervous.

"What else is it?" I asked.

"Nothing. I'm just glad you're alive."

"Laura, I'm a cripple in a hospital bed, stewing in his own shit and piss. It can't be that bad."

She breathed out slowly and shook out her wrists. "Well... you were in a coma for a month and the doctors—"

"A month?" I cut her off, my jaw dropping. No wonder I could sense the muscle atrophy.

"And three days," she clarified.

"That long, hooked on life-support in Iron City's finest with no insurance? How the hell is that possible?"

And then I saw her features darken tellingly. She was hiding something, and we didn't have that sort of relationship. *I* hid almost everything while she always told the truth, futilely hoping that might eke more out of me.

"Laura, how is that possible?" I asked again.

She swallowed hard and turned away. "They, uh, didn't think you were going to make it, and you have no next of kin, so I... I had to pay the hospital not to pull the plug."

"You mean your dad?"

She shook her head. "No, me. He said it was hopeless and time to let you go."

"And you didn't listen..." I grumbled.

"What was I supposed to do?"

"Let me go." My head slumped back into the pillow. "How much, Laura? How much was keeping me around worth?"

"You think I only did this for myself? I saved your life, Reese. The least you could do—"

"That's my job!" I smacked the stupid little plastic tray hovering over me, spilling a cup of ice chips I hadn't seen brought in. They trickled over the side into my worthless lap. I gave the tray a shove, sending it banging against the wall.

Laura's purse was on it too, and now, its contents were all over the floor. She flinched, turning away, with her hands extended as if to stop some unseen force. And in that brief moment, I saw primal fear flash across her features like it had in that alley. Only this time, I was the trigger.

"I. Save. You," I said, panting, barely able to see straight my head ached so bad. "That's how it works. Not the other way around. You have a daughter, an apartment, loans. And you wasted it on a guy who almost rolled himself into a river because he's got nothing left?"

Raising my voice strained my already hoarse throat too far, and I started coughing into my sling. Any time I tried to keep talking, it escalated. As I did, Laura braved getting closer again. She half-sat on the side of the bed, rubbing my back like I was a little kid or some kind of an invalid. Why couldn't she just walk away?

"But you didn't," she said softly. "You don't get to play God, Reese. And yeah, maybe I did want to keep you around. You barely talk to me, yet you say more than my father ever does."

I peered up at her, each breath rattling out as the phlegm cleared. My temples throbbed.

"How much?" I asked.

"It doesn't matter."

"Spit it out, Laura."

Her fingers covered the back of my head, tangling in my sweat-soaked hair. She tilted my face toward her. I knew the expression she wore. She'd earned it while fighting for her life. That look, which said she wasn't going to budge no matter what.

"It's just money," she whispered.

I jerked my head to the side. "I'm going to pay you back."

"What are you going to do, get a real job? They don't pay people to sit at home draining bottle after bottle and waiting for their names to pop up on the news."

I grunted. "So, a month," I said to her after a short pause. I gave the room a closer examination. "And not a single card or bouquet?"

It felt like no time for me. All those romantic movies about people falling into comas and miraculously waking, having heard all the conversations of their loved ones... they're all bullshit.

Laura chuckled. "I see you're still you. Moody and never satisfied."

"You know me oh-so-well."

Smiling, she made her way around the bed and started cleaning up her things. I leaned over like I was possibly gonna help from my bed. A rush of blood to my head stopped me anyway.

A gentle knock at the door snagged my attention, giving my head another rush as I turned. My nurse peeked in, her hair up in a bandana to keep it tidy. She was pretty, no question. Like a homier Diana Ross.

Great... She'd had the awesome opportunity to prod around at all my worthless goodies downstairs.

"Hi, Miss Garrity. We have a few more tests to run if you don't mind?" she said.

"I'm fine," I blurted, even though my hand was over my eyes while I rubbed my temples between my thumb and middle-finger to try and relieve the ache.

Laura ignored me. She popped up, having mostly restocked her purse. "That's okay, just give us a second." Her eyes shifted toward the clock over the door. "Oh, is that the time? Shit."

Sensing the urgency in her tone, I said, "Don't leave me with her."

Nurse whatever-her-name-is ignored me and stepped outside to review her clipboard.

"I have to go relieve Michelle's babysitter because Dad's busy with campaigning," Laura said. "And then I have to get some extra work done, so my boss gets off my back. So, can you do me a favor?"

"What?" I grated.

Laura raked the last bit of loose change and a set of keys into her purse. "Sit here and behave until they say you can go home."

She bent down one last time and rose holding the SuperBall, which she slapped down on my gut. Then, she returned to her chair to retrieve her leather jacket slung over the back of it. My Laura. Professional, badass-looking lawyer who didn't quite succumb to societal pressures, despite how privileged she'd grown up.

"I'm sorry for yelling," I said, low. "I don't like hospitals."

She sighed and moved to the end of the bed. Placing her palms on it, she leaned over me, the sheets stretching across my calves. Man, did I wish I could feel that pressure. And there I went again, imagining miracles. That truck had truly scrambled my brain.

"You don't like anything, Reese," Laura said. "So, just be glad you're alive and stop complaining."

I bit my lip, then let my chin fall to my chest. "I'll try. But I'm going to pay you back, I swear."

"You saved Michelle's life. Consider us even." She patted the bed and cracked a frail grin. I think she even tried to wink. She was terrible at them. "Just sit tight."

I sent a grin right back at her. Or forced it. My head was so out of sorts, I wasn't sure what I was feeling. Maybe a little confused that no matter how hard I tried, I couldn't die. I really was like a cockroach. It'd take a nuclear bomb going off in Iron City to take me out.

"Tell Michelle 'hi' for me," I said after Laura turned and headed for the exit.

"You can tell her yourself," she replied. "Over dinner. The moment you get out of here." She stopped in the doorway. "By the way, did you really hurt that kid?"

"What kid?"

"The one that came to your house."

"If I did, he had it coming," I said, having completely forgotten about that component of the incident until then.

The frustration in Laura's sigh was palpable. "Oh, Reese... Well, you're lucky your incredible lawyer denied everything."

"I don't have a lawyer."

Laura straightened her posture and adjusted her collar. "You're looking at her. Not that it matters. The kid and his mom dropped the charges after you got hit. I guess they figured you were punished enough. Maybe something to think about?"

"Laura Garrity. A lawyer and a shrink," I murmured.

She chuckled. "I'll see you later."

"Yep." By the time I looked up, prepared to say, "Thank you," her heels clacked down the hall until they blended with the rest of the footsteps. And just like that, I was back to being alone with my thoughts, and not a bottle of anything in sight. My head again fell back against a pillow that I'd only then realized was as stiff as a brick.

I closed my eyes and tried to doze off, but as tired as I was, now that I was off most of the pain meds, my mind cranked along with nothing to dull it. Then, my nurse re-entered.

"It's incredible the way she's been there for you," she said.

"You should have pulled the plug and saved her the time and money," I replied, turning away from her.

"Very nice."

"The truth rarely is."

She took my arm, and I pulled away.

"Mister Roberts, I need you to stay still," she said.

Too exhausted to think of a snappy comeback, I let my arm fall slack. Or maybe I was too weak to resist her. "Just be gentle," I said.

She wasn't. She returned to poking and prodding me, and now that I was fully conscious, I wanted to squirm out of my skin. Her breath reeked of stale cigarettes. Anything to stay awake, I guess. I never got into that particular vice, but maybe once I returned, I'd add it to the drinking. Couldn't hurt.

After she was done with me, I think I made it an hour or two following Laura's advice to stay put. Then, I started to actually itch all over, which got me hollering for my nurse to return.

This wasn't my home. Wasn't my bed. And I'd put enough men in hospitals to know that they couldn't hold you against your will.

Not if you were of sound mind and body, and qualifications are awful low in an overcrowded downtown institution desperate to turn over beds to turn a profit in fair Iron City.

Nurse Chain-Smoker took some convincing before unhooking me from all their fancy new medical apparatuses while I signed my release. I could be a pain in the ass when I wanted to, and in a city like this, emptying beds for new patients came at a premium. I even got my old clothes back, sporting far fewer bloodstains than expected. They even fit a little better now that a month without solid food had me so slim.

The best part of feeling nothing waist-down is that the catheter slips right out. Before I knew it, I was loaded onto a hospital-provided wheelchair while my nurse rattled off all the things I should do to avoid ailments. Lots of fluids, rest, stay off my feet—you know the deal.

I nodded along, barely listening, eyes on the clock. She'd already seen every bit of me exposed, how could ailments get any worse? I didn't care how much my body and head ached. I had to get out of this place.

I glanced up at Nurse Cigarette as she rolled me to the elevator. She wasn't too young, though it was hard to tell with how flawless her dark skin was. But she was effortlessly pretty. No time for makeup since, judging by the bags under her bloodshot eyes, she likely hadn't slept in days. Every few seconds, she gnawed on her fingernails, hardly sanitary for a nurse. She clearly needed a smoke.

The elevator chimed again, and a doctor holding a clipboard blocked the doors while everyone else got off. I was rolled out and through a busy lobby. A queue snaked away from the information desk. Families waited to get cheap grub from the café. Glass was everywhere, letting in too much light thanks to a contemporary design part of Downtown's recent facelift.

Why does everyone like everything so bright? What the fuck is so important to see?

We made it halfway across the airy space until Nurse Marlboro stopped me for a line of school children filing behind their teacher. What a shitty field trip, even for an inner-city school.

Look, kids, that guy got hit by a taxi. And over there, that woman is giving birth to a kid who's gonna grow up in the shit part of town.

I looked to my left, only to see more hospital employees and visitors. To my right, the same. Footsteps pitter-pattering all over. Voices big and small chattering nonsense.

I closed my eyes, pushed my nails against my palms, and breathed in slowly. I could sense them all looking at me, wondering why a bearded bum was getting this royal treatment. Wondering what stunk of moldy cheese.

"Can we get a move on?" I grumbled. I tried to take the wheels myself, but the nurse slapped the top of my right hand. She hit harder than expected. The sting was a welcome distraction until the children finally marched by like ducklings, and she returned to pushing.

"I've never met a man so lucky to be alive and so impatient," she mumbled.

"Pleased to make your acquaintance."

Her groan made me feel worse than expected before she guided me right out onto the sidewalk at the drop-off circle on 3rd Ave. The moment I was outside, our brief transaction was complete.

"Here you are," she droned. "We're gonna need the chair back."

I lifted an eyebrow at her. "Do you plan on dumping me out on the pavement then?"

"Sir, please. It's been a long ass shift." Nurse Cigarette looked like it. I could tell she was inches away from snapping at me if she didn't get her fix.

I looked down at my legs and spread out my hands as if to present them. I expected her cheeks to go red and for her to throw herself on the ground in apology. I got nothing. Her head went back, and she unleashed a sigh of epic proportions.

"Oh, right." She rubbed her eyes. "You don't got anyone who can bring you yours?"

"Sorry. Mine got run over."

"I'm not paid enough for this shit," she muttered. "You didn't hear it from me, but if no one knows you still have it, we can't come chasing you for it. So, I'm gonna leave you sitting here, and whatever happens to the chair after that, I'm not gonna see."

She forced a smile just to be polite, then wandered over to a doctor leaning on the window nearby to bum a cigarette. They seemed to get along, probably enjoying complaining about me and all their other patients. Not sure about what, considering she was the one who forgot I was disabled somewhere between my room and the front door.

A few cars cruised by, dropping people off, picking others up. The many not-so-impressive towers of Iron City's downtown stretched out before and above me, all dwarfed by one covered in cranes. Aurora Tower was being constructed primarily to house Aurora Technologies after Mayor Garrity somehow lured their main offices to Iron City. The glassy monolith would stand a monument to man's ingenuity and ability to waste money on the worthless while so many people in Harborside enjoyed living in cardboard boxes and shitting on the streets.

I didn't pay enough attention to the news to know how far up they'd build. What's the price for reaching the heavens? Tower of Babel, attempt numero dos.

Ads on all the rooftops below it popped up like oversized, neon gravestones. This type of Soda. That insurance company. This TV show. Hell, a cab even told me what candidate to vote for if I wanted jobs back in Iron City, and it wasn't Mayor Garrity.

Man, did people love their high-dollar distractions, all paid for by the CCTVs set on almost every streetlight and corner Downtown as part of the Garrity Act's latest phase. Whatever kept Iron City's richest and most influential citizens safe so they could slowly drive out the rest of us. Imagine a city without the plebeians, peasants, piss-class.

But even here, where suits, ties, and pin-skirts were the duds of choice, the air smelled faintly of roasted almonds and sewage. Might as well have been flowers to me after spending time in a sterile box. I breathed it in deep and relished the chill in my nostrils. A month in a coma had brought the cold of winter's edge to the air.

There I was. Reese Roberts. The Roach with nine lives, and nothing left to do with them.

CHAPTER FOUR

I headed to my block, under the overhead light-rail tracks. The metal columns hummed and shook like a mini earthquake had hit as one of the old cars screeched along. One day, maybe the city would be safe enough to update the people-mover beyond just Downtown before it all falls apart.

A light drizzle left puddles in every crevice on sidewalks in desperate need of repaving. My hands and sleeves got soaked by the water flicked up from the tires and pushrims of my crummy new ride.

I passed my street's resident bum. Tinman, as I called him, wore the wrinkly metal sheets head-to-toe, including a cone atop his head, and a ratty blanket lined with the stuff to sleep under. He never asked for money. He only wanted people to listen. Closest thing to a superhero in Iron City these days.

Ignoring him like usual, all I could focus on was the street outside my townhouse. There wasn't even a blood spot where I'd been hit. Just burnt rubber, then a few blemishes on the pavement to join the countless others, eventually all to be paved over.

A skid mark on some backstreet in Harborside. *Splat.* What could have been a more fitting grave for the Roach? What can I say? I'm a sucker for irony.

I stopped nearby, just staring. I didn't care if anybody was snooping from their windows—nor did I give the slightest shit about the driver beeping at me to move. Who knows, maybe a coma was all I'd needed to rid myself of the last ration of fucks I had left in my reserve. This was Iron City, and here, I looked as normal as anyone in a wheelchair in the middle of the road with a scraggly beard down to my chest. Five years of slogging around like a useless sack of meat, absorbing liquor and TV dinners, and I finally had a chance to die a hero again. For someone who might *actually* give a damn too.

The headlines... Jesus. All those ungrateful pricks like Chuck would be fawning over me with no idea who I really was. But not Chuck. He was still an asshole.

RACES TO A YOUNG GIRL'S RESCUE.

Redemption, after his last article about my fatal exploits. The city would probably have named a street after me. Maybe a bench. At the very least, a sewer cover.

I couldn't even do that right.

"Your chair absorbed most of the impact," they'd said. Like a damn exoskeleton—an insect's carapace. I almost wanted to look up, or down, and wink at the God I didn't believe in.

But it's funny, isn't it? If I'd died, I'd be romanticized as a hero. There'd be stories. A made-for-TV movie, with me played by Rob Lowe or some shit. All of it. Yet the moment I woke up, it was just another day in smoggy Iron City. Unworthy to grace the pages of the *Bulletin* or even the gossip rags. Where was the tragedy to draw the eager eyes of readers who loved seeing what they believed could never happen to them?

"Get out of the fuckin road!" some guy yelled at me, half-leaning out of his clunker's window.

I tore my gaze off the street and gave him a curt wave.

He beeped again and hung on the horn. Next thing I knew, I'd dug the SuperBall out of my pocket and flung it at his windshield. It ricocheted off, then bounced on down the road where it'd eventually find a sewer grate and be out of my life forever. Last time I'd try to buy a gift.

The guy drove around me, cursing, and nearly banging the edge of my chair. I gave his rear bumper a whack on the way by. All it did was leave my aching shoulder sore and my hand red. Then he was gone, his wheels leaving another mark over the ones that had almost ended my life. Bye, bye memorial.

I chewed on my lip as I rolled toward my flat.

"What?" I grunted at my left-hand neighbor, a middle-aged man who'd kill to live anywhere else, I suspected. Might've helped if he spoke anything but Polish. The townhouse on the other side was boarded up. A far more preferable neighbor, though I suspected hooligans used it to smoke crack, the new drug of choice for Iron City's vagrants.

One month away, and it felt like I was gone for ages. And it wasn't just that sleeping anywhere other than my cot made me itch. My house smelled different, too. Sterile, like the hospital.

The normally musty front hall greeted me, and I slammed the front door shut behind me. Dust didn't shake loose like usual. Even the living room's single window sparkled like Mr. Clean's bald ass had been here. And the drapes were drawn to brighten everything inside. Magazines and papers were neatly stacked on my coffee table. No crumbs covered the couch. The booze stains were still there, but fainter. The bottle I'd left behind was missing too.

"Laura..." I sighed and shook my head. She couldn't help herself —wanted me to live like a human. Only, I was always around when she visited, and I never let her do the deep cleaning I know she longed for. But man, was she thorough.

I closed the drapes to envelop myself in the familiar comfort of darkness, the turned the dial on the TV to its only working channel.

"With only two days until Election Day, the Mayoral race is

heating up," an anchorwoman said. "Challenger Darrell Washington is rising at the right time. Experts believe this is due to his promise to cut police funding in order to improve our city's infrastructure and living conditions in what he calls the 'Forgotten Districts' beyond Downtown Iron City and the waterfront. Maybe, it's just time for a change. Our own Nancy Lockhart is Downtown, speaking with—"

I lowered the volume to just above a whisper. I may've liked to be alone, but a little background noise never hurt anybody. My entire life, I'd been around people. Not talking with them. Not seeing them. Just hearing them, distantly. I found strangely comforting, but with half the street now vacant, Harborside just didn't provide like it used to.

Continuing into the kitchen, I spotted a paper bag atop the stove with a note taped to it.

EAT, OR YOU WON'T BE ABLE TO SAVE HER AGAIN. XOXO

I checked inside. Six cans of Corbell canned soup—the good flavors. Lots of meat. Laura knew me too well. Cooking is such a waste when a perfectly hearty meal comes in a tin. They used to can them in Iron City, too. Now, I think some poor, emaciated kids do all the work in China.

I wasn't hungry. Plenty of hospital Jell-O held me over, and my stomach was out of whack from all the drugs and not drinking for over a month. I slid the note into a drawer for safekeeping, then checked my cabinets.

"Couldn't grab anything else?" I asked out loud.

My last bottle of whiskey remained missing in action. I checked the fridge. Not even a beer. The shelves were spotless, though. There'd been a dark smear on the left side of the middle rack for about a year now. I'd been watching it slowly grow hair. No longer.

I shut the door. After what I'd just been through, a stiff drink was required. Doctor's orders be damned. I wasn't about to let some little coma make me sober. So, I set off back for the front door, and on my way by, I noticed something wrong in the one room Laura knew never to mess with.

Books were out of place in my study. Only a few, but still, they were never out of order. Always organized by date of publication.

My foster mother was an obsessive reader, though it got her nowhere. After I escaped the foster home, I taught myself to read and scoured everything I could to do just the opposite and wield knowledge as a weapon.

But I remember how Mother taught me, Steven, and all my other unfortunate foster-siblings the consequences of things out of place. I could still remember the weight of a book on my knuckles whenever I messed up.

"*History belongs in order*," she'd scold. "*You can't change time.*"

If only.

Presently, *The Great Gatsby* was switched with *Count of Monte Cristo*, which was now over *Twenty Thousand Leagues Under the Sea*.

"No, no, no," I muttered as I quickly fixed them, having to lean up on the arms of my new chair to reach one. The thing was rickety as one would expect from a free hospital chair. I collapsed back into it, a wave of dizziness smashing my frontal lobe.

I probably should've stayed at the hospital.

Breathing out slowly, I dragged myself toward the kitchen. I couldn't see straight. Couldn't see much of anything, really. I patted along the wall, knocking my phone right off its hook.

The dial tone zoned my senses in and allowed me to locate it. Another measured breath and my head started to clear up.

"It's uh... work time," I said, taking a glance at the time over my stove. "Work. What's Laura's number?"

I'd it written down somewhere from a while back, but I wanted to remember. What other challenges did I have left to undertake? Doctors could screw themselves. I'd push this brain until it ran right off the tracks.

As I rubbed my temples, I noticed the calendar thumbtacked to the wall beside the phone. Laura, in all her generosity, had flipped it ahead to November. If Election Day was two days away, that made it the 1st. A Sunday.

"No work. Right, okay." One spin at a time. The familiar whirl-click of the rotary centered me as I put it in her home number. And wouldn't you know it, someone picked up.

"Hello?" a tiny voice said on the other end of the line.

My throat caught. "Michelle... Is that you?"

"Who is this?"

"It's Reese."

"Who?"

"Uncle Reese."

"Oh."

"I... uh... How are you?"

"Michelle, who is it that?" I heard Laura holler in the background. Michelle didn't answer, and all that came through were what sounded like footsteps and hushed whispers.

"Reese, is that you?" Laura asked.

"There you are," I said. "What, did I scare Michelle off again?"

"Is everything all right? I—Wait. Where are you calling from?"

"Home."

"Reese, you—"

"I'm fine. I had to get out of there. Too crowded."

"Did the doctors say you were okay to leave? They told me they wanted to monitor you another few days at least."

I gritted my teeth. Sometimes, Laura didn't understand that I didn't need a mom. I was handed over to a crummy enough one when I was a kid, courtesy of our fair government. Two, I suppose, if you count whoever the woman was that pushed me out screaming, then gave me away like an unwanted Christmas present. I guess I was re-gifted. Whoopie.

"They said they've never seen anyone so healthy. Discharged me just like that." I cut Laura off again before she even got out the first syllable of a response. "I didn't think I'd come home to a place as sterile as that white box, though."

"I won't apologize for making you live like a human," Laura replied.

I knew she'd say that.

"Reese, what is it?" she asked. "Are you okay? I'm slammed today after taking so much time off the last mo—"

She stopped talking for a second, but I knew it was just because she didn't want me to feel guilty. I wasn't about to. She deserved to be made a saint after what she'd done even though I wish she'd have just let me die.

She cleared her throat. "I have to prep a whole case file for my asshole boss. Thank God Michelle has daycare tomorrow so I can go to the firing range and blow off steam, or I think I'd lose it." She paused. "Reese?"

I scratched my beard. What was it I needed from her again?

"Reese?" she repeated.

"When you cleaned up, did you touch the study?" I asked, finally remembering.

"No. I'm not insane."

"You sure? You didn't move any books around trying to get downstairs and clean?"

"No. Last time I tried to go down there to check on you after you didn't wake up, you nearly bit my head off."

"Right. Well, good. There's nothing for you down there. Nothing for anybody."

"Why are you asking, I..." She exhaled. "Do you need me to come by? You sound... out of it."

"No, I'm fine. Really. Just a headache. I think I just need some real sleep."

"That's a good idea, since, apparently, you can't stay at a hospital with *real* doctors."

I blew a raspberry. "They just want to rack up my bills. *Your* bills," I corrected.

"You're..." Michelle whined for Laura in the background and interrupted her. "Reese, I have to go," she said. "It's Michelle's lunchtime. Are you sure you're okay?"

"Never better."

I think she was about to respond, or maybe she took a deep breath. I hung up too fast to know.

So, it wasn't Laura. I trusted her, and that didn't come lightly. If she'd cleaned my study, she'd have told me straight away and explained why I was being both ridiculous and neurotic in harsher terms. Put me on the stand. That's how she was.

But she'd never understand that she couldn't be involved in that part of my life.

I returned to the bookcase, head feeling a whole lot clearer. Reaching behind a worn copy of Mary Shelley's *Frankenstein*, I found the switch and signaled the stack to swing open. Then, I wheeled into the lift.

Maybe when I was drunk the night before the accident, I forgot how to go down and rummaged through the bookcase. Right? It was the most obvious answer. Though, that'd be a first. It'd take something a whole lot stronger than liquor to disrupt that muscle memory.

Unlike the rest of my apartment, the lift remained filthy as ever. It ticked along like a heart with a busted valve. And the folding doors needed that same extra push to open all the way after reaching my lair.

I flipped on the light, and the metal-halide lamp took a few seconds to reach peak brightness. My gaze swept across the room. The corner of some of my newspaper clippings had folded back down as tape peeled off the vending machine glass. Not surprising. They always did.

An empty bottle still lay against my cot. My computer monitors and radios were all switched off and coated in dust, like usual. My stacks of folders, empty except for dust... And then I saw it.

My heart clenched. My throat grew dry.

I'd witnessed things most people's nightmares couldn't even

fathom. Men disemboweled on butcher's hooks by mobsters. Women preserved in concrete by psychopaths.

All that, I could handle.

But the upright display case for my suit was broken open. As the light continued to bloom, I saw the specs of glass all over the metal and concrete floors. The mannequin stood alone, naked.

My suit had been stolen. Mask and everything.

I had been stolen.

CHAPTER

I sat, panting, my lungs struggling to keep pace.

I didn't even remember tearing my lair apart, but all my newspaper clippings coated the floor. My mannequin was tipped over and cracked, crates of empty folders littered the concrete.

I wanted to throw up. Worse, I wanted to peel my flesh away and scream. Imagine someone going through a teenage girl's diary. Or digging up a grave. Or a father telling his son he's special as he touches him in places no father should.

While I lay in a coma, someone had violated me. They'd suffer consequently. Did they want to expose me? What ham-fisted title would the papers come up with? THE ROACH UNSHELLED. That's what that hack Chuck Barnes would use if he got the scoop.

Yeah, something cheesy like that. I could imagine the vultures circling at every news outlet. Eager to spin their stories over how I'd been a villain, despite how they'd once called me everything from *hero-vigilante* to *guardian angel*. Before the mayor and his army in blue pulled the wool over their eyes and made everyone think that it was *them* who'd cleaned up Iron City with the Garrity Act.

And the crowds would form outside my door. Oh, would they

form. Everyone pushing, and shoving, and jockeying just to get a look at the face of the inglorious Roach. Their feet would scrape, and their cameras would click. I could hear it. Hear them.

My ears started ringing. I squeezed my already tired eyelids as tightly as I could to try and drown it out. I almost sagged off my chair but caught myself on my desk below the array of box-shaped monitors stacked one atop another. My forehead pressed against the edge, dangerously close to the self-destruct button as I quickly inhaled and exhaled. Was I hyper-fucking-ventilating?

When I reopened my eyes, stars formed in a broadway dance across my vision. A dark vignette pulsed in my periphery. I breathed. Heaved. Finally, things started to normalize, and I noticed the bundles of wires running down beneath the grating installed above the old concrete platform.

Cameras! I'd hidden security cameras all around my home, even outside on the stoop and sidewalk. Just in case. The one thing in common between my lair and Garrity's Downtown Iron City.

Pushing off the arm of my chair to reach the desk with one hand, with the other, I dragged a keyboard closer. The whole installation had been built at a time when, well, reaching things wasn't an issue for me.

I pecked at the keys with a single finger. There were about twelve monitors, and only three winked on. One was so staticky, I couldn't even see where it was pointed. Another faced the street, where Tinman staggered along, pushing a shopping cart and picking cans out of trash. The other aimed at me from above.

I glanced up. I couldn't spot it. I really had hidden them well. The camera tech was high-end stuff in its heyday, stolen from a research firm no longer headquartered in Iron City. They didn't miss them. And my lair needed to stay secure.

Offering a wave, the screen displayed me with choppy motions. In the left-hand corner, my suit's display case was visible.

"Got you," I said.

I backed up and rotated, bumping the desk in my haste. Things used to be easier with an office-chair. Then, the reality of who I was now came crashing down like a packed airliner.

"No. no, no, no, no." I hit eject on one of the few memory stacks that still turned on, and the tape it spat out came with a web of tangled film reels. The tapes had run out. Even what was once state-of-the-art surveillance needed upkeep, and for years, all I'd done was record absolutely nothing.

"No!" I grabbed a fistful of film and yanked, dragging one of the units out of the stack. It crashed onto the desk and didn't even spark. Might as well have spewed out dust and webs. One reel got stuck around my arm, and I screamed at the top of my lungs as I flung it, slashing the bottom row of monitors.

I pounded on the desk, over and over, shaking off dust from years of neglect. Glass crumbled into one of the broken monitors. The ones still-active flickered, my pathetic, haggard form displayed in the upper left corner. A still-operating VCR ticked as it attempted to play until a thin stream of smoke filtered out.

Buzz. Buzz.

I didn't realize the sound was my front doorbell and not from the machines until someone rang it again. The second time, it was like a bomb. I'd have jumped out of my shoes if I could jump, I was so startled.

The working screen displaying the sidewalk outside my townhouse was slumped too low to see who it was, but the shadow of a person standing at the top of my stoop was cast across the view. They held something. A briefcase? A bomb?

"Who in God's name..."

I swept onto the lift and up, hoping maybe this was a joke. A prank by Laura. If anyone in the world, maybe, potentially, might be allowed to come down here, it was her. But she knew better. She wouldn't betray me.

Buzz. Buzz.

I barreled out into my study, wheel hitting the bookcase and knocking over a few tomes. What did they matter now? I ran them over, then across the living room where my TV discussed some bullshit political march somewhere.

Throwing open the front door, I screamed, "What the fuck do you want!?"

I glared straight into the face of a middle-aged man holding an umbrella. Nobody I recognized. Nobody threatening. A bald spot, potbelly, mustard-stained slacks, and a workman's briefcase.

He seemed stunned, like mine would be the worst response he'd get from knocking on doors in this rundown neighborhood. The guy was in over his head.

"I asked a question." I might as well have growled.

He blinked. "Uh, sir... could I interest you in—"

"No."

"But you didn't—"

"And I won't."

I rolled backward and pulled the door with me. At the same time, I spotted someone else watching us from an alley across the street, half-crouched behind a garbage can the Tinman currently rummaged through. Somebody wearing an Iron City Marauders hat that covered their face in shadow.

"Out of my way!" I blew by the salesman and hit my ramp hard. The wheels of my crappy hospital loaner nearly misaligned as I bounced along the sidewalk and splashed water everywhere. The trip down that ramp was an eerie reminder of the last time I'd rushed like this to save Michelle. I took the briefest of moments to look both ways for mail trucks before barreling along without a care.

"You, what are you looking at?" I shouted.

Was I paranoid after what happened? Absolutely. But innocent people don't take off like bats out of hell, do they? The shadowy stranger bolted, knocking over the Tinman's cart on his way by and tripping. The bum hollered some unintelligible nonsense.

That gave me a chance to gain ground. My hands pushed along the rims of my chair, taking me to the road. Nobody beeped until I flew across Fisher Blvd. without looking. The snoop checked back and nearly tripped again.

But he was fast. Even with adrenaline and rage pumping through me like back in the old days, I couldn't keep up. He zipped down the next block.

What I lacked in speed, however, I made up for in knowing my turf. Tip number one for all would-be vigilantes—know where you live. Decades, I'd kept my headquarters a secret, but I was always wary. My mind, even in its foggy state, was a living map of Harborside.

"Get back here!" I barked as I emerged from the alley, and he looked directly at me. He spun around fast and sped off again around the corner.

These roads were freshly paved. Fast. I could still smell the asphalt baking in the sun. I cruised down the bus lane, and the snoop scrambled to keep ahead. Whoever he was, he was nervous. Stumbling, tripping over curbs. He knocked into a poor lady strolling down the sidewalk and plowed her over.

And then, unlike most criminals I'd ever pursued, he stopped to help her. I grabbed the side-mirror of a parked delivery truck outside a bodega to whip myself ahead and hopped the lowest part of the curb.

"What the hell do you want from me?" I screamed.

The snoop released the woman and sprinted down the nearest alley, throwing down a garbage can to impede me. I rumbled over the spilled refuse, then slalomed around the ass of a sleeping bum tucked under a tarp whom the snoop stumbled over.

My shoulders burned as I pushed them to their limits. Like with Michelle and the truck, I got lost in the thrill of being the real me again. It gave me tunnel-vision, which backfired the moment we burst out onto Bleak Street.

I hit a lip in the sidewalk, veered, and slammed into somebody's back. My chair dumped me, and I skidded across the hard, wet concrete, scraping up both hands.

The squeals of people all around sucked me back into the present. Women shrieked, asking if I was all right. Seeing me exactly how I saw myself in the mirror—more fit for a casket than a bed.

And not only the standard, light street traffic which was usual for west Harborside. But a proper crowd. Who knows what they were there for? A parade? Some new music device to keep them distracted while the filth took over their city? More likely, another useless march about taxes.

It didn't matter. Nearly a dozen eyes fell upon me. People reached down. I froze, transported back to the twisted games my foster father used to play. I could hear the feet shuffling against the barn floor like battle drums. The blood crusting under my fingernails as they dug into dirt to dull the pain. Everyone watching in silence as father whipped me for misbehaving. Mother telling them this was the way.

"Don't touch me!" I swiped at the gathering crowd like a feral cat. I scrambled for my toppled chair, digging my fingernails into the sidewalk, hoping the blood scratched off. I squinted, so I didn't have to see all the saucer-eyes watching me, dreaming up their own sad origin stories.

"Please, sir. I'll help." A hand wrapped my forearm.

Next thing the guy knew, he probably had a broken wrist. He staggered back and yelped. I grasped my chair and dragged it closer with a screech akin to nails across a chalkboard. Not that I'd know that sound. I'd never been to a normal school.

"Shit, shit, shit, are you okay?" someone said, shoving through the people gathered to watch my sideshow.

I spotted the Iron City Marauders hat as he leaned over me. My hand shot out, grasping a wad of shirt and choking the spy with his own collar.

"Hey, get off him!" some nosy bystander demanded.

He and others grabbed me by the back and dragged me away, but I had a grip refined by years of pushing my own wheelchair. They were the strongest muscles I owned. It wasn't like Professor Xavier, and his magical floating chair nobody ever explains. I still had to do all the work to move around.

My grip only relented when dog tags swung down out from under the shirt, clinking off each other. The people behind me collapsed, me on top. Isaac fell in the opposite direction after I let go, hitting his ass on the sidewalk.

"Lunatic," someone moaned.

"Fucking bum," cursed another.

One by one, they rolled out from under me and gave me space. I focused on the dog tags. It helped to do that while stuck in crowds. Focus on one small object like it was the only thing in the universe. As a child in the foster home, it was mostly bales of hay. I could pretend I was walking alone through golden plains, free of everything.

Until Steven and I found a comic book in the neighbor's garbage one night when we snuck out. Well worth the whipping I got after when I took the blame. I couldn't read back then, but the pictures told their own story. I could pretend I was off battling some grand villain instead of wrestling with foster brothers.

Then, I became the Roach and realized it's all fiction.

And in being the Roach, sometimes saving people meant having to delve into the sweat-and-drug-addled madness of clubs and malls. So, I refined my focusing trick to keep myself centered in crowds and stop my heart from bursting through my ribcage. Though, it helped when I had a chance to prepare.

"You planning to leave me down here, kid?" I grumbled.

Isaac peered up through thick glasses. With the hat knocked off his head, I immediately recognized the messy-haired runt I'd saved from bullies. That same one whose pathetic squeal kept me from rolling myself into the harbor, and then nearly got Michelle killed by fibbing. At least he gave me a chance to play unrequited hero again.

"Are you deaf?" I said.

"I... I thought you didn't want help?" Isaac stammered, voice as gentle as I remembered.

My gaze swept across all the ogling faces, and my heart skipped a beat. Now that I had my wits about me, I noticed all the angry protest signs the people held, against city conditions and in support of mayoral challenger Darrell Washington. Phrases like, SAFE AND HOMELESS, or, WE'RE STILL HERE.

Which one of them was a journalist? Which one of them would jot down their story of the wheelchair bandit who broke up their march? Plaster it in the papers, right where nobody told the story about me saving a little girl.

Not that I cared. Laura would have squashed the story anyway. I knew she didn't want her father knowing how much time she spent around me. There were too many lies swirling around my very existence. Too many dark secrets for ambulance-chasing hounds like Chuck Barnes to dig up that might put the Garrity Act in jeopardy and leave Iron City vulnerable to monsters again.

It was never about the clippings—who I'd saved or how I'd done it. It was about what the stories represented. A city paying attention. It was about making bad people afraid, because that's all the news really is, isn't it? Fearmongering. Keeping the people controlled and confined. At least the Roach's exploits told civilians where to stay away from. And it warned bad men that I was always watching. Ready to wipe them off the street.

Until I wasn't.

"Just get me up," I grunted, spotting two cops pushing through to find the cause of the ruckus.

Isaac retrieved his hat, then scampered over. He helped lift me by one shoulder while I pushed off the ground with the other. I felt the back of my clunker sag behind my weight since my ass was permanently numb. Before the kid could get a word in, I zipped back into that nearest alley. Only once I faced the dark passage, walls covered in blood-red graffiti, did I feel like my lungs could inflate again.

"Hey, Mister Roberts!" the kid called after me, just a bit louder than the protestors still discussing what the hell they'd just witnessed.

I rolled along, like a diver coming up for air. Even the stench of the bum sleeping beside a dumpster was welcome. Sometimes, I wondered if everyone else were the loons, struggling to slot into quaint homes on a pretty little grid. Maybe the haggard men on the streets like Tinman were the geniuses. Maybe, we were all in some TV program aliens watched for fun.

"Mister Roberts!" Isaac shouted, racing up ahead of me. He hunched over on his knees to gather his breath.

"How do you know my name?" I asked.

"That cop outside your house said it."

"After you assholes followed me home, right?"

No answer.

"Right?" I repeated.

"Th-th-that wasn't me. They wanted to have some more fun with you."

"You didn't stop them."

His lip twisted. "I... Are you okay?"

"Just golden." I stopped and turned to face him. "So, why the hell were you watching my house, then? Still helping them have some 'fun?'"

He hung his head, opened his mouth, then closed it again.

"You better tell me now, kid."

"Because it was my fault," he blurted. His eyes glazed over, and his lower lip started to tremble. "I shouldn't have let that jerk come and get his mom causing trouble. I lied for them, and because of me, you got... you got hit..." He couldn't finish the rest of the sentence, so I did it for him.

"By a Jeep. Pretty simple."

The lump in his throat bobbed. His shoulders sank. It was then I realized, Isaac wasn't really that scrawny. He just comported himself like a weakling. Took half-a-foot off his height by hunching like the weight of the world was constantly crushing him. Wore clothes that barely fit and let his crazy hair stick out from under his hat like spaghetti. It was no wonder bullies flocked to him. He practically wore a neon sign.

I breathed deeply. The protestors' sounds were completely gone now, and all that remained was Iron City's daytime ambiance. The rumble of cars. A horn here and there. A distant siren. A can being rattled for spare change.

"Was that your first time seeing anything like that?" I asked.

Isaac nodded, slowly. "In person."

"In-person is all that ever matters, kid. Don't let the boob tube lie to you. But look at me, I'm fine. Apparently, I'm invincible."

"But... it was my fault."

"It was a lot of people's faults. But now, you see what happens when you let bullies boss you around."

His cheeks flushed so dark I worried he might pop.

"I don't judge victims," I went on. "I only ask they learn from their mistakes." I rolled toward him, pushing him back against the brick wall as my wheel nearly ran up over his foot. A few feet above, an artist had scrawled the words, THE ROACH IS GONE, complete with my logo engulfed by a mushroom cloud. Not a bad bit of art, to be honest.

"What I do judge, though, are kids breaking into my house," I said, a harsh edge to my tone. "Stealing my things."

"W-w-what?" Isaac stuttered.

"Someone broke into my house while I laid in a hospital on life-support. I'm wondering if that person was you? Or maybe your two shithead friends."

"Me? No, it wasn't." He emphatically shook his head side-to-side, causing his glasses to slide down the bridge of his nose. "I swear, it wasn't."

I rolled a little closer. "Says the kid staking out my house. Hiding in the shadows. Just admit it: you saw your chance, and you broke in, and—"

"I only wanted to apologize, that's it!" he blurted. "But I worried you'd..." His words trailed off, and he pushed his glasses back on.

I studied him, head to toe. And it wasn't hard to confirm that it wasn't him who'd done it. I have this problem, you see. Anyone I meet, I see both the worst they're capable of, and the worst I'm capable of doing to them. An endless stream of dark thoughts dancing in the chaos that is my mind, predicting futures. Impossible to dam off without alcohol, and thanks to young Isaac, I was sober as a Buddhist.

My assumptions were rarely, if ever, far off.

This kid. He followed rules. He loved rules. Dead military dad, who was likely never home. Working, probably single mother doing her best, like Laura. Leaving him to entertain himself outside of school. That's the problem with wars. They ship strong men off and leave everybody else to pick up the pieces. Eventually, the death toll tallies up to a country filled with broken homes.

No, I knew it. Rules were the only thing that kept the balance in Isaac's lonely, friendless life. Rules kept him from swinging back at bullies he could probably take down by drawing on his rage. He wasn't a coward, but he wasn't brave, either. Something right in the middle. The definition of average.

I backed away and licked my lips. "You thought I'd what?"

"Nothing," he huffed under his breath.

"Scream at you? Beat you? Trust me, kid, if I thought you deserved that, I'd have rolled straight by you guys the other day, or month, or whenever it was. And I can tell you didn't break into my house, but what about your friends?"

"They aren't my friends. They're seniors."

"Whatever you say."

"And, it couldn't have been them," he said.

"Why not?"

"I told Frankie's mom what really happened after... you got hit. They got grounded so bad I haven't even seen them outside school."

Yep, average. The kind of kid that would call the cops at the drop of a hat. It's how most people are—sheep relying on sheepdogs to protect them from hungry wolves. Justice wasn't Isaac turning his bullies in. It would've been him taking a bat to Frankie's arm and *really* breaking it. Though, at least now I knew they were in school with him, potentially underage as seniors. Always a toss-up. Damn did I get lucky.

"They're going to beat your ass next time they see you," I said. "You know that, right?"

"They already make school the worst," he griped.

"Which is why you don't rat."

"I did it because it was the right thing to do. My mom—"

"You shouldn't have."

"I thought you died!" He stomped forward. I didn't flinch, but I was honestly proud. Some average people, they can be drawn out of their safety nets. Learn to fend for themselves so that the Roach didn't have to. It was a rare feat, but it happened.

Then, young Isaac sunk back, a tear rolling down his cheek. What a disappointment.

"I even came to the hospital," he sniveled. "Saw you lying there with tubes sticking out of you. How are you so mean and your daughter is so nice?"

My brow furrowed. "My what?"

"That lady who took care of you."

"She's not my... Look, you—" I caught myself, then blew out hot air. It wasn't worth an argument. My head was already killing me. "You're right. Sorry, kid. Just been a long day."

I gave my wheels a push and rolled myself back onto the street.

He trotted to keep up. "So, somebody broke into your house?"

"Don't you have something else to do?" I said. "Homework. Anything?"

"It's Sunday."

"Right? That's when most kids are rushing to get their homework done."

"Why don't you call the cops?" he asked. "They can get fingerprints, DNA, all that stuff."

"You watch too much *Miami Vice*, kid," I said. "All cops do is make a mess of things. If they even show up."

"They *have* to show up."

"You sure?"

His quizzical expression drew a smirk out of me. Not everyone gets a first-hand display of how the world really is when they're young, like I did. Any time me or any of my foster brothers called the authorities, a cop or a suit showed up, cleared the home, and we got punished. Steven tried a handful of times, even after I'd given up.

A few seconds went by in silence. Then Isaac offered a confident nod, as if in response to a conversation occurring in his own head. "Yeah, I am. The Roach can't be everywhere at once to pick up the slack."

"The Roach can't be anywhere anymore," I replied.

"What do you mean?"

"What do *you* mean?"

His eyes lit up. "Oh, right. You were in the hospital! Some people are saying he's back. My mom used to always say he was only making things worse, but I don't know. I've always thought he was cool."

I grabbed him. "Hold up, kid. What do you mean, back?"

"I mean back. He's saved a few people already. Here, I'll show you."

Isaac jogged on ahead like we were two kids on a playdate. My protests fell upon deaf ears as I pushed my exhausted arms to keep up. He approached a newsstand on the next corner and skipped all the major papers—those pillars of community that documented my entire career from start to silent finish.

"Dammit, kid," I said, breathless. "What are you on about?"

He passed a row of plastic-wrapped porno-mags and rifled through the next rack, plucking out this week's copy of the *Weekly Iron*. I don't think I'd ever picked one up in my life. Journalists were a pain, always trying to spin their angle about me, but accuracy mattered on their pages. Not to the *Weekly Iron,* or any of the soul-sucking, celebrity magazines on display near it, practically worshipping people whose only skill was playing make-believe.

The *Weekly Iron* was no different. It wasn't real news. A glorified tabloid focused on the most famous Iron City residents. Right on the front cover was a headline about our divorced mayor finding romance again. I knew the guy. He wasn't finding anything. Not since Laura's mother fled to the West Coast for some ridiculous dream of acting and never looked back.

He'd probably bought the pages for the article just to seem more human to his constituents before the election. Or to sneak in a picture of him talking to a woman outside of gleaming Aurora Tech Tower.

The entertainment tabloids like these were trash rotting the brains of our nation's people. Spinning the truth into popcorn clips. Especially the movies they promoted about my former line of work. Like the *Incredible Lion Man* and his overdramatic exploits striking fear into the hearts of New Sterling City's lowliest criminals. My existence had sparked a recent renaissance of superhero films and comics. It never stopped. And every time, the hero only hid who they were because they didn't want their loved ones getting hurt.

Ridiculous.

Anyone doing what I do—did—can't have loved ones. How could they? How could you hide sneaking out every night and coming home with bruises and burgeoning darkness in your soul? You can't. Real hero-vigilantes wear masks because that's all they are.

How do I know? I'm the only real one out there.

"Look." Isaac flipped through the pages, drawing my focus.

"You read the *Weekly Iron*?" I asked. Even speaking the title gave me a bad taste in my mouth.

"My mom makes me pick it up. She loves the dating column... or something." He shook his head. "It doesn't matter. There's been a new column in the last two issues about Roach sightings."

"People make that shit up all the time to see their names in the paper."

"Maybe five years ago."

The nonchalant way he said that wasn't meant to cause harm. I knew that. But it hurt anyway, as the truth often does. For the year after me being shot, everyone wanted to break the return of the Roach. Then they forgot, and I was as real as the films I inspired.

"When you were, what, six?" I said.

Isaac ignored me, stopping on a page toward the back of the issue and exclaimed, "Right here!" He pointed so hard he almost knocked the paper out of his own clammy hands.

"I know it doesn't look like it, kid, but I do really have things to do," I lied.

"Just look."

He knelt and held the paper in front of my face. I blinked hard to try and concentrate. The font was too small and page too white for my aching head. As if noticing my struggle, Isaac wiped away some rain droplets and ran his finger under the title as he read, "'The Roach Resurfaces Again.'"

"Give me that."

I snagged it and skimmed. A typical fluff piece, light on detail, high on drama, about how the Roach—well, clearly not the Roach—saved a dancer from a mugging. Pretty standard stuff. She couldn't see his face through the mask, blah, blah, fucking blah. As real as the story on page four about England's pregnant princess being eager to divorce her royal husband. Right.

But it was the next page that earned my attention. The picture was blurry, like any paparazzi photo taken at night. However, this specific one was of someone wearing *my* suit and mask. Or a perfect replica, at least. Only difference from when I last saw it was that the Roach symbol was bright and distinct, as if repainted.

Whoever the copycat was, the photographer caught him running down an alley into the shadow. That's right. Running. On his own two feet. Meaning, it was either an old photo someone managed to snap when I was active, or whoever had stolen my suit now paraded around in it playing hero.

I was so worried about someone trying to expose me after I found my lair broken into, that this eventuality hadn't even crossed my mind. Somehow, it felt even more violating. Not just robbing me, but wearing my skin.

The paper groaned as my grip tightened, stretching the binding.

Isaac was lucky I was busy holding it, or I might have accidentally struck him out of fury.

Sure, it could have been a rip-off costume. I'd worn my suit down by the harbor that day, and nobody looked twice. It was a popular Halloween costume in Iron City, or, at least, it was. And it wouldn't be the first time a copycat tried to pick up where I'd left off only to quickly wind up behind bars. But the timing was uncanny. Even worse still, was the name at the end of the article.

"Chuck fucking Barnes," I said out loud.

He was the one disgraced journalist who'd chase this story no matter what. Who'd push to get it in print with the *Weekly Iron* since no reputable publication would ever run anything by him anymore. Maybe because he really believed the Roach was back. More likely, to get under my skin and force me to tell the truth.

I clenched the paper and wheeled around without a word.

"What is it?" Isaac asked.

"Hey, you gotta pay for that!" the newsstand operator yelled.

I wouldn't have cared, but yet another cop was buying the day's paper, and I didn't have the time for trouble. They seemed to be everywhere these days, and yet never where they needed to be. Like helping Isaac fend off bullies in that alley.

"Pay the man. My wallets at home," I told Isaac, then continued along.

Someone had spent the last month pretending to be me. Wearing the only face of mine that ever meant a damn. I was going to get to the bottom of it.

CHAPTER

"C'mon, you runt," I muttered to myself, rolling back and forth on the sidewalk of the Stacks district, imagining I was tapping my foot. At least it'd stopped raining.

I'd sent Isaac up to his apartment to get the previous issue of the *Weekly Iron*, featuring the first appearance of my copycat. No time to scold him for leading a relative stranger to the place where he lived. To his credit, he didn't invite me up.

Probably didn't want his new friend to see the one-window box he and his mother were stuffed into without daddy. You don't expect a backpack-on-both-shoulders and glasses-wearing kid like him to live in the Stacks, but welcome to Iron City. If Harborside was the city's crotch-stain, this was its taint. The shittiest side of a city with plenty of shitty sides, filled with rundown projects mostly housing minorities. If it wasn't boarded up and covered in graffiti, it would be soon.

Hey, Darrell Washington should have put that on all his campaign posters stuck up around the area, most fallen and trampled.

In my heyday, I could've cleaned the crime and the gangs out, but I wasn't Robin Hood. I had no gold to offer the poor and disenfranchised. Isaac's building was a hodgepodge of broken windows, entry door half off the hinges, brick so discolored and chipped you could see the walls' innards in places. And that was just superficial.

Homeless and strung-out crackheads littered the sidewalk out front. A tattooed guy in a hoodie dealt crack at the corner by a scrapyard. A group of youths played hockey on the street with sticks and a banged-up beer can, blasting their grating music on a boombox with only one working speaker while an old blind man on his stoop yelled at them to keep it down.

It didn't matter who was in charge of the city, the grime was never scraped away. At least Mayor Garrity came down hard on organized crime and the drug influx, but there were some bullies even the Roach couldn't touch; those high up in Downtown Iron City's few ivory towers counting their piles of cash earned off mothers like Isaac's living in projects like this.

No. I wasn't like a silver-screen-superhero. I knew my limits. And the county jails and morgues could afford to deal with the reachable bullies *I* had put in them.

"Got it!" Isaac announced, shouldering through the door, panting. He waved another edition of the *Weekly Iron* in the air like he'd won a game of capture the flag.

I snapped my fingers to hurry him. He obliged, rushing to slap the magazine down in my hand. I was about to scold him when I noticed he already had the correct page earmarked. Some flamboyant crew of superheroes for a new movie donned the cover—*The Liberty Squad*. Apparently, that was the theme that had inspired the Roach column.

"Sorry, Mister Roberts. My mom asks a million questions," Isaac said.

"For God's sake, just Reese," I replied. "And she just lets you roam around out here? Alone?"

He bit his lip, looked away. "Yeah, on weekends. As long as I'm back for dinner." He was lying, that much was obvious. I didn't care to press further.

Flipping to the earmarked page, I used my own finger this time to help me focus and read yet another column by Chuck Barnes. Same deal as the latest story, minus a picture of someone in my suit. A masked robber hit a bodega down on 73rd Street, at the border of Harborside and the Stacks. Held the cashier at gunpoint until the false Roach barged in.

According to Chuck, the cashier said it all happened too fast to comprehend much. Some shots went off and shattered the storefront, as indicated in the attached photograph of the location. Then, the robber dropped his bag and fled. The copycat vanished soon after.

There was a time nobody in Iron City, let alone Harborside, would dare attempt such a brazen act and risk my judgment. I always have the local news playing on at home—the channel with the blonde bombshell and the plastic-haired putz. It happened now from time to time. The Garrity Act couldn't erase it all, especially far beyond Downtown, where there were no CCTVs yet. Cops had to eat. Sleep. Follow their rules.

When I prowled the city, if a robber tried to take some poor soul's livelihood, they earned the same fate. I'd find them, break into their place, take everything they had, and toss it out onto the streets for anyone to take.

Hm, I guess I was sort of like Robin Hood.

Anyway, then I'd break their gun-hand and leave them for the cops alongside any proof I'd managed to dig up. The things it takes to dot whatever I's and cross whatever T's police need to get criminals locked up in county.

Hammurabi had it right a few thousands of years ago with his "eye for an eye" idea. Even if it was my foster mother who'd quoted his laws when someone got in trouble. The cradle of ancient civilization and he figured out what we, in the most advanced country on the goddamned planet, can't. I'll never understand when we humans got so fucking soft.

"Does that help?" Isaac asked, breathing down my neck.

"It's something." I stowed it alongside the other edition.

"Why do you care, anyway?"

"What?"

"About this stuff."

"I don't."

Isaac slid around in front of me, wearing the sort of mischievous grin I didn't think he was capable of. "No. You want to meet him, don't you?" he asked.

"Just keeping busy, kid." I started to roll in the direction of that bodega.

He caught up fast. "No way. You were wearing a Roach costume that day we met. I remember. You're a faaan."

I didn't care for the sing-song way he used that term. 'Fan' was so derogatory. It meant, 'adoring follower of someone that can do what they aren't capable of doing or willing to try to.' It was how people got lost in dreams instead of working to get out of this dump.

"And *you're* starting to get on my nerves," I said.

"Well, what then?" Isaac asked. "You think he can find out who robbed you?"

"Sure. Let's go with that."

"What did they take?"

"None of your business."

"Well, I still think you should just call the police," he decided, crossing his arms over his chest, which looked awkward as he walked beside me. Who the hell was I to judge? At least he could walk.

"That's because, like all kids, you're a moron," I said, turning my head toward him.

"Hey, I get straight B's... mostly."

"My point exactly. You still haven't realized it's all bullshit." I tapped the magazine. "Thanks for these, I'll be seeing you around." I veered off the curb and onto the street. Isaac stopped me with a shout.

"Hey, I can help!"

"No, you can't."

His lips parted. No words came out.

"Go home, kid. You've done your community service. Find an arcade or see another movie or something."

Without bothering to look, I crossed the street. A few cars stuck at a red light honked horns as if I'd run over their cats. I squeezed by one and that rule-adoring teenager back across the street didn't follow me. He simply watched, disappointment clear as day upon his face. Then, he huffed and kicked the street. He didn't go anywhere, just took a few aimless steps.

Poor kid. I knew what it was like to grow up without any friends. But one day, he'd understand how much better that was than caring about people only for them to throw shit in your face. The other shoe always drops.

Except with Laura. I swear. That woman is a goddamn saint.

I took 3rd Ave down through the edge of Harborside. It was a near ten-block roll, but I needed the crisp air to keep my blood from boiling at the thought of someone staining my legacy. Besides, cabs were a nightmare. Watching some schlep try to load my chair into his trunk, groaning the whole time. Trapped in a tiny backseat with a stranger? No thanks. People are way too trusting.

And don't get me started on the city's rickety light-rail transit system. The people-mover running through Downtown and encircling the metropolitan area was too packed for people on legs, let alone in a chair. The very thought of cramming in a metal tube like a sardine with all the sweaty, grubby businesspeople, teeth chattering as we rumbled along rusty tracks a decade overdue for repairs, gave me a shudder.

I stopped across the street to case the location, and if I'm being honest, give myself a rest and massage my temples to quell a headache that seemed to always be there these days. The bodega called CORNER MARKET was as unassuming as its name.

A four-way intersection made it an easy target. Plenty of directions for a robber to run. Enough foot-and-car traffic to get lost in and cross-up any patrolling cops, though not quite enough to make me overly anxious. And this was at about 5:00PM. Later in the night, the place was the kind of easy-pickings that might have started me off on a long shift of crime-fighting.

The panel of the storefront from the picture remained boarded up. Beyond that, the inside seemed back to normal: row after row of snacks, crap, and half-rotted fruits. There were fridges along the back, with only one reserved for the good stuff.

I only then realized that I'd been sober all day—a rarity since the gunshot. I'd only reward myself with sweet nectar after solving this latest mystery. Maybe I'd roll back to the harbor, wearing *my* suit again, and finish what me and Mr. Daniels had started. Or was it old Jimmy Bean?

A bell dinged as a middle-aged woman opened the door and held it for me on her way out.

"You're welcome," she said as I moved in, without waiting for a 'thanks' from me even though she'd stood like a dolt in the space I needed to go through and made things even more difficult.

A guy at the counter was buying a pack of cigarettes. I slid in behind him and waited my turn. His knee banged the edge of my wheelchair as he finished up, and instead of a "Sorry," I earned a "Watch it." And now, it's clear why I don't bother saying "Thank you" every time someone holds a fucking door, right?

"How can I help you, sir?" the cashier asked, leaning over the counter to look down at me. A bronze-skinned immigrant from somewhere in the Far East, working his ass-off only to be robbed. I couldn't quite place the accent.

"This story." I slapped the magazine down on the counter, folded at the correct page. "Is it true?"

"Yes, sure. Now, what are you buying?" he replied without even really looking.

"Answers."

"Excuse me, sir, but there are others behind you."

I peeked back and saw an older, moon-faced man waiting to buy a carton of milk.

"After you." I waved him along, then rolled around the side of the counter. While the cashier dealt with the man counting change, I waited at the opening to get to the register.

The cashier's eyes darted nervously to me until he was finished with the customer. Then, once the old man left the building, the cashier scowled at me. "If you aren't buying anything, you have to leave, sir."

I raised the magazine and poked the page three times. "Is. This. True?"

"You can read it. Please, we are very busy."

I scanned the store. A few adults perused the shelves. A bum kept warm. Two teenagers were in the snack aisle, smuggling who knows what. That's it.

"C'mon, I can't see well and lost my glasses." I gestured down to my wheelchair. It had nothing to do with reading, however, it was a move that usually worked on people. I hated using it, but desperate times...

The cashier clenched his jaw then crept over. He kept his voice low. "Please, sir, I already said everything I know to the police and reporters."

"Right, Chuck Barnes, crime-chaser extraordinaire." I made myself comfortable leaning over my armrest and against his counter. "So, a robber comes in here, guns blazing and you—what?"

"Who are you?" he questioned.

"An interested party."

"Please, sir, I have much work to do."

"Mr... uh..." I glanced down at the magazine. I'd read his name enough times on the way over, but the information refused to stick. "Patel? That you?" I said. "Just calm down and talk to me. I'm only after the truth."

He exhaled through his teeth as he checked the counter only to realize nobody was close to buying anything. Those teenagers scrammed right out the front door, bell chiming, and he said nothing.

I'd sized Patel up by then. Being foreign, he had a please-everybody mentality—something we spoiled Americans could learn from. Everything about him said, 'I just want to fit in here.' From his three-button shirt with the little alligator to the way his accent seemed weaker only when he focused on hiding it.

"Are you with the insurance agency?" he asked. "I told you people everything over the phone. I just want a new window!" He pointed at the boarded-up storefront and rattled off what sounded like curses in his native language.

"Oh, right, I forgot to introduce myself," I said. "Yeah, they sent me out to evaluate the case in person."

"Ah! Well, that is good, yes?" Patel clasped my hand and shook it enthusiastically. I didn't even have to offer it. "I will tell you anything that helps, my friend."

"Excellent. Sorry, I uh, banged my head, and haven't been thinking clearly." I cleared my throat. "So, start from the beginning and be as specific as possible, because this article says all you heard were gunshots and then they were gone. I imagine you had to see something."

"Yes. Yes. It was almost closing time when a very shady man in a hooded sweatshirt came in. He turned quickly, and I did not see his face. He checked that fridge, over there." He gestured toward the beer. "When I looked back again, he wore a ski mask and aimed a gun at me over the counter. He threatened to shoot me if I did not open the registers and fill the bag."

"What bag?"

"A garbage bag. He threw it at my face. His pupils were very wide. I remember that. And he shook, out of control. Perhaps on drugs or something. So, I did what he asked." Guilt swarmed his expression as he looked toward the floor. "I am only trying to make a living in your country, you understand? I did not know what else to do."

I shrugged. "I'm not judging."

"I filled the bag most of the way when someone burst through the door. I only got a quick look before I ducked, but he wore a dark brown suit. Or maybe red. And a gas mask, with tubes like this." He imitated wide arcs down from his mouth with closed hands. "I only arrived here four years ago, so I did not realize this was the famous Iron City vigilante known as the Roach."

"What a welcome party for you," I said, nodding toward the broken storefront.

"Yes," he replied with a tinge of melancholy. "Anyway, the Roach must have surprised the robber because he spun around and fired his gun right away."

"And that's it?" I said. "The robber missed some shots and then ran off?"

Patel shook his head. "No, he did not miss."

"What?"

"His first shot hit the Roach right in the chest." He tapped his own, just above the sternum. "The Roach flew back onto his bottom."

"I thought you were hiding and couldn't see anything?"

"I was, but I heard... and maybe I snuck a few looks. I do not know, I was terrified, you see. It is all blurry. The robber was scared, too. He held his head and started pacing, like... uh... like a madman. Cursing that he had shot somebody. And then, like magic, the Roach rose back up to his feet. He charged the robber, and a few more shots went off into the glass."

Rose back up. I wish. But that confirmed something for me—this copycat was definitely wearing my skin. The Roach wasn't only a name. It defined me. Struck fear into the hearts of bad men like my tiny namesake would someone shitting in their bathroom when one crawls out of a crack in the floor. They're nearly unkillable, which, I mean, I took a bullet to the spine and a car to the chest and survived both times. My suit had Kevlar inlays that had saved me from dozens more bullets. All except that one sneaky bastard that took my legs.

It was expensive labor, crafting that suit, but I had money back then from working for the city. It's amazing how far cash goes when you don't waste it on all the trivial, decadent crap people in this city love to even when they can't afford it. But, that's not my war.

"Then what happened?" I asked.

"Then nothing," Patel replied. "When I crawled to safety and looked again, they were both gone. The robber left the bag of money behind."

I scanned through the column in the *Weekly Iron* one last time. "I don't understand. Why is so little of that printed in the story Chuck wrote? You told him the whole story?"

Patel nodded, then shrugged. "Maybe he wasn't allowed enough words or something. I do not know."

"And the cops?"

"I told them the same. They said there was no blood, and that it was probably a... copycat. I think that was the term they used. That was when I learned about this Roach character."

"Excuse me, I'd like to buy this!" an elderly shopper croaked, shaking some dreadful beef snack near the register like it'd summon its operator over. She wore a scowl as deep as a toad's, with wrinkles even deeper.

Poor Patel immigrates here from god-knows-where and has to deal with people robbing and scolding him every day. When in the end, all he'd done was properly report a crime instead of pretending the money had been stolen and trying to pocket some extra insurance cash like many savvy, Harborside storeowners would have.

"I will be right over," Patel said, somehow maintaining a polite demeanor. Then he turned back to me. "I really must get back to work now. I hope my explanation is sufficient."

"It's the best I'll get," I said.

Patel's gaze elongated, as if he were looking at something far away. I knew the type. The look of a man who'd stared death in the eye and returned unscathed... on the outside at least. He'd never walk the streets the same way again. Every footstep behind him would be like a time bomb. Tick, tick, tick, until the stress got the better of him and he snapped at someone. Hopefully, not the wrong person.

"Sir," the old bat spoke firmly.

I watched Patel's fists clench in real-time. Before he snapped or did anything to lose a customer, thanks to me prodding into his trauma, I gave him a pat on the arm and said, "You did good, Patel. You'll be fine now."

"Thank you, my friend," he said, eyes finally snapping back toward me. "Whoever that Roach is, he saved me. I cannot afford to lose anything here. I will never forget it."

"Sounds more like he got lucky."

I forced a smirk, then rolled my way out from behind the counter. The elderly lady stared daggers at me. As I went to return the look, I realized that I had to be precisely where the robber would have been when he shot my copycat.

What kind of vigilante would be sloppy enough to burst through the front door?

And then I remembered... me...

There was a time in Iron City before I was the Roach. I know, who'd have imagined that?

I'd escaped the hell of my youth, growing up on a farm in a foster home that made cults seem like child's play. A few years, surviving and scrounging for food in town after town across the Midwest, and there I was, in a bustling big city. Iron City was in its golden age then, the many waterfront factories casting it in an eternal haze and browning the Horton River.

And even though there were people everywhere—so many that my heart raced at every block I turned onto—I soon realized that, here, on the streets, even though people were all over, they were rarely looking.

They were wrapped up in their own little worlds. Their jobs.

Their wardrobes. What to eat. Who to take home that night. I was surrounded by hundreds of thousands of people at any given time, and yet, in most of the city, I felt alone. Just how I liked it.

Of course, I could barely afford something in lower Harborside with the money I'd earn taking petty jobs across the country. And I had no applicable skills besides farming, brawling with foster-siblings, and getting revenge on foster parents. Write that on a resume. See how far it'll get you.

But all that was okay because I was finally free.

So, what does a young man with no skills and barely any money do in a city? He gets a job nobody else wants. And so, that's where I found myself, working maintenance in the sewage and water lines down with the roaches and the rats. Getting home every night with my face and hands covered in blood, sludge, and worse. Even the factories willing to hire anyone out of the Stacks didn't want me.

I didn't mind. It kept me busy and with enough spare change to survive without begging anymore. I never understood how any coworkers complained about it, but they all did. A job, a roof, food, nobody beating up on you or forcing you to beat up on others—it was a goddamned paradise.

There was this one guy I worked with that talked too much. Billy Price. I don't remember everyone I took down in Iron City, but you remember your first. The moment I looked him in the eyes, I knew he was scum. Every day, while we ate sandwiches behind a divider at whatever underground station we were working in, he'd bitch about everything under the sun. And nothing more than his 'nagging' girlfriend, Alexis Bradley, who got too many looks as a diner waitress.

I wanted to punch him after every lewd comment about how he shut her up, or how her body made it worth it, but I restrained myself. That's what a decent member of society does: he holds back and behaves when all the whispering little voices in his head are begging him to lash out.

Months went by in my simple life. Billy talked and talked, and then one day, the girl he was telling a story about spending the night with wasn't Alexis. He looked at me then, right in the face, and said, "You know how it is. A guy has to go fishing, but it's all good as long as he returns to port."

Then he cackled like a horny teenager and the other workers with him. He even nudged me, the joke too funny for me to possibly not get. I pretended to laugh as, yet again, I held back. Because that's what a decent member of society does.

Those little voices told me to keep paying attention, though. So, I did. I got beers with Billy and the fellas after our shifts. I found out where he lived when I followed his drunken ass home. A ramshackle flat on Jefferson Avenue, a few blocks past Horton Point in the shadow of the abandoned Iron City Marauders Stadium before they built the new one out in the 'burbs.

I hid and watched. Alexis got home later that evening, wearing her pink, polka-dotted uniform complete with a frilly skirt. She looked like a barbie doll, all covered in unseen bruises.

The moment she got inside, Billy chewed into her. Asking where she'd been. Yelling that she was screwing somebody else. He had her to tears by the time I heard the unmistakable sound of her being struck, followed her body hitting the floor.

Others might have called the police and waited for them to ask questions while Billy got away with it. Others might have listened while she decided to defend this asshole that was ruining her life. I knew what it was like to be a prisoner in a place with no exit. You start to feel like it's what you deserve.

But I'd heard enough. I raised my hood and then put my heavy boot through the front door. I didn't even have a mask on. I can remember the screaming, though, I'm not sure who said what. I pummeled into Billy, sending him flipping over the counter. His head hit a corner, and he was out cold in seconds. Then, I fled.

Running down the streets that night, I hadn't felt more alive since watching my foster home burn to the ground. I swear, my heart raced a mile a minute. It was euphoric. Like how junkies explain the first time they dropped acid.

Billy Price never showed up to work again. Not with a bandage on his head, not with anything. Apparently, he'd cracked his skull open on the counter after I pushed him and died of a brain hemorrhage before the ambulance even got him to the hospital.

Me and all the other maintenance guys from our team went to the funeral—I had to. Had to avoid suspicion. But there were no witnesses besides Alexis, who'd seen nothing. Not in Harborside, where everybody's out for themselves.

What surprised me about the funeral, however, was how sad I felt. Not for Billy. Hell no. I'd killed before. Not by choice, but they all had it coming, and so did he.

No, I felt bad because sweet Alexis cried over that piece of shit like I'd never seen anyone before. And there, sitting in the house of a God I didn't believe in, while desperately longing to feel something so beautiful as blind faith, was where the Roach was born. If I'd merely broken Billy's hand so he couldn't hit her, then in a few weeks, maybe Alexis would have realized he wasn't worth staying with.

His crimes weren't equal to death, and that imbalance broke Alexis. I don't know where she went after that, but because of me, she had to uproot her entire life just to stop feeling sad over a guy that deep down, I know she wished she didn't care about.

Still, I knew I'd finally found my purpose. Saving the helpless, the trapped, and the battered. Like any sword against injustice, my point just needed to be sharpened. Refined...

"Mister... I'm sorry, I didn't get your name. Are you okay?"

Patel's voice drew me out of the reverie about when I too was young and clumsy. I sucked down a mouthful of air and looked from side to side. The memory was so real. Now, I sat in a fog, as if waking from a lucid dream. The old woman had already purchased her beef sticks and left.

Had I passed out? Fallen asleep like an old geezer?

"Sir?" Patel said.

I shook the cobwebs out of my skull and clutched my wheels. "I'm fine."

He asked something about his insurance money, but I kept going. I figured I was still out of whack from the accident, but if that happened when something important was going on, it would end ugly. I couldn't worry about that now, though.

I needed to keep digging. The copycat was real, not just some piece of Chuck's imagination sold to a tabloid to fit a superhero theme. Whoever it was, they clearly had no idea what they were doing. A recipe for getting someone killed... or killing someone. I knew that from experience.

CHAPTER SEVEN

Next up on my list was the copycat's second recorded save. A woman going by Roxy, who we'll call a dancer. Hard to define anyone who worked at a rathole like the *Bleek Street Gentleman's Club* as that. There wasn't anything frowned upon in the place so long as you had the cash, but I digress.

People needed to make a living in a city like this somehow. As long as they only hurt themselves, they're beyond my purview.

That didn't mean I had to play along with the cracks in society's pavement, though. I couldn't stomach the thought of willingly entering the club. A place for everyone to stare at the hermit in a wheelchair who they'll think needs to pay to get his rocks off? Sometimes, I wonder what the hell I was fighting to protect when people are so willing to wade in the sludge for a few cheap thrills.

Clubs like this were a breeding ground for the types of scumbags I took down religiously. Men who couldn't get a handle on their baser urges, needed someone to tell them how 'special' they were every damn second of every damn day. A sweating, drugged up, gyrating throng of men at their most primitive.

This specific venue happened to be mob owned. I only mention that to note that since I'd driven away most of the other gangs warring over corners of the city, they were one of the few name brands left. Mostly because they were a pale shade of what they were when I first got on scene. The feds took care of that. Now, they were essentially crooked businessmen with deep pockets.

I couldn't even say what other relevant organized gangs remained operating. Occasionally, the news reported on some initiation gone wrong by remnants of the River Kings, or the Iron Riders hitting a delivery truck on I-75 beyond the city limits. These days, all they really amounted to were groups of people with the same skin color wearing matching tattoos.

After the Roach and the Garrity Act, gangs in Iron City barely got their hands into more than selling drugs on street corners and being a bad influence on inner-city school kids desperate for cash. They all became too preoccupied, worrying about who was in charge until their turf slowly evaporated—exactly my intention when I used to pick them off from the top. Tough as any gang member claims to be. They're all out for themselves without someone bossing them around.

But the mob had stuck around to some degree, even when the Bratva moved to greener pastures. Sure, they caused trouble sometimes, but mostly, they behaved. Iron City was just one of many outlets to the rest of the Midwest. Like a minor trading hub for weapons and drugs, usually moving them right on through.

Probably wasn't that hard, considering everything these days is made in China. Not much I could do about it. They were Mayor Garrity's problem now.

The truth is, Italian, Black, Mexican, Russian—they're all the same to me. All capable of the same evils. What does it matter if someone looks or talks differently? In Iron City, as industry slowly abandoned us, everyone had their chance to be disenfranchised or taken advantage of by foreign influences until they left too.

I rolled right by the black-clad bouncer standing at the club's front entry, wearing his sunglasses at night.

"Taking the song a bit literally, aren't you, pal?" I said to him, but he wasn't listening.

I rolled into an alley around the corner. I'd saved plenty of women behind strip joints, cornered by creeps who believed the lies whispered to them in champagne rooms in the name of higher tips.

A young black woman leaning against a dumpster wore a fur coat so red it looked like she was on fire. She took a long drag of a cigarette, relishing every second of blowing the smoke through her ruby lips. A blonde in a jean jacket two sizes too big stood across from her, hands tucked under her pits for warmth. The jacket probably belonged to a boyfriend I'd never want to meet.

I approached them. They should've fled at the first sight of a stranger back here after dusk. They didn't. I'd cleaned up the streets so well back in the day, I fear it knocked the common sense out of people. Or it was just impossible for someone to be afraid of a guy in my... condition.

"Doors on the other side, sweetie," the black woman said to me, face lost behind a mask of smoke.

"I'm not looking for the door," I replied.

"Well, you ain't getting anything out here." She stretched her neck in the direction opposite me and continued to focus on her cigarette.

"Don't be rude, Candy. He's cute." The blonde sauntered toward me. She grabbed a clump of my beard, but I shook my head free.

"Says the girl who gives all her tips to bums." Candy chuckled. Her name really fit her outfit.

"I'm no bum," I said.

"Says every bum."

I bit my lip.

"Don't listen to her," the blonde said, tracing her finger along the back of my neck. It made goosebumps rise all over me, all the while, reminding me of the part that couldn't rise. I shrugged her off out of instinct.

"What, you don't like being touched?" she asked.

"He's probably some weird virgin who just wants a look-see," Candy added.

"Look," I growled, then took a moment to calm myself. I hated this part of the job—acting like a detective, scouring for information. Not every situation was as cut and dry as a robber with a switchblade or an abusive ex. Sometimes, it took a bit of finesse. The difference was when I got the information I needed, I could act on it instead of wading through miles of caution-tape.

"I just need to ask Roxy a question," I said. "Do you know her?"

Candy puffed on her cigarette. "Roxy, who?"

I didn't know. I grabbed that issue of the *Weekly Iron* and thumbed to the page, only to find that I wasn't being forgetful. Her full name wasn't listed, because Roxy was most certainly not her full name. The girls inside venues like this protected their identities, same as I did.

"I don't know her last name," I admitted.

"Oh, stop messing," the blonde said to Candy. "Yeah, Roxy. A pretty blonde, just like me." She twirled a strand of her hair around her finger.

"And only a dozen years older," Candy remarked.

"You're such a bitch." The blonde punched her in the arm and earned a yelp. "Candy is just jealous because Roxy's been getting a *lot* of attention recently."

"What kind of moron walks Murdock Park at night, girl? But no, for her, the fuckin return of the Roach swoops in and saves the day. Now every nerdy white guy in Iron City wants a dance from her just so they can ask what he's like."

The blonde flashed me a grin. "Like I said, jealous."

"My ass. She's a fuckin liar who was on her way out. Ain't no Roach. Not no more. Everybody knows that." Candy dropped her cigarette and ground it into the pavement with a sparkling, oversized heel as bright as red licorice.

"So, she's been bragging about the Roach saving her?" I snuck in the question before they kept arguing. The more they talked, the more it felt like I'd vanished into the shadows, which would've been ideal at any other time.

"Oh, so that's what you want?" Candy said. "Another weirdo after her ridiculous story?"

"Be nice," the blonde said. "He's crippled." She grasped the handles of my wheelchair and leaned in over my shoulder. That was when I got a whiff of her breath and a good look at her glazed eyes. She was wasted. One of her heels slid out as she attempted to push me. She caught herself on the dumpster, and Candy stopped me by grabbing both my chair's wheels.

"Girl, he's just another bullshitter in Iron City," she said. "I bet he can walk, too."

Candy gave my chair a shake. By pure instinct, my hand shot out and clutched her wrist. I saw a wave of fear pass across her face.

"Get off me!" she squealed.

"Sorry," I stammered, letting her go and allowing my chair to roll back a few feet. "I swear, I'm only here to talk to Roxy. I think she's lying, too."

"Hey, don't touch her!" the blonde shouted as she pushed my shoulder. For such a skinny thing, she was remarkably strong—drunk muscles. My chair rocked, and I needed to shift my weight to keep from tipping. I blocked her next push with my arm, which she misconstrued as an attack and shrieked even louder than her friend.

My attempts to calm them were useless.

"You fuckin creep!" Candy yelled. She went to kick my chair, but her heel got stuck in a spoke, and she tripped. Her fur-coat got snagged on the dumpster handle and tore.

And so there I was, a drunk girl pushing on me, another on the floor looking like she'd been through the wringer. I knew what it looked like. I'd seen plenty of situations like it from afar and been the hero to leap in and take down the offender.

How many muggers had I thwarted who were merely caught in a misunderstanding, in the wrong place and time? I doubted many. I always looked straight into the men's eyes and saw them for what they really were. You can't hide it there. But still, nobody's perfect, even the Roach.

I wondered... if this copycat looked into my eyes, what would he see in them?

Suddenly, the back entrance to the club flew open. A bouncer with a body probably as unnatural as half the dancers inside appeared in the doorway. His biceps could pop my skull like a walnut. His bald head looked like yet another bulbous muscle popping off his shoulders.

The blonde was still carrying on and pushing while Candy struggled to pull her heel free.

The bouncer cursed and charged me. All I had time to do was wish I'd sucked it up and entered through the front door. I braced for an impact likely to be equivalent to the truck that ran me over when a bloodcurdling scream echoed from inside the club.

Not like the ones these girls unleashed, who only worried they might be in trouble. A real one. The kind that could only come bubbling out of a throat when its owner has no time to think or react. Something primal. Elemental. Fear in its purest form.

The juiced-up bouncer stopped in his tracks and looked back toward the door.

Maybe it was because of the accident, I don't know. Something switched on inside me, and I reverted to my more formidable, former self. I lifted back on my chair, popping Candy's heel free, then zoomed for the door. The bouncer grabbed at me and said something I didn't hear.

I was too busy delivering three strikes. One to the side of his knee, then stomach, followed by a jab to the throat, until the brute was on his knees, gasping for air. There's a lesson for you. All the muscles in the world aren't good for anything if you don't know how to use them.

I raced down the club's back hall, kept dark for obvious reasons. The stench was appalling and burned my throat.

The club was still pumping. Girls on stages, swirling down poles with neon light glowing all over them. Men in suits watching from sofas all around them, flicking singles at high heels. Tattooed, wannabe gangsters having their meets in a booth. Drunks getting themselves kicked out for being too handsy.

Security, however, amassed in the center aisle between two curved stages, being barked at by their boss. I didn't recognize the man. I was too out of the loop, but I knew he had to be in charge. Black suit and a bright purple tie. Always with his chin jutting out.

It takes a certain level of influence to walk around in what's essentially a costume and avoid ridicule. People in power do it. Take a look around at any boss of anything. Even celebrities. They have their special little ways of sticking out. The skin they choose to wear.

The boss sent them scattering throughout the club to shut things down. I gathered my bearings and noticed many of them dispatched to lead an exodus of patrons from the hallway on my left. Doorways covered with beaded drapes lined it, behind which all rules were off, depending on the wad in your wallet.

I held my breath and delved through the mass of scared patrons and dancers. Knees bumped my chair. Curses were flung my way. But the good thing about being eternally half-height is it's easy to get lost.

One of the dancers crouched against the far wall, bra half-off, crying hysterically. A member of security comforted her. It didn't take me long to figure out why. The bead-drape of one private room still swished. Behind it, a young woman lay flat on the floor, arms and legs spread, completely naked.

She was face up, a deep gash running from her privates up to her sternum. Her eyes were frozen open, stuck in a state of pure horror.

She wasn't alive. She'd died like that, with her mouth stuffed full of cockroaches. One by one, the bugs crawled out of her gaping mouth.

Her head was turned to the side. A silver necklace draped down across one breast, the pendant in the form of a name: ROXY.

"This is some Jack the Ripper shit," one girl said behind me, voice shaking.

She wasn't wrong. I'd seen brutality. I'd caused brutality. Felt throats crunch within my very own hands. And I'd dealt with plenty of monsters and maniacs who thought they'd make a name for themselves by taking down the Roach. Even a cartel boss attempting to extend reach into the northern states who was tired of me busting up drug rings, so he put guns in the hands of Hispanic kids throughout the Stacks. I pulverized his followers until they abandoned the city completely. Mayor Garrity probably took credit for that too.

The point is, every enemy who focused on me would send messages in perverse ways. I was never surprised by them. And not because comics told me that every hero's journey winds up causing them to generate their own arch-nemesis, but because it's simple psychology. People who think they're powerful always want to challenge the best out there. They have a constant need to prove themselves.

However, back then, I was an active vigilante who'd send messages right back to criminals in my own ways. Two wishy-washy stories in a tabloid about the Roach's not-so-triumphant return didn't equate to a message like this.

And make no mistake. Roaches in a dead woman's mouth was a message—a brutal, savage one.

"Get over here!"

I turned to see the bouncer I'd knocked down outside hollering at me. He flung a patron out of the way, then wobbled into the wall, still dazed.

A strange, hobo-looking creep rolls up to a club, asking questions about a dancer. Dancer winds up dead. The only punchline to that joke is that even if the timeline didn't line up, I looked as guilty as Charles Manson.

"You can't be back here!" barked the bouncer who had been comforting the dancer who'd undoubtedly been the one unfortunately enough to find Roxy carved up like a puzzle.

He fell into a grappling stance like it was second nature, but even the mob didn't train bouncers how to fight a man in a wheelchair. He hesitated as he sized me up, and in one smooth motion, I ripped a strand of beads off the doorway and whipped it at his leg, snagging his ankle and pulling his legs out from under him. The momentum as I tugged spun me around, and I barreled down the hall at the other bouncer.

A patron exited the private room directly to my right, naked like Roxy, but for very different reasons. He covered his junk with bundled-up clothing. I shoved him hard in the back. His clothes went flying as he flopped into the first bouncer like a wet fish. They both went down hard—pun sort of intended—and I ran over one of their wrists on my way by. Didn't matter to me whose it was.

Zooming out of the back halls, I skirted the upper tier of the club by the bar. I got lost in the crowd stampeding for the exits. The very notion of being amongst them had me gagging. I focused on the string of neon running along a seam on the floor to stay calm.

Sirens wailed outside. Cops on their way, as late as I was to save a young woman trying to make ends meet the best way she knew how. All I knew was that I couldn't be caught anywhere near the scene.

I stuck to a narrow space between the wall and the amassing crowd as I squeezed outside and rumbled along the sidewalk. Blue and red flashed down Bleek Street from both directions. I turned perpendicular onto the nearest avenue, and as I did, who did I see speeding down toward the club in a banged-up station wagon but Chuck Barnes? I'm not sure if he'd noticed me, but he wore the determined look of a journalist chasing ambulances.

He'd soon see the consequences of celebrating a vigilante he had to know was a copycat. Because if he truly believed I was the Roach like he'd spent years accusing me of being, then he knew it wasn't me jumping through doors and taking bullets.

Now, some psychopath had carved up a woman to send a clear message to the Roach. I had no idea what it was, or who would do such a thing, but I knew who'd earned a visit from me next after I laid low for a bit and let the heat die down.

Chuck Barnes.

The fool who'd breathed new life into the legend of the Roach onto the gossip-ridden pages of the *Weekly Iron*. I'd put it off far too long already.

CHAPTER

EIGHT

I reached my block before I stopped for a rest. My head hammered. I couldn't see straight. When the nurses advised me to take it easy before they discharged me, I really hadn't planned to do the complete opposite. Honest.

Leaning over into my palm, I closed my eyes tight. My racing mind promptly rewarded me with images of poor Roxy in her butchered state.

That was another issue of mine I'd honestly forgotten about until then. Not sure what the doctors would call it, but when I saw something horrific, I obsessed over it until I made it right. I'd see the scene, again and again, like a stuck record. Now, imagine you couldn't take the record off until the player broke on its own.

It'd be like that with Roxy. I'd keep seeing her, gutted like a fish, and stuffed with bugs until I stopped whoever was responsible. It appeared to be the work of a psychopath with twisted sexual fantasies —maybe a serial—but to do it in the back of a crowded club?

That just didn't add up to others I'd dealt with. And the personal note for me. Serials always seemed to do did it for their own warped self-satisfaction.

Was this an old enemy thinking I'd actually returned? Or was this the copycat himself, prepared to desecrate my legacy? Angry didn't begin to cover my feelings. Violated either. I was starting to run out of adjectives.

My finger sliced along the rusty ridge of my wheel's pushrim as I squeezed it as hard as I could without realizing.

"You'll figure this out," I told myself, sucking the wound. "You always do."

"Are they talking to you, too?"

I whipped around too fast and strained my neck. Tinman pushed his cart along, his metallic blankets crinkling and his cans rattling. I don't know how the hell I hadn't heard him. I'm usually more attentive. Am I getting old or tired? Or both?

He, on the other hand, wasn't anywhere near as old as you'd expect a homeless man to be. Maybe a Vietnam vet—I'm not sure. He was always too wrapped up to see if he had any tattoos that might give it away. A dirty sanitary mask with yet more tin taped to it even covered his mouth and nose, so only a leathery forehead showed.

"I wish," I muttered.

His eyes twitched as he adjusted his tin hat. "They always are, man," he said, voice muffled. "You just gotta listen. It's obvious. So obvious."

I offered a polite grunt. Then, another cop car zooming by a perpendicular street, blaring its siren, spurred me along, and Tinman continued on his noisy way. I had to massage my neck to get the knot out. Add it to my growing list of injuries.

Laura's Subaru was parked a few spots down from my place. Japanese piece of crap. This city used to be known for producing high-quality American automobiles. She was lucky I noticed. Otherwise, when I opened up my door and found somebody inside, I might have done something stupid.

"Reese, is that you?" she called.

"It's me," I replied.

I threw my keys down, then ran my fingers through my beard and hair to try and clean up a little bit, which was useless. The freshly Windexed mirror over the credenza told the true story. But as much as I needed to shower after a month of unconscious sponge baths in the hospital, I didn't have the energy.

I rolled across my living room, expecting to see her in the kitchen. Something in there smelled, well, decent. Laura was no chef, but she tried.

"Laura?" I asked. I moved a little farther, then spotted her in my peripherals. She stood in my study, staring at my false bookcase, which I hadn't realized I'd left ajar before chasing Isaac earlier in the day. A different obsession had engulfed me. Good Lord, I'm getting sloppy.

"Laura," I said, low and brooding, angry at myself more than her. "What are you doing?"

"Don't worry, I didn't go down," she replied, still staring.

I entered fast and pushed the case until it locked. Then I started fixing the disordered books.

"I was here, wondering if I should," she said. "Wondering if maybe you were down there, drunk or dead since you weren't upstairs."

"Sorry to disappoint you." I slid the last book in.

"It's not funny, Reese. Your call, it freaked me out. Why couldn't you just stay at the hospital one more day?"

"Do you really need to ask that?" I turned to enter the kitchen.

Laura moved ahead of me. "Jesus, what happened to you?" Her eyes pored over me as she reverted to her default character: caring, substitute daughter. She rotated my arm until my hand showed, all covered in scrapes from an eventful day.

"I fell," I said, pulling back. Not a lie, per se. I continued into the kitchen. "I'm sorry, Laura. I can barely remember when I called, I was so out of it. I think I was seeing things."

"Which is why—"

"I 'should have stayed at the hospital.' Got it."

Her nostrils flared. "Well, you don't smell like booze, so that's a start. Though, I'm not sure what it is you do smell like." I was about to answer when Laura cursed and blew by me.

The stove beeped, timer at triple zeroes for who knows how long. She pulled it open, and smoke puffed out. Fanning it with one hand, she used a dirty rag to reach in and pull out a tray of blackened... I-don't-know-what.

She dropped it onto the counter and cursed some more, running her hands through her hair like she wanted to peel her scalp off.

"It's fine," I said.

"It's not fine. I fucking burned it!" she snapped. Rage contorted her face in a way I wasn't accustomed to seeing. Her bloodshot eyes were sunken back behind black rings too. She looked exhausted, frustrated, angry—all the above.

"It really is. All I wanted was soup anyway. I swear. I'm still not that hungry."

Laura drew a strained breath. "I'm sorry, there's just so much going on. The McDonagh Case just won't quit, my boss is on my ass, and my dad barely has time to watch Michelle when I can't because of the campaign."

"I thought she was here with you?" I hadn't even looked to see if Michelle sat in the living room when I entered. Or if the TV was on low, how I liked it. I hadn't even thought of it until right then. I needed to get a hold on myself, fast.

"After your call, I didn't think that was the best idea."

I sighed. "Fair enough."

"One night, just one night, I beg Dad to help a little extra so I can check on a man who doesn't even want me here."

I got as close as I could and took her hand. "That's not true."

"I told you I was coming over, and instead, you're out doing Lord-knows-what."

"I lost track of time. Honestly. Here, c'mon, sit down. You look beat."

"There's a word for it."

I tugged on her arm, but she didn't budge.

"No, you need to eat something," she said.

"I'm perfectly capable of heating up a can of soup. Let's go." She finally moved, and I led her to the kitchen table. She fell back into one of my cheap, wooden chairs as if it were a bed.

"What're those?" she asked, looking at the magazines tucked between my butt and the chair.

"Trash," I said. I tossed them across the table, hoping she wouldn't notice the earmarks. I didn't want her worrying about this copycat, and I knew Laura Garrity didn't read sensationalist bullshit like the *Weekly Iron*. It might color her opinion of me differently if she thought I did.

"Now, close your eyes," I said. "Take a load off."

I returned to the counter and picked up one of the cans of soup she'd left for me. I placed it on the stove before initiating a kitchen-wide search for a pot.

"I'll get it," she said.

"No. Sit."

I threw open another cabinet to no avail. If Laura didn't keep reordering my very limited belongings, it might've been easier, but now wasn't the time to scold. Though, truthfully, I loved that she did it. I'd subconsciously feared for a long time that if she ran out of things to help me with, she'd stop coming around. Which was fine when I had been ready to die, but now I had a mission.

I may not have liked Laura taking care of me as if I were a toddler. Still, just a few minutes spent with her in a bad mood, and the images of Roxy's mutilated corpse plaguing my mind grew less vivid.

I didn't mean for it to happen, I don't even know when it had, but Laura Garrity centered me.

"Here. Got it," I said, finding the pot buried in the last possible cabinet I could reach. "Not so useless."

"I'm supposed to be taking care of you," Laura muttered.

"I'm a new me." I slapped the pot down onto the stove. "Can opener, can opener," I whispered to myself, back on the prowl. This time, I found it on one of my early tries. After opening the can over my lap to get proper leverage and spilling just a bit, I reached up to dump the congealed lump of liquid and meat into the pot.

I stretched my hand out as far as I could to turn the dial. My townhouse wasn't exactly designed for a man in my condition. Though I'm sure very few are. Usually, Laura helped with this part when she was around, even as I argued, but as I glanced back after finally getting the burner on, her eyes were closed.

After dumping in the prescribed portion of water, I watched her as I waited for my liquid meal to boil. The way one strand of her soft, brown hair got stuck in her mouth, rising and falling with her tiny, bubbling breaths. She was true beauty. Iconic. The men who frequented that club wouldn't realize it if she hit them upside the head.

Not long after, I started to picture Roxy again, lying on that grubby, neon-washed floor. Her glassy eyes were fixated on me, silently asking why I couldn't have gotten there sooner. Only this time, it wasn't Roxy's face I imagined on the body, but Laura's. And we weren't in the club, but out on the streets. Back in that alley, where my whole life turned over. A roach crawled up and perched on her eye, wiggling its antennae my way.

Something hot sprayed my face, and I shook my head. Steam poured out of the pan as my soup boiled over while I got lost in my own nightmares.

"Shit, shit, shit." I fumbled to get parallel again and reach for the dial. I got the stove off but forgot to pull the pan off the heat first. The scalding liquid burned the top of my hand as it splashed across the handle.

"And you don't think you need my help?" Laura asked.

I looked back and saw her blinking. The hungry roach skittered across her eyes. I squeezed mine tight to drive away the image and exhaled slowly.

"No, I just like it hot," I said, blowing on my hand. That particular extremity had been through hell the last twenty-four hours.

People outside of a wheelchair don't realize how much you rely on them. I get it. We're primates, we all use our hands and thumbs for everything. But it's different when they're the only limbs you've got.

"Are you okay?" Laura asked.

"Fine." I wrapped the pot-handle in a hand towel and carried it while I rolled to the table with one hand. The wide-arc one wheel in motion took me close enough to place the pot down before I pulled myself in.

I breathed a sigh of relief, then realized my mistake. "Crap, a spoon."

"Stop," Laura said. "I'll get it."

This time, I let her do her thing. She fetched one, then dropped it in the pot, so it circled the rim once before settling.

"Do I need to tell you to blow on it first, like Michelle?" she asked as she returned to her seat.

"Very funny." I didn't add that, yeah, she did. The moment I got my hands around the spoon, I'd been ready to dig in. My stomach had nothing but Jell-O and ice chips swashing about in it, and my head vacillated between feeling light and pounding.

"So, Michelle's with your dad?" I asked.

"Yeah," Laura replied. "Heaven forbid he take a day off campaigning to take care of his only granddaughter, so he's dragging her around with him. As if anything this late will change the outcome."

"His fourth term isn't going to win itself."

Laura nodded begrudgingly.

I finally braved a taste of the hot soup straight out of the pot. I didn't wait long enough, and it burned my tongue. I didn't care. The moment it touched, vicious hunger took hold. I spooned it down my gullet so fast I forgot to breathe.

"Is it bad I hope he loses?" she said.

I swallowed a mouthful and came up for air. "Do you realize who you're asking? As far as bad thoughts go, that's pretty tame."

She chuckled. "True."

A bout of silence passed between us as I kept slurping. Laura was usually never at a loss for words, so I could tell exactly how worn out she was.

"I'm sorry I didn't listen to you about resting," I said. I wasn't, but she needed a win.

Laura put her hand behind her ear and folded it forward. "What was that?"

"You heard me."

"I know. I just wanted to hear it again."

"Then it wouldn't be special."

She shook her head, grinning her picture-perfect white teeth. "It's fine though, really," she said. "I think I know you well enough after all these years to know when you won't listen. I just get worried. Especially after what you told me about the harbor. You can be so closed off, Reese."

"You don't have to worry about that. You know how my mind is. Sometimes, I can't control the thoughts racing through it. I just have to follow them to their ends."

"I know. It's just me being a mother now, I think. Any minute I lose track of Michelle, my heart wants to explode out of my chest."

"And I promise, there isn't a kid in this world who doesn't wish his mother was like that." I reveled in the bashful smile that comment lured out of her. I think it was the truth. I wasn't sure. If I grew up with a mother like Laura, or a real mother at all, who knows what would have become of me. Maybe *I'd* be a mayor somewhere or, maybe, I'd have grown up too soft and died.

Would the Roach ever have existed?

"If it makes you feel any better, I wasn't down by the river today," I said out loud. "I was at a club."

That really got her attention. She arched one eyebrow. "A club? You?"

"Yeah. A club for, uh..." I took another sip of soup and lowered my voice. "Gentlemen." My cheeks went hot even before I said it. I felt dirty. I couldn't worry Laura with the real reason I was there, and

I wasn't even sure why I was telling her at all. I suppose I just didn't want to add to her concerns. I am a hero, after all. So, some say.

I expected her to retch at the very notion, but instead, she put on a goofy expression. Her nose wrinkled in the peculiar way it does when she's having fun. Her hazel eyes sparkled with flecks of gold.

"Reese Roberts, I never would have guessed that," she said.

"It wasn't what you think."

"Suuure."

"I'm serious."

She leaned back in her chair, looking absolutely delighted. "How was it?"

"Crowded," I grumbled.

"What did you expect?"

"I don't know, Laura. For fuck's sake, just drop it."

She slid her chair around the table closer to me. "I'm sorry. You brought it up! I'm not making fun of you, I promise. That's just... unexpected."

I slurped from my spoon and glared at her over the rim of the pot."I get it, Reese. Really, I do," she said. "After what happened, you realized it's finally time to get close to somebody, didn't you?"

"I'm close with you," I said. "Doesn't that count?"

"I mean with someone outside this prison you call a house."

"I hate meeting people."

"That doesn't mean there isn't someone out there. But someone like you won't find her at a club like that."

"Someone like me?" I asked, pushing my tongue against the back of my teeth.

"That's not—"

"It's fine. I told you. That's not why I was there."

She ignored me. "That's it, Mister Roberts. From now on, I'm dedicating myself to setting you up on a real date. When's the last time you went on one of those?"

"I can't remember."

I could. The answer was never. When I escaped my burning

foster home and survived like a street rat for years until reaching the big city, it was like teleporting through time. I didn't know how to talk to the people. How to fit in with society. Then I became the Roach, and the closest I came to dates were the overly grateful looks some women offered me after I saved them. The more appreciative, the faster they chased me off.

"Well, I'm going to do it," Laura declared. "I meet people through work who maybe could tolerate you."

"Laura..." I exhaled.

"I won't take no for an answer. You have so much to offer, Reese. I know you don't think it, but I want you to see that the river is the last place for you."

"Enough, Laura. Now isn't the time." She was reaching. Desperately trying to concoct ways to stop me from ever rolling up to that riverside again because she didn't understand it. Couldn't understand it.

"You aren't *that* old," she said. "Why not share with somebody?"

"What about you?" I said, a harsh edge creeping into my tone. "Single. Young. Beautiful. Great job. Why are you spending your time with me when you could be out there dating? Finding Michelle a real fatherly role-model?"

Her face scrunched. She'd pushed, and I'd cut deep. I wished she would stop doing that as much as I hoped she didn't notice I'd called her beautiful.

"Don't worry about me," she said, remaining calm. "I see plenty of people every day. This is about you, alone in here. Holed up like some hermit when—"

"Enough!" I slapped the table. She winced. "Please, enough. That's the last thing I'm thinking about."

"Because you refuse to open up."

"Nobody wants to see what's inside."

She took my hand in both of hers and turned me toward her. There was that look. Not the normal Laura I knew, but that grateful sparkle of someone I'd saved and all the expectations it brought with it. It showed itself from time to time.

"I do," she said softly. "And so will somebody else. You just have to let them in."

"And tell them what?" I asked, pulling away. "Say we go on a few dates, and somehow she isn't scared off just by the sight of me. Great. Then she wants to come over. Maybe she takes off my shirt, sees my scars, and starts asking where they came from. What then, Laura? What do I tell her? The truth? Or worse, I lie. Make up some bullshit just like all the scumbags in this city.

"Either way, by some miracle, maybe she stays. Another date. Another kiss. Then she reaches down and discovers that I don't even fucking work." I slammed on the table again. "But she doesn't care about that. She's a saint, she likes me for who I am. She only wonders why when she touches me, I look like I'm going to vomit. What a lucky girl. What a fucking fairy tale."

Laura didn't back down. "You're more than the Roach, Reese. You just have to see it, like I do."

"I'm fine with my life the way it is," I said.

"That's because you won't see it any other way." She looked around my meager kitchen, filled with unstocked cabinets with doors that didn't quite shut properly. "What if you moved out of this place? Cemented up that damn tunnel downstairs and left it all behind. I can help you pay for it all."

"No, absolutely not. Not after the hospital." I returned to my meal so she couldn't reel me back in.

"For the last time, it's just money. I make plenty of it because *you* kept me alive. I don't care what they called you. I'm a lawyer in Iron City. I've looked straight into the eyes of heartless murderers, and you aren't one. Not at all."

"Then what am I?" I asked, teeth clenched.

Laura tilted my head back toward her. The cold touch of her fingertips on my cheek gave me a welcome shiver that, from anyone else would have me squirming. I stared at her soft lips, watching her breathing, matching my cadence to it, letting it calm me.

"Lost," she whispered, succinctly. No hesitation whatsoever, like she'd known exactly what she'd wanted to say for years.

My throat went tight. I nearly dropped my spoon.

"It's okay you've never been with anybody, Reese," she said. "It doesn't matter. Someone out there is going to see you for who you really are and they're going to love you for it. Like I do."

I don't know what happened. My head leaned into her palm until she supported its entire weight. I felt like silly putty—another useless toy I would absolutely *not* be buying Michelle.

I could have fallen asleep right there, the lilac scent of her shampoo wafting over me. In a city with a copycat stealing my identity and a rogue killer on the loose, somehow, I felt safe in her hand. But we're never really safe, are we? One step out onto a street and a car might skid out. A visit to the bank and a masked guy with a shotgun might come knocking.

The whole world was chaos. Anything could go bad. That was part of the gig. Trying to make the chaos just a little more manageable by cleaning out the people who bask in it. Safety was fleeting, even if you plaster it all over campaign posters. Fickle as the wind.

"Now, it's getting late," Laura said after not long enough. "I'm hoping to sneak in some time at the firing range. Then I have to relieve my dad before he starts teaching Michelle how to work a crowd." She removed her hand, and my head hung as if cradled by her energy. I didn't want to move.

Did I love Laura? I have no idea. Do real parents teach you about that sort of thing?

She was right though. I'd never tried to care about anybody, even kept her at a safe distance. Never laid with anybody by my own choice. It all felt so personal and exposed—having someone see right through you into the depths of your soul, and all the weaknesses that dwells there. And all the terrible darkness.

If Laura saw it, really saw it, I knew, she would run too.

"Just, please, think about it," she said, standing. "You've got a second chance, again. You need to start finally becoming Reese Roberts and stop living in the past."

"Wow," I said. "And you thought I needed to pay to talk to a shrink?"

"Hah, hah," she mock-laughed.

She squeezed behind me to gather her belongings. A bout of silence passed between us before I said, "Tell Michelle I say, 'boo.'"

"Tell her yourself next time I bring her over."

I nodded. "And, uh... make sure she knows that what happened wasn't her fault."

"She knows."

"Laura, please. I know how kids can blame themselves for the awful things that happen around them. I don't want—"

Laura stopped and kissed me on the top of the head. My heart filled to the brim. Whatever love meant, her simply being around was enough for me.

"Stop that," she said. "She knows, and so do I. Get some rest, would you."

"I will."

She backed away, and I let the moment sink in. By the time I looked up, she was halfway across the living room. "And you too," I said, not even remembering to roll myself to the portal between rooms so she'd hear me.

She stopped at the front door anyway.

"Reese, can I ask you something?" she asked.

"Always," I said.

She didn't turn all the way, just peered back over her shoulder. Her lips were drawn in a straight line. Her face was pensive.

"When you went after Michelle and pushed her out of the way, why didn't you keep rolling with her?" she asked. "Was there really no time, or did you..." She took a strained breath. "Did you want to be hit?"

My lip twisted before I answered. "I honestly don't remember."

That was the truth. It was all a blur of chaos, arguing, and screeching tires. I had no idea if I'd had a chance to get myself out of the way too. But for the first time since, I found myself truly glad that it wasn't the end, glorious as it would've been. The thought of Laura, all by herself, crying at my funeral like Alexis Bradley over her shit-head boyfriend—that was worth me slogging along. And protecting my legacy from imposters, of course.

"Really?" she asked.

"Really," I said.

"Well... If you ever feel like you did that day again, you call me, you hear? At least until we find you someone you'd rather call."

"Impossible."

She flashed a sad but hopeful smile, threw on her coat, and started out the door.

"Laura," I said.

She got her arm through the sleeve and stopped. "Yeah?"

My tongue fidgeted around in my mouth. I'm not sure what I planned to say. I didn't want her to leave, even though I knew she had to.

"I'm going to pay you back for the hospital," I said.

"Yeah, yeah." She dismissed me with a wave and closed the door behind her. I sat, staring at the doorknob who-knows-how-long until the calming effect of her presence drained away, and I was left circling the drain of my current predicament.

I reached over the back of my couch and dug through the cushions to find the remote, prepared to see news about Roxy, who I currently pictured dead and covered in bugs in the corner of my vision. Not yet.

Sunday Night Football flashed on, a break from the news and election week madness. The Marauders were playing in the swanky new stadium built outside the city limits to both alleviate traffic and keep visitors outside of Harborside, where the old stadium fell into disrepair. I'm sure millions around the state were tuned into that, distracting themselves from the big bad world. A war overseas, a looming recession, crack infiltrating every ghetto, and brutal murder on the streets from a new monster stalking Iron City.

I moved to the stairs, slid myself off my chair, and planted both palms on the first landing. One-by-one, I pushed off to ascend a tread at a time, reaching down to drag my legs up after me. My scraped-up hands stung each time. My muscles burned.

Laura insisted I move to a one-story place after I first got shot, but she didn't have a secret lair underneath her home. And she grew up in a home—a real one. Broken by her overworking father and a mother who'd abandoned them, but a home, nonetheless. Better than bunks lining the cold, dirt floor of a barn amidst cow shit.

No, this place had become my home. There wasn't anywhere else like it.

"Pandemonium strikes inside the *Bleek Street Gentleman's Club*," I heard over my own groans. I stopped and peered through the railing. The game had reached halftime, which meant a quick break for a local broadcast.

They transferred to a reporter standing on the street, awash in the pink neon of the club's sign. "Police say a performer was stabbed to death in a private room tonight," she said. An ambulance behind her was being loaded with a body bag. "No more details are being released at this time, but we spoke with some patrons who happened to be inside when all hell broke loose."

They cut to a guy with tattoos everywhere—even his face. He wore a backward hat—at least it was the Marauders and not some schlep team from New England. "Crazy things happenin lately around here, man." He was definitely high on something. "I was just inside with some friends when everyone started shovin us to the doors. I heard girls screamin. Thought, for sure, we was gettin safer but, stabbins, strikes, Roach sightins..."

Another person ran to the camera. "The Roach is here to help us take back our city! The mayor ain't doin—" They bleeped out his last word as if lips couldn't be read.

Then, the feed transitioned to one of the dancers. The drunk blonde I'd encountered all too closely. Her oversized leather jacket was draped around her shoulders, and she could barely get any words out.

"Just... what kind of monster would do this?" she forced through snivels. A cop pulled her away and extended a hand to block the camera.

They cut back to the field reporter. "We'll bring you more on this developing story as soon as we can," she said. "Back to you in the studio, John."

"A horrible, horrible story from a district that has seen far too many bad things. In other news, mayoral challenger Darrell Washington spoke at a charity dinner in the Stacks in support of children of broken homes."

There Laura's father's opposition was, making his final push before Election Day by calling on the city's poorest to support him. He called himself a man of the people, not tainted by years pleasing donors and lobbyists.

All I saw were 'civil servants' in suits and gowns sitting at tables covered in white tablecloth, dining on prime rib, and drinking wine as they celebrated their own generosity. All playing the same game, which never seemed to stop more broken homes and abused children from popping up.

I reached the top of the stairs by then and missed the rest over my huffing. The cops were staying tight-lipped about Roxy. Because why tell the city that there's a killer on the loose who's out to send a message? Why tell everyone to be on the lookout for a Roach copycat who was clearly a key to something?

That all just made too much fucking sense.

Or maybe, they really hadn't put it together yet, even with the gruesome message filling Roxy's mouth. The Roach's return was merely rumors at this point. Unsubstantiated stories in a gossip paper by a hack journalist who'd pissed off everyone in the city that mattered.

"I have to do everything, don't I?" I asked the world. Nobody answered.

After another beleaguered succession of heavy breaths, I slid into the bathroom like a slug. First things first, I had to make sure I didn't fit the profile of the dirty, bearded man in a wheelchair spotted causing trouble at the club when the murder was discovered.

Grab bars installed in my shower helped me yank myself up to a built-in seat. That gave me enough height to pull my pants off one leg at a time. Then underwear, shirt. A whole big-to-do over something that used to be so simple, only to leave me sitting there as half-a-person, with the rest dangling down from my hips like soaking wet towels.

Water sputtered cold out of the showerhead first, beating along my shoulders. The scars crisscrossing my back from lashes still tingled all these decades later.

Shaving cream and a razor were on a shelf to my left. I extended as far as I could to get them one at a time.

The bottle fell and clanked across the tile. I cursed and tried to stop it, causing me to slip off my seat onto my ass. I considered trying to get back up, but I was too tired. So, I sat there, like a baby who'd fallen after his first time learning to walk, letting the water wash over me. Brown strained out of my hair and beard, gushing down my leathery skin.

First damn shower in over a month, and it felt like it.

The shaving cream was crusted over from disuse, and it took a hearty shake to get even a smidge out. It'd have to do. The water started getting hot just in time for me to start. Hair fell in clumps from my chin, circling the drain beneath my stringy legs.

"Look how handsome you are," Laura would say on the few occasions I'd shaved since we'd met—one being our little charade to get my settlement. And even little Michelle would sit closer to me, like it made me more human.

With no mirror, I stopped when my cheeks felt smooth. Enough hair plugged the drain to have the shower basin looking like a swamp.

I noticed a flit of movement across the shower and raised the razor to defend myself. A cockroach cowered in the corner, fleeing the rising water.

"You too?" I couldn't help but chuckle.

It scurried around the edge, probing with its antennae until it found a crack in the caulking and vanished just as soon as it had appeared.

"Showoff," I said.

I let my head lean back, so the base of my skull found a comfortable position on the shower seat. I hadn't even noticed how bad my headache was until then, but steam relieved it a bit. My eyelids drew closed. Even the minuscule weight of the water dribbling down on them made them nearly impossible to reopen.

CHAPTER

NINE

A strong, gloved hand clutched my arm, jolting me awake. Grasping the empty shaving cream can, I smashed whoever it was in the head with the bottom corner, where the folded metal was hardest. He fell back and broke a few tiles off the wall as he groaned and grasped at his head. The floor was slick from a layer of water and grime that couldn't drain through my freshly shaven hair. The shower remained on, but the water was freezing. How long had I been out? Long enough for the hot water to run out.

A foot stomped toward my abdomen. Lying flat on my back, I pushed off the wall to slide sideways out of the way. The man's other foot slipped as he tried to recover and forced him into a split. I elbowed him in the balls, then dragged his face down through my shower seat.

I rolled out from under his body before it collapsed. Then, I crawled across the bathroom. At first, I didn't realize there were two guys. I didn't feel the hand around my ankle, but I felt him pull on me. Peering back, I saw the second guy stomping toward me, boots splashing in the water.

My fingers caught the knob of a cabinet, and I whipped it open, the momentum helping me flip onto my stomach. The door smashed into his elbow but didn't slow him long.

He yanked harder. The dirty water, which had apparently pooled and leaked out across the whole bathroom after I'd fallen asleep, made it easy to move me. I snatched the hem of a towel hanging from the bar on the wall and used it to catch his punch.

I twisted him right into the sheetrock, then left into the sink. The crown of his head cracked against the porcelain.

It was all instinct up until then, when I had enough time to realize the two of them wore dark-colored, matching uniforms. The details were unclear since I remained in such a fog from waking.

And because of that, I didn't notice the third attacker, who was entering through the bathroom door, until it was too late. A baton smashed across the back of my head, leaving me stunned and seeing stars. The other two recovered and charged me, pushing my head down against the tile and restraining my wrists.

Next thing I knew, I was slung over a shoulder, naked as the day I was born, bouncing as we went down the stairs. I think I squirmed, but I can't really be sure. I heard the slam of a door that blocked out the white noise from my TV, felt the chill of outdoor air, and bounced more as my carrier descended my front stoop.

Whoever it was, promptly tossed me onto the backseat of a car. Breath filled my lungs as my torso finally wasn't crushed against a shoulder.

"Get up," someone said from the front seat.

You can't imagine how hard that was to do in a backseat, dizzy, without use of legs, my arms cuffed behind me, naked, and soaking-fucking-wet. I had to wriggle forward until my shoulder found the door, then stuff my chin into the gap beneath the handle, using my neck to prop my body up onto my twisted elbow.

"You have no idea who you're messing with," I groused. Well done, self. I looked as threatening as a chihuahua in a pit bull fight, slumped against a door with my cheek squished against the window.

"Actually, I'm one of the few who does," my attacker replied.

I blinked hard a few times and concentrated on the rearview mirror. He was right. So many hits to the head throughout my life made it difficult to identify many people, but not this guy. Lieutenant José Montalvo of the ICPD, 12th precinct. He'd been a rookie when he happened upon me saving Laura during his beat and put a bullet in my spine.

Staying quiet and helping the mayor with our coverup had earned him quite the rash of promotions. I guess it didn't matter that *I'd* been the one saving the mayor's daughter that night. Right place, right time for old José. He'd probably be a captain soon, as long as Mayor Garrity kept his position. Maybe even Commissioner.

"You?" I said, incredulous. "You couldn't knock?"

"I knew you wouldn't answer," he replied.

I wanted to wipe that smug grin right off his face. It'd been a while since our last encounter, but José seemed to take pleasure in my misery—like it was the only way he could get off since he couldn't brag about gunning down the city's—no, the country's—most famous vigilante.

"How are your buddies?" I asked.

"They'll be fine," he said.

"You warn them what they were up against?"

"They only know what they need to. Now, put this on before you stain my backseat. I cuff meth-head bikers cleaner than you. You look like you shaved with a hacksaw."

He threw a clump of clothes back at me. The same dirty outfit I'd peeled off before showering. They were damp in places from lying on the floor when it flooded.

"You mind taking these off then?" I asked, twisting my back toward the front seat.

"Long as you promise not to run."

I didn't hear him snicker, but I knew he was inside. I now recalled why my blood boiled the first time I heard he'd received a rushed promotion. It wasn't the lack of qualifications. It wasn't that he'd shot me—I was going to kill a man that night to be fair. Most Iron City cops would've walked away and let me do my thing—as was our unspoken agreement for so long—but José was immature then. A young Latino from the Stacks, looking to make a name.

No. I was pissed because he was a prick.

"Can we just get whatever this is over with?" I said.

"Hold still."

I stared out the window as he reached back and squeezed my wrists way tighter than necessary to unlock my handcuffs from the driver's seat. His sleeve came up enough to reveal meaningless tattoos covering both his tan arms. The kind street kids get just to look cool.

The glow of dawn loomed low in the mostly-navy-blue sky. A trickle of civilians already headed to a people-mover stop up a block or the bus stations, off to slave for a handful-of-bucks-an-hour they'd soon waste on Christmas presents.

"There," José said as the cuffs fell free with a jingle.

One of the other cops who'd attacked me slammed the trunk outside, then offered a thumbs up to José. A line of blood ran down the crease of his nose.

José hit the gas, and I slid back, barely able to catch myself before I'd be forced to do the gymnastics required to get upright again.

This early, the city actually seemed peaceful. It used to be my favorite time—that hour of twilight before the sun creeps over the horizon and while the moon vanishes below it. It's funny, humanity's most tranquil period is when there's nothing above looking down on us.

Gangsters had to sleep. Junkies passed out. Even the bums were rolled up in their ratty blankets, not bothering anybody for nickles. It was almost like a change in shifts before the criminals in suits came out to play Monopoly in their shiny towers, creating more gangsters, junkies, and bums in society's vicious cycle.

"What is this about?" I asked José while I maneuvered to get my pants back on.

"Our mutual friend sent me to have a little talk," he said, keeping his eyes on the road.

"What is the car bugged or something? You can say his name."

"Bad habits repeat themselves."

I groaned. "Whatever you say."

"We know you were at that club last night on Bleek Street."

"What brilliant detective work brought you to that conclusion?"

"You do realize who owns that place, right?" he asked.

"Sure do. They help fund the mayor's campaigns, right?"

He didn't bite. "You can see how a man in a wheelchair with the skill to take down two of their security could be a bad look for someone in your particular situation," he went on, disregarding my response.

"I take it you got the message from our killer then?" I asked.

"No message. Officially, it was a junkie who hit the crack-pipe too many times and lost it."

"That's the story you're going with?"

"For now. Our illustrious mayor built his entire platform around cleaning up the streets and strengthening the police force. 'A safe city, strong as iron.' Look around. Before him, this place was a war zone."

"Yeah. You're strong enough to beat a cripple in his shower," I remarked.

"You should be happy," José said. "The mayor picked up where you left off. It all worked out in the end. But a lunatic carving people up and filling their mouths with bugs? *Mierda,* that's a rough story a couple of days before the election. If that pansy Washington has his way, we'll only be carrying nightsticks like the Brits. We'll see how fast the gangs flood back in across the city after that. All your work." He clapped his hands together, then imitated an explosion. "Adios."

"Okay, so keep what happened to that girl quiet if you want. What do I care?"

"It doesn't matter if you do or not. Stories about a copycat Roach in a superhero-themed tabloid column, that's all good fun. It isn't the first time other maniacs put on masks and ran around in tights, punching people because of you."

"Body armor," I corrected.

"Whatever. The stories help keep good people occupied and others fearful. But clearly, somebody isn't so scared. They want a piece of your legend." He looked back, and his nose wrinkled in disgust. "If only they saw the real thing." Turning the wheel hard, he sent me sliding across the backseat into the opposite door.

I rubbed my still-aching head and moaned, "Get to it. And please, tell me you don't think I did all this to get back at some copycat?"

"Nah. You're a different kind of insane."

"Then what?"

José turned the car back in the other direction. This time I braced myself. I wasn't, however, prepared for what lay ahead.

The serene, morning glow was disrupted by harsh, orange and flashing red. Leaning forward, I spotted two fire trucks down 73rd Street. More cop cars were parked on either side, controlling a crowd of curious citizens. A column of black smoke swirled up through the broken windows of Patel's bodega. Embers danced in the darkness within it.

"No..." I whispered to myself.

"I figured you'd recognize the place," José said, pulling along the side of the road a few car-lengths away from the fire trucks.

"What happened?"

"Officially, a spark fire from a bad outlet. Patel was asleep in the back room and didn't realize until it was too late."

"He was—"

"Inside. Yeah."

I let out a rash of curses. I'd seen what had happened to Roxy and had totally forgotten about the other public recipient of the new copycat's rescuing. I should've headed straight here, not home to be distracted by Laura's presence. I should've at least called and told Patel to hide, but it'd totally slipped my mind.

I could've blamed being out of it from the accident. I could've blamed being overtired, barely out of a coma, and sober for the first time in years. But really, it was me. This useless shell of the Roach trying to play hero again and focused on all the wrong things. I wanted to puke.

"What's the *unofficial* story?" I managed to force through my lips.

"Someone broke in after closing and used what we assume is his blood to paint the Roach's symbol all over the outer wall. Then they lit the place on fire with him still inside," José said.

My hands balled into fists. "And let me guess, you people were all too late to save him?"

"Save him? He was fried in minutes. Probably hurt less than if he'd bled out all that time. Nobody could have saved him. Not you in your prime. Not us. That girl at the club, either."

"No, that's right," I snarled. "You're all only ever on time to clean up. Or should I say, cover up?"

José rotated all the way in his seat and glared at me. His hand rested on the passenger's seat, only inches away from the grip of his semi-automatic Colt M1911. A far cry from the revolvers the ICPD carried five years ago. The mayor had been upgrading. Those, body armor, and SWAT teams with fully automatics if situations escalated —all part of the Garrity Act.

"We can't predict the future, and neither can you," he said. "What, you think that you saved everybody back in the day? Were you there, castrating the River Kings' boss who'd forced my brother to run drugs while I was still riding a tricycle? Got him killed. I earned this badge to stop that from happening to any other kids. Then, I fucking grew up."

I stared into José's eyes as the smugness gave way to raw, unbridled anger.

"You can't help everybody, Roach," he said. "Better to have an army of us keeping the animals at bay, than a freak in a costume."

I swallowed back a harsher response, then said, "So, the courts can set them free a few years later on good behavior?"

"At least the mayor makes sure they get locked up now."

"Because people change that fast, right? All you boys do is

recycle the bad guys, but me? I sweep them away for good." I leaned forward, arm on the back of his chair. "I bet you wish you could too, don't you? I see it in your eyes. You wish you could issue a little cartel justice."

"No. Because I'm not a murderer."

The air seemed like it was sucked from the car. I didn't answer. *Murderer*. The term was so broad and lacked context. Yeah, sometimes there was collateral like those three immigrant girls, but minus a few accidents, I only killed those who truly deserved it. Those silver-tongued devils who probably would've gotten away with the awful things they'd done. Men who could work a room of malleable peers; who could afford corner-cutting lawyers without a conscience.

José was right, though. If the truth about me ever came out, that's all people would see—a murderer who killed some girls they didn't even know or care about, but a murderer, nonetheless.

"I'm not sure you needed to drag me out of my house just to throw insults," I said.

"I brought you here to see that." He pointed at the smoke. "I'm sure you want to go after whoever is doing this. I'm sure you want to find this copycat, if he's real. But that right there? That is your legacy. Death. Brutality. Lawlessness. That poor man traveled across the world from a warring country to be here, only to die in fire all the same, in the name of the *Roach*."

He spoke the name like he was spitting poison. I swallowed the lump forming in my throat. Life had made me hard. It was easy to bury my feelings in a stony lair, but when it was my fault and not some bogus propaganda piece spun by journalists, it was different. It made me want to kneel on my bed and lash my own back like father used to.

The cops couldn't get to Patel on time, but I'd forgotten about him entirely. Plain and simple. Now, a respectable, hardworking immigrant was dead because of it. The kind of good man that made old Iron City worth preserving.

"You can't help," José said. "Not anymore. We're going to find the bastard who did this our way."

"Then do it," I said, grinding my teeth. "Make it public. Someone out there knows about this copycat and might come forward. You can bait the killer."

"Our. Way." He emphasized each word.

"What, driving around flashing pretty lights and badges, asking questions to people who won't answer?"

"The way that keeps this city from tearing itself apart in fear and going right back to how it used to be. When kids got shot on street corners."

"And keeps our honorable mayor in office," I noted.

"May he keep doing what it takes to save this city." José pushed his door open and stepped outside. He opened my door, too, before heading to the trunk.

"Now," he said, barely audible over the cacophony of sirens from every safety institution Iron City had to offer. "You're going to roll on home, lock your doors, and stay fucking quiet."

I leaned out of my open door. "Or else what?"

"Or else, maybe we find another way to get you locked up for good—fraud on your injury statement. Beating up a kid. I don't know, we can get creative. And don't say it," he added before I could get a word in. "We know you won't tell anybody anything. Because I know your deepest secret. The thing you really fear."

"Oh yeah?"

José closed the trunk and moved to my door. "Yeah. The entire city peeling your mask off and seeing you for what you really are. A monster." He unfolded my wheelchair and set it on the sidewalk. "Get out."

I glared at him, fuming, reminding myself that now was the time to act like a decent member of society. Taking a cop's gun and shooting him to return the favor wouldn't help me figure out who was playing games with my legacy. As good as it might feel.

"You're really not gonna drive me home?" I asked.

"A nice, long ride will give you some time to think about how much better Garrity has made the city than you ever could. Now, c'mon." José grabbed me and hoisted me out onto the chair. My elbow hit the armrest. My ass nearly missed. Once I was in, he gave me a hard push so I rolled away from his car and couldn't retaliate.

I hated how true what he'd said about me was. He and our mutual friend clearly spent these years building a profile on me, just in case. Finding ways to protect themselves if the coverup got out. I even wondered if that was why Laura really came around so often. To poke and prod and learn my fears for her father so they could be wielded against me.

"No," I shook my head. "She wouldn't."

"What?" José asked, pausing on his way to sit back in the driver's seat.

"Nothing."

"Good." He sat and closed his door, then rolled down the window. "Stay out of it, Reese. And for God's sake, stop making Laura take care of you. Let her move on."

"I wish she would..."

José smirked, then offered a mock salute. "Enjoy the walk." His engine roared on, and he whipped around, spraying my legs and chair with the pool of something gathered against the curb.

I watched him go, wishing that maybe an arm of fire might arc out from the bodega and grab him. Or maybe another firetruck would speed around the corner and smash him to pieces. The city wouldn't miss one man in a uniform. It had plenty.

I did find relief in his last comment about Laura. That meant they weren't using her.

What was wrong with me? I don't know how that could even be a thought. Though, mine was the same compromised brain that couldn't even remember a simple phone call to save a man's life.

The sky brightened with each passing minute, but not over Patel's store. Smoke cast it in eternal night, a wave of heat splitting the brisk, late-fall air. Coroners carried out a bag filled with remains that could never be sent home to his family. And maybe they'd receive insurance money from the fire, but I doubted it. Rows of cops and caution tape would make examining the bodega for whatever clues the blaze had missed impossible. Sneaking onto a crime-scene wouldn't be easy with my wheelchair getting stuck on the tape—a waste of time.

I focused on the embers dithering in the blackness of the interior. Fire always brought me back to my childhood. I could picture my foster farm, burning. The house, the barn, the hay—everything. Razed to the ground with those excuses for foster parents still locked inside, their grubby hands roasting so they couldn't lay them on us anymore.

José was wrong about one thing—I wasn't going to stop. They could arrest me on whatever charges they concocted, so be it. All they cared about right now was an election. On maintaining their little Iron Kingdom that the rest of the country seemed to have forsaken. Not saving lives.

That was what made the Roach different.

No distractions.

No feelings.

No politics.

I may have been out of practice, but Iron City truly did need me again. They didn't know it. They didn't need to know it. I did. And instead of shriveling up and heading home to sleep in my lair like I'm sure José had intended with his threats—I felt more like me than I had in a long, long time.

CHAPTER

An infernal buzzing noise pierced my brain. Made the hair along my arms stand on end. I'm not sure why people made apartment buzzers so shrill. Like we're dogs waiting for a treat.

I sat in the entry of Isaac's apartment building, slowly raking my hand down the intercom buttons and saying his name. I'd wanted to stop for a drink after seeing that Bodega on fire. Craved one. But, it seemed fate was destined to deny me.

Dawn. The one time of the day or night when even the seediest bars are closed for a break. When any corner store that sells booze is still closed. The time when nocturnal beings were usually fast asleep, yet here I was.

I hit another intercom button, the buzz making me wince. I had no idea what unit Isaac was in. Judging by how long it took him to go up last time, I started at the top.

Most residents didn't answer. A few yelled at me. But it was dawn—up and at 'em. Better than being ripped out of the shower, cold, wet, and bloody.

"Mister Roberts?" the intercom for unit 1023 finally replied just as I was about to move onto the next one.

"Kid, is that you?" I answered, lunging at the button.

Seeing Patel's shop burn made me feel like I'd chugged a dozen black coffees, and coffee was something Iron City did right. It kept all the factory workers who'd once populated it alert as they repeated the same menial tasks over and over. Now, I suppose it fueled property-deals and lawsuits Downtown.

"Yeah, it's me. What—" Isaac yawned.

"I need your help with something that requires legs," I said.

"Mister Rob—uh, Reese. It's a Monday. I have school today."

"Call in sick."

"I can't do that..."

"Sure, you can."

"I—"

"You can either help me save lives, or you can go learn about... numbers or whatever they teach these days. You can go in late one day."

"I have to get all the way Downtown!"

"Why the hell do you go to school that far away?"

"Because I... Mom got me in a better one."

"C'mon kid, it's one morning. Adventure calls."

I sat in silence for what seemed like at least half-a-minute before saying his name again. No answer. Sighing, I turned toward the street. Strangers went about their business. Some tattooed teenagers loitered by the corner store, smoking before school, hopefully just weed. Garbage trucks picked up heaps of bags with flies buzzing around them. A homeless man rolled out from under one, using it for warmth.

I didn't have much to offer, but I could probably get that guy to help now that he was awake. The homeless were my secret weapon in the days of the Roach. People underestimated them. Thought they didn't see anything, and truthfully, most didn't. Most were barely sane, like Tinman. There were a few gems, however, who truly had lost everything when the city's industry tanked and had nowhere else to live. They wouldn't dare talk to cops—not in the Stacks or Harborside—but they used to talk to me.

I tried to open the door with just my arms but couldn't get much leverage. The thing was heavy. My wheels pressed against the glass as I pushed hard as I could until a hand above helped me get it the rest of the way.

"How did you know where I lived?" Isaac asked.

I glanced back. He had a sweatshirt on with the hood up, his Marauders cap on, and a pair of women's sunglasses that probably belonged to his mother over his eyeglasses. His head tilted.

"You shaved," he said, incredulous.

"Tada," I said as I ran my hand across my chin, feeling all the hairs I'd missed.

"What do you want?"

"We may want to go outside. I annoyed a lot of people pushing all those buttons."

He exhaled. "You're going to get us evicted."

"Let's go. This won't take long."

I squeezed the rest of the way through the door and out onto the sidewalk. Isaac caught his sleeve on the handle, stumbling out to meet me after he pulled it free. It was getting easier and easier to realize why the kid was bullied despite his stature.

"What won't take long?" he asked.

"I need your help getting up some stairs," I said.

"Me?" He looked at me like I had two heads.

"Yeah, you. Everyone else I know is working."

And connected back to Lieutenant Montalvo, and the mayor, and Laura. There weren't many others. If I'd asked my neighbors, they might call the police just from the shock of me talking to them. But Isaac seemed to be a good kid, and the last thing he needed was more lessons at a frilly Downtown school on subjects that wouldn't help an outcast like him survive long enough to become an adult.

"Come here." I waved him over. He hesitated but eventually listened. I swiped the sunglasses right off his face.

"Hey!" he squealed as he reached for them with one hand, covering the glasses lens over his left eye with the other. I held the sunglasses behind my head.

"What are these for?" I asked.

"I don't want anybody to see me outside of school."

"They'll all be *in* school. Show me. C'mon."

His lips sagged before he slowly removed his hand from his face, revealing a bruised left eye.

"Jesus," I said. "You look worse than me."

"It's not that bad," he muttered.

I tugged his hand down and tilted my head to get a closer look with the wound contorted by his thick glasses. The bruise looked fresh, with splotches of purple and red, like the pattern on a flower somewhere exotic that I'll never visit.

"Those same assholes again?" I questioned.

He nodded.

"You know you could pummel them, right?" I said. "Bullies only see straight forward. But guys like us—scrappers—we do whatever it takes."

"I tried!" he exclaimed. "I swear. They didn't get close this time. They pegged me with a can of soda as they rode by. I was just picking my mom up some soup..."

"Pegged you with a—" I rubbed my face. "Don't you have any friends you can walk with?"

He chewed on the side of his lip. "Nobody around here..."

"All right. You help me, and I promise that we'll set aside a time for me to show you how to make sure they never mess with you again."

"I can't kick them in the nuts if they're on bikes."

"No." I snickered. "You can't. But there are better ways to make a bully back off."

I don't know what it was lately. My mind kept returning to events I believed I'd forgotten. I thought about the oldest kid at my foster home when I was probably seven or eight. Can't be too sure since I don't know my real birthday. Just a bit too young for father to really care about me yet.

The older boy would make us give him extra food simply because he was enormous, especially poor, spineless Steven. And we didn't get fed much more than the pigs. After a few futile attempts to fight him, he stole our comic book and tore it in half. So, I tried a different approach.

I dug a hole out back in my spare time and convinced Steven to help me. Spent months on it all while letting the bully take food from us. When it was deep enough, one night, I fought back and got him chasing after me. I jumped, and the boy tumbled into that dark hole, so deep he couldn't pull himself back up.

He spent the entire night down there in the dead of winter, because I'd dug it in the one corner where his cries didn't carry for anybody who mattered to hear him. Steven begged me to help him out. Cried over how after he escaped, he'd kill us.

I held strong. We tossed him some scraps of our dinners, so he didn't starve, covered in dirt and spit. The bully held off, but by the time I tossed a rope down to pull him up the next morning, he'd devoured every last bit.

And you know what? He never made me or Steven, or anyone else, give him anything ever again.

I hadn't hurt him, not really. What'd I'd done was show him exactly how we younger kids felt every time. In doing so, everyone saw how weak he really was. We all heard him cry that night. A month's worth of digging simply to humiliate him left him terrified of me.

Probably the other kids too, since nobody but Steven ever talked to me much again. Even he mostly just hung around, never saying much. Deep-seated fear and the unknown of how far I'd go—it made the bully's size irrelevant.

"Well, what are they?" Isaac asked me back in the present, eyes pleading for answers.

The memory almost had me smirking. Almost. Nothing was good

about where I grew up. I'd won that battle, but we were all too young to realize that in our fighting with each other, we didn't fight the ones in charge. Nobody else was going to save us.

"You'll see," I replied.

I focused on the shine from Isaac's glasses to keep myself focused on the present. Which was difficult, since I couldn't help but picture Steven in them. Whatever. Better than seeing Roxy all cut up or imagining Mr. Patel, a charred crisp. I placed my hands on the pushrims of my chair and started to roll, then paused. My shoulders burned.

"I need a break. Do you mind..." I swallowed hard. "Do you mind taking the handles and pushing me?" I asked him, unable to believe the words coming out of my own mouth.

"Uh... sure?" He didn't move, as shocked as I was. Like he was worried I was pulling a prank.

"Get to it, then. Lives hang in the balance."

"If you say so."

Isaac took the grips and pushed. I hated the sensation of being so out of control that someone had to guide me around, but my aching body was yapping, and I finally listened. I needed to save my strength for whatever the hell was to come.

"135 Park Avenue," I told him. "It's a bit of a hike."

"Why don't we take the rail?" he asked. "There's a stop up nearby."

"Absolutely not."

"That's like twenty blocks," he whined.

"Good. You can use the exercise if you ever want to stand up to those guys."

He moaned, then asked. "Who are we saving, anyway?".

"Maybe the entire city. Maybe nobody. A good sidekick doesn't ask unnecessary questions."

For what's it's worth, he didn't after that. I lowered my head to ignore the confused stares thrown at us by all the locals. What an odd pair we made. My chair rumbled over the rough concrete and misaligned gaps, shaking my body. Horns beeped, people hollered, awful smells shifted with the wind—all part of Iron City's endless symphony.

Never beautiful. Always unique.

Isaac talked and talked as we moved, pointing out landmarks where he once did... whatever kids do. I don't know, he never shut the fuck up. I ignored basically all of it.

We escaped the heart of the Stacks after circumventing a gathering on a closed-down street where Darrell Washington addressed downtrodden locals by megaphone in his last-ditch-effort campaign of trying to speak plainly and directly with Iron City's constituents.

Then we moved toward the fringes of Harborside, where things got a bit nicer, and Mayor Garrity's improvements could really be felt. There weren't quite so many shady characters hanging out in alleyways and under scaffolding, either.

Well, minus the group of homeless under a tree in nearby Murdock Park, crowded around a garbage can. And the graffiti all over the side of the church down at the end of the block—a Roach being crucified like Jesus Christ himself in one image. And the trash bags lining the sidewalk, which apparently nobody felt like cleaning up yet. And the beat cops on every corner. But hey, renovated warehouses have great character.

"I think this is the right address," Isaac said, stopping.

That particular sentence drew my attention back to him. I glanced up at the overhang. 135 Park Avenue. I knew it well from surveillance missions years back. This was the apartment building housing my pen-wielding adversary, Chuck Barnes. A five-story walk-up where he, of course, lived on the fifth story.

"Well done, kid," I said. "Now, roll me in."

Isaac positively beamed from the compliment. The kid's mother must've always been at work for him to get that happy over nothing.

The inside of the lobby was much like any other around here—cold, stark, and unadorned. A tackboard by the mailboxes was covered in business cards and flyers that nobody would ever read—guitar lessons, singing lessons, lost dog this, lost cat that. The floors were simultaneously clean and dirty. You know, that way things in cities always are? Someone probably cleaned it often, but the filth gets so engrained, janitors just polish right over it.

A young woman leaned against the wall by her mailbox, unlit cigarette between her lips. She was pensive, probably thinking about where her life went wrong. I couldn't help but picture Roxy in her place, pale as a china doll, eyes like blank marbles.

"Okay, kid, now here's the fun part," I said, turning away fast. "I need you to carry me up to the fifth floor."

Isaac's smile vanished. He stopped in the center of the scissor stairwell, stared straight up, and asked, "All the way to the top?"

"Don't put on that face. You think this doesn't hurt my pride enough? But my arms aren't what they used to be, and snail's pace just won't cut it today."

He gulped. "What's up there?"

"A man causing trouble."

"What kind of trouble?" he asked.

"What did I say about sidekicks and unnecessary questions?"

"That's really high."

I sucked through my teeth. "The guy who wrote those columns in the *Weekly Iron* about the Roach's return? He lives up there, and I need to know why he's lying."

Isaac squinted upward, then turned to face me, brow furrowing behind his lenses. "Who are you?" he asked.

"You know who I am."

"No, like... What do you do?"

"Consider me a rival journalist who values the truth above all else. So, when somebody makes something up just to sell a bogus story, it personally offends me," I said, hand over my heart.

"Who do you write for?"

"Anyone." I rolled forward and nudged him with my chair. "Kid, please. Don't make me beg."

He looked up again, back to me, then re-adjusted his glasses. "Fine, I'll try. But you have to tell me what all this is about after."

"Ah-ah-ah, I already promised to teach you how to fight back."

He crossed his arms, and one half of his lips lifted into a smirk. "Fine then. Maybe I'll go tell my mom about the *white* adult who's making me work for him for free."

"That what this is about?" I would've smacked him if I wasn't proud of him for standing his ground. "Money," I lamented. "Always getting in the way of things. How about I tell her you ditched school?"

"Those kids can't touch me in detention," he said, grin spreading to the other half of his face.

I clenched my jaw, releasing a low grumble. I didn't have time to barter. People were dying, and Chuck was the single thread connecting them. A fraying stitch ready to pop.

"Okay," I conceded. "You get me to the top and back down, I got a Benjamin back home with your name on it. That ought to pay for whatever useless algebra lessons you'll have missed this morning."

His smug expression fully faded. "No, no, I-I'm sorry. I was just joking around. I can't take that from you."

"Why not? I already agreed."

"No, I can't—"

"What? Say it?"

"I..."

"You can't take money from a cripple?"

All the color fled his cheeks. I slapped him on the back.

"Listen to me, kid," I said. "You don't want to keep getting bullied, stop worrying so much. Bad guys feed on fear like sharks to blood. But they scare just as easy."

I rotated and moved in front of the steps. A resident with a crying baby stayed as far away from me as she could. She even switched the swaddle to her other hand.

"Now, help me before I change my mind," I said.

Isaac moved around to my front and studied me like I was one of those tri-fold boards at his school's science fair. He extended his arms and bent toward me, then stopped.

"What?" I asked, patience wearing thin.

"How do I…" He leaned back in and wedged his hand under my thigh. I punched him in the gut, knocking the wind out of him. He fell back onto the third step, gasping, hands over his face as if preparing for another blow. The shock in his eyes probably matched mine. It was purely reflex.

"What the…" he huffed. "Fuck?"

"Watch your mouth," I said. Then, I quickly added. "Sorry. I don't like being touched." I patted him on the shoulder. "There you go. Cough it up."

He shrugged me away. "If I can't touch you, how am I supposed to carry you?"

"Not through the legs, for one. Here, arm around my waist, then heave me up on your shoulder. I promise, I'm not as heavy as I look. These legs are all skin and bone."

Isaac wavered.

"You're fine. Look." I tucked my hands behind my back.

He chewed on his lower lip as he inspected me for a few seconds longer before saying, "What about your chair?"

"Worry about that once we reach the top."

He drew a deep breath. Then, he dove right in, lowering his shoulder into my gut and wrapping one arm around my back. I pushed off the seat with my other hand to help him, moving slowly so as not to alarm him and get dropped on my noggin.

"There you go," I strained to say as my flabby pecs were compressed against his shoulder. I could feel him quaking; hear him stifling groans. I had a view straight down at his collar, at his father's clinking dog tags.

"Brace yourself on the railing with your other hand," I instructed. "There you go."

I clung to the back of his shirt as he swayed a bit.

"Got me?" I asked.

He moaned what I suspect were meant to be words.

"There, you've got it," I said. "I knew you were strong enough. Just take it slow. One step at a time. You drop me, and I'll stuff the money I owe you right down your gullet."

His throat bobbed, but Isaac kept quiet as he followed my directions. The few residents trickling down eyed us like we were a circus show. I closed my eyes, deciding to take my own advice and stop worrying so much about how pathetic this looked. This was what needed to be done. That was my creed. If it needed to be done for the good of the city, I could stomach it.

"Can we... break..." Isaac groaned as we rounded the landing for the third floor.

"Are you serious?" I asked. "Don't drag this out."

"Please..."

Isaac could barely get the word out and didn't wait for a response. He lowered me onto a step, my back pressing hard into its edge. Far from a gentle landing.

I was about to scold him when I realized that he'd flopped next to me, sucking down air like a fish out of water, beads of sweat rolling down his face as if he'd actually been underwater.

"You have a minute," I said.

Too breathless to reply, he offered a halfhearted thumbs up.

"Stand up," I told him. "Stretch on the wall. Hands above your head. You'll get more air that way."

"I can't..."

"Just do it."

Grasping the railing, Isaac pulled himself to his feet and hunched over it. He lay his palms flat on the wall and stretched back like a cat. His breathing started to steady.

"See?" I said.

He released a high-pitched grunt and nodded. I smirked and let him enjoy the break.

"Everything okay here?" a nosy resident asked, approaching from the third-floor hall.

"We're fine," I said.

The guy glanced between me and Isaac.

"Keep staring, and you won't be able to walk either," I growled. His jaw dropped before he squeezed by to go down the steps. "There you go. Move along."

"Great example for the kid," he scolded on his past.

"What was that, asshole?"

His footsteps clacked along faster. I turned to Isaac. "You good?"

"One more minute?" he said.

"Think your dad got to ask for one more minute? No. You want to be like him, you have to push through pain. Use it as fuel. That's what it takes to win a fight."

Isaac remained against the wall, head sinking between his arms.

"Did you hear me?" I asked.

"My dad died in Vietnam when I was barely four... and then we moved here," he said softly. He peered back, eyes welling with tears, chin scratching against the chain of his dog tags. "I don't know what he's like."

Now it all made sense. Isaac wasn't the skinniest twerp. Yeah, he wore bug-eyed glasses, and two-strapped his colorful backpack, though he didn't seem like a nerd either—he'd skipped out on school to help me after all. But his dad wasn't the victim of some recent war caused by the charlatan currently in the White House. This was long-lasting damage.

I wasn't big on people fighting in wars when our own streets were in so much trouble, but I respect the bravery. Those poor men, though—returned from hell on Earth to ridicule and resentment. I'd encountered enough of them living on the streets, ghosts of the evils they'd done to survive haunting their expressions. It made them ripe pickings for street gangs like the Iron Riders to exploit back in the day, if they weren't busy getting into trouble themselves.

Very few hard criminals earned my pity like vets. I did what had to be done, of course, but I probably wouldn't have had to do it as much if they'd returned to parades instead of picket signs. When society gives up on you, where else is there to go?

Maybe, I went too far sometimes, though. Maybe, I could've taken their rage and their pain and invited them to join my crusade.

As for young Isaac, a mixed-race new kid living in the projects would have a hard enough time fitting in with any group, let alone one who grew up without a father from that early on. It made him different. Like a boy who doesn't like sports. Or a girl who hates dresses. Or a quiet foster child in an overcrowded home that preferred to be left alone.

Children are mean sons of bitches.

"Stop that," I said. "You know what he was like."

"I don't!" Isaac snapped. "I can barely remember his face..." He squeezed the dog tags, and I half expected him to tear them off. I scooted along the steps closer to him, needing both arms to slide my ass along.

"Right or wrong, he believed he was doing what he had to do to protect you."

"He didn't have to join the war," Isaac sniveled. "Mom says he wasn't even drafted. He just wanted to. It was almost over, and he-he left instead of being with us. And then, she made me move here, and... and..."

"It's never that black and white, kid. Trust me. There are far worse parents you could have than a dad who gave his life for his country, whether or not it accomplished a damn thing. Hell, at least you know who your dad is. And you know he was brave. Foolish, probably, but brave."

Isaac wiped his nose on his sleeve as he sat beside me, leaving a trail of boogers like a snail trail. "You didn't know your dad?" he asked.

"What?" I said.

"You said I'm lucky to know mine. Does that mean you didn't?"

"Kid, this is about you, not me. Now, let's get a move on." I smacked the step. "You've still got to make good on your end of the deal, like your father did with our government. Best thing we can learn from our parents is how to make better choices."

Isaac tucked his dog tags into his shirt and stood. "Mom says dad was perfect."

"Good for him."

I stuck out my hand, averting my eyes, so the sting of needing to be hauled like a sack of manure was diminished. Somehow, the second time hit me harder, but not him. He didn't even sway. I bet he imagined himself in the jungles of Vietnam, hauling a wounded soldier like daddy might've.

I pictured it, too. It took a bit of an edge off the embarrassment.

Still, when he lowered me to the top landing, the relief was akin to what those guys must've felt in the back rooms of the *Bleek Street Gentleman's Club*. My sigh was blissful. Isaac kept his composure this time. I could tell he was wiped, but he stayed upright and controlled his breathing.

"Now, the fun part," I said. "You get to go grab my chair."

"You said this was the fun part."

"Whatever. Get my chair."

Isaac's groan of frustration shattered my impressed vision of him. He threw his hands behind his head as he stomped back down.

While he was gone, I followed the signs, dragging my body backward toward unit 524. It wasn't as easy on the dingy, gray carpet as on tile, but I made my way. Half the hall lights were out. Ceiling panels were missing. The building may have had an old-world charm on the outside, but it was clear why it didn't have an elevator, and why a journalist who probably couldn't sell a story to a major outlet if he personally caught the President being blown by his secretary lived here.

"Reese?" Isaac whisper-shouted from the top of the stairs.

I leaned back around the corner and waved him along. By the time he reached me, he was back to being out of breath.

"How do you move so fast?" he panted.

"Practice," I said.

He parked the chair right in front of me. I felt his fingers tighten around the back of my shirt, but I called him off. My pride had taken enough of a trouncing for one morning. All I could do was hope that I could convince Chuck to carry me back down. That, I might have enjoyed. Hearing him huff and puff. Maybe he'd even drop me—easy way to get him off my back for good.

"That's the room," While I pulled myself up onto the chair using the doorknob of a maintenance closet, I nodded toward unit 524, the last digit hanging upside-down.

"Okay," he said. "Now what?" Isaac breathed down my back, as if waiting for me to fall. Made finding my seat all-the-more satisfying.

"Now, nothing," I said. A series of pops sounded from my back as vertebrae adjusted to my weight. I cracked my neck next, then knuckles. I was back in action as long as Chuck didn't flee down a fire escape.

"I don't get it?" Isaac said.

"I need you to wait out here."

"But I carried you all—"

"You did. And I need you out here, keeping lookout. He's not going to like the chat we're about to have, so if he runs..."

Isaac's eyes sparkled. "You'll need me to stop him?"

"Exactly. You can trip him. Or, better yet, kick him in the balls."

"Roger that." He eagerly rubbed his hands together. "Lookout. I can do that."

I gave my exceedingly-average, overeager companion one full look over. Is this what Batman felt when he recruited Robin? Maybe Isaac needed a costume and an alias. Call him the Inch Worm or something cute like that.

No! I scolded myself inwardly. The Roach worked alone. Connecting to someone like that, sharing the life—it was a fantasy for comics. All sidekicks ever were, in the end, were a way to undermine the hero. This was the last time I'd involve him.

"Back around the corner," I shooed him. "Go on."

I waited until he was out of sight, then moved to Chuck's door. Only right before I knocked did I consider the fact that maybe he'd moved. It'd been, oh, I-don't-know-how-long since I'd tracked him here. I wouldn't have been surprised if he'd been crashing on couches for years or living down in the Stacks. Maybe spending a night or two here and there under Horseshoe Bridge with the crackheads.

"Too late now," I muttered to myself. "Chuck, open up!" I shouted as I rapped on the door three times.

I heard a *clatter* inside. Followed by a *thump*.

"Chuck!" I knocked again.

Now came footsteps, moving away from the door, then back toward it.

"Chuck, I can hear you in there. Open the fucking door!"

"Who is it?" he asked. His voice was ragged, oozing urgency. Chasing ambulances for stories wasn't easy work. Even worse when the subjects of his ridiculous column were turning up dead. Did he worry he was next?

"You won't be able to see me down here through the peephole, so just open up," I said.

"Reese? Reese Roberts, is that you?"

"I'm not gonna ask again."

Something else inside fell. Chuck cursed.

I sighed. I'm not sure why I thought he'd make things easy. He never did.

Studying the door, I realized that even though it was a piece of shit, I couldn't bash through it in my state. I looked back and noticed Isaac peaking around the corner. He nodded toward the door, as if I was supposed to read his mind.

Convincing a minor to carry me upstairs, maybe I'd get a slap on the wrist from authorities. Convincing him to pull off a B and E, different story. That'd give my pal Lieutenant Montalvo the ammo to lock me up in a heartbeat.

I pinched my nose and racked my brain for answers. Chuck Barnes was the only lead I had, which meant the men in blue would likely come talk to him once they caught up. This was my chance at getting a leg up before they swept this under the political carpets, metaphorically speaking.

The lock clicked. The door creaked open.

I didn't give Chuck a chance to change his mind. Shoving the door with one hand, I pushed inside.

"Chuck, do you realize how much trouble—" I lost my train of thought as I heard yet another *click*.

I looked right, and there Chuck stood, eyes bloodshot, nostrils flaring. He aimed a revolver at the side of my head. Nothing new, looked bought from some gangster right off the streets. And he didn't wear his usual mustard-stained slacks and vest. No.

Chuck Barnes wore my suit, a freshly repainted Roach symbol stamped on the chest.

CHAPTER ELEVEN

"You're alive?" Chuck asked. "Was it you? Did you do it?" Words spilled out of him like he was on something. He for sure hadn't slept soundly in days, if at all.

"Chuck, what the hell are you wearing?" I asked, slow and steady. My rage over seeing him in my suit had to take a back seat with a gun aimed at me. Survival instincts, thankfully, kicked in.

"Was it you!" He pushed the barrel of the revolver into the side of my head.

"You're asking me that while you're playing dress-up?"

"Stop playing games, Reese! Did you kill those people just to get back at me?"

I turned, the gun sliding around my scalp until it stopped right in the center of my forehead. I rolled forward, glaring at Chuck the entire time while the barrel pushed so hard it'd surely leave a circular imprint.

Is that what people thought of me? Decades cleaning up the streets, and the one man who'd might have put it all together thought I could murder innocent people in cold blood. I don't know if I was more hurt or enraged.

I never took a night off as the Roach. Never. Not a vacation, even when my day job strained me to my limits. When Iron City's downtrodden screamed, the Roach answered.

"You think *I* killed those people?" I asked.

"Who knows what you're capable of." His gun-hand shook as I leaned into it, but I didn't make my move yet. Maybe he actually *was* on drugs. He smelled like he hadn't even showered in days, had a bruise near his right eye, and another on his left cheek.

"Reese, are you okay?" Isaac's squeaky voice asked from behind us.

Chuck's arm whipped toward the doorway, his eyes wide with fear and adrenaline. Survival be damned. Without hesitating, I pushed off my chair and rammed into him. One of my hands flew toward the gun and he fired, blowing the top half of my pinky off as I re-directed his aim. The slug burrowed itself in the doorframe.

The gun flew out of his hand as we tumbled to the ground, thrashing and punching. Isaac froze in the doorway like a deer in headlights. I'm not even sure it was from almost having his head blown off. His gaze was fixed upon a guy wearing the suit of the infamous Roach.

I crawled for the firearm, but Chuck kicked me in the gut. I caught his already bruised face with an elbow to break free.

A second before reaching the gun, Chuck pounced on my back, constricting my throat with the familiar tube of a gas mask. He wrenched my head back, and as I elbowed more, my bones met the heavily-reinforced armor of my own suit, and I learned why so many criminals had broken their own hands trying to take a beating to me back in the day.

Chuck wrenched my head to the side, crunching my ribs against the edge of a desk. I managed to stuff my now pinkyless hand under the tube, and the blood made it slick enough for me to get free. Not for long. Chuck wound up and smashed me across the face with the gasmask.

I flew flat onto my back. By the time my squishy abs helped me sit up even the slightest, Chuck aimed the gun at me again. A fresh cut over his brow had a line of red snaking down over his eye.

"Don't move, either of you!" he yelled, aim snapping between me and the doorway.

"He's just a kid, Chuck," I said, raising my hands. I'd never lost a part of a finger before. Broken them plenty, but never this. Weirdly enough, it hurt a lot less. Probably only the adrenaline, or maybe my body had gotten so used to missing legs, a tiny finger was nothing.

"What is he doing here?" Chuck demanded.

"He helped me get upstairs. That's it. Let him go, and we'll talk."

"Y-y-y-you're the R-r-roach?" Isaac stuttered. He didn't have his hands up. Didn't move his feet.

"The Roach is dead," I said. "He's just a guy playing dress-up."

Chuck turned the gun back on me. "If the Roach is dead, then I'm seeing ghosts," he said. Isaac's stance shifted, and Chuck's aim shifted right back to him.

"Chuck, let the kid go."

"So, he can call the cops?"

"He knows better. Right, Kid?" Isaac was too busy gawking to acknowledge. "Besides," I went on. "You don't think anybody heard a gun go off?"

"You know how many guns still go off in Harborside every day?"

"How many aimed at the head of a teenager?"

Chuck exhaled slowly through his teeth. More a growl than anything.

"Kid, just back up and close the door," I said. I snapped my fingers. "Isaac. Listen to me."

He remained completely frozen. Terror, awe—his face looked like it'd gone through a blender of the two and then some.

Chuck took a hard step toward him, and fear took complete control.

"Chuck, think about this!" God, if I had legs, I'd have tackled him straight out that puny excuse for a window in this shithole. But all I could do was lay like a slug as his revolver got close enough to Isaac to blow a baseball-sized hole in him.

"Chuck!" I yelled.

Isaac's lower lip started to tremble. The front of his pants went dark. I couldn't judge him for it. They might've taught me to manage with catheters, but when you're a drunk, you forget, and I'd pissed myself enough the last few years to fill a bathtub. Chuck lunged. I winced. Then he grasped the edge of the door and slowly pushed it closed. The moment it clicked, he pulled the bolt-lock and turned on me with the revolver.

"Goddammit. God. Dammit!" He kicked my mask as hard as he could, sending a crack up one lens. I could almost feel the pain vicariously through my left eye. Hurt worse than my missing pinky.

"Watch it," I said.

"You were dead," he said like a petulant child. "They said you had no chance of waking up."

"Aw. Nice to see you too."

"They wanted to pull the plug."

I shrugged. "I woke up."

He ignored me and rushed across his room. Leaning across the window, he peeled back the blinds to peer out while keeping the gun on me. With my wheelchair across the room, there was no way I could reach him even if I managed to get the jump.

"What the hell is wrong with you, bringing a kid here?" he asked.

"I thought I was coming to ask a journalist some questions, not a maniac," I spat.

"Like you can talk?"

"I'm not the one aiming a gun, chief."

I surveyed his studio apartment now that I didn't have Isaac to worry about. A pile of dirty laundry lay beside a desk cluttered with more than a dozen notepads filled with colored tabs. A cheap polaroid camera hung from a framed black and white photo of two parents and a young boy in the middle, wearing ball caps and standing outside the old stadium.

The place was a pigsty, and don't get me started on the bathroom. Wet towels on the floor were covered in red. The shower curtain had mold creeping upward from the bottom. It certainly didn't look like the residence of a sane man, though, people might look to my lair and say the same. And while Chuck Barnes didn't have a surveillance station in a lair—nonoperational or otherwise—he used the wall at the foot of his bed for an investigation board.

Thumbtacks pushed in dozens of photos and clippings, each surrounded by notecards. Surprisingly, considering his living conditions, they weren't covered in mad scrawls, but neat, perfectly legible words, with strings connecting one to the other.

A photocopy of my old Water and Sewage Authority ID picture was at the center of the diagram. Around me were both familiar and unfamiliar faces. A line between a picture of a blank figure and myself branched off, also connected to Laura, the words HER RAPIST appearing above it. Then, FATHER? below, alongside Michelle's photo. Just the thought that Chuck had stalked them enough to get a polaroid of Michelle sent my anger soaring, but I tried to keep my composure and keep studying.

Then, there was Mayor Garrity next to the word COVER-UP in bold. Officer José Montalvo. The Police Commissioner. A handful of other cops I'd never seen or met before. My old boss at the Iron City Water and Sewage Authority. The insurance agents and lawyers who'd handled my case, where a ceiling had partially collapsed and "led to my paralysis," and subsequent settlement. Even the Doctor who was documented for treating me. I knew that he'd retired to Florida a few years back, and so did Chuck's notecard beneath him.

I'd never realized what a tangled web of lies we'd left behind that night until seeing it laid out like this. Chuck had been busy. He had it all. A missing piece here and there, like who Laura's rapist actually was, and no credible sources to back it, but he had the story. My gaze kept going back to the faceless representation of the man who raped Laura. Chuck had circled it and written, FIND HIM, in Sharpie.

That there was the missing piece of the puzzle. The man was on the bottom of Horton River, tied to a cinderblock, courtesy of my co-conspirators. The bloody foundation of the Garrity Act and the end of the Roach. Figures, Vinny had been an architect, too.

But he would never talk. Never have a say in being Michelle's dad.

And me? I got my payment for saving Laura's life. Got to stay hidden to the world in exchange for handing over every ounce of dirt I'd gathered on every group operating in Iron City, from gangs like the River Kings to Mayor Garrity himself. I was too angry at my body back then to care. And with me out of the way, all the credit went to the mayor for making Iron City into a city again rather than a war zone.

And Laura? She got to be the public martyr. The victim of an unknown assailant in a district out of control, where only the night before, three young girls in sex slavery died when I took down a Bratva-run brothel. A district in a city so foul that it gave birth to the Roach. A city that only a better-armed and more-prepared police force could tame.

Everybody got something they wanted. All it took was one asshole dying.

I'd call it a fair trade. Investigators' views might differ, but hey, I played outside their rules. Always had. A part of me respected Mayor Garrity for bending them and playing dirty to get the job done.

I only wished he'd left what happened to Laura out of it. Though, I understood that, too. Every movement needs a pretty face behind it these days. Have you watched TV? Looked up at a billboard?

The sweet, young, and brilliant daughter of our beloved mayor got attacked, and half the city finally woke up and wanted to smoke out the filth, people from every race, creed, religion. Garrity used her to drive drug-slinging organized crime out of Harborside in order to lure in new businesses like Aurora Technologies and hope that one day, Iron City might find a new identity and flourish.

What did it matter who got the credit, right? Do what needs to be done; that's how I lived. For Iron City and for Laura, my legacy was erased. But presently, as my gaze filtered back to the journalist playing dress-up.

"Jesus fucking Christ, Chuck," I said, unable to believe his vast web of conspiracy and meticulous research was real. "Is this what you've been up to all this time?"

"Digging and digging." He continued looking between the window and me. "I tried to sell the story everywhere. Over and over. But without Laura's attacker, it was all conjecture. You all did quite a job covering this up."

"I have no idea what you're talking about."

"Oh, cut the crap, Reese!" he snapped. "You think I have a tape recorder in here? Huh?" He stormed across the room and started flipping things off his desk. Then he swiped a pile of notebooks onto the floor. In the mess, he fished out a tape recorder that was turned off.

I pushed off the floor and propped myself higher on the wall. "The cops are going to find the connection between your Roach column and the murders. They'll be here soon. And when they find all of this..."

"They'll what? Disgrace me? Pin it on me?" He tapped his head with the barrel of the gun. "Keep up. Not much further I can sink." He returned to the window. "I offer the conspiracy of a lifetime, implicating a mayor and the country's most famous vigilante, and nothing. Buried at every turn. I offer a few cute, heroic stories about the Roach returning to fit a theme? The *Weekly Iron* gobbles it up like Thanksgiving turkey and wants to keep the column going."

"And two people wind up dead."

"You think I wanted that?" he seethed. "It was just more proof."

"Of what?"

"That nobody wants the truth anymore."

"The truth is that you stole the Roach's skin," I said. "You walked around wearing a lie, making a joke of his legacy! You're lucky it's only two people who wound up dead, you goddamn lunatic."

Chuck stared at me for a few long seconds, then started to laugh.

"You think this is funny?" I growled. I clutched two handfuls of his shag carpet. The fibers scratched my missing pinky and finally made it hurt like it should. I welcomed the pain. I wished it was his hair.

"'Skin'," he said, still enjoying his own private comedy club. "That's the word you use for this, and I'm the lunatic?" He stretched my suit's sleeve. "It's a fucking suit! A costume. Strong enough to slow a bullet, though, I'll tell you that."

"You're not gonna get away with this."

"And you won't rat me out. Don't forget, Reese, I've followed your whole career closely. Street justice, that's your code, right? Well, except during million-dollar cover-ups funded by the mayor."

My fists lifted me higher. My teeth ground so hard I gave myself a headache—or maybe it just hadn't gone away yet.

"Two deaths are on your hands," I said. "You know the Roach so well, what do you think that earns?"

He scoffed. "Two deaths is nothing compared to you."

"You think that gun scares me?"

"No, but I bet prison does. I die, with all this research in here? A journalist who's been publicly seen outside your home arguing with you. Hard to cover that up. Hell, there's no loyalty amongst thieves. They'll probably blame you for the killings, too. Say you wanted to protect the Roach's... what did you call it? Legacy?"

"Worth it." It felt like I was breathing acid. I begged my legs to give one last push so I could reach him and strangle the life out of him.

"What about my legacy?" he said. "A few too many questions at the mayor's office after your 'accident,' trying to piece timelines together, and I lose everything! I got arrested for domestic abuse. They planted drugs, too. Did you know that? I didn't even do it, but still my fiancé left me after. Then the *Bulletin* fired me. Nobody else worth a damn would even take an interview. I can barely afford a camera. Talk about a joke."

I didn't know about the arrest part, though it was hard to feel bad after he stole my identity, and aimed a gun at Isaac. I knew women-beaters like I knew child-beaters. They always thought they were right. They had to teach a lesson.

"Oh, boohoo," I mocked. "Poor Chuck Barnes. Loose with the truth his whole career until he decides it matters."

"Why—because I had the balls to write the truth about the Roach?" he said. "To question that maybe the guys who wound up dead from your justice only deserved to serve five to ten. Maybe they were completely innocent, like those three Slavic girls you got killed whose only crime was being born. Who'd ever know?"

My fingernails dug into my palms, wincing at the pain in my pinky. "The Roach made a move against the Bratva back then because nobody else had the balls to."

"I saw the crime scene. You rushed in, sloppy. Not like your other work."

"They used children!" I roared.

"Dead ones, now. All swept under the rug after what happened to Laura Garrity, even though nobody was ever caught. Maybe that was a lie, too."

"I'll kill you."

Chuck pointed out the window in dramatic flair. "The simpletons out there may have lapped up the legends of our dark guardian vanquishing evil, but that doesn't make you a hero, Reese."

"I never asked to be."

"Cut the crap. You loved every second of it. I saw your trophies down in your tunnel." He crossed the room again, found a photograph on his desk, and flicked it at me. I watched it flip through the air and settle nearby. A picture of my lair and the wall of clippings I kept for myself.

"I thought about sending that to the press," he said. "Or this." He showed me a Polaroid of my suit's display case. Then another of the broken tunnel I once used to access Iron City's innards and move around undetected.

"I had it all," he went on. "The evidence I needed. What were you going to do about it, lying in a hospital at death's door? And then

I realized the headline they'd spin it with... THE ROACH DIES A HERO." His whole face shuddered with revulsion. "Dies, saving a little girl, redeeming himself for past failures."

I knew he'd think of something corny like that.

"And I thought: 'They don't deserve the story,'" Chuck said. "Not you, not the papers, not the police. None of you deserved the fluff piece I knew your unveiling would be turned into. They'd shrug off decades of broken bones and corpses, and fawn over the Roach's great sacrifice. No." He aimed the revolver straight at my head again. "You don't get that happy ending."

"And look where we are now." I squeezed my head, palms tugging on strands of hair until they stung, and let out a groan. "What was the plan, Chuck? You wear the suit a few months, come forward, and you get to be the hero you once despised?"

"It doesn't matter now." He released the blinds with a *snap* and ducked quickly. "Shit! They're here."

"Police?"

"Yes, police. I knew that little twerp would call."

"They were bound to come knocking."

"Your friends?" he asked.

"I have no friends."

He pursed his lips, then grunted. Tearing across the room, he yanked a duffel bag out of his closet, pulling down a few hangers with it by accident. I slid along the floor a foot or so while he was distracted, but as he returned to his desk, he aimed the gun at me.

"Don't move."

"Wasn't planning to," I said. "This looks like it's going to resolve itself."

He continued aiming as he shoveled all his research into the bag, including the pictures of my lair. He even swiped his entire web of conspiracy off the wall, though not before snapping a picture of it with his Polaroid. He shook it out to develop it as he grabbed my mask, taking a moment to stare at himself in the reflection of the lens, before stuffing it in as well.

"We've got to get out of here," he said as he crouched down low and patted along his carpet, searching for something else while continuing to shake the Polaroid until the image formed.

"We?" I almost burst out laughing. "No, I want front row seats."

"Do you want to stop the killer or not?"

"I plan to."

"Well, then you need me." He tucked the gun and the photo of his conspiratorial findings into my suit's belt so he could use two hands to reach.

"I promise you, I don't."

"Aha! Got it." He rose, holding half my pinky between his thumb and forefinger. He gave it a shake. "Do Roach legs reattach?"

"Come over here and test it," I replied.

Chuck sneered, then put it into his bag before zipping up. Compared to stealing my identity, a finger barely affected me. It would've looked nice crammed down his throat, though.

"You do need me, because I know who the killer's going after next," he said. "Whatever there is between us, I had no intention of getting anybody killed. You help me stop him, then all of this." He gestured to the duffel. "You can burn it, for all I care. All that matters anyway is that I was right about you."

"Or, you tell me where and I clean up your mess," I offered.

He shook his head. "It doesn't work that way."

"Fine, help me up then." I extended my bloody, four-fingered hand toward him.

"You think I'm stupid?" He grabbed my chair and tossed it over next to me. "I know how you operate, remember? Get on yourself." He pulled the gun again and wagged it at me. "Make a decision, Roach. Stay here and wait for them to question you? Or handle things like you used to."

I glared straight down the barrel of his revolver, wondering if he'd loaded it with more than just the one bullet he'd already shot me with. I wasn't going to risk it. I let my gaze move toward the chair, then him. Straight into his overtired eyes. In them, I saw a man who couldn't be trusted. A man capable of things beyond even what I'd thought. Like I said, sometimes my intuition about people is a little off, but usually, they're better than I expected, not this.

Chuck was right, though. The moment the police found me, Officer Montalvo would be involved, and I'd be cut off from stopping more deaths. If Chuck could help find the killer he'd inspired, I owed it to Iron City to follow the breadcrumbs. Then, when it was settled, Chuck would pay for his violation. Like my foster parents had.

I didn't indulge him with an answer. Instead, I grasped the side of my wheelchair and started to drag myself into its seat. His bed frame offered a nice bit of leverage.

"Thought so," he said. He pulled his coat off a hanger behind his door and threw it on, zipping it all the way up to his neck, so it covered the emblem on my suit.

"You're not even going to change?" I asked as I settled into my seat.

"No time. Here." He opened his door, then tossed the duffel at me, leaving me no choice but to catch it. In that moment, he moved behind me, and I felt the revolver's barrel at the back of my head. He really had done his homework on how to handle me. Or, I'd just lost a step.

Chuck pushed me out into the hall, closing his door but not bothering to lock it. I kept an eye out for Isaac as he retraced our route. The kid was nowhere to be found.

"Stop," I said as we rounded the corner, hearing the crackle and chatter of police radios echoing from the lobby.

"Shit." He stopped me, gun-barrel tickling my earlobe.

"Is there another way down?"

Chuck thought for a few seconds, then spun me as he blurted, "Fire escape."

He picked up the pace this time, zooming by his unit. We whipped around the next corner, down to the end of the hall, to a hollow metal door. Chuck parked me beside it and squeezed by. He opened it slowly to look. I could've had him then. Gun at his side while he focused elsewhere.

I was glad our lengthy conversation gave me some time to stew in my anger. There was no reason to turn the tables on him yet, especially with no time to squeeze him for information.

"Looks clear," he said.

"Did you think they were going to bring SWAT to chat with a pathetic tabloid columnist?" I laughed.

Chuck reached around my back and gave me a hard push out onto the landing, so my knees banged against the door to get it all the way open. I bit my lip and controlled myself. The city needed me.

Closing the door behind us, he took one noisy step down the escape, before pausing and looking back and forth between me and the stairs. "Crap. How do you do this?"

"By myself." I threw the duffel back at him. He dropped it in his panic, and it rolled down to the next landing. He chased after it like a crackhead jonesing for a fix.

I slid off the front of my seat onto the grated metal, then looked down through the spaces, mapping the layout. Going up was tough. Down, not much easier, but I could stomach Isaac helping me. Not Chuck. My meter for embarrassment had already run full for one day. Probably for a whole year.

Rolling beneath the railing, I dug my fingertips into the space in the grates to rotate myself before grabbing the ledge and letting my body hang off. Chuck scooped up the duffel and ran back to the top level.

"Are you insane?" he whisper-shouted.

"Grab my chair, too," I said. "It folds."

I dropped, catching the next landing, and thankful I'd given my untested muscles a break earlier. My busted pinky screamed, but that was only pain. One floor at a time, I dropped, grabbing each landing. It wasn't as smooth as it used to be when I was the Roach, but I still beat Chuck down.

My pinkyless hand finally gave out at the last landing. A pile of garbage softened my fall, minus what were, presumably, soda or beer cans poking into my ass. I rolled off them, flat onto my back, and stared up at how far I'd come down. The tight walls of the alleyway made five stories seem like a skyscraper.

A smile tugged at the corners of my lips. I still had it.

"You are insane," Chuck panted, who-knows-how-long later. He stopped nearby and struggled to unfold my wheelchair. A curse and a good kick got the job done.

"Get up," he said, waving the revolver. "My car's parked on the street."

I tilted my head all the way back along the dirty pavement to regard my chair. Then I coughed and stuck out my hand. "Help me up, would you?"

CHAPTER TWELVE

Chuck had me in the passenger seat of his station wagon, gun aimed at me across his lap as he drove with one hand. The floor was littered with fast-food wrappers and empty coffee cups—the diet of an ambulance-chasing, vigilante-impersonating loon.

We'd made it a few blocks before some cops raced by, but none in the direction of his building. The officers there had probably already knocked on Chucky-boy's door and found he wasn't home. They'd either walk away or go in and find a mess, but nothing incriminating. Maybe a smidge of my blood on the carpet if they looked close enough. They wouldn't—there was no reason for them to believe a crime had happened there, after all. Well, no crime outside of a gutless, worthless nugget of shit like Chuck Barnes breathing the same air as someone like Isaac or Laura.

Other residents might talk about a paraplegic carried up the stairs by a teenager, or a gunshot they'd heard from somewhere, but this was Iron City. Weirdness abounds. Besides, if those cops were really there to talk with Chuck—and honestly, I wasn't sure—the most likely case was they'd leave and come back later. It wasn't inquisition time yet. As far as they knew, he was an everyday working schmuck, and these were normal work hours.

"How long?" I asked when we got stuck at a light.

"How long what?" Chuck said, leaning into the horn the millisecond it turned green and speeding right up the ass of the driver in front of us before cutting off someone else on our left.

"Slow down," I told him. "Drive normal. Blend in."

"Is that how you did it?"

"Christ on a fucking bike, would you just listen?"

He muttered something under his breath, but the station wagon slowed. He fell in with the steady flow of city traffic, like ants in their tunnels. It's why I didn't care for cars. People in them focused only ahead on getting where they needed to go. They probably forgot why they needed to go in the first place, they just did it. Routine. Gather food, feed the Queen, make more ants.

"So, how long have you been parading around as the Roach?" I asked.

Chuck's jaw clenched. "Would you just say you're him already? My God, you're ridiculous. I already know."

My jaw set right back at him. I knew what he wanted. I'd never outright told anybody I was the Roach. Not even Laura. She knew, of course, as did everyone directly affiliated with that night, but I never had to say it. I certainly had no plans to make Chuck Barnes the first.

"How long?" I repeated.

"You read the columns. A few weeks."

I laughed. "I was down for a month, and you only stopped two crimes?"

"Hey, I don't have much practice." He turned right, and as his car straightened out, so too did his features. His chin dropped to his chest. "Only one crime," he said softly.

"What?"

"That Bodega up on 3rd? I uh... I set it up after a night of driving around, finding nothing I could stop."

"Are you out of your damned mind?"

"Hey, I'll give it to you. You and your pals in blue really cleaned this city up from how it used to be."

I grunted.

"I paid some strung-out punk in the River Kings to pretend he was robbing the place," Chuck continued. "I'd already checked to make sure Patel didn't keep a gun. It was going to be easy. The Roach's grand entrance back onto center stage... until the guy got himself spooked and shot me with my own gun."

"Patel died so you could sell a fake story?" I said, half-seething, half-wondering why he was telling me all of this. I wasn't a confessional booth priest ready to dole out five hail Marys and an Our Father. I was closer to ripping the revolver away from him and offering five bullets and a punch to the throat.

"Why do you think I want to make it right?" he asked.

"You can't make it right, Chuck. That's the first thing you learn. You wrote that last article about me, remember? The three dead girls. Collateral is collateral, but at least I stopped something real around them." By the time I finished, I was squeezing his armrest so tight, my knuckles were pale as fresh snow.

He pursed his lips. "Yeah..."

"Where's the guy who helped with the store?"

"Guy?"

"The druggie kid. Where is he?"

"Oh. Gone, I guess. Haven't heard from him since."

"What's his name?" I said.

"I felt safer not knowing anything about him, or him me."

"Like a drug deal."

He chuckled meekly but nodded. "It worked though. The *Weekly Iron* was desperate for a good Roach story to fit their latest issue, so I told them I had a scoop on recent potential Roach sighting. Gave them the article, all buttoned up with Patel's interview and everything."

I rubbed my temples. "And here I was, thinking a real copycat tried to take up the mantle."

"Roxy was real," Chuck said. "She was nice."

I shot him a sidelong glare.

"Hey, don't judge," he said. "I'm single now in the shit-end of Iron City and barely have a job, thanks to you. Roxy talked to me like a real person."

"She wanted your money," I said.

"Yeah, maybe, but... well. She told me her problems. I told her some of mine. I didn't even care if she danced after a while, or for whatever any of the other stuff people pay for in those backrooms. I just liked being around her."

"So, she pretended to get attacked for your column?" I asked.

"No." Leather from my suit's reinforced gloves creaked as he clutched the wheel. "She told me all about her scumbag ex. I pretended not to notice the bruises on her thigh. One night, I don't know, I had a hunch or something, so I followed her instead of meeting with another contact like I was supposed to. We had an ATM robbery all planned for me to prevent. But it was like, uh, destiny, you know?"

"I don't."

"Yeah, well, her boyfriend and some drinking buddies caught her walking alone after a late shift. They got rough. I already had the suit on in my car, so I pulled over, jumped out without thinking, and just went at them until they were all on their backs, spitting up blood."

His face lit up like a menorah. He smiled broadly and said, "It was... incredible." He turned left and checked the street signs. I knew it was just to hide his expression from me.

"Boyfriends," I murmured, deciding not to bring up the fact that my first take-down as the Roach was an abusive boyfriend. You know, Billy Price. The irony was not lost on me. It was as if him wearing my skin had slowly stripped away who Chuck was... metamorphosing him into me.

"The check I got for that column was the best I'd gotten in a long time," he said. "And I promise, before you came along, I spun a few good stories. I went back to the club the next night and let Roxy tell me all about the 'Roach Reborn' while I handed over twenty after twenty to keep the conversation going. She deserved the money anyway, right?"

"Why are you asking me?"

"I don't know. This is what you did."

I stared at him, dumbfounded.

"I'm serious," Chuck said, voice shaky now. "I'm not trying to trick you into saying anything, Reese. I just... I helped her, and for once, I got it. I understood what it was like to be you. And now she's dead and I... I don't know—" He choked back words and tears, then focused back on the road. "It doesn't matter. Maybe I can't make things right, like you said. But I can make her killer pay."

I studied the quivering, pathetic, lump of a man who was my arch-nemesis. He who called me a murderer countless times in writing, even a serial killer. The same shit-for-brains who broke into my home and stole from me.

A part of me felt pity. He'd learned the hard way how people get hurt in my line of work. I wondered, if Alexis Bradley had died that first time I acted in Iron City instead of Billy, would I have spiraled into a wreck like him? If I couldn't save Steven Dixon from his bullies or escape our foster parents, would I have become like them?

"All I know, is that the Roach didn't sell stories celebrating himself," I said, reminding myself who he was and what he'd done. "He didn't worry about making money for people he liked or chatting them up in back rooms. Maybe if you'd focused on the lives, Roxy would still be living."

"Don't tell me you never got distracted," Chuck countered, wiping his eyes with the heel of his palm. "All that time fighting, nobody ever got close to you, and then you get shot one night? C'mon. I told you mine. You tell me yours."

Laura's terrified eyes flashed through my brain. Looking at me like I wasn't even there while Michelle's father had her way with her. It was no different than any other rape I'd ever stopped. Why had my rage then sent me over the edge?

Was it her? Was it the article Chuck himself had written blaming me for the deaths of girls I'd done everything in my power to stop? Was it, as he'd said: destiny?

Now, we were in a car together. Two Roaches, speeding down the tunnel of modern civilization in our vehicular apparatus, ignorant to everything around us.

I battled the temptation to lose focus and looked to my right. I recognized the newsstand Isaac and I had shopped at only the day before. We were nearing my neighborhood, nestled between the Stacks and the park-slash-junkie-hideout they'd turned the old Marauders Stadium into, where I'd dare anyone brave enough to visit after dark.

"Why are we here?" I asked.

"You'll see," Chuck replied, right back to his snobbish, bitchy self.

"That's not going to cut it."

Without answering, he turned right, heading straight up the avenue my street branched off of. The usual crowd loitered outside the barbershop. My liquor store zipped by on the left. Bodega on the right. They sold the best hot dogs.

"Chuck?" I said, muscles tensing.

"Relax," he answered, which only served to make me want to shove his head through the car window even more. "It's all in my upcoming third column. I rushed it to the editor before the deadline last night, after I'd found Roxy... You know."

He turned onto my street. Mine. The wheels thumped over a sewer grate which hadn't quite settled. Tinman was on the corner, shaking a can at the sky, then listening to the open end like it was a phone.

"What did you do?" I asked timidly.

"It should be on newsstands already—a column about how the Roach saved a middle-aged white man in a wheelchair from being hit by a speeding car on Fisher Blvd. Seemed fitting, considering what you did. Really heroic stuff."

I squeezed the armrest again.

"You put my name in that rag?" I said. It took every ounce of my willpower not to make my skull-into-window-smashing thoughts a reality.

"No," he said. "Unnamed. But the killer seems pretty resourceful. How many others living around here go by that description? I got so caught up with Roxy, I didn't have time to actually hit the streets. So, I figured, why not send the killer after the one person who could take him out?"

Chuck started to pull into a spot on my street.

I lost it.

I lashed out, bashing his head against the window to disorient, but managing to restrain myself enough not to break it. Then I ripped the revolver free. In an instant, I had the gun aimed at his temple. He released the steering wheel and raised his hands slowly.

Most people with a gun to their head piss themselves like Isaac. To his credit, Chuck remained calm, staring forward as if the threat wasn't real.

"You should be flattered," he said. "It was the best plan I could come up with. The real Roach kills the Roach-hunting killer. You're telling me you don't want that?"

I was, expectedly, not calm. Fuck trigger discipline. My finger twitched there, begging to pull back on that four pounds of pressure and blow his pencil-necked, prepubescent-mustached face off his brainless skull.

"And if you didn't, the city clearly has an interest in protecting you, right?" Chuck rattled on. Now the fear was beginning to settle in. I could tell by the throbbing veins in his throat. "We'll lay a trap and take him down."

"If the police already linked your column to the killings, they'll be here too," I said. "Maybe faster."

"So, call your friends. Tell them the plan. This can work. I'm telling you. The killer will see the article, and come for you. Just like the others."

I pressed the gun harder. Now, Chuck started to tremble from head-to-toe.

"If that's the case, then what do I need you for?" I asked.

"I can help! Wear the suit or something. He's after the Roach. If things go bad, or whatever, it'll distract him. Then one of us shoots him in the back. Case closed."

"I don't shoot in the back." I slid the barrel down to Chuck's chin and used it to tilt his face toward me. His pupils were fully dilated—heavy drops of sweat beaded on his forehead.

"I have to help!" he insisted. "Please. I caused all this. You can kill me after—I don't care. Nobody would come looking for me anyway. I have nothing."

Tears gathered in his eyes as I held his gaze. He didn't piss himself, but I could smell his fear. The pheromones give off a certain aroma—you start to recognize them after a while—and the smell got thicker as I ground the barrel of the gun into his flesh.

I couldn't do it, though. Chuck Barnes had earned punishment, but not death. Not yet.

"Fine," I said, tapping the gun against his nose. "You can help. But afterward, you're going to turn yourself in. You're going to admit that you made the costume and invented this whole charade to fix your pathetic career or feel special, or whatever you want to call it. That the deaths are on *your* hands, not mine."

Chuck rolled his tongue around inside his cheeks. He bobbed his head. "Whatever."

"Good. Now, get out." I shoved him into the door. He groped for the handle, and I pushed him again, causing him to fall through.

"I'm going, geez," he said. "You know, you must see the irony of you making *me* out myself for causing deaths. What about you?"

"Don't worry about me."

I waited for him to bring around my chair. While I got myself in, he retrieved the duffel bag full of his years of research desperate to prove who I was and why the Garrity Act was founded on a lie. Then, we headed to my townhouse.

"Open it," I said, tossing him the keys.

Chuck was a bag of nerves. It took him long enough to unlock it, and then he cautiously peeked inside. I rolled up the ramp and gave him a push in the back of the legs with my footplate to get him going. Before I joined him in the foyer, I checked from side to side. Nothing on the street seemed out of the ordinary. The same blather of strangers who didn't work or go to school as always. Old lady on a walk with her dog. Guy tending a pathetic, dying garden. Trickle of cars cutting through to more exciting places.

It wasn't a busy block. Too rundown and far away for downtowners and too expensive for most Harborsiders. A perfect vacuum for me.

"You coming?" Chuck whispered, crouched by my stairs so he could see in every direction.

I moved all the way inside my house and closed the door behind me, leaving it purposely unlocked. Chuck was out of his depth, but he was right. The killer clearly had a pattern, and these types stuck to them. He'd come for me, and if the one way inside was locked, he might just burn the place down like Patel's store. I wanted him to feel welcome to stroll right in, thinking a cripple was easy prey.

"Check upstairs. I'm sure you know the layout of my house already," I said, taking zero effort to mask my disdain. I'd work with Chuck. I didn't have to like it.

His nervous gaze flitted toward my mess of an upstairs bathroom. The door hung crooked after my scrap with José Montalvo's men.

"What if he's in here already?" he asked.

"Scream loudly," I said.

He extended out his hand and made a gripping motion. "No way. Give me the gun."

"I don't think so."

"Then check it yourself."

Stifling a groan, I rolled into my kitchen and left him there, checking every corner for something out of place. Laura made it easier with her cleanup. The TV remained on, more election talk playing just too low to understand.

Everything remained pristine as she'd left it except the kitchen, which was how *I'd* left it. My empty pot of soup sat on the table, hardened vegetables sticking to the sides. The dirty spoon lay beside a puddle of spilled broth. All my other pots, pans, and utensils seemed to be where they always were.

I checked the study next, where all my books remained in proper order, and my lair's secret passage remained locked.

Satisfied, I tucked the revolver into my waistband. Moving to the kitchen counter, I slid the knife-holder close enough to reach the handles and pulled out a carver.

"Use this," I said, offering it to Chuck after rolling back across the living room.

"What if he's got a gun?" he asked.

"Don't get shot in the face."

"Very funny." He kept waiting, then his brow lifted. "You're serious?"

"You've got body armor, you'll be fine." I tossed the knife, and he jumped out of the way, letting it stab down through the wood floor. The metal hummed as it wobbled.

"You're insane, you know that?" he complained as he pried it free. "All right, I'll go check. But if he kills me, that's on you."

"Oh, how would I ever deal with that?"

He grimaced before moving on, climbing cautiously, keeping his footsteps as furtive as possible. As if a killer wouldn't have heard that we were already home, or what our plans were, or the way the seventh step always creaked.

This was where I took control of the plan. Back to the kitchen I returned, to my phone. This time, I had no problem remembering the number to dial, even if it was the first time I'd used it since being a child back in the home. The men who answered the call back then had done absolutely nothing.

A simple number for the simple answer to normal people's problems.

"911, what's your emergency?" a call-taker answered after a few too many rings. In a city like this, I imagined they were always busy fielding calls from nutjobs.

"Hi, I need to talk with Lieutenant José Montalvo, of the 12th precinct," I said. "I have information about the killing in the *Bleek Street Gentleman's Club* last night."

"What's your name?"

"I'd rather not say."

"Can I relay a message?"

"No, it has to be him. There's not much time."

A brief pause before she said, "One moment, please."

Did I sense a hint of annoyance? As if the solving of a brutal slaying was getting in the way of her relaxing day?

"Hello?" Montalvo answered a minute or so later, interrupting the gentle buzz of the open line.

"There you are," I said. "It's Reese."

"Reese, you..." He held the phone away from his mouth and muttered something I could only imagine was foul. "I thought I told you to stay home?"

"That's where I'm calling you from."

"I don't have time for this."

"You do. Have you seen the latest issue of the *Weekly Iron*?"

"What about it?"

"Ask someone for a copy. I'll wait."

He groaned, then I heard a *thunk* as he placed the phone down. I covered my receiver and shouted, "You alive up there!" to Chuck.

"What the hell happened to your bathroom?" he yelled back.

That was all the answer I needed. I lifted the phone back to my ear and listened. José barked loud enough for me to hear now, browbeating some inferior officer. "Goddammit! I told you to get me the issue as soon as you saw it!"

Is it wrong that I grinned until José returned to the phone? And he took his sweet time too, probably flipping through a copy of the magazine to find Chuck's article.

"Those morons," he said, finally. I think to me. "We left a message for them not to run anything about the Roach."

"Issue was probably already printed," I said. "You think they'd eat all that cash without you guys spilling what the hold was really about?"

"If you're trying to make a point, save it."

"Not trying anything."

"Did you tell Barnes to write this? We haven't been able to get in touch with him since the bodies turned up. You just couldn't play along, could you, Reese? Poking sticks at authority like a fucking child!"

"How about you slow down and let me talk?" I said, calm as I reveled in his frustration.

"How about I come over there and do what we should have done last time?" he said.

"This is a courtesy call, Montalvo. The killer's likely to come for me. Let me take him out if he does."

"No way. This is our city now."

"Keep it. I only want him. And if he sees cops roaming around my block, he might stay away. Hold them off and let me do what I do best."

"You know I can't sign off on that."

"Then don't tell anybody. I'm sure you're all busy enough securing election parties and expensive champagne for the bossman. Why complicate things? The trap's laid. I'm the bait. Nobody but me gets hurt if things go wrong, and if that happens, then I'm out of your hair. Everybody wins."

Again, José clonked down the phone. I could only imagine the internal argument in his head, knowing how right I was. Making him endorse an act of vigilantism—I'd never tell Chuck, but he had my gratitude for presenting this opportunity.

"Okay," he muttered after a bit.

"What was that?" I asked.

"I said, 'okay.' We'll do this your way. But never again. I swear it."

"I wouldn't dream of it."

"Nobody's up—" Chuck said as he approached me, stopping once he noticed me on the phone. He mouthed, "who is it" with only his lips. I lifted a finger.

"One condition, though," José said. "If you get the fucker today, we get the credit. And if you take him alive, I'll make it worth your while. You can move out of that shithole and find another city to torture."

"Of course," I said. "A little boost for the mayor."

"A favor," he retorted. "For letting you play superhero again."

I didn't say anything. Chuck continued plying me with mimed questions.

"Reese?" José said.

"Good luck in the polls," I replied, then hung up.

"Who was that?" Chuck asked.

"Doesn't matter. But the cops won't be an issue. They're giving me my shot."

"Ha!" Chuck slapped the doorframe. "I knew you had connections. I knew it."

"You're just a regular old genius, aren't you? Now, take off my suit."

He went from arrogant to serious in a heartbeat. "Wait, what?"

"You heard me. We're going to lay a trap for this asshole together, but there is no way I'm doing it with you looking like that."

"Not a chance. It's pretty clear I'm no superhero. It'll protect me."

I lifted the gun and aimed it up at him. "Think it'll block this?"

"It did in the store."

"But I know where I'm aiming." I waved him toward the floor. "Now, strip. Right here. It's going back down where it belongs."

"I have nothing on underneath. I'll return it after. I promise." I kept my expression from corkscrewing with rage, but it took every muscle on my face. Chuck wasn't only wearing my skin; he was going commando in it. Really taking the Roach out for a spin. Seeing how snugly it fit.

"I don't give a damn. Take it off, or I put a bullet in your head and peel it off myself!"

He flinched, but he didn't back down. Instead, he turned around and headed for the door, putting my statement about not shooting people in the back to the test. He stopped, kneeled to pick up his duffel bag of evidence, and returned to the kitchen.

"I'll tell you what," he said. "You can take all of this for now. After it's done, we'll burn it, whatever you want. Then I'll give the suit back for your trophy case."

I glowered at him.

"If something happens, he won't expect the Roach here. We can catch him off-guard, and I'll be protected enough to help. You know I'm right. It's like writing a story. You need all the surprise factor you can get."

More time glowering ticked by, before I finally snagged the duffel bag and heaved it up into my lap. Then I rotated and started to roll toward my study. He went to follow, but I aimed the gun at his crotch and stopped him.

"I go down alone. You set foot down there ever again, you die," I threatened. "Hear me?"

Chuck chewed on his upper lip, then nodded. "Fine."

"The moment this is over with, you take that off."

He nodded. I went to continue along, but he scrambled to stop me.

"Wait. What's your plan for taking out this guy?" he asked. "We hide behind the bookcase... W-wait... you're not going use me in the suit as bait, are you?" The lump in his throat bobbed.

"The plan is simple," I said, ramming by him and squishing him against the wall. "He's going to stroll right through the front door, and I'm going to kill him."

CHAPTER THIRTEEN

I lay on my couch, as familiar a position as I could remember lately. Though, no bottle of anything in hand. Clarity was needed for what was to come. I didn't care about what would come after, and I liked that—just a city to protect.

Chuck was upstairs, peering out the window, still wearing my suit. No, I wasn't happy about that, but personal feelings had to be set aside. Him helping take down the killer was the contingency plan, and he'd have a better shot in body armor.

I'd brought my working surveillance feed up for him too—the one hooked to the camera aimed just at the base of my stoop. If anyone approached my door, he'd see it, and let me know through the walkie-talkies I'd scrummed up from a bin of supplies in my lair.

Was it my most complex plan? No. But simple often worked best. My front door was unlocked. I was prey, visible through the living room window, with my empty wheelchair backed up against it. If the killer decided to use a gun, I'd be toast, and I couldn't guarantee he wouldn't. His pattern was new and unpredictable.

Sure, he brutalized people saved by the Roach. But Roxy had been cut open and filled with bugs, while Patel was gutted and used for an art project before being burned. Both were personal messages used to taunt me—or, well... Barnes, I guess. The Roach, either way. Still, why the fire? Did it mean something, or was the killer simply lighting a beacon? Setting a signal in a big city as if to say, "Hey, morons, look over here. This was me, too."

"What do you think of these rumors about the Roach being back?" asked Donna Carlson, the host of the daytime talk show, stuck on my TV. Hearing my name drew my attention. When she wasn't showing people how to cook stuff they'd never have time to cook, she talked tabloid nonsense.

"Bogus," her male cohost said. "Bogus! The Roach is gone."

"If he was ever real," spoke the youngest of the three, a woman with big, poofy, feathered hair and a short dress that hugged her hourglass figure in a way that made me unsure if this was appropriate for children. She must've used a whole can of hairspray a day to get it to stay that way. "You know I've always believed he's just urban legend. A scare tactic."

"Oh, stop that," Donna said. "How could you ignore all the proof. Thirty-three deaths are attributed to the Roach vigilante and countless more arrests; bodies hogtied and left outside precincts with evidence taped to their forehead."

"You sure did your homework, didn't you?" the male cohost said.

Donna laughed. "I always do! I have kids now, and all the time they say how cool it'd be to see the Roach in action."

"Hey, I've always wondered what he looks like under all that leather," the youngest woman said in a sultry tone, flashing a wink at the studio audience and earning a laugh.

"You would. But no, no, I'm honestly scared." Donna turned to face the camera, which zoomed in on her face. She feigned a look of desperation, and the crowd grew deathly quiet. "Legend or not, the Roach comes from a dark time in this city's history. Like I said, I have children now. What does it mean if there's a killer dressed like a comic book character running around, dishing out justice?"

"Killer!" the big-haired woman said, incredulous.

"It means Iron City is cool again!" the male cohost pronounced, standing up and raising his arms to elicit cheers.

Donna broke a smile as she waved for them to quiet down. "Or dangerous. Why did he disappear? Because his work was done? Why would he come back now?"

"Maybe it's someone else," the young woman said.

"Or a hoax," the man added.

"Maybe," Donna said. "All I know is I don't like the thought of a serial killer—"

"Gosh, Donna," said the other woman.

"—on the loose in our city. Because make no mistake, that's what he was. Good or bad, people wound up dead whenever the Roach was involved. I mean, am I wrong?"

A mixture of cheers and boos rained down upon her. I'd heard this same self-righteous argument from so many talking heads before. Deep down, all the sheep knew what I was doing was right. They just had to lie to themselves in order to feel like good people. Let it be their daughters who got assaulted. See how fast they wished I'd leaped down from a building and massacred the offender.

"I may not agree with your terminology, but I'm with you, Donna," the young woman said. "I'm Iron City born and bred, and we can stand up for our own city!"

More cheers.

"Well, I have a surprise guest for both you killjoys," the man said. The other's looked to each other in exaggerated shock, and then the man reached behind his chair pulled out a knockoff Roach action figure.

"The Roach is here!" he tossed the toy at Donna, and she acted so startled she nearly fell off her chair. My effigy bounced off her desk once, then hit the floor where a leg broke off. Nobody even cared to pick me up. Just left me there to be trampled by the audience on the way out.

I squeezed my walkie-talkie tight, then brought it to my mouth. "Anything yet?" I asked Chuck.

"Nada," he replied. "Just some lunatic in a tinfoil hat who keeps walking by."

"Keep watching."

"What if he doesn't come?"

"He will."

Chuck's end went quiet, and I leaned my head back. The revolver jabbed into the small of my back, making things uncomfortable, but it helped me stay awake. The five shots remaining—and yes, I checked it—would ensure the killer never killed again. I wasn't used to all this excitement. I focused on a brown spot on my ceiling, letting the TV fade to white noise.

Minutes ticked by. I used to roam out into the darkness and find my prey, research them. Learn what made them tick before I undid them. Now, here I was, laying traps like a hungry spider with a man I detested to my very core. Laura would be proud, though. It wasn't what she meant when she said I should talk to new people, but beggars can't be choosers...

"Reese?"

I shot upright, clutching the walkie-talkie. Had I dozed off? My eyes stung.

"Anything?" I said.

"Did you fall asleep?" Chuck asked, using a harsh tone I'm not sure I approved of.

"No." I fidgeting to get comfortable. My couch had taken a pounding over the years. The cushions barely cushioned anymore. I suppose I never thought I'd live long enough to need a new one.

"What is it?" I asked.

"I, uh, just wanted to say. I'm sorry. Yeah, I'm sorry."

Now it was my turn to use a tone. "*Sorry*? For what? This I gotta hear."

"I don't know, everything. The articles, I guess. It just hit me as I was sitting here. You didn't only keep the good ones. You kept mine, too."

"Yeah, well, they aren't trophies."

"Then why?"

My gaze angled back toward the TV. The news was back on, discussing polls, showing Mayor Garrity talking to a crowd in front of sparkling Aurora Tower, then Darrell Washington in the Stacks. To be honest, Mr. Washington's crowd looked bigger. No mention of a killer or copycat on the loose though—just smiles and shaking hands, and bluster.

"Reminders," I said.

"Of what?" Chuck asked.

"Just keep watching."

"Reese, I... I get it now. Yeah, I had to wear your 'skin' a few weeks, but I get it."

"Well, you can't erase all the things you wrote. That's the whole point of it."

"You act like I was the only one who didn't approve of a vigilante? Hell, you should love me. I'm the only one out there who didn't forget you the moment you stopped showing up at crime scenes."

"Please," I scoffed. "You wanted a big break. The story of a lifetime. 'The Roach Unshelled.' You exaggerated your bullshit until everyone saw you for the fraud you are. That's what happened, Chuck. Conspiracy? You did this to yourself. They just twisted the knife because you wouldn't shut the hell up."

"Bullshit?" he said. "I never lied. You just didn't like the truth."

"Oh, and what's that?"

"That the underworld of Iron City didn't revolve around you. That you couldn't save everybody alone, just like you didn't save my paren—" he caught himself, but not before finishing enough of the word for me to figure it out.

"Your parents?"

He sighed. "I was just a kid when they took me to a Marauders' game at the old stadium. Right around when legends of the Roach were becoming popular. We left early out one of the rear gates because I got sick and... a robber showed up. My parents gave him what he wanted, but he got aggressive, shook my mother... I can still remember her scream. Then he shot them both right in the alley. My childhood died that day, though I got to spend the rest of it in a home. And all the kids raved about was the crime-fighting Roach, but not me. Never me. Because you didn't fucking show up to save us."

And there it was. The origin story of Chuck Barnes, who had been given almost as good a reason to seek retribution as I had, but had turned his back on it. Everyone who's ever done anything has one. I recalled that black and white picture that Chuck had on his desk, which seemed so out of place in his pigsty of an apartment, but now I understood.

He couldn't blame the robber in a city full of them, so he blamed me. A lifetime vendetta because I hadn't been there. That was when I knew. Chuck Barnes wasn't my arch-nemesis; I was his. I was the cops who showed up at my foster home time-and-time again and glanced right over the scars on our backs because father was the son of some oil baron, paying their salaries.

"January 12th, 1957," Chuck said. "That was the date. Where were you, Roach? Who did you save that was more important?"

I swallowed back the lump in my throat. "I wish I could tell you it was someone who mattered, but would it change anything?"

"No."

"I tried to be everywhere. It's a big city, Chuck. And it was hell back then."

"I get it now," he said. I could hear how choked up he was, even through the static of the speaker. "Maybe I always did and just didn't want to believe it. Needed to blame somebody."

"Or blame everybody," I said.

"Yeah, that too. I know it wasn't your job to save everybody. It was the city's, and Iron City failed itself. That's the only reason you even exist, isn't it?"

I had no answer. I never liked to question the past because there was no changing it. I wound up here in a place that needed me by chance, but I'd seen enough of the world. Wherever I settled down, the Roach would've been necessary. Just like he still was. Even in the safest city in the world, there's someone needing saving and monsters lurking.

The Roach wasn't a symptom of Iron City. He was a symptom of humanity.

"I can't go back and be at that stadium, Chuck," I said. "And I wouldn't even if I could. Whatever I was doing that night needed doing. Your parents died so you could live. You think they'd be happy with all this?"

"I don't know," he answered. "I can't ask them."

"You know."

"Yeah?" Chuck said. "What do your parents think about what you've become?"

I thought for a second. "I don't know. I can't ask them."

A snicker came through the walkie-talkie.

"Well, the Garrity Act would've never happened without you," Chuck said. "Everyone official in this city was too afraid of the scum who really ran it until you killed enough of them."

"Was that a compliment for the Roach from the journalist who had once called him: 'No better than the people he's fighting?'"

"Nope. Just a fact."

"Well, of all the stories I ever read about the Roach back in the day, yours were the only I remember. It's like you were in my own thoughts." I took a deep breath. I'm not sure why I kept talking. Maybe it was because, for the first time, someone else knew what it was like to wear my suit, however limited and disastrous as his experience might be. It felt like a belt loosening from around my chest.

"Those girls who died?" I said. "You were right. I heard about kids being traded into sex slavery through a shipping yard on Horton Point. *Kids*. I didn't take the time to do my homework. I rushed in too fast." My lower lip started to shiver. It was a strange sensation for me, but as I spoke, I could hear the bullets in that place clanging. The screams of young girls in Russian as they were caught in the crossfire. The crunch after I lost control and chased down the Bratva boss who'd put them there and collapsed his throat, all while kids bled out. All while I should have been calling an ambulance for them.

"It broke me..." I said, shuddering. My eyes glazed over, and I don't think it was from being overtired this time. "Maybe you didn't know you were writing the truth, but there it was. Clear as day, and nobody likes to see their own reflection."

"You got shot the next night because of it, didn't you?" he said. "Because of me..."

"And here we are. The authors of each other's origins, without even knowing it."

My throat went so dry I could hardly breathe. Is this what Laura wanted? For me to admit the truth out loud. Did she realize it, too? That a bullet didn't end the Roach, the truth did. The truth that maybe, just maybe, I could've saved one of those girls like I'd saved Laura, or Alexis Bradley, or Steven Dixon, or so many others. That I could have been patient, taken my time to stake out the place. That after decades fighting crime, anger pushed me just a hair too far too fast, over the ledge and into the darkness.

"I guess s—Wait, Reese, I think someone is coming," Chuck said.

I released a shaky breath and straightened myself. Back to action, I knew the drill. No time to dwell. I closed my eyes and pretended I'd fallen asleep watching the TV. All I could do was picture that night when decades of seeing humanity at its worst took over. Then Laura, being raped. Roxy, cut up and fed bugs, her glassy eyes aimed through me.

"*That, Roach, is your legacy,*" José had said. "*Death.*"

"Reese, are you hearing me?" Chuck asked over the walkie.

I leaned on the button and transmitted without opening my eyes. "Shut the fuck up," I whispered.

As carefully as I could, I slid the walkie-talkie behind my back so he couldn't say anything and ruin the trap. Then I wrapped my fingers around the grip of the revolver.

The front door's handle jiggled. This was Iron City, so naturally, nobody in my neighborhood would stop a stranger, let alone notice him.

Fighting every urge in my body to peek, I held steady. Lack of patience had ruined me before. Not this time. The Roach was back, and this fucker who'd already killed two innocent people would pay.

The door clicked, then squeaked just the slightest bit. He was good, I'll give him that. Quiet. I barely heard his footsteps, and had I actually fallen asleep, he'd have slit my throat with ease. But I didn't move at all. Might as well have been a corpse.

The fifth plank inside my house creaked, like always. I sensed the lurch in his step as he realized, but still, I didn't move. I heard the soft *whir* of his controlled breaths. Felt the subtle heat change of another presence.

Closer and closer, he drew. Around the couch, moving to where he could get a good position over me like he was ready to carve a turkey. I never heard the gentle rasp of a blade coming loose, which meant he had his weapon in hand. So did I.

His foot brushed up against the bottom of my sagging couch, making me glad I'd never replaced it. I felt his breath on my face, warm and rancid, like he hadn't brushed in days. The Tinman had better dental hygiene, for Christ's sake.

Time to move.

Peering through my eyelashes first, I spotted the glint of silver in his left hand. I rolled into him, my left elbow bashing him at the forearm so he couldn't stab down. My other hand came free, and I opened my eyes, the barrel of the revolver aiming toward the soft spot of flesh right under his jaw. My finger started to squeeze the trigger.

Until I saw *his* eyes. I could never forget them. Not a million lifetimes, let alone one. A shade of brown so rich they were almost red—demonic—like everything else in the world was below him. All at once, terrified and unhinged.

It was him...

***

I held a younger Laura by the shoulders. An undergrad at ICU. Bright-eyed, pretty—she had the whole world ahead of her. Kudos to her for letting her origin story make her stronger, but in that moment, she was far from it.

Her dress was hiked up, her underwear around her ankles, fresh scrapes on her knees from being smashed against a dumpster. She could hardly breathe, let along talk. Just a mess of fear and quaking nerves, muscles like stretched rubber. Like my foster brother Steven when Father brought out his whip or undid his belt.

Vinny Statman, the coward who'd raped her, lay on the ground nearby, hyperventilating from the shock of my arrival. I gripped the knife I'd taken from him and stalked toward him. He crawled away.

I couldn't hear whatever senseless nonsense he rambled between breaths as he begged for mercy. His eyes were utter chaos—like raping girls unlocked something deep in his soul. His pupils dilated from too much coke. His face was gaunt, almost skeletal, like he tried too hard to stay handsome, and his dark suit made it seem even more so.

I didn't move fast. I wanted him to experience every ounce of fear that his victim had. I wanted him to bleed like she did. To slip into a waking nightmare like she had. His hand slid on a discarded newspaper, covered in grime, but with the lead story visible as ever.

HERO OR VILLAIN? CITY DEMANDS THE ROACH COME FORWARD AFTER SHOOTOUT AT HORTON POINT LEAVES THREE UNDERAGE GIRLS DEAD.

My heavy breaths rattled through the hose of my mask like a cicada. Every night I was the Roach, but on special occasions, I played the grim reaper.

Vinny wouldn't get prison. I wasn't some comic book hero with a no-kill rule, believing my own morals were more important than cleaning out the trash. I stopped and hovered over him. Even after two decades, the filth kept drifting up to the city's surface. For every distributor I removed, a new one popped up, selling some new brand of drug. Feeding the errant masses.

I'd wiped out the River Kings. Devastated the mob and the Iron City Riders. Yet still, there were men in my city trying to trade in underage girls or loading up just to go out and fuck anything that moved.

Whatever sickness plagues humanity, there's no curing it. You can just squash out the germs one at a time, and that's all Laura's attacker was. A disease.

His face flinched as I glared down at him. It wasn't the drugs. He knew what was coming. An entire life of worthlessness flashed in front of his eyes. For the first time, he must have realized how small he truly was.

"Drop your weapon!" someone shouted from the mouth of the alley.

I turned. A beat cop stood, gun aimed at me, gaze flitting between Laura and her attacker. Officer Montalvo couldn't have been more than a year on the force, tattoos up and down his arms. Better than becoming a street ruffian. Sweat beaded on his forehead like it was his first day. Fear rippled across his features.

"Walk away, kid," I said, voice distorted by my mask.

He took a step forward and raised his gun higher. His trigger-finger quivered. "I said, drop your weapon!"

I exhaled slowly. Cops and journalists like Chuck Barnes had a hard-on for me for years. Everybody wanted to know who was behind the mask. I did a fine job avoiding them, and occasionally when a cop caught me beating up on some punk who deserved it, they'd look the other way.

Montalvo stood his ground. Young and eager to prove himself without knowing the true nature of our city yet.

Usually, when I ran into cops like him, I'd make myself scarce, but I saw red after looking into Laura's eyes. And I could hear the echoes of the Brava bullets from the night before, the screams of more young girls having their innocence stripped away without a chance.

I squeezed the handle of the knife so tight I almost ripped through my gloves.

"Don't!" Montalvo yelled.

"They were all kids!" I shouted at the top of my lungs.

Montalvo hesitated, as young men often do. I brought the knife plunging down, neutering Laura's monster like the dog he was. His howl was squelched by a deafening *bang*. I'd heard plenty of gunshots, but that one was special. The way it exploded, like the golden gates of heaven slamming shut on me.

Next thing I knew, I was on my back. My suit was reinforced everywhere it could be, but everything's got a weakness. Superman has green crystals from space; I have a bullet that entered through a seam on my side, at the perfect angle, and plunged through my spine.

I gasped for air, patting at the wound. This was the time when I'd usually get up and run, regroup for another night and force a veterinarian to sew up yet another future scar. Not every cop was on board with my special brand of justice.

But my legs didn't move.

A chill spread throughout my body as I lay, facing up at a cartoon-looking full moon made blurry by Iron City's ever-present smog.

Laura watched me, still huddled against the dumpster, and paralyzed with fear. Her monster grabbed at his missing crotch and wailed, both our blood pooling beneath us and mixing into a macabre cocktail. I clawed at the concrete to drag myself toward the knife.

I couldn't stop. Vinny had to die. Had to be wiped off the face of this Earth, not just marred.

Montalvo appeared between us, kicking the knife out of reach before I could reclaim it. He cursed under his breath in Spanish, clearly unsure what to do. Men like him are trained to do everything right up until the bullet enters a perp.

He panicked and stowed his firearm. Then he grabbed the newspaper by my feet and pressed against my wound.

"Hold this he—"

My hands shot forward before he could finish his sentence and wrapped his throat. I couldn't roll over, so I held him above me.

"They were fucking kids," I growled as squeezed harder and harder, watching his eyes and veins bulge. Saliva bubbled on the corners of his lips. All I had to do was get him out of my way, and Laura's monster could get everything he deserved.

But young José Montalvo was a scrapper. Grew up on the streets, ran with the wrong crowd until he straightened his life—I figured that out about him in a second. My paralyzed legs were stuck open, and he kneed me in between them. I didn't feel it, but I did feel the impact in my terminally-abused spine. He broke free, redrew his gun, and bashed me across the face.

The back of my skull slammed on the concrete, and my head rolled to the side, but I wasn't unconscious. My right hand landed right on an empty bottle. Montalvo coughed, completely dazed from lack of oxygen.

My fingers wrapped the cold glass, ready to keep fighting through him when a hand fell upon mine. My gaze locked with Laura's, and for the first time since I'd pulled Vinny off her, she was focused on me. She saw *me*, mask and all.

And I stopped fighting....

"You?" I think I whispered, back in the present. I could barely even get the words out.

My finger froze on the revolver's trigger. All I could picture was Vinny, pinning Laura. But as he returned my gaze, the only surprise in his expression was that I'd caught him.

He clearly had no idea who I was. He'd never seen my eyes, only the Roach's mask.

I couldn't believe it. This fucker was dead. "Removed from the equation," Mayor Garrity had put it oh-so-eloquently, way back when. Killed by a vengeful father. Yet, here he was, stooped over me like I was one of his girls. No question about it. It didn't matter that his suit was swapped out for a baggy shirt and pants. Or that his once flawlessly gelled hair was wild and unkempt.

Vinny slapped my hand away, shifting my aim. I pulled the trigger a hair too late, and all the bullet did was knock dust and sheetrock off my ceiling. His knife hand fell with force, the blade sinking into my gut a few inches west of my belly button.

White-hot lines of pain shot up my abdomen. Nothing like my finger being blown off, even adrenaline couldn't dull it. As I reeled, he went to steal the revolver, and with only half a pinky, I couldn't maintain grip.

The recoil from him ripping it free sent him tripping into my coffee table. He fired once more as he fell. I snapped to action, clambering over the back of my couch. The bullet scraped along the meat of my shoulder before I fell and hit the floor hard.

"Reese!" I heard, followed by two more *bangs*.

Chuck tumbled down the stairs, fully decked out in my Roach suit and mask. Against all our plans for him to be the secondary support, the idiot came rushing in again, not even learning from Patel's shop. He pulled the lowest banister of the stairs loose as he reached the bottom, slowing his fall before his back slammed into the wall.

Dust clouded him. I couldn't see if the bullets pierced my suit on his body or not. Chuck coughed and stabbed the floor with his knife to drag himself forward. Another shot blew the blade out of his hand, and he fell forward, my mask cracking on the floor.

"I got him?" the killer said, his voice like blades to my ears. He shrieked with laughter. "I got him!"

It was Laura's monster, no doubt. I could still hear him begging me not to kill him. I should have fought harder, through José, and done it. Ended him. How was he still alive?

I crawled toward Chuck's knife, every pull burning deeper in my gut. I'd forgotten what this kind of pain was like. I couldn't focus. Couldn't see straight. All I could do was watch as Vinny approached Chuck, who could barely stay on his knees himself. Two flattened bullets lay near him, proving my suit still worked... in the right hands, at least.

"Aren't you gonna finish me off?" I rasped, desperate to get the killer off guard. We still had the numbers, injured or not. Just one opening, that's all we needed.

But I might as well not have been there. The killer kneeled before Chuck like he'd found a treasure chest. Slow movements, full of wonder and disbelief; hands and lower lip atremble. He used the bloody tip of his knife to lift Chuck's head back and peel the mask up. The moment Chuck's face was revealed, the killer's brow knitted.

"You?" he whispered, same as I had earlier. "No, no, no, how could it be you?" He staggered back, hands rushing to his head and revealing scars up and down his forearms. The blood on his knife smeared across his hair and forehead. He didn't care. The barrel of his gun ran through hair that hadn't seen a comb in years. He looked like he'd just been electrocuted.

"Statman?" Chuck said, breathless. "You're the killer?"

I had no idea how, but the bastard knew him. He even knew his name.

"You said we could get the men who did this to me!" Vinny screamed, pacing around my living room like a maniac. "You were the first person who didn't think I was insane. Who believed me."

I stared at Chuck as I continued in my futile efforts to drag myself, my expression asking everything while all my lips said was, "He's dead."

Shame darkened Chuck's features as he shook his head slowly. "I had a hunch it was him. So, I talked to his old firm. Found him in Coalville Mental Hospital a few hours upstate after you got hi—"

"Don't talk to him!" Vinny barked, brandishing the revolver. He barreled across the living room, knocking over a vase and curling the corner of the rug. "You talk to me."

"What the fuck did you do, Chuck?" I asked out loud. "He's dead."

"Was this your plan?" Vinny said, walking along the stairs and letting the gun bang against each banister. "To set me up? Five years in that hell wasn't enough!?"

"No, V-V-Vinny, you have to listen to me," Chuck stammered.

Vinny whipped around, and his foot smashed down on my fingers before I could reach the fallen knife. The revolver pressed on the back of my head, squishing my cheekbone against the floor so I couldn't see much of what was going on.

"Who is the cripple, huh?" Vinny asked. "Your little sidekick? I'll put a hole in his head!" His knee plunged into my upper back. The pain was blinding. I screamed, my voice muffled by the floor. I squirmed but was too wounded to even shake him off—a roach under a boot.

"Vinny, for God's sake, listen to me!" Chuck shouted, voice cracking.

"I broke out just to find you," Vinny said. "Then, I saw the articles. I thought they were for me. I thought we were a team—making the Roach and the people who did this to us pay for destroying our lives!"

"Vinny, please—"

"But it was you!"

He pressed against me so hard, I couldn't breathe. This was the end I'd always expected. Undone by a raving lunatic I thought was dead, and an enemy I was too foolish to trust. See Laura? This is why I don't like talking to people. They always disappoint.

"Get off him!" someone that definitely wasn't Chuck shouted.

Vinny flew off me, and he and this new stranger rolled across the floor. I struggled for air as they wrestled. Chuck crawled to help me.

"I swear, I didn't know," he said. "Reese, he was so drugged up... it was useless. Another dead end."

Chuck rolled me onto my back, eyes widening as he saw the deep gash in my gut leaking blood like a running faucet. He pressed once, then removed his hands, gawking at the red covering them.

I squeezed my eyelids, fighting back the blinding pain, and looked right. The man who'd charged Vinny caught him in the midsection with a kick. Vinny flew back, snapping another banister in half. He used the railing to keep himself from hitting the floor and aimed the gun.

My savior lay on the floor across the room, head turned away, eyes closed, and hands raised in surrender. He wasn't a man. It was Isaac, under the aim of a gun for the second time in one day. He tried to speak, but nothing comprehensible came out.

All the air I'd managed to gather fled my lungs just as quickly as I unleashed a guttural scream. I shoved Chuck aside and pushed off the floor to lunge, but the wound was too deep. I collapsed far short of my target.

Vinny tittered like a lunatic, closer to a hyena than a man. Isaac's eyelid's clenched tighter. Vinny pulled the trigger.

Click.

Once, then again. Vinny shook the gun like that'd magically generate more bullets before realizing he'd wasted them all. The Roach would have been smart enough to know the count and when it was safe to come out of cover during the reload.

My recent fantasy that I was back eroded as quickly as the idea that this rapist was dead at the bottom of Horton River.

"You piece of shit!" Chuck shouted. He swung at Vinny with one of the loose knives—I couldn't keep track anymore—but he was no Roach. Vinny ducked, then pistol-whipped Chuck across the jaw with the empty revolver.

Vinny looked at the gun, shrugged.

Chuck recovered and swung backhanded, but Vinny caught his arm and twisted him around, bashing his head deeper into the sheetrock hole he'd already caused by falling. Vinny ripped the knife out of his hands and lowered it to Chuck's crotch.

"Let's see how you like it, Roach," he said, laughter behind every word.

I extended my arms to try and rise. "He's not—" I said before they gave out in pain and exhaustion.

Distant sirens blared, giving Vinny pause as he playfully dragged the sharp blade along the inside of Chuck's thigh without cutting. Vinny wrenched Chuck back around and held the knife against his throat.

"Please... I'm not..." Chuck was hysterical, tears and snot running down his face. So much for walking a mile in my shoes—now, he knew what I'd faced every night.

"The city's right," Vinny said, glaring between Isaac and me over Chuck's shoulder. "Why rush it? We'll take things nice and slowly. Like they did with me."

"No, please!"

Chuck's cries were cut short as Vinny squeezed his throat with his forearm and dragged him back through the open front door. As they did, Vinny bent slowly to retrieve my mask and gave it a playful shake. "Wouldn't want to forget any pieces."

"I didn't know..." Chuck cried, trying to break free. "Reese, I didn't know!" As he twisted left, I spotted the Polaroid Chuck had stuffed into the back of his belt—a snapshot of his web of conspiracy. All his evidence was safely in my lair except for that. In my increasing lack of attention to detail, I'd forgotten about it.

"Reese!" Vinny tightened his grip to shut Chuck up. Then, he made eye contact with me once more before they backed out through the opening, still with no clue who I was.

No amount of rage that instilled could get me to my feet. I was close enough to use the stair to pull my torso upright, but it felt like my entrails were going to come spilling out as my abdomen stretched. My shirt was so red I couldn't even remember what color it'd been.

"Reese!" Isaac blurted.

He hooked his arms around me, keeping me from crumpling back onto my face. My weight dragged Isaac to his knees.

"I know you said leave, but I-I-I followed," he stuttered. "I heard gunshots, I... Oh, Jesus, Jesus! You're bleeding a lot, Mister Roberts."

"Focus, kid!" I clutched his forearm hard enough to cut off the feeling to his hand. I didn't want to hurt him, but my fingers were beyond my control now.

"Kid, we have to get him." I coughed.

The police sirens grew louder. Maybe not turning onto my block yet, but close. Officer Montalvo couldn't keep it in his pants.

"You need a hospital," Isaac said. Maybe his father was a combat medic back in 'Nam because he composed himself far better than expected. Yeah, his panicked voice currently sounded like it belonged to a little girl, but seeing blood like this made most people faint.

"You hear the sirens?" Isaac said, cradling me to the floor. "They'll save you."

"No!" My other hand gripped his collar, forcing him to face me.

"You need—"

"No. My chair..." My throat clenched, a coppery taste flooding it. "G-get me on my chair. No cops."

I wish I could've seen Isaac's reaction, but in my state, I saw three of him. My body fell back, and blackness closed in around my vision before I felt him manipulating my body. He had my chair against the couch, straining his entire body to try and lever me up until I slumped over the armrest.

Somehow, he did it. I slid my hands up my numb legs to my stomach, searching for the epicenter of pain. I held them against my wound.

The sirens were loud now. Red and blue flashed through my living room window.

"Reese, are you sure—" Isaac said.

"That way," I interrupted, pointing toward my study.

He rolled me through the puddle of my own blood, running along the grooves in my floor. The tracks would lead cops right to my secret bookcase, but I had plans for that. As long as I could stay conscious. Not easy.

Isaac whipped me around the corner and helped wake me the hell up. I caught glimpse of Laura's note on the fridge as he did. The man who'd turned her life upside down was still alive. I focused on picturing her eyes that night. Her tears. I let it fuel me.

"Here," I said, stopping Isaac at my bookcase. I reached toward the proper book to start the combination, but merely removing my hand from my knife-wound sent tendrils of pain bursting through my abdomen.

"There," I told Isaac, only with the strength to point with my jaw. "A switch, behind it."

He stuck his hand around the book's spine, patting to find it.

"Faster!" I urged.

Isaac got spooked, brushing some books off and sending them thudding onto the floor. *"History belongs in order,"* my foster mother used to say. Well, now the dead were still alive and killing, so... Fuck her, and fuck order.

"Found it!" Isaac exclaimed. "Now what?"

"Another one, there." I tried to point and winced. Air didn't seem to want to stay put in my lungs. I had to huff a few times before I could show him the last switch in the correct sequence. The bookcase unlocked.

"What the heck?" Isaac said.

"Focus, kid," I said. "Open it. Onto the lift."

He pushed the bookcase all the way open and scrambled back to get me, slipping on THE GREAT GATSBY and banging his knuckles on a side table. For what it's worth, he stifled a squeal and successfully pushed me onto the lift. As I rolled in, pulling the bookcase shut behind me, I heard the sound of car doors slamming and cops shouting.

This was it. A reason for Mayor Garrity's loyal hound, Officer Montalvo, to send his goons in publicly and find blood belonging to four people all over the living room. My eyes fluttered closed as I pictured it: them dragging me before a judge to be evaluated by a handful of peers who didn't give a shit about anything. Was this the plan? Wait until right before Election Day to make the big reveal of the Roach and soar to victory?

All while Vinny Statman got away with it. Also, how the hell was he alive? Did Laura know?

"Reese?" Isaac asked.

My eyes snapped open, and I looked up. Dust tingled in them. The lift had stopped, and it was almost pitch black except for the thin blade of light cutting down the shaft from upstairs. Without thinking about the fact that I wasn't alone, I grasped my wheels and rolled myself to the lighting controls.

My bloody hand wrapped the handle, and Isaac had to help me lift it all the way. The metal-halide light slowly bloomed, purposely revealing my lair to someone for the first and last time.

"Where are we?" Isaac stepped ahead of me, looking around with childlike awe as the light revealed my lair. He spun slowly until his gaze fixed upon my suit's display case, adjacent to a wall filled with dozens of newspaper clippings mentioning the Roach. My suit may have been missing from the mannequin, but Isaac wasn't stupid. Foolish enough to try and help me, but not stupid.

"You're..." His words trailed off.

"There, at the workstation," I said, speaking through my teeth and sucking air between every word. "There's a red trigger."

He spun to face me, layer upon layer of confusion nearly making him unrecognizable. Or maybe it was my inability to see straight.

"A trigger?" he asked. "What?"

"Underneath," I said. "On the right side. Like something in a spy movie. I need you to hit it."

"Why?"

"Do you always need to ask questions?"

Isaac moved as leisurely as one could possibly move, considering the situation, but he reached my pathetic surveillance station. Chuck's bag of research was nestled underneath. After he hit the trigger, I'd never have to worry about it getting out. It'd be blown to smithereens. That made the thought of what was going to happen to my home easier to bear.

Thinking wasn't easy at the moment anyway.

"Under here?" Isaac asked as he groped beneath the table. I didn't have the energy to answer. I just watched him waver in and out of my failing vision until he called out, "Got it!"

"Now what?" he asked.

"We get out of here before it blows," I said. I nodded toward the opening in the concrete wall down a level that blocked off this station.

His brow furrowed. "Before what blows?"

"The C4 in the lift, the floor, the ceiling. Everywhere."

His eyes went wide. "Are you… joking?"

I think he could tell by my expression that I wasn't. How would I know, I'd lost all control of my parts. He sprinted over, grabbed my chair, and raced for the opening. The few working monitors in my surveillance station blinked, offering a grainy vision of a countdown timer set to two minutes.

At least that still worked.

I'd always known the day might come when the wrong person entered my home. So, I'd set up a way to bury everything. I wouldn't give José or Vinny or anyone else the pleasure of finding this place. Chuck had messed up enough after he did.

Isaac said something as we rumbled into dank tunnels I used to know, then retched as the stink of stale sewage greeted his nostrils. I couldn't hear him. Instead, I stayed focused on my lair, listening, hoping that my wiring was still good, and C4 hadn't gone bad.

Turns out, I'm not a complete failure. A deep *boom* resonated, enough to seem loud even to my impaired senses. Dust shook free from above us, causing Isaac to lose his grip on my chair and staggered through the muck, into a wall. It was too dark to see anything, but we were both coughing.

A smile lifted one corner of my lips. I was back in the darkness again, back where I belonged—invisible—the way I needed to be if I hoped to stop a dead man from hurting anybody else.

How was he alive?

"Isaac," I said.

He yelled my name in response. I couldn't see him. Couldn't see anything.

"Isaac..." I whispered again.

Nothing. No answer. Only silence answered, and blackness...

CHAPTER FOURTEEN

My eyes were crusty, but shapes took form. I was on my back, lying on something soft. Maybe a bed. A woman sat on a chair nearby, watching me, or rather, leaned into her palm in exhaustion. It was dark, so she was probably asleep.

A dream. A nightmare. That's all it was. Apparently, I'd never woken up from my bed in the hospital after the accident. Probably passed out soon after Laura had left and now, she was back. Always checking up on me.

Or maybe I was still on my couch, and Vinny never came. No killer, if there ever even was one. A lifetime of head injuries finally catching up to me and making me imagine things.

"How many times do I have to tell you to stop coming around?" I asked, throat hoarse. This time I wasn't actually irritated by the fact that she'd wasted her time with me. All right, yeah, it was a waste, but man, did I need to see her.

I went to prop myself up.

Nothing like deep, excruciating pain to suck me right back to my awful reality. There was no blood rushing to my brain from head trauma, you know, like being hit by a truck. Instead, my gut burned as if someone plunged a firecracker through my belly button.

I lurched, muscles seizing as I grasped at cushions and found that they were loose.

This was no bed. It was a couch—not much cleaner than mine to boot. And the room wasn't all white tile and sterilized counters, but a living room, complete with family photos, a TV with a working antenna, and a bowl of fake apples on the coffee table to tie it all together. Who could live without one of those?

"You need to sit back," a woman said.

She leaned over from her chair and placed a cold, wet towel over my forehead. She wasn't Laura, but somehow, I recognized her voice. The ache in my gut dulled a bit as I sank back into a pillow and turned my head.

It took a few tries to focus my vision enough to make out her face. Definitely, not Laura. For one, Laura wasn't black. Two, she'd never be caught wearing pajamas. Not her. Not since that day when that bastard showed her humanity's ugly face, and she always made sure she presented a strong facade.

Vinny Statman. That's right. He was alive—ready to pick up where he'd left off and haunt her. Was this part of it? Was this all his twisted game to get back at me for neutering him and whatever had happened after?

"Who..." I froze and bit on my lip, drawing blood. Twisting my side to get a better view sent a bright line of pain shooting up my ribs.

"I said, sit back."

A gentle push from the woman forced me right back, flat on my back. Groaning, I peeked down through my eyelashes and realized that my shirt was off, revealing enough scars to look purposeful, like tattoos. I promise, most weren't. One wound was fresh. Bandages wrapped my abdomen, stained a dark red like they'd been there for hours.

"Don't touch it," the woman said as I went to peel them back. She clutched my hand and pressed it down to my side.

"Ow."

"Sorry."

"No, not that," I groaned. "It hurts. They say you can't hurt in a dream. I think they're wrong but, I wasn't dreaming, was I?"

"If you're wondering if you really bled all over my son, then, yes—not a dream." She scooted along the floor on her knees and lifted my bandage so she could inspect. Skin stretched, and I felt the familiar pull and prick of fresh stitches.

Studying the walls of the cramped two-bedroom unit, I spotted a shrine near a kitchen table covered in magazines, including many copies of the *Weekly Iron*. Pictures lined a credenza, with some sort of military award hanging from a velvet case. Images of a pale man with freckles and fire red hair were everywhere, and in the photo on the left, there was Isaac in his elementary school uniform, with bug-eyed glasses and hair way too unruly. All knees and bones.

"Isaac's your kid?" I asked, turning back to the woman. The mixture of her and that soldier, no doubt, led to Isaac's unique and bully-friendly appearance.

"And you're the new friend he told me about," she replied. "I was hoping he meant someone his age."

"Nobody likes kids his age."

I earned a single chuckle. She glanced up at me. First, I smelled cigarette breath, then I noticed the bags under her eyes. She was the nurse who'd rolled me out of the hospital, only for my entire life to get shit on by a ghost. Why didn't I stay in that nice, comfy bed?

"Cigarette nurse?" I asked.

"Still got your chair, I see." She smiled and released the bandage. I winced.

"You know how weird that is, right?" I spoke through my teeth. "A nurse putting that shit in her. Tsk, tsk. You wouldn't want Isaac picking up the habit. They target kids, you know. Cartoon mascots. Some kind of bullshit, if you ask me."

Mrs. Isaac turned away and drew a deep breath. "You can't be serious right now."

"What? Someone's gotta look out for him."

"The only reason—" she started loudly, then lowered her voice and pointed at me, her plastic gloves stained red. "The only reason I haven't called the police is because Isaac told me how you helped him with those bullies before that truck hit you. He says you hurt yourself cooking, but I'm a nurse." She gestured toward my wound. "That's no accident."

"He's got quite an imagination."

"You realize how much blood you lost. A few minutes later, you might have died."

"It's not that bad," I argued.

Mrs. Isaac stood. She was impressively tall when exhaustion didn't have her plodding around a depressing hospital in scrubs.

"You think this is a joke?" she snapped. "He's just a kid. He's not supposed to be pushing around handicapped adults with... with stab wounds."

"It was an accident, all right?" I said.

"Don't lie to me. That boy is my life."

I rolled my shoulders. "Then maybe you shouldn't let him go off with strangers instead of school."

"You really are an asshole."

"I..." I sighed. My insides burned, and sarcasm just didn't seem to work. "Look, your son saved my life. You think I'm proud of that?"

"My son would have called the cops. My son would have gone to school. He's not like all the other kids who grow up around this shitty neighborhood. Isaac knows better." She looked to the floor. "At least, I thought he did."

"Yeah, that's probably my fault... Look, I don't know. A thief stabbed me and stole my wallet. Isaac came out of nowhere and got me here, what can I say? Just keep him away from me and get me onto my chair. I need to go."

Out of this place, to start. Back to the streets. Back on the prowl. If this wasn't a dream, that meant Vinny really was alive. He had Chuck, who he believed to be the Roach. He'd figure out that wasn't true pretty quick if he even had half a brain left. Oh, and he'd find that damn picture with my face on it, and so many other faces easily revealed by a magnifying glass.

Chuck knew the truth about everything that had happened. Knew who I was, who Laura and Michelle were. Incinerating all his evidence with my lair was a step, but I should have broken his brain. And mine, considering I forgot to confiscate that damn Polaroid from him.

"Go?" Isaac's mom said, incredulous. "You can't go anywhere like this."

"This is nothing," I said.

I gripped the cushions and used them to push off. Agony all over, but I slid a few inches. Then, a wracking pain overwhelmed me, my hand shifted, and I slipped off the couch. Mrs. Isaac rushed over to help me. I cursed and swatted her away.

She tried again. "Here just—"

"Leave me!"

She threw her hands up in frustration and crossed the room, gnawing on her fingernails. She was itching for a cigarette, that much was clear.

"I'm only trying to help," she said.

"I know, but you charge in to touch me too fast, like your son."

Her jaw dropped. "Touch you... what?"

"No, not like that." I slapped my forehead. "I'm sorry. I can't think straight. I helped the kid with those bullies, so, he's been helping me get around a little, that's it. I was supposed to pay him, but then..." I gestured down to my wound.

"Oh. Wow. That makes me feel better." She accentuated her sarcasm with another chomp at her nails.

"Like you all can't use the money?"

"Right. Because we're black, we need a side hustle?"

"No. You—Hey, if he told the truth faster, maybe I wouldn't have gotten hit by a truck."

She chewed her lip. "You know, I thought Issac was visiting the hospital more last month to see me."

"I was in a goddamn coma," I said. "I didn't ask him to visit, and I don't blame him either."

"Good for you. And now he's caught up in whatever you're up to."

"I didn't put a leash on him. He saw a crippled man in need and jumped to action. You should be proud."

"What I am, is in need of a new couch."

I peeled my body up slightly and saw what she was talking about. I think the couch was supposed to be green, but it was brown beneath me.

"I'll pay for it," I said. She could throw it on my tab along with paying back Laura for keeping me on life support.

It was the least I could do after Isaac dragged me out of hell. Which reminded me: the self-destruct had gone off, and I'd need to find a new home too. My lair was buried beneath enough concrete that it'd take months for anyone to find any proof that I was anything other than a retired city worker living on benefits. All Chuck's research would have been incinerated from the charges under my surveillance station.

With it, had gone any records he had of Vinny's full identity. Clinging to life, I hadn't thought about it. Yet another mistake by the best vigilante Iron City used to know.

"Why the fuck did she have to keep me alive?" I groaned.

"Don't say that," she replied.

"Would have been a whole lot easier."

"Trust me, I've seen people in a lot worse shape than you." She checked through her medkit, pretending she was busy.

"Oh, have you?"

No answer.

I grabbed the coffee table and gave it a yank out of place, startling her.

"You don't know a fucking thing about me," I bristled. "You hear that. Nothing. You don't know what I've lost. And now I'm here, and they're out there. That liar is wearing my... I'll kill him." I tried to move again and failed again. She kept me from falling off the couch with a lot less effort than it should have taken for a man my size.

"Would you just calm down?" she said. "You're gonna hurt your-damn-self."

"Calm down?" My hands balled into fists. I raised my voice. "Calm down???"

Unfazed by my behavior, she leaned around me and shifted the pillow under my head. The movement sent a wave of discomfort down my entire body, paralyzing me. I don't know if she meant it to, but it did calm me, and the position I wound up in was a hell of a lot more comfortable afterward. She offered me a feisty nod that said, 'I know how to make you hurt if you don't behave.'

I leaned back and drew a deep breath. That's the thing about nurses, doctors, and barbers. Piss one off, they're as deadly as serial killers in a playroom filled with knives.

"Where is the kid anyway?" I asked, lowering my volume. "I have to thank him."

And make sure that he keeps quiet about what he saw, I didn't add. Last thing I needed was to be a headline when I had to go hunting. And the underground explosion in Harborside? Easily explainable for the mayor and his goons while they searched for me. Gas leak. Bad boiler. Whatever they wanted to say.

Mrs. Isaac nodded toward a closed door at the end of their four-foot-long excuse for a hallway. "He threw up a few times watching me stitch you up after he showered. Then, he conked out. I've never seen him so tired."

"You should get him into sports," I said.

"Yeah, right," she dismissed with a weak chuckle.

"Did he tell you anything crazy-sounding?"

"I told you what he told me."

I nodded proudly. "Good kid."

Mrs. Isaac moved to the edge of the couch and leaned over the end, looking awfully serious. Her arms flexed, her smooth skin glistening with sweat. I didn't often meet fit women like her, so it was difficult not to stare. She wouldn't ever need my help. She'd beat the shit out of any robber dumb enough to make a run at her. I liked that.

"Isaac brought you here because he's smart enough to know that, sometimes, I help some of the residents who can't afford a doctor," she said. "A fever, a broken finger, accidents... but not this. I'm gonna need to know what happened. What *really* happened."

Her firm glare made me feel small, inconsequential. The size of an insect. When she wasn't fidgeting, she wielded a matronly fire I could only imagine growing up with. Somebody who'd kill for me. And yeah, maybe she worked all the time just so they could afford to live in this rundown dump on the wrong side of a bad town. Maybe she didn't watch Isaac as closely as she should have... but she'd kill for him. I could see it written plainly on her face.

I pushed my tongue against my lower lip. Would it hurt to tell her the truth? Even as much as the thought of it made me feel sick. Would it actually hurt? She'd saved me after all. Stitched me up before I bled out instead of calling the authorities or dropping me on the hospital doorstep. She was in this now.

"It's got nothing to do with Isaac," I managed to say. A half-truth. It didn't, and it wouldn't ever again. This was personal now—between me and Laura's monster. I'd put Isaac in harm's way twice already. He was one spare bullet in the chamber away from being a corpse, thanks to me.

"Tell me, my son is safe," Mrs. Isaac said, low and menacing. Ready to kill.

I nodded. "He is. As long as you get me out of here. I don't care how much blood I've lost, you need to put me on my chair, and I'll roll far away from here."

She stared at me blankly. Her lower lip twisted. I'd learned the look from Laura. She was struggling not to glance over at the shrine to her fallen husband. Trying not to imagine having her heart ripped out again, the way ordinary people do. When you grow up with nothing like I had, in a home filled with bullies and abusers, you learn to keep your heart outside your chest.

I didn't want that for her or for Isaac. They'd been through enough.

"Just take a day off work and stay with him," I said. "No school. Nothing. I promise, you'll both be fine."

"He's off for Election Day," she answered. "His school's used for voting."

"Good." At least, it seemed that way until I realized I'd lost a day. That meant Mayor Garrity would be having one of his lavish parties somewhere with no expectations of possibly losing to a newcomer. Not the white knight who'd saved Iron City from the brink of chaos without any help from good old Roach. The same mayor who'd told me that Vinny wouldn't be a problem anymore—who'd told me that Officer Montalvo had taken care of him.

Did Laura possibly know? Did she realize that Michelle's dad was still out there?

"Who are you?" Mrs. Isaac asked.

"Do you really want to know?" I said.

She gnawed her thumb, then shook her head. "You know, I was so happy he made a friend. School in the Stacks was so tough for him after we moved, we got him transferred Downtown. But I think it's even worse for him there."

"Nah. There're some bullies, but he can take them," I said. "I gave him some pointers, and I know bullies. Your son is as brave as any man I've ever known, Mrs—" I stopped before embarrassing myself by calling her Mrs. Isaac out loud.

"Clarice. Clarice Johnson," she said, chin raised high. Proud of her name in a way I'd never been. Proud of her family and her heritage.

"Well, your husband would be damn proud. I find most people are disappointments, but Isaac... He's what makes this city worth saving."

"I know he is..." she said softly, choked up.

"No. You don't," I said. "Not yet, but you will. He makes the Roach look like a fucking pussy."

She wiped her eyes and half-sniveled, half-laughed. "Don't let him hear that. He worships the Roach."

"Oh yeah? Maybe one day he'll meet him."

Her left eyebrow raised.

"For now, you need to get me out of here," I said. "The guy who did this to me, I don't think he's going to stop. I have to find him."

"So, it wasn't a robber?" she asked.

I swallowed hard, then shook my head. "No."

"Well, you aren't going anywhere without a new dressing," Clarice said, moving on fast. I took the hint. She didn't want to know more, for Isaac's sake. She was smart.

Skirting around the couch, she kneeled right in front of me. She pulled an open medkit across the coffee table.

"You know, I treat gangbangers and addicts every day," she said. "Gunshot wounds. Stabbings. Overdose. How is it that you've caused me more trouble than *any* of my patients?"

I stared at her, or rather, through her, my gaze fixated on the shrine to Isaac's father—on a man who died for something more than himself, even if I didn't agree with it. Would Laura do the same for me whenever death came calling? Or would she slowly forget and realize how much better off she and Michelle were?

"I'm the Roach," I said, matter-of-factly.

My heart thumped against my ribs, but it surprised me how easily the words escaped my mouth. I'd never tried them out loud before, but why not with her? The mother of a boy who was more worthy of the title now than I was, or perhaps, ever had been.

Clarice dropped the medkit, spilling its bloody contents all over the carpet—another thing I'd need to replace.

"*Was* the Roach," I clarified.

Her lips parted as she searched for a response, then closed.

"You don't need to say anything," I said. "You don't even need to believe me. But I figure that kid of yours is going to tell you one day what he did. That he saved the Reaper of Iron City. The Haunt of Horton River." I chucked until a sharp pain made me grimace. "The Roach."

Clarice stared in silence. Usually so good at reading people, I was at a loss. Was she horrified? Impressed? Angry? Would she abandon her principles and call the cops now? I wondered if I'd done something to offend her like I had Chuck, which sent him hurtling down a path toward finding a lunatic and inspiring him to return home.

Instead, she steeled herself. "Hold still," she said as she fixed her medkit and began unwrapping my bandage. As strong as she was, she had a gentle touch. I still had to close my eyes as her fingers wandered near my navel, and she cleaned the wound. But I didn't swat or push her away, just clenched my jaw and let her do what she was best at.

When she finally helped me sit upright, I sported a freshly cleaned wound. Every breath stung, every movement ached at a musculoskeletal level—but she'd done a hell of a job. I wished I'd had her around back in the day. My nurse of the night. I'd probably have cleaner scars than the ones caused by me stitching myself up.

"Thank you," I whispered as she finished wrapping and cut the bandage. I had to focus on the ceiling and away from the scissors in her hand to keep calm, but I meant it.

She grunted softly, then dropped the scissors onto a clump of wet paper towels and stood. The space between us finally allowed me to breathe. She crossed the room without a word, vanished into her room, and returned, holding a plain green T-shirt. She held it against the back of my wheelchair and rolled it over, pushing the coffee table out a bit to make room.

"All right, it's time to go," she said. She stopped, regarded the shirt with a forlorn expression for a few seconds, then said, "Here," and tossed it at me.

"Perfect," I replied.

"I'm sure I could tell you that if you exert yourself, you'll pop the stitches."

"And I'm sure I won't listen," I said as I stretched the shirt over my head. I knew who it had to have belonged to, but I kept my mouth shut.

I started to push off the couch to try and load myself onto my chair, forcing Clarice to have to help me, per her nursely nature. My muscles just didn't want to obey me anymore. To be fair, after the last month, if I were them, I wouldn't trust me either.

But Vinny couldn't wait. What if he'd already gotten Chuck to spill everything? About me, and the mayor, and Laura, and... his biological daughter? I had to end this twisted-fucking-Greek-tragedy, once and for all.

"There you go," Clarice huffed as my ass hit the seat, and I sunk back. She pushed off me, and for a moment, we made eye contact. I think I half-smiled. She quickly averted her gaze like I was a car wreck she didn't want to get caught ogling.

"Just promise me you'll stay away from my Isaac," she said.

"Nothing would make me happier," I replied. "Tell him I died."

"He doesn't do too well with death." Her eyes flitted toward the shrine.

"Right. Then tell him that I had to go far away to escape the guy who did this, but if I'm ever around again, I'll come ringing. Don't worry, I won't." I cracked my neck, then gave pushing my wheels a try. It certainly didn't feel good, but I could manage. The pain would keep me sharp, focused.

I set off across the living room but barely escaped the rug before I slowed. I couldn't help but stare at Isaac's door, a blade of light slicing through as it was cracked open. It wasn't night. Clarice just had the blinds drawn, that's why it as so dark.

The light drew me like a fly to fire, even as Clarice hissed at me to stop. My wheel bumped the door and nudged it just enough for me to see into his eight-by-eight box. The kid had action figures along a shelf, movie posters everywhere. More than a few were of the local legend, the Roach, along with some of the small-time comic lines I'd inspired.

Isaac slept on a twin mattress he'd grown too big for. He didn't even fit it under his Star Wars patterned sheets. And he snored like a fifty-year-old man with a stuffed nose.

"Not everyone gets to meet their hero," Clarice whispered, slowly wheeling me back out of the room. I cut the wheels and turned to face her. Her pretty, walnut eyes were welled up.

"I got hooked on some pretty bad stuff after my husband..." she sniffled, bit her finger. "The River Kings owned the Stacks, but the Roach made them weak. I lost my dealer, and it, uh, forced me to get clean because I wasn't strong enough to do it for Isaac on my own..."

"*Hero*," I scoffed. Then I looked back toward Isaac. "You're right. I'm lucky to have finally met mine."

Her throat bobbed as all she could manage was a sad chortle and a nod. She backed up and let me by.

"Do me a favor and tell him thank you," I said as I approached the door.

Clarice hurried to my side and grabbed the door handle before I could. Fear hardened her features. "I won't tell anyone about you. Swear it."

"Thanks," I replied. I believed her, for whatever reason. I wasn't scared at all. And maybe it was because I knew there was a better chance of Vinny and Chuck revealing my secret to an ungrateful city. Or I was too injured to think straight. But maybe, just maybe, saying it out loud had changed me. I doubted it.

"Just so you know, I would never hurt you or the kid," I added. "Just be strong enough now. Screw working so hard. Who cares if you have to live in a box together? A mom like you, that's the one thing keeping Isaac from growing up like me."

I took her hand and slowly removed it from the handle. She didn't fight me.

"Oh, and one more thing. Tell Isaac to keep aiming for the balls," I said.

Before she could answer, I opened the door and rolled out into the dank hallway, ripe with stains, broken lights, and missing ceiling tiles—a crackhead passed out on the ground outside his door down the other way. It almost felt like I'd taken a brief stay in heaven and now returned to shitty old Earth. Not my time to rest yet.

I squeezed my pushrims tight to fight back the sharp aches elicited by every movement, making sure Clarice wouldn't feel a hint of guilt about doing what was right and kicking a patient out.

Some people... they have no idea how lucky they are. Yeah, it was a small one, but they were a family. I used to have dreams of waking up in a home full of love and lost love, no matter how shitty the building. I hated them more than the nightmares.

Like Laura and Michelle, Isaac and his mother would be better off with me far away. How the hell did I keep getting embroiled with these families clinging to a chance at normalcy?

"Wait!" Clarice called just as I reached the elevator lobby.

I glanced back and saw her run out into the hall in her slippers. She caught up and offered a pill bottle.

"You need these more than I do," she said. "Nothing crazy. They just... they'll help with the pain. That's all." She bit the side of her thumb as she waited for me to take them, her shame evident.

As the Roach, I stayed away from drugs like this. No matter how bad my bruises, or if I'd taken a tumble off a roof—I couldn't risk my focus. Now that it was clear I wasn't capable of being the Roach anymore, just a disabled, aging drunk... why not?

I snagged the bottle and deciding not to mention the fact that it was unmarked and clearly not prescribed. So, Clarice wasn't perfect, but who is? She'd probably stolen them from work. Percocet or some other opioid the hospital gave out to keep the sheep from baying.

Offering a nod and a rattle of the bottle, I looked toward an elevator lobby filled with campaign posters for the men running for mayor. Darrell Washington's—a Stacks native—were mostly untouched. Mayor Garrity's weren't so lucky.

"Mr. Washington is going to change this city," Clarice said.

I stared at the posters. He'd been given Garrity devil horns, a mustache, and a crooked crown. The vandalization trifecta. Seeing him helped my thoughts settle. Somebody wasn't being honest about what had happened the night Vinny raped his last victim, and he was at the top of the pyramid.

Now that I was back on my feet, figuratively speaking, I'd find the truth if it killed me. Chuck had mentioned having located Vinny through coworkers. Smart. Where better to start than with the kinds of people who sat next to him every day, thinking they knew him?

"Clarice," I said. "Do you have a copy of the White Pages?"

CHAPTER

In a city that had, for so long, forsaken design for factories and cheap housing, there weren't many architecture firms worth a damn. Downtown? There was one—right on the precipice of Harborside, but still inward enough to look down on everyone else.

Beaulieu Architecture, the oh-so-lucky employers of Vinny Statman, once upon a time until he was sent off to the loony bin. I'd known he was an architect, but I had to scan through Clarice's copy of the White Pages until I saw a company name that rang a bell.

Iron City was buzzing on Election Day—that wonderful, semi-holiday where people get to believe their voice counts for something. And maybe it does. Maybe that thin sheen of hope passed down to us from ancient Athens is all people need to be content. The idea that they can change the fate of the city, or a country, or even the world.

I've said it plenty, but nothing seems to change no matter who's in charge. Sorry, Clarice. One thing improves, something else takes a dive. Mayor Garrity didn't regenerate the waterfront or cure vagrancy, but well-armed police and lower crime-rates attracted certain types of corporations and creative-types Downtown.

Give and take, and the world goes round. That's all I ever needed to know about politics, and I can tell the story of every election. But if it quells the masses, keeps them happy, then I'm all for it. Better than them out rioting or burning society to the ground. I'm no anarchist.

There's just such a thin line between rules and structure, and oppression. Take my foster home, for instance. I learned to be on time and get my work done efficiently, or risk the whip. Those aren't necessarily bad attributes, but what happens when the reward for a job well done is equally awful? Being in a safe city means higher taxes, for instance.

Give and take. Nobody ever really wins; you simply hedge your bets. Which mayor will make my life just a bit less shitty? Who'll keep my wallet a hair thicker?

I stopped pushing my wheelchair and drew a deep breath. What the hell was I thinking about? My mind raced in random directions. A side effect from whatever pills Clarice had given me, or maybe of too many bangs on the head in quick succession. One bonus, I was almost in Downtown Iron City, and my insides weren't threatening to fall out from pain. My arms weren't even sore from pushing.

It felt like I was gliding over the uneven sidewalks, potholes, and puddles from the light rain. Every store I passed, I squinted through the wet storefronts to check TVs for news playing about Vinny or another killing. Nothing.

I followed the overhead light-rail line. One thing the old people-mover was good for. All the active routes led Downtown these days, little veins and arteries feeding the city with working people instead of blood cells.

People. I barely even noticed all the people. Children off from voting location schools meant extra crowds everywhere.

Flyers for the election were everywhere Downtown. Darrell Washington put in the work, that's for sure. He had his face on a bill-board over a brightly lit Ford showroom. He'd lose, but it was a valiant effort this election cycle, at least. Forward-thinking ideas are nothing compared to familiarity. And Iron City knew its award-worthy parent, blue-suit-wearing mayor well. Even many people from the Stack who he'd all but abandoned would cast their ballot Garrity because they knew how to spell his name by reflex.

A line snaked down from a public middle school filled with voting booths. I had to cross the street just to get by without dealing with an even bigger crowd, not easy considering congestion down here. If it wasn't a protest, it was construction on a glassy high-rise or a new swanky coffee shop location. There seemed to be one on every corner.

I rarely ventured this far Downtown, but I witnessed the revitalization now, clear as day. Why worry about the boarded-up buildings out in Harborside or the Stacks and their brown running water? This was where Iron City needed to shine. Along Main Avenue, straight down to Garrity Bridge over the Horton River to the new Iron City Marauders Stadium.

You could live in this tiny little bubble of luxury apartments, expensive restaurants, shops, and showrooms, and think Iron City was the gem of the Midwest. Even City Hall was power washed, with marble columns as white and triumphant as an ancient Roman temple. All in exchange for CCTV at every intersection playing the role of big brother.

A whistling traffic cop helped me cross the multi-lane avenue, and I rolled up to the marble stairs of an art deco low-rise sticking out like a sore thumb. *Beaulieu Architecture* had its office on the first floor.

Made sense, a bunch of stuck up designers would plant themselves in here—bundle up with coffee and draw little doodles all fucking day. Some assholes never grow up. There were lots of jobs I didn't understand, but this was one of them. People needed homes, needed offices, but didn't need to live in fucking works of art. Wastefulness at its damn finest.

No wonder the place let a rapist like Vinny infiltrate them. Too busy looking up and imagining what could be and not looking down and seeing what is.

I rolled into the lobby, all mahogany and white walls. It looked like a temple. And standing proudly on a table to my right was a scale model of Aurora Tower. Light shone down straight on it like some holy edifice. All the while, the irony didn't escape me that Mayor Garrity's most significant achievement would be conceived here.

I couldn't help but wonder as my eyes ran up the model to the spire that almost touched the ceiling—had Vinny designed parts of it? Five years was a long time, but it was a big tower. Could have taken that long. Fuck if I know how any of this works.

"Good afternoon," the pretty, young receptionist greeted me, craning over the front desk to look down at me. "How can I help you?"

No way. I rolled around the side so I could get a straight look at her. College girl, no doubt. Working in her off time. Probably a lot like Laura back when... I shook my head. Vinny must've enjoyed chatting up whoever used to be posted here.

"I'm looking for someone," I said as I examined her desk. Brand-new-looking phone system. Custom pens, pads embossed with the Beaulieu family crest. This firm had done well for itself, teaming up with Lord Garrity.

Her brow furrowed as she appraised me head to bottom of my wheels. I knew the look. What could a ragged cripple like me need in a place like this? Was I homeless and looking for a handout? An escape from the chilly air?

"I don't think you're in the right place, Mr..."

"Barnes," I lied. I couldn't risk Montalvo hearing that I'd been here, causing me more grief. "An old friend works here, and I'm passing through the city. It's been a long time since I've seen him. Figured I may try dropping by."

"What's his name?" She dropped her pen and stood. "Oh, crap... Would you like some water? So sorry about that, I'm supposed to off—"

"It's fine."

I rolled in her path. She grimaced but sat back down. Everyone always wants to help.

"Vinny Statman." Wasn't easy getting his name out attached to a word like "friend." Felt like pushing puke through a spaghetti strainer. "We were school mates."

"Statman..." She started to nibble on the end of her pen. In fact, every single one in the jar on her desk seemed to have suffered from her oral fixation. "Doesn't ring any bells. You're sure he works here?"

"Well, it's been a while, but he did last I heard."

"Hmm. Maybe he left the firm, then? I just started last week."

Before I could answer, a man rapped his fingers across the top of her desk. "Jenny, before you go tonight, can you do me an itsy-bitsy favor?" he asked, not even noticing me.

Light gray hair slicked back like that was to hide the fact that he was balding. A ridiculous tan for this late in the fall. Decked out in a white... I don't know what... it wasn't really a suit. Guy looked like he was trying to do his best Jesus impression.

"Hey, Mr. Beaulieu. Did a Vinny Statman ever work here?" receptionist Jenny asked.

He blinked. For a moment, his skin didn't look so golden. "Who's asking?"

"Me," I said. I reversed and moved back around the desk. Man, his face when he realized someone had heard him say "itsy-bitsy..." Priceless. Made this whole detour worth it, even if it amounted to nothing.

"I'm an old friend," I continued. "Thought he might still be working here."

Beaulieu leaned on the desk, shoving his elbow into poor Jenny's workspace. He tapped his polished shoes on the hardwood flooring. Made a show of it. "So funny. A reporter came in a few months ago asking about him, too. Hadn't thought about Vinny in years."

"Very funny."

"Well, like I told him, Vinny he hasn't been with us for..." He turned back toward the office bullpen and shouted. "Hey, John! When did Vinny Stacks leave again?"

"Like, five years, I think?" an employee called back. "Last time the Marauders were in the playoffs."

"Right, yeah." Beaulieu put on a scant grin and slowly shook his head. I couldn't imagine the memories being dredged up by a guy they called Vinny Stacks. "Very serious guy. Let loose at the Christmas parties, though." He chuckled and nudged his elbow further Jenny's way. "You'd have liked him, Jenny."

"I bet," she agreed.

He leaned down so she couldn't see. "Liked the, uh—" he scratched at his nostril, "—a bit too much."

Yeah. Sure, you would have *loooved* him, Jenny. I bit back my tongue and squeezed the arms of my chair. I should not have come here. Memory lane is a road best left unpaved.

Beaulieu let out a wistful sigh. "But yeah. I don't know what happened. I'd just told him I was planning to name him a partner, and next thing I know, he has a psychotic break. Cops said he'd attacked one of theirs."

"No way," I said, dragging out the word, feigning interest. It took all my willpower. All I could think was about how Beaulieu knew Vinny wasn't dead, and I didn't. Had I been that blind to never see it? That drunk?

"Yeah. Imagine, attacking one of the boys in blue? Gotta be crazy. And he was, I guess. Totally delusional. Had to be institutionalized. Yep," he said, sighing. "Haven't heard from him since. Couldn't handle the pressure, maybe. I—You really didn't know?"

"Well, we were pals in high school. A long time ago."

"Oh? Where abouts?"

Jesus, this guy and his small talk. And I thought Garrity loved the sound of his own voice. "P.S. 131," I answered. Thank you, Isaac.

"Oh yeah? You know, my father actually designed that back—"

"I can't believe that happened to him," I cut him off. Every part of me was beginning to itch from the senseless chit-chat. "Any idea where he was taken?"

Beaulieu shook his head. "No clue. Lots of work and client

turnover after he left. Busy time. I guess we all just sort of..."

"Moved on," I finished for him. Not surprising. Completely forgotten, like the Roach would be one day.

A guy like Statman wouldn't have actual friends, just people he entertained. A joke at the water cooler someone could barely remember. An ass groped at an office party that all these schmucks shrugged off as being 'fun.' People don't want to see monsters, like what he undoubtedly was. They resist it with every fiber of their being.

But I see. Always have. The moment I looked into his eyes in that alley, I knew attacking Laura wasn't some spur of the moment mental lapse. *That* was him. The monster hiding behind narcissism, good humor, and a nice suit and tie.

"Makes me feel sick saying it, but yeah," Beaulieu said. Then he smiled, a physical representation of erasing memories. "Well, if you manage to get in touch with him, tell him I say 'hello.'"

"Will do."

He nodded at me, then tapped on the desk again, and headed out the front door with a hop to his step. I looked back up at Jenny, still gnawing on her pen's clicker and barely paying attention.

"Oh well," I said.

"I'm so sorry about that," she said.

"Moral of the story," I said, starting to spin my wheels, "don't wait too long to catch up with people, I guess."

"So true. Is there anything else I can help you with?"

"Actually, is there a bathroom I could use before heading out?"

She smiled. "Sure thing." She went to stand and lead me when the phone rang. She muttered a curse. "I have to take this. It's down that hall, to the right. Can't miss it."

I thanked her and went on my way into the offices. This was a trick I'd learned. Nobody—*nobody*—said no when I asked about a bathroom. Even if most of the ones in this city didn't have grab bars, they'd let me go. No need to buy something or be coherent and sober.

I rolled along down the side of the bullpen, past a dozen or so neat little desks with paper-thin dividers. Photos of families and building sketches were pinned to all of them—their own minuscule worlds.

Some watched me go by like a UFO landed outside the window. Others didn't notice me. Others, still, made believe they didn't notice me.

All familiar reactions. I followed Jenny's directions to an auxiliary hallway, looked up at the bathroom door, then turned and found the file room.

No lock. People are so trusting. There were piles of rolled up construction drawings everywhere, but those weren't a help. I found the boxes of files until I saw one labeled employee records. Naturally, it was on a shelf above my reach.

Grabbing one of the cardboard tubes containing drawing rolls, I poked it up and nudged until the box scooted loose and fell on my lap. Luckily, I couldn't feel how much it should have hurt. But my numb legs gave it a soft landing that nobody would hear. Even the shockwave it sent through my body didn't register through the painkillers.

"Where are you?" I whispered, rifling through tabs until I saw one for Statman. I yanked it out, flipping through to his contract and scanned the pages for an address. Guy had a pretty decent salary. Would have had a stable, normal life if he'd been capable of that.

"Here we go."

I tore the address off the page just in case my aching head decided to play any tricks on me, then I pushed the box into a corner so it wouldn't be too obvious. *111 City Place, Apt 1020*. That was where Vinny used to live. It wasn't much to go on, but a man like him with nowhere to go might be drawn back home.

It was worth a try.

"Excuse me?"

I turned, seeing a middle-aged guy in glasses standing in the doorway—sweater vest, fitted pants, timepiece—the works.

"Sorry, I was looking for the bathroom," I said, then rolled on by him.

CHAPTER SIXTEEN

111 City Place was a fucking lovely apartment building. Seriously, one of the nicest in Iron City. It made where Isaac lived look like a third world country. And yeah, the lobby appeared freshly renovated, but Vinny's salary wasn't nice enough to live here.

The guy must have been house-poor, stretched himself to the very limit just to look richer than he was. Bump elbows with the city's few bigwigs.

A doorman opened for me like I was royalty. The security desk just inside was manned by a lazy wage slave. Feet up, listening to a game on a radio hidden behind it.

I didn't stop or slow down. That was always the key to sneaking around places. Either be invisible or act like you belonged. I rolled right on by, not even looking at him and showing no signs of hesitation.

He didn't say a word. I'm not sure if he even noticed me. Maybe he felt too bad for me to say anything. All I know is that next thing I knew, I was in one of four elevators, shooting up through the building. Four. Chuck's place didn't even have one, and these pompous fuck-nuggets had four. Heaven forbid anyone wait more than a few seconds to catch a free ride.

An old woman in a flowered dress got on when I got off. Like the guard, she didn't pay me a passing glance. Maybe everyone just felt so safe in this tower, far from Harborside and the Stacks, they'd all grown complacent.

Apt 1020 was as far from the elevators as could be. I needed to catch my breath when I got there. The last hanging *zero* was crooked, but otherwise, it looked like any other door in the brightly lit hall.

Looking side to side, I took out a paperclip I'd swiped off Jenny's desk on my way out. You can do amazing things with one of them that had nothing to do with paper. From jabbing an eye to picking a lock—even works as a makeshift toothpick after a particularly fatty steak.

I pressed my ear to the door and worked the thing. A little rusty, but after a minute or so, I got it to click. Then, I clutched a razor blade, also compliments of Beaulieu Architecture. One of those overpaid preschool arts-and-crafters was cutting up pieces of whiteboard to make a model with. Snagged an extra one right off his desk.

Slowly, I pushed the door open. If I was wrong about Vinny coming here, all I could do was hope nobody was home in the middle of the workday.

Snap!

I heard it first and ducked my head out of instinct. A fire axe swung through the opening, shaving some strands of loose hair off the top of my head. It sank into the wood of the doorframe with a heavy *thunk.*

My pulse throbbed in my ears. I missed the sensation. Primal. Fight or flight.

Looking up fast, I saw all the clever strings set up to work the axe. Someone had jury-rigged a trap for when the door opened. *Someone.* Vinny, obviously. If I'd been Montalvo or any other cop checking in on him, I'd be down a top half.

Saved by the one thing I couldn't fix.

Without hesitating, and spurred on by a lifetime of close calls, I sliced the axe free with my blade and tore it out of the wall. Then, I pushed myself in, axe ready to go.

A tang of iron wafted across my nostrils, like stale blood mixed with cleaner. And there, hanging by a shirt from a ceiling fan in the living room, I found Chuck Barnes. His naked body had cuts across his chest that formed my Roach emblem, the knife stabbing through that Polaroid of all his research and into his heart. I don't need to spell out exactly what Vinny did to him from the waist down.

I moved closer, checking corners. Vinny didn't seem to be home, but who knows. He'd managed to turn his old home into a lair damn quick. Of course he hadn't found new digs after escaping the nuthouse. And where did he end up? Back at the place he knew best.

Lucky guess by me? Maybe. Or human nature. Because that's what animals do, don't they? They return home, to familiarity, to nest and dig in for the winter.

I gave Chuck's body a poke with the butt of the axe handle. His jaw shifted farther open, tongue fat and bloated. Blood dripped down his legs and toes, staining a carpet where a coffee table had been moved aside, a half-eaten box of pizza on top of it. Seeing him like that gave me momentary pause. Nobody deserved such a gruesome end. I couldn't be sure Vinny had marred his body while Chuck remained alive, but I'm pretty sure I knew the answer.

"Was this worth the story?" I asked him, as if he could hear me.

A muffled scream replied. I squinted at Chuck, wondering if it was my head playing tricks on me again. Then, I heard pounding—faint, like it was coming from a bedroom.

I wheeled around and rushed for the door down the short hallway off the kitchen. An axe wasn't the best weapon without leverage, but it's about working with what you got. Peering around the corner, I saw nothing but a clean master bedroom—king-sized mattress covered in useless throw pillows. Dresser. Jewelry. It all looked untouched.

More banging, only now that I was closer, I realized it was behind me. Damn expensive building and their solid walls.

The apartment had a second bedroom with the door closed. I used my axe to push it open, wary of another trap. There wasn't one. Only a bedroom that looked like a unicorn had thrown up in it. Pink everywhere. Baby dolls on a twin bed. All of it contrasting band posters on the walls that I wouldn't call porn, but pretty close. Like a little girl was in the middle of finding herself, growing a bit older, not yet wanting to let go of the past but still wanting to move forward.

Sounded a bit like someone I knew.

My chest clenched as I rolled across the soft rug to a folding closet. The handles were tied closed by a wire. Nothing my axe couldn't bash through. I swung them open, and a freckled young girl cowered from me, screaming into a sock duct-taped to her mouth. She looked around Isaac's age. Not a child but, still a kid. Innocent, like we all are before life makes us anything but.

"Hey, it's okay. I'm not going to hurt you," I said softly with the voice I used with Michelle. Was she too old for that?

She screamed louder, kicking across the floor of the closet to hide in the corner. Her wrists were tied behind her back. Ankles bound, too.

Her bright green eyes focused on my axe, and I quickly threw it aside.

"See?" I said, showing my empty palms. "I'm here to help you."

She yelled something else, muffled. I edged in closer and reached for the end of the tape on her mouth. She turned her head away and wriggled her body.

"Oh, would you just..." I tore the tape off. The very start of her yelling 'help" escaped her lips before I covered her mouth with my palm.

"Sh. I don't know where he—" she bit the soft, fleshy chunk of skin between my thumb and forefinger. I yelped.

"Help!"

I fought the pain and covered her mouth again, this time, careful to press tight and not allow her a biting vantage.

"Please," I huffed. "I swear it, I'm here to help. Look at me." I held her gaze and tracked it down to my wheelchair. "I'm nothing. Nobody. That's right, just breathe. It's going to be okay."

I inhaled with her. Let it out. In and out, one at a time. I needed it too.

"Good girl," I said. "Now, I'm going to let go, and I need you to tell me who did this to you, okay? I'm going to get him."

A few more breaths and I slowly released my hand. She swallowed hard. Fear seized every part of her, down to her marrow. She looked like Laura had. I could hardly bear to look at her.

"Are you police?" she sniveled, tears running down her cheeks.

"Something like that. What happened?"

"He... my parents, they're on anniversary and... he..."

"Calm down," I said. "Just breathe. You're okay now."

She exhaled slowly through lips chapped by tape. Who knows how long he had her like that.

"Some guy knocked on the door... I answered and he-he—"

"Did this to you?"

She nodded.

"What'd he look like?"

"He looked crazy. Like he..." she broke down into sobbing. Before I knew what I was even doing, I had my arms around her neck, hugging her. I stopped pressing and held her there, let her get it out. And eventually, she started to whisper.

"He put a knife to my throat..." she whispered. "I thought he was going to... but then he said he couldn't do it, so he tied me up."

"Did he... touch you?" I asked, barely able to say it. Of course he had in order to tie her up, but she knew what I meant by the way I said it and shook her head. What a load off my heart that was.

"Oh, God. Are my parents home?" she said after a short bout of silence. "Where are they? Did he—"

"No, they're not here. It's just you and me, okay? That's it." I straightened my arms to look straight at her face. "Did he say anything about where he was going?"

Her nose wrinkled, bunching up a constellation of freckles. "I don't know... I..."

"Anything at all?" I probed.

"Before he left. Something about a party to, uh, meet an old friend... yeah. He stole one of my dad's suits, asked me how it looked... I'm sorry, I..."

"Hey, you're doing great. That's great." I stroked the side of her face with my thumb. With the other hand, I reached into my pocket and drew the razor blade. She winced.

"Do you mind if I free your arms and legs?" I asked.

She looked like a deer in headlights, looking at the blade. Vinny must've really gone at her. Maybe he really was going to kill her, but then couldn't? That didn't add up. He was leaving her like a trail of breadcrumbs. All part of some twisted revenge scheme.

"I'm just going to cut them. Real quick." I angled her to the side. Her shaking intensified, but I made it quick, slicing the tape on her wrist's first, then her ankles.

Before I could make another move, she crawled out to the foot of her bed and sat there, knees cradled against her chest. The bruises on her wrists... Just seeing them made me want to explode. She looked like those Russian girls, or Laura, or my foster siblings—why do pieces of shit have to involve kids?

I moved to her nightstand, to a bulky pink phone covered in faded stickers she'd probably put on years ago. I stretched the curly cord over to her and planted it in her hand until she took it.

"I want you..." I paused. It wasn't easy to tell her to call who I was about to. They'd never done a thing for me. Made my life hell if I'm being honest. But it was the right thing to do. I couldn't stay here, and I couldn't leave her alone. Not like *I'd* been left alone.

"Call 911, and tell them where you are," I forced out.

She didn't answer or couldn't. I'm not sure which. She just stared blankly at the wall.

"Nod if you understand me. Hey. Nod."

Her head bobbed ever-so-slightly.

"Good." I rolled to the axe, picked it up, and placed it down by her feet. "Now, I want you to hold onto this and stay right here."

All the frantic terror flooded back through her, and she clutched at my chair. "Please, don't leave me..."

"I have to," I said, removing her hands. "I'm going to get the guy who did this to you, okay? So that you'll never have to be afraid again."

A lie, but it was all I had. She'd always be afraid, just like Laura was. Always flinching at night when she heard a noise. Squirming in her skin whenever a guy she didn't know came close. Vinny Statman would be another person's monster.

"Okay?" I repeated.

Again, her head bobbed.

"Good. Now whatever you do, you don't leave this room, okay? Don't go to the living room. Don't get water. You stay here until a cop walks through your door, and you ask him for his badge number. Got it?"

Nothing this time. Her blank stare returned as her toes curled over the handle of the axe, sliding it closer.

"You'll be okay, I promise," And as I lied to her, I placed my hand on her shoulder. I think I was shaking as much as she was. Then, I wheeled around and back out the door. I waited at the entry to the living room until I heard her spinning the dial, then moved on through, gaze flitting over the swinging body.

I'd have traded anything in the world not to find that girl like that. For her to have been at a friend's house, or off on vacation with the parents who'd left a child here to fend for herself. Like pizza money was all a kid needed to grow up safe in this fortress where I'd just rolled in like I owned the place.

My grip tightened. My jaw hurt from clenching so hard. Vinny was still out there, and now I knew where. The only party happening tonight that mattered, filled with old friends. You know, the kind that ruined his life and locked him away.

Mayor Garrity's election night party.

CHAPTER

SEVENTEEN

I exited the apartment building, shrouding to the shadow of a tree with boughs clinging to a handful of browning leaves. My wheel barely missed a pile of dog shit, but at least it was quiet, and the tree blocked the rain. Less exposed.

What if Vinny was watching my every move now, wearing his new suit like a mask to blend in?

"Focus," I told myself. "Ignore it all. Where would the mayor have his party?"

I looked up and across the street. My brain immediately wondered when someone would come sweep away the homeless-looking guy in a wheelchair talking to himself. I couldn't remember the last time I'd felt so out of place. I'd never minded the streets of Iron City because it was easy to get lost in them, but not anymore. Not looking like me.

Where was the stink of stale trash, sweat, and roasted almonds? It smelled so clean here, like the hospital. Sterile.

I rolled out a bit farther to see more of the avenue. A few men in suits walked by, wriggling their noses like they got a whiff of Harborside trash.

Oh, hey, that's just me.

"Keep walking," I grumbled. They looked back at me like I was a freak, then laughed with each other over some unheard joke.

My gut started to ache. Which—no shit, I had a knife wound the length of my middle finger there. My chest grew tight as another wave of people got permitted across a camera-monitored crosswalk and headed my way. Gathering as much saliva as I could, I forced down another of Clarice's pills.

Focus, or be able to move. I had to stay in the happy medium.

I looked the other way, and my gaze froze on the city's crown jewel, down at the triangular intersection of Main and Verner Street. Aurora Tower was so much bigger and more modern than any other in Iron City, it was almost laughable. Its glass lobby had an indent above, where the main stop for the Iron City people-mover slid through. The future home of Aurora Technologies would soon serve as the city's core, like a heart with many arteries carrying lifeblood to a city on life-support. Here, the metal tracks barely even hummed, let alone shook.

What would be the result of this bustling Downtown to which all roads led, with not a homeless man nor pile of garbage in sight? With police checkpoints outside voting locations, keeping everyone safe. Cameras like digital eyeballs, always watching. A shopping hub on Voyage Street, eternally blocked off to serve as a square where all the happy businesspeople could spend their lunch hours buying useless shit or drinking martinis.

Fuck me. Is this what I fought for?

What would happen to people like Clarice and Isaac when this cancerous revitalization spread just a bit further and they couldn't even afford to live in their piece-of-crap building? When the Horton River was cleaned up, and the waterfront becomes an attraction instead of fuel for industry? I guess every city needed an identity, and we'd lost ours overseas to child labor and cheap factories.

There I was again, not worrying about what mattered in the

moment. I slapped myself on the cheek a few times to get the blood flowing to my brain.

It worked.

Aurora Tower was where Mayor Garrity was having his election party. A place to show off for the city's richest and most connected inhabitants and celebrate a victory he knew he had in the bag. Maybe grease a few palms, make a few deals.

I took off so fast, even the pain meds couldn't dull the sting. I didn't care. I was already behind the clock. Vinny had an entire night and day to continue his revenge tour. Getting there was another issue. I had to push and ram my way through human cattle. Horns laid into me as I crossed in front of a green light. I didn't have the energy to flip them off. Only enough to get up the ramp and onto Aurora Towers' generous sidewalk. Seriously, I'd never seen anything like it. Spotless pavers spanning at least twenty feet wide surrounded a bronze sculpture of... Apollo I think? I never went to school, remember?

He stood proudly in the center of a fountain as big as my townhouse, with planters and dedicated benches. Back in Harborside, you were lucky to get sidewalks that fit two people side-by-side, let alone dotted with fucking plants instead of steaming sewer grates.

Stopping to catch my breath, I got the lay of the land. The entire lobby had been transformed for a swanky white-tablecloth event, but this was no Fort Knox. Glass walls were everywhere. Soon-to-be reelected Mayor Garrity was peacocking for the cameras, that's for sure.

Two of his personal security detail worked the door, and there may as well have been a velvet rope. Men and women decked out in trench coats and gowns with big ass shoulder pads got out of cabs. I spotted what could only be a few players from the Marauders towering over everyone else. Up next was the fill-in-the-blank of hotshots and bullshitters. To name a few? The District Attorney, chief of police, superintendent of this tax-funded this and that tax-funded that.

All the city's players down from their penthouse suites. I swear, five years ago, Downtown Iron City needed the Roach. But this? Garrity had built his own little kingdom, and fuck all, it wasn't that little. Through the glass, I could see him, shaking hands, posing for pictures, and wearing a big bogus smile. Red, white, and blue streamers ran down from a mezzanine level in the back atrium, all around a giant banner with his name and face on it, along with his campaign slogan: A SAFE CITY, STRONG AS IRON.

I think I'd asked it before—or maybe it was Laura—is it bad I hoped he'd lose? Yeah, he'd kept my secret. But Vinny was alive so... what other secrets was he keeping? From me. From Laura.

My grip tightened on my pushrims, and a surge of energy surged through me. I rolled my neck from side to side, getting the knots out, and drove right up to the front door. It was early. People were still slowly trickling in, which was a much better time for me to confront him. Avoid the crowd, so I could focus better.

"I'm sorry, sir, this is a private event," one of the guards said, barring me with his arm as I tried to slip behind him. Sneaking into places in a creaking wheelchair wasn't as easy as it used to be. The Roach would have scaled a neighboring building, hopped a crane, and made his way right down into ducts above the lobby.

"I'm a friend of the mayor's," I said.

He looked at me like I had a monkey growing out of my ear—whatever the hell that means. "Name?" he requested.

"You're really going to put a man in a wheelchair through all this?" I asked, mustering my whiniest tone.

"Name?"

No bullshit with this guy. The other guard checked a list and let in a couple who looked ready for the opera. I recognized the bald, wrinkled husband. He ran the Iron City Water and Sewage Authority, you know, the group who went along with fabricating my crippling 'accident.' His eyes passed right over me like I was a stranger.

"Reese Roberts," I grumbled.

My guard scanned through his own list. It was worth the try.

Maybe Mayor Garrity was feeling generous and put me on. Maybe Laura begged him to and was on her way to pick me up for a surprise night on the town, introduce me to some friends, revitalize me like her father had done to Downtown. What would happen when she found my house in shambles, my blood all over the couch and carpet?

"Sorry, you're not on the list," the guard said. He waved the next couple along.

I nudged him with my wheel and said, "Check again."

"Sir, I really don't have time for this."

"You think the mayor's going to be happy that you booted one of his closest friends?"

"Let's go. I won't ask again."

His hand fell to his holster, but a glower didn't follow. Just a pitiable expression, like he thought I was some loon with his mind gone, desperate to get inside for a shitty buffet and warm air.

"It's about the killings, you shit stain," I growled. I don't know where it came from. Did Clarice's drugs make me even more ornery than usual? Was that possible? Too late to back down.

"You know, roaches in mouths," I said. "Dead strippers. Burning shops. Ring any bells?"

The guard closed his eyes, took a measured breath, and muttered to himself, "Jesus Christ. Today of all days?"

I snapped my fingers up toward his face. "Hey, I'm still here. You want more people to die?"

"That a threat?" the guard said, looking to his partner. Guard number two stuck out a palm to stop the line before talking into his radio. All I needed to do was get spotted by Garrity. He'd have no choice but to talk to me. Five years, I'd been a good soldier. He'd know something was wrong.

I rolled around the guard, right up to the glass, and pounded. "Garrity, get out here!" I yelled. A few suits inside nearly jumped out of their loafers.

Shouting and radio chatter erupted behind me. I kept banging until across the room, I noticed Mayor Garrity notice me. And all he did was shrug and keep talking to whichever ass-kisser had his attention, like I was fly buzzing around his ear. He, the uncrowned king of Iron City.

"Garri—"

Hands grabbed at me before I could get his name out again and ripped me back. The other kept my wheelchair upright. They couldn't just spill a paraplegic onto concrete out in public—bad optics.

"Let go of me!" I shouted, twisting to get free. Blinding pain seized my core, and I lost track of what was what. White spots danced as they dragged me away.

"I need to see him," I gasped, over and over.

Admittedly, not my finest infiltration job. But it worked. After a brief struggle, they stopped and placed me down. My body settled first, then my vision. Enough to witness an angel strolling toward me.

I'm not sure there's a word for how Laura looked that day. Gorgeous? Radiant? They don't quite cut the check. I'd seen her with makeup on and all the fixings, but never done-up like this. Her brown hair was blown out and cascaded over slender shoulders left bare by a blue, sequined dress with a slit up the side of her left leg as if to say, "Fuck the world and men like Vinny."

My ears rang from the pain, so I couldn't hear whatever she'd said to the officers, but she had her lawyer-face on. Giving them a stern talking-to from Iron City royalty. One by one, hands came off me, and the suddenly apologetic officers backed away.

I couldn't begin to imagine what I looked like in Isaac's dad's green T-shirt, probably soaked with sweat and worse. At least I'd shaved recently.

Laura kneeled in front of me, and her mouth moved. I shook my head out to hear.

"Reese, what's going on?" she asked.

"I just need to talk to your dad, that's all. And these *assholes* wouldn't let me in," I replied. I pursed my lips so she wouldn't see me tightening my jaw. No doubt, I'd popped a stitch or six.

"They're just doing their job."

"So am I."

Laura sighed. Then she placed her hands on my knees and leaned closer. "Your eyes... Have you been drinking again?"

"Not at all," I replied.

"Reese, what do you want? You couldn't just call? I'm sure dad would've set aside a time to talk."

"Yeah, right."

She stood, rubbed the bridge of her nose, and groaned very similarly to how the guard had. "I can't deal with this today."

"Laura, this is serious. You know me. I wouldn't be here if it wasn't. I hate it Downtown."

"I don't know anything anymore," she said. "I thought maybe the accident would be a turning point for you."

"It was. It is." I grasped her hand and lowered my voice. "Please, Laura. Someone knows about what happened that night. If I don't talk to your father and get ahead of this, who knows what might come out."

Her features darkened. "Someone knows about—"

"Yes," I interrupted, so she wouldn't have to stomach saying it.

"Okay, I'll bring you in," she conceded. "No theatrics, deal?"

I nodded.

"I swear, Reese, if you cause any problems in there—"

"Then you'll never have to see me again," I said. "You can roll me right into the river if I'm lying. But I promise, I'm here for *you*. That's all."

Laura's lips twitched at something resembling a smile before she rolled her eyes. "Stop being so dramatic. Let's get you out of the rain."

She spun, the rift in her dress splaying open and revealing one smooth leg. I slapped myself lightly in the face and looked away. What was wrong with me? I didn't want to view her like that, ever—only protect her from scum like Vinny.

"I like the shaved look, by the way," she added as she approached the doors. "You look dashing."

My hand instinctually rose to my jawline, and I stroked the stubble. All the while, my tongue lashed around aimlessly in my mouth as I fumble for a response. I settled on a very eloquent, "Pfft. Right."

She reached the security guard who'd barred me at the door. "Sorry about the confusion," she said to him. "He's with me. Just gets a little confused sometimes."

"Who is he?" the guard replied.

"An old family friend."

"All right, Miss Garrity. Next time, please let us know beforehand."

"Don't you worry. This is the last time I bring him out in public." She flashed me a simper, and my muscles unconsciously returned the favor.

I lightly slapped myself again. Now wasn't the time for games.

"Let's go, Michelle!" Laura called back. "Everything's okay."

Scanning left, I spotted little Michelle, waiting patiently by the curb. She moseyed over, her hair blown out like mom and gobs of eyeliner and mascara on. Looked as if Laura let her apply it herself, just for fun. And while her dress wasn't as revealing, it matched her mothers' blue.

She skipped along until she saw me, then stopped in her tracks, her feet shuffling awkwardly.

"Why is she here?" I asked Laura.

"It's a party for her grandfather," she said. "It's called being there for your family, no matter how little they do to deserve it. Say hi to Uncle Reese, sweetie."

Michelle played coy and batted her eyelashes. Laura took her hand and pulled her inside. The girl didn't fight it, though she certainly wasn't eager. No interest in attending a big, boring adult. She stared at me the entire way, her line of sight aimed straight to my gut.

I glanced down and I hadn't been wrong. I was soaked with something far worse than sweat. A spot of fresh blood blossomed on my shirt. Rustling to hide it under a fold, I surveyed our surroundings, all the strange faces walking by and inside. Michelle being around wasn't in my game plan. I'd have preferred her locked up in a vault somewhere. What if Vinny was out here, watching?

"Are you coming?" Laura asked.

I grunted and rolled inside, through a wall of warm air shooting down from expensive modern strip-vents.

"Enjoy your night," the guard muttered before returning to his duty.

The doors sealed behind us. Some Peter Gabriel or Genesis song played throughout the room, I never knew the difference, and I found myself face-to-face with Iron City's other half. Did people have fun at soirees like this? Picking nibbles off silver trays, jabbering about nonsense around tall, seatless cocktail tables, faking remembering names. I wanted to slink into the shadows, but Aurora Tower's airy lobby didn't have them. Everything was open, with clean corners, glass walls, and no unintentional clutter. Suddenly, I wished it was my hand Laura was holding as she and Michelle delved into the pompous throng.

"Aren't you going to ask if I'm okay?" I asked Laura, desperate to distract myself. To close my eyes and focus on the soothing melody of her voice.

"Why wouldn't you be?" she replied.

"You didn't hear about my house going—" I stopped myself. She had more important things to do than keep tabs on me every second of every day, and I was glad about it. If she didn't know about the fate of my house, that meant Lieutenant Montalvo was still keeping it quiet. Better not to involve her.

"Never mind," I said.

She stopped and turned, brow furrowed. "What are you talking about?"

"Laura, you made it!" exclaimed a guy in a suit pulled too tightly around his bloated midsection, complete with a red polka-dotted bowtie.

"You did tell me to leave early, Mr. Rickman," Laura tensed upon hearing him, then drew a slow breath, put on a big smile, and turned.

I knew the name. This was her boss. Though, the way he pulled her into a big hug with his waist thrust forward certainly wasn't professional. His hand wandered a bit too far down her back, and I had the urge to snap it off before he finally let go.

"And you brought your daughter," Rickman said, only then noticing Michelle and sounding very-much disappointed. What, did this slob think he was going to score with his brightest young employee? People make me sick.

"My God, she gets bigger every time I see her." He knelt, pretended to steal Michelle's nose, and got no reaction.

Michelle clutched her mother's leg and hid her face, proving she wasn't a tough crowd only for me. Though, Mr. Rickman here wasn't much competition, what with his clammy, grabby hands.

"Sorry," Laura said. "She's in one of her shy phases."

"All mine ever want to do is watch TV." Rickman needed to put both hands on his knees to stand up straight. Then his embarrassment was cured by a pretty server walking by with a tray of some sort of raw hors d'oeuvres that'd make someone from Harborside sick.

"Have you seen the man of the hour?" Laura asked.

"Yeah, he's over by the big banner, wheeling and dealing." Rickman laughed as he scooped up two of the delights.

Laura put on another polite smile before Rickman went chasing after a tray of champagne flutes. She kept her head high as we continued through the patrons.

It didn't matter if she worked for a dog. Laura would be powerful one day. I knew it.

What else I knew, was this party made me feel ill—well, more ill than lately—and it was barely full yet. I had to stare down at my own lap and half hold my breath not to taste the lies of all the overdressed sycophants. Each of them probably glanced over and wondering why Laura was with a sad sack like me.

"Sweetheart, there you are!" Mayor Garrity pronounced,

weaving through the dozen or more ten-person dining tables arrayed in the two-story atrium area at the back of the enormous lobby. "I was just talking about you with Mister Aurora here."

"Only good things I hope," Laura said, a slight chuckle. I'd never seen her in professional mode like this. She sure knew how to play the game.

"He sang your praises," another man said. "It's lovely to see you again, Laura."

"And you, Benjamin."

I braved looking up to see Benjamin Aurora take Laura's hand and kiss it. He wasn't old, though not too young, but undoubtedly handsome. More than me at least. The billionaire tech mogul moving into my city had an iron jaw refined to a point. Her father eyed them together like a proud miser, and if I didn't know better, he'd planned for Mister Aurora to be around when Laura arrived. What better match than them?

"And there's my beautiful grandchild." Mayor Garrity scooped up Michelle and planted kisses on her head until she actually unleashed one of her rare, but delightful giggles. What a showman, able to deceive even children who see through everything.

I rolled right up to them and cleared my throat loudly.

Garrity lowered Michelle and stared down the ridge of his bulbous nose at me. I couldn't help but wonder what he might look like outside of a suit. I'd never seen it. This was his costume, complete with American flag pin and red tie, and he wore it well. He was fit enough to be appealing, though not too much, so he could seem the everyman. His hairline receded, but what was left of it was thick and gelled over, and the bushy mustache hugging his upper lip more than made up for what he was missing.

"Reese, what a nice surprise," he said, in a tone which completely undermined his words.

"I thought so, too," I replied. "Nice place you got here, Benji." I looked around, snagged a flute of champagne out of Aurora's hand,

and took a sip. I don't know how people stomached the stuff. It made me retch. I tossed the rest over my shoulder.

"Reese!" Laura scolded.

Benjamin Aurora looked appalled. Garrity whispered something to calm him and moved closer to me.

"What the hell are you doing?" he questioned, ditching the gracious-host act.

"Have you seen my house?" I asked. "You really should. I had to remodel because a ghost came knocking around and made a real mess of things."

"Are you insane, coming here?"

"I just think we need to have a little chat. That's—" I froze. A man walking down from the mezzanine stared at me, chaos in his bloodshot eyes. He smirked.

"Son of a bitch!" I dropped my glass and raced toward him before it even shattered. I pushed through partygoers, around tables. A woman yelped. A man cursed. More than one person toppled over.

Snagging the first officer I found on the other side of them, I yanked his face toward mine expecting to see Vinny. He wasn't. Hell, the guy was Asian and wearing a pin-straight suit. They didn't look anything alike.

"Reese, what is wrong with you?" Laura asked, grabbing the back of my chair and whipping me around.

I caught my breath, searching from side to side. What the hell was in Clarice's pills?

"I thought I saw..." I panted. I stuck my finger out at the mayor. "Garrity, we need to talk. Now."

"You're lucky I don't have you thrown out," he spat.

"Go ahead, but first, we talk. Unless you'd rather me tell everyone the story of how we met."

Garrity faked a laugh and gave Aurora a slap on the back. "Charity function, for injured city workers." He turned to Laura and ushered her aside. "Laura, darling. Care to keep our guest here occupied while Reese and I take a few minutes to catch up?"

"Are you sure? I can take him outside," Laura whispered in his ear, probably thinking I couldn't hear her. I looked between her and her father's legs and shot Michelle a goofy wink with my tongue out to the side. She covered her mouth and stifled a chuckle.

See, I could entertain her, too. I just needed someone to warm her up first.

"It's fine," Garrity said, straightening his tie. "Walk with me, Reese. Let's have a chat before everybody gets here."

I ignored his obvious slight. "How many friends do you have?" I asked.

"Too many."

He placed his hand on my shoulder and guided me toward a hall branching back behind a reception desk being used by the catering staff to hold glasses and plates. A green wall of what I think were live plants rose up through the two-story atrium behind it. The logo for Aurora Technologies carved in the middle—through stacked, curvy lines.

I glanced back at Laura, who was busy having her ear chewed off by the wooing billionaire. She regarded me, that all-too-familiar look of concern plastered upon her face as she held Michelle tight with one arm. A wink to her didn't have the same effect as it did with Michelle.

Garrity schmoozed with everybody we passed. Shaking hands, grinning, pretending he knew them. Laughing like he heard some of the best jokes in the world. It actually made this ride through the growing crowd enjoyable. Absurdity is the best kind of distraction.

"I thought we discussed keeping our public interactions to the bare minimum?" Garrity said before we even made it around the corner. "That was the deal."

"You think I want to be here?" I replied. He took his hand off my back, and I let myself drift a few feet before wheeling around.

"I *think* you're a drunk who needs a hobby."

"Why don't I get into construction, huh? Rebuild my house now that it's a pile of rubble."

"What are you..." He caught himself and waved me through a door into what I assumed would soon be a mail room or something when the building was completed. For now, it was an empty, polished-concrete space.

Garrity nodded to an officer posted down the hall by an emergency exit, then closed the door behind us. "What are you talking about?" he asked.

"Officer Montalvo didn't tell you?" I said.

"Tell me what?"

"We were using my house to lure the killer into, so that—"

He checked his watch.

"Do you have someplace better to be?" I said.

"I'm a very busy man. Lieutenant Montalvo said he was on top of the situation."

"On top of it?" I scoffed. "I was handling everything until that fucking ghost walked through my door."

"What ghost? What in God's name are you talking about, Reese?" He stomped forward and leveled a steely stare at me. "I have a lot of guests out there, and a city I plan to keep running long after tonight's over and Washington is put in his place. Laura may enjoy your games, but not me. She's still too young to spot a bullshitter."

"What ghost?" I rolled across the room away from him, barely able to suppress a laugh. "The man who assaulted her, remember him? I do. Which, how is that possible considering you told me he was out of the goddamn picture?"

"He is." I didn't have to face him to know Garrity was lying. I could hear the hesitation. The lump in his throat tempering his basso voice. Not drinking really did make it easier to notice the little things.

The pills still had me extra agitated, though. "He was in my house!" I shouted, spinning back to him.

"That's impossible." Garrity dismissed me with a swipe of his hand. Like he was waving a magic wand, making all this insanity disappear.

"Then tell me what the fuck I'm missing, *Eugene*," I said, his first name slipping through my teeth like a mouthful of diarrhea.

"Maybe you're just losing your mind. Too much drinking and whatever else you do all day, locked up like a hermit."

"Would you listen to me!" I slammed on the wall, crunching a bit of new sheetrock. Whoops. They never tell you that part. Even in the fanciest, newest buildings, the walls are just as fragile as anywhere else.

"The rapist who attacked *your* daughter is in Iron City, out for revenge," I explained. "Not just on me now, but on everybody involved in that night. That pain-in-the-ass reporter, Chuck Barnes. He found him and all the beautiful theories about us bouncing around his stupid little brain that just so happen to be true."

Garrity stared, dumbfounded. I huffed to catch my breath after my rant, wanting to reach into his mouth and yank on his tongue just to get him talking.

"Fuck!" he cursed, finally, biting his lower lip to keep his volume down.

"Ah, now he's paying attention," I said.

"This can't be happening." He ran his fingers through his thickly gelled hair and yanked on a clump of it. A few more curses rattled out.

"Care to share with the class?" I asked.

"He was never supposed to get out," he said.

I rolled closer. "Out of where?"

"We didn't kill him, Reese."

"No fucking shit."

I felt like I could breathe fire. My fingernails dug deep lines in my palms and no pain pills could dull the sting.

"How is this possible?" I asked. "You built all of this on top of his corpse."

"We didn't kill him," Garrity repeated, emphasizing each word like that would change anything.

"I'm aware. Apparently, everyone knew, even his boss. Everyone but me." I moved until my wheel bounced against one of his shiny shoes. "How could you not kill him? You had one fucking body to bury for this city. That's it. And you couldn't go far enough? You know how many monsters I buried because nobody else had the balls? Mob. Bratva. Cartel. He raped your goddamned daughter!"

"I know what he did!" he shouted. The vein running down the center of his soaring forehead pulsed. "Don't tell me about going far enough. This wasn't some half-measure. I thought we knew that about each other. We don't resort to that. No, I didn't have him killed because that was too easy. He didn't deserve easy for what he did."

I bit back a scream. My missing pinky throbbed along with my gut.

"What did you do?" I questioned.

"What he deserved." Garrity grabbed my wheelchair by the arms and leaned in, his breath reeking of champagne and cocktail shrimp. Gone was his dignity and mayoral disposition.

"We beat him and shot him up with enough smack to scramble his brains since he loved getting high so much," he said. "Then, we dropped him at a mental hospital upstate. Told them and his bosses at the brokerage he worked for that he mutilated himself while he rambled on about the Roach's hissing breaths. He was fit for a straight-jacket when we left him there to rot for the rest of his miserable life."

"Well, he got out," I growled.

How far is too far? That question kept popping up in my head, but the universe is pretty good about slapping you in the face with answers you don't want to hear, if you're patient. Five years after that mess with the Russians and then, with Laura—I had my answer.

Too far was risking everything only to make it personal.

Garrity clenched my wheelchair until his knuckles blanched, then pushed me back and groaned. "What did that damn journalist say to him?"

"No idea," I said. "But whatever it was, it happened already."

"What does that mean?" Garrity asked.

"Vinny fucking castrated him," I said. Then, when I wasn't sure the self-righteous prick understood, I added, "Chuck's dead."

"Shit!"

"Understatement of the year," I said under my breath.

"I knew we should have had that nosy bastard thrown into the Horton."

"But wasn't destroying his career and his life so much more... cathartic?" I replied.

"You don't get to look down from some high horse. You didn't stop it. The only reason you're here, in this room, and not sinking to the riverbed with him is because you saved the right man's daughter."

"Because that's what you cared about, right? Not your precious Garrity Act, or your big old mahogany desk, or the fact that you get to be Iron City's savior? Laura's a tool for your campaign, that's all. An accessory like this tower."

"Don't you fucking dare."

I didn't back down. "She gets assaulted, and I bet all you saw were dollar signs. You probably begged her not to have Michelle, but you spun it in the end. Can't lose the religious vote. God forbid."

"You get the hots for my daughter and think you can preach at me?" Garrity bristled, checks red as tomatoes. "Everything I've ever done is for her. The biggest mistake I ever made was letting you stick around and drag her down into the gutters with you. So, why don't you go home, Reese? Curl up with a bottle in your sad little lair and die alone where you belong."

I laughed. "You don't listen to anybody else, do you? My home is gone, thanks to you." It hadn't really sunk in until I phrased it like that out loud. A tightness in my chest took hold and refused to relinquish.

My home. My lair. Gone. For good.

Garrity glared at me, more curses ready to explode through his lips as if they could wound me. That's the problem with politicians. Eventually, they spew so much bullshit, none of it matters anymore. They're all just empty words. He probably actually believed that all the things he'd ever done were for Laura and not for him.

A knock sounded at the door before he could talk.

"Mister Mayor, are you in there?"

Garrity stared a short while longer before he opened the door. Lieutenant Montalvo stepped in, decked out in full ICPD regalia, with long sleeves beneath to cover his tattoos.

"Well, you were right," Garrity said. "He came right here."

Montalvo sucked on his lip and shot me a sneer. "Men like him are predictable."

"Oh, great, now it's a party," I groaned.

Garrity squeezed his arm, hard, wiping the smirk right off Montalvo's face. "You already let this get way out of hand. Take care of it, or I'll find somebody who can."

"It'll be my pleasure," Montalvo said.

"It'll be your ass." Garrity released him and smoothed his tie. "Now, if you all don't mind. I have a party to enjoy."

"You don't get to leave," I said. "That monster is out there ready to hunt. Do something if you claim you care about Laura."

"Lieutenant Montalvo will handle it from here. It's been nice catching up with you, Reese." He smiled before stepping out. That haughty, self-important smile. All the crime lords I'd taken out—they wore the same kind. Had I missed the worst of them? Put him in control?

"Get back here, you coward!" I barked as his shoes clacked away.

"He doesn't need to hear any more," Montalvo said.

I rolled forward, but Montalvo strode in and dropped a heavy duffel bag in my path, blocking my wheel. He gently closed the door, like he took pleasure in hearing the latch click.

"Quite a mess you left at your house," he said. "I guess that's what I get for trusting you to take him down. Some legend."

"It's not the time for a cock-fight, Montalvo," I said.

"How could it be? Mine works."

"Very funny." I wheeled around the bag, and he stepped in front of me. "You know Vinny's full name. His information. Put out an APB. Use the city's cameras. Get Garrity's blue army to do *something.*"

Montalvo sized me up. "It's sad, seeing you like this. Imagining things."

"I'm not imagining anything."

"You may have mutilated him, but I knew Vinny Statman. I put him in that place. He was a smooth talker, but that's it. There's no way he's capable of all of this."

"You don't know that," I said. "Who knows how many other girls he raped. I looked into his eyes that night and that wasn't his first time. Did you ever even ask him?"

"I warned Garrity about you," Montalvo said, ignoring me. "I warned his daughter. You're a delusional drunk."

"Call them then," I said. "Call the hospital and see if Vinny's still there. I know what I saw."

"You should be in that place with him," Montalvo said. "Hell, maybe you deserve to be there even more."

"Why don't you dig through the rubble of my house while you're at it. His blood's in there along with mine and Chuck Barnes'."

"What rubble—"

I didn't let him finish. "Or, wait. Maybe you knew it was him all along. Maybe you told Chuck where to find him. Get your chance to finally catch the bastard who raped the mayor's daughter and help him win by a landslide. That'll get you a captain's seat."

"What. Rubble?" Montalvo pronounced more loudly. I noted how he didn't deny my accusation.

"My home!" I said. "Where you sent your men in when I told you to stay out of it. Because of them, I couldn't go after Vinny."

Montalvo's chin fell to his chest. He exhaled. "Reese, your home is fine. You detonated one old C4 charge that blew open a wall into another tunnel. Specialists removed a few other faulty charges. Otherwise, your house is fine. Just a messy living room with enough blood types to drive forensics wild, and an unregistered basement against code."

"What are you talking about?"

"If I was there alone, I'd have kept everyone out of your lair, or whatever you want to call it," Montalvo went on. "But it's all on record now. I'll tell the mayor... after he wins, but we won't be able to stop the press. At least I got that bag of evidence out. How sloppy can you be?"

"How the—what?"

Montalvo gave the duffel bag a light kick, and I regarded it with more than a cursory glance this time. It was Chuck's, the zipper opened a tad to allow me to see the piles of research notes and photographs inside. Years of work, trying to pin me as the Roach, dating back to even before I got shot.

"No... I..." My tongue swelled. I couldn't talk. My hand slipped and wheeled me straight to face a wall. I leaned on it, feeling like I was choking on a SuperBall. If the self-destruct hadn't worked as intended, that meant cops went crawling around my dusty lair like hungry spiders, plucking out evidence. Examining. Putting their grubby little hands all over everything.

"I told you we'd find a way to pin this all on you if you couldn't stay out of it." Montalvo leaned in and whispered in my ear. "'The Roach Strikes Back at the City That Forgot Him.' I can see the headlines now. Maybe they'll make a movie." He laughed. "I'm tired of all these films celebrating what men like you do. Time people see the real face of super*heroes*." He accentuated the second part of the word with a push to the side of my head.

In a fit of rage, I elbowed at him, but he was ready for it. Dodging left, he used his boot to upturn my wheelchair. I crumpled into the wall, then slumped down it. Sharp pain in my gut had me seeing stars again. No doubt from another stitch popping loose. I may have been numb from the waist down, but I could still feel the warm, fresh blood sticking against my shirt.

Lieutenant Montalvo towered over me, grinning and slapping his police baton in an open palm. No matter that there was a killer on the loose, it was time for him to get off. Time to finally put the Roach down like he'd failed to last time and prove his rise through the ranks wasn't a lucky break.

I pawed at the floor to try and prop myself up, but the polished concrete was too smooth and now, coated in my blood. Instead, I slid backward.

"José, he's out there," I said. "Do whatever you want to me, I don't care. But you call that ward and ask. He's after all of us, everyone mentioned in that research. You're in this, too."

Montalvo grabbed my wheelchair and flung it across the room. He knew the best way to face me. Flip me and get my torso on the far side, like an upturned turtle. I wished with all my heart that my legs would learn to kick again.

"I'm in this, thanks to you," he said. "I've got a girlfriend—a kid on the way. I'm sick of covering up this bullshit. Iron City is strong now. I'm not going down because the mayor has a soft spot for a damn vigilante. He pulled me off the streets. I won't let him ruin what we've built over you."

He stretched his neck and pulled down his collar, revealing a rose tattoo that I'd never seen before. He'd done an excellent job masking it to get through the academy, but I spotted the underlying symbol of the crowned 'R' and 'K' from one of my old rival gangs.

"I got out of that life," he said, tightening his grip on his baton. "And I'm not going back."

CHAPTER

EIGHTEEN

I reached the corner of the room, crawling on the ground. Nowhere else to go.

"What the hell did you do?" I asked Montalvo. "Did you tip Chuck off?"

"It's always about what everyone else did with you," he replied. "You know how many kids I rolled with in the Stacks got battered by you? Killed? Kids with every chance to make something of their lives like I have?"

"Sure. They just would have turned our city into a junkie cesspool first," I groaned. "Worse than it already is."

"We survived however we had to when the jobs left."

"Like you are now? Please. You traded in their colors for a new gang. You do this, you're only proving my point."

"We were smalltime. You wiped the River Kings out so worse motherfuckers could come in. Sell girls. Heroin. Crack. You paved the goddamn road for them. They didn't care about the neighborhoods, just ripping it all down."

"You don't get to choose who's worst," I said. "Bad is bad."

"And you don't get to choose who dies."

The Roach wasn't a talker, but I had to keep Montalvo going as I rifled through my weary, drug-addled brain for a way out of this. That's the thing with lies like the ones that forged the Garrity Act. Eventually, someone loses their nerve and spills.

"What will you tell Laura?" I asked.

Montalvo grinned. "That you wandered into traffic. Got squashed like a roach—"

His head snapped to the side, blood splashing onto the white walls like a Jackson Pollock painting. He didn't make a *thud* when he toppled over, the concrete was too thick. Another man stood behind him, and before Montalvo could make another move, the newcomer bashed his skull again. Then a third time.

My gaping eyes darted between the new man and Montalvo's twitching body. The newcomer lifted his head and wiped the blood off his cheek with the back of his hand.

Not a man. Vinny Statman. The way his bony cheeks cast a shadow down his face made him appear eternally hooded, but it was him. I wasn't insane.

He had his hair gelled back just like in the alley and wore a thousand-dollar suit that hung loose on his emaciated frame. His striped, yellow tie looked like a kid had done the knot. And in his right hand, he gripped Chuck's revolver, the handle now stained with Montalvo's blood.

"You know, I never thought I'd see him again," he said. He pressed a shiny loafer against Montalvo's cheek and tilted his face toward him. "Yeah, that's him, all right. You know, they really made me believe I'd done everything to myself. They really, really did."

"Vinny, you—"

I winced as he smashed Montalvo in the skull with his heel, spattering more blood and brain matter. I'd never been affected by brutality, but the room's emptiness seemed to heighten my senses. The way the sickening *crunch* reverberated. I could almost feel it in my own skull.

"Crap. I got these, brand new, from my old place. Owner won't miss them." Vinny snickered as he tucked the revolver into his belt, then crouched to wipe the blood off his shoe. He froze.

"Well, look what we have here," he said, each word lingering with delight. He moved to the duffel bag and gave it a kick, knocking out materials. "Good ol' Chucky said he had a gold mine buried under your house, but damn."

"What did he tell you?" I asked.

I eyed his gun, then Montalvo's. I needed to get one of them, assuming his was reloaded. Wasn't hard to find ammo in Harborside.

"Did you see all this?" he said as he rummaged through the bag. "Ah man, he had you pegged." Vinny's nightmare eyes went bright. He removed a sheet of paper from the bottom. "My Coalville admissions record! Signed by officer José Montalvo himself. The guy used his real name. Chuck must've grabbed a copy when he'd visited." He shook the paper at me, then let it fall into a puddle of José's blood.

I flattened my palms against the floor and steadied my body upright. I didn't have a good move, but I had to be ready. Montalvo's body had his gun. It was a small distance away, but it might as well have been a country mile. No shadows to hide in or furniture to hide behind—just empty space. Exposed.

"What did he tell you?" I repeated.

"He talked real fast after I found a picture of all this," Vinny said. "I barely had to ask. Made it pretty easy to know he wasn't the Roach. No, I met the Roach and he wasn't a talker. He was a growler."

"I know what you did to him!" I barked.

"See, a growler. Just. Like. You. And then, I remembered the way you looked at me back at your house, and it all clicked." He poked the side of his head. "The Roach gets to live a happy little life in a decent place while I'm off to the loony bin."

"I had no idea about that."

"Shut up!" He pointed his bloodied baton at me. "Just shut up. The doctors always wanted to talk, talk, talk at me. It's my turn."

His eye twitched. He licked his lips. If I kept pressing, I knew he'd kill me without a second thought, especially now that he seemed to know who I was. Looking back, I preferred being under Montalvo's watch. At least he had limits.

"Chuck told me everything," Vinny said. "When he came up to visit a few weeks back, I didn't even think he was real. But something he said made me start hiding my meds under my tongue."

He stared like he was waiting for me to invite him to continue. I didn't give him the satisfaction. He popped to his feet and twirled on the tip of his boot using José's slick blood.

"He told me the Roach did this to me. Nobody up there even thought you were real, but..." Vinny snickered. "Here you are. It's you." His laugh deepened as if I wasn't even in the room with him—like some sick joke played on repeat in his own perverted noggin.

I opened my mouth to say something, but he screamed at the top of his lungs, his voice cracking. "You took everything from me!" Saliva peppered my cheeks. He crept toward me, his fingers wriggling and eager to crush something.

"Do you want to see what you did?" he asked, reaching toward his pants zipper. "What they'd convinced me I did to myself?"

He got close enough to give one of my useless feet a kick. My legs splayed outward. Then he drew the revolver from his belt. He aimed it right between my legs, the scarred-up track marks along both his forearms plainly visible.

"Do you want to feel what I felt?" he asked, clicking the hammer. The thing was loaded, all right.

"Go ahead," I laughed. "I won't feel a thing."

He moved closer, shoving the gun right against my crotch and staring me square in the eyes. I locked in on his pulsing jugular. Just a little closer and I'd tear it out with my teeth. It takes a monster to slay one.

"No," he said, jumping back before I could make my move. He paced back across the room, murmuring to himself and treading right through Montalvo's blood without a care.

"That's right, you only pick on skinny girls," I said. "Pussy. Come here and finish it."

He whipped around and aimed at me, his dark eyes like two more barrels. But he didn't pull the trigger. Instead, he lowered the revolver and shook his head.

"That's no fun," he said. "Not at all. You'd miss the show."

"You sick fuck. How do you think this ends?"

"I don't know? Isn't that great, not to know?" He covered his mouth as if to hold in hysteria, then looked around. "This looks just like my empty room, but there's no curfew. No doctors with pills then water, pills then water."

Static suddenly crackled on Montalvo's police radio, causing Vinny to flinch and take aim.

"*Lieutenant Montalvo, you there?*" an officer on the other end asked. "*We've got a situation. Mister Hennessy was caught with powder in the bathroom. He's a big donor...*"

"Now it's a party," Vinny cackled before I could hear any more.

"They'll come looking for him," I said. "There's no way this goes that you get out alive. You killed a cop. You killed Chuck. You tied up and gagged an innocent girl!"

Learning that I'd seen his apartment didn't even seem to faze him.

"You think I care about that?" He swiped his hand down his face in exhaustion, stretching out his mouth and jaw. "I'm only here to meet all my old friends. So, c'mon now, I can't be late for Mister Mayor." He took a skip step toward my chair, lifted it upright, and rolled it into the wall beside me. "Or, well, I guess he's family now. Do I call him grandpa?"

My worst fears were realized. He'd gotten Chuck to tell him about Michelle. Anger burned through me, and I ignored another stitch popping as I dragged myself up against the chair.

"Is little Michelle out there?" he asked. I didn't answer, but his eyes sparkled. "She is, isn't she?" He licked his blood-covered fingers, then combed his gelled hair with the revolver. "How do I look? Anything in my teeth?"

"If you touch her..." I hadn't felt rage like this since that night in the alley. Maybe since even before that, since back in my foster home, the night Father went too far. I could have punched through the concrete, if only I could reach him.

Vinny took a step toward the now-open door, then pirouetted on his heel. "Wait. Can't forget all the family pictures!" He scooped up the duffel bag, then winked at me the same way I'd winked at Laura. Like he'd been watching all along.

"Hurry up, *Roach,*" he said as he vanished into the hall, his cackle echoing.

"Statman!" I yelled, pushing with all my might to climb back onto my chair. My body was a searing heap of failing muscles, and I just needed what was left of it to obey. Pain was irrelevant now.

"Get up," I told myself. "Get up, you sack of shit."

I pushed on the seat, triceps burning. One last burst of strength; that was all I needed. One last time getting up into my god-forsaken chair. But the more I pushed, the more my stomach threatened to rip open. Or maybe that was the seat's stitching tearing. Likely both.

Tears stung in my eyes. My throat constricted. My pulse pounded away in my temples and behind my ears, making it impossible to hear anything.

"Get up," I willed myself, wheezing. "Get. Up!"

My mind strained to keep fighting through the agony. The fires of rage erupted deep within me. They roared up and through me, dragging me back to the night they'd first consumed me.

A night worse than when those girls died, or when I first met Laura.

The night my own monster came to life...

I watched the whip crack against one of my foster brothers' backs. So many nights, it was me on the post against the back of the barn, earning punishment for anything mother and father saw fit. There was always someone on the post, whether they'd really done something wrong or not.

This time, the skin on the big bully who used to steal Steven's food split open. Red lines formed like hieroglyphics upon his back. It had been years since he messed with us, though I still couldn't help but feel a bit of satisfaction. Better him than me.

However, that's not what made it a particularly special evening. No. Every so often, the best helper around the property got rewarded with spending a night in the main house. Against all odds, my bunkmate Steven Dixon earned the honor.

I don't think his back could have taken another night on our stiff bunks. And I wasn't always there to protect him from the bigger kids. No matter how old we got, he still hadn't sprouted. More bullies came out of the woodwork to pick on him. Give him bruises. Steal his food. Pour shit into the fresh whip wounds along his back until he cried and slept under the bed.

Like in Iron City, I couldn't be everywhere all the time.

But not that night. Steven was getting a much-needed break from hell, rewarded for the long, grueling hours we'd put it on the fields. I was happy to give him all the credit. To quietly disappear into my shadows where I was comfortable. People were too scared to mess with me by then.

I'd never seen Steven so happy. A smile, ear-to-ear. He practically skipped up the trail to the main house. The other kids made fun of him, but fuck them. I was so happy for him. One night in paradise can make years in hell worth it. As a kid growing up in our home with no hope of escape until eighteen, that's the only way you can think.

A real meal would do Steven well, too. Help him grow just a little stronger. Anything was better than the gruel we all ate daily. At least they didn't feed it to us using troughs like the pigs, though, that might have been cleaner. And the barn smelled like pig shit anyway.

I'll admit, I got a little jealous watching him. Other kids got rewarded and went up to the main house, and I was glad for the extra space, but not Steven. Not my only friend. The only one of them worth talking to. He couldn't read either, but we used to look at the pictures in our comic book and imagine their worlds. We'd pieced it back together as best we could after his bully ripped it.

The big cities. The noble heroes. All that impossible stuff of dreams.

Looking at it alone wasn't the same. So, I hid it under my pillow, and I snuck out of the barn, shushing the cows on my way by. I scaled the main house using a lattice and checked through windows, one by one until I found Mother in a rocking chair in the sitting room of their master bedroom. A palatial suite to me. She spooned pie into her wrinkly gullet as she read a book with her black-and-white RCA tabletop television playing in the background, volume blasting.

I wondered if Steven got to try a slice of pie. I remember imagining what it smelled like. I didn't even know what flavors existed, but just something sweet to wash away the foulness of life. Or maybe it tasted as rotten as mother was.

Moving to the next window, the first thing I spotted were candles. A lot of them. On every ledge, every piece of furniture. Like they'd been planted for a satanic ritual.

Then I saw the luxurious king bed. I swear, it was big as the room our bunks were all lined up in. Steven lay on it, belly swollen from a lavish meal and pushing up the bottom of a shirt two sizes too small. His head rested on more pillows than I'd ever seen. We used sacks of wheat in the bunks.

He stared across the open-plan suite, struggling to watch the TV through Mother's head. We never got to watch television. Even a lousy view of that tube of imagined worlds was like seeing a dream come true. All the stories we invented to pass the time, brought to life. Better than a tattered comic book we couldn't read.

Mother cackled at some joke she read and scared me so much I nearly slipped. I caught my shoelace on the gutter, nearly snapping it. Even her laugh rang wicked. This was the woman who stared, silent and beady-eyed, as father cracked his whip on us.

I checked my footing, then returned to the window and pressed my face against the foggy glass. Steven wasn't alone. Father laid beside him across the gargantuan bed, above the covers, wearing nothing but underwear. His one hand rest atop his grotesque, hairy belly and the other slithered across the sheets toward Steven's pants. My friend winced as it went further, but he didn't stop it.

He couldn't stop it.

Father was heavy enough to crush him.

I froze, gawking in utter disbelief. There were no girls in the foster home—just fantasies. We had our ratty comic and the chesty heroine who arrived halfway through. Others had bullying. Others jerked off after dark. Anything to pass the years until eighteen meant being an orphan no longer mattered. We were thrown out to become decent members of a society that forced us here.

Steven froze, focusing on that TV across the room, no doubt imagining he was there instead. It didn't matter where. Anywhere else.

I wanted to scream at him to get up! But I couldn't summon the words. And every time I thought about breaking through the glass, the whip-scars along my back burned white-hot. Leaving the barn at night would earn me more lashings than I could imagine—a night in the pen with the snorting hogs, shit for a pillow.

Father's hand went further and further down Steven's pants, and I wished the candle flames would catch and burn him alive first, then mother, who stood to raise the volume on their TV so her husband's perversion wouldn't distract her from her book.

I wished I could save Steven, but I. Did. Nothing.

That night, I'd seen Father for who he truly was, and I vowed never to do *nothing* again. The next time they invited someone up, I made sure it was me, and I burned it all down. The main house, the farm, the barn—everything. I used mine and Steven's comic for kindling, and after that, I never saw any of them ever again.

I screamed, rage venting from deep within my soul as the memory flooded my senses.Pure anger powered me like a rocket—a chemical explosion through my veins. My muscles gave every ounce they had until I found myself back on my chair, ready for one last fight.

The bottom half of my shirt was wet with warm, slick blood. My arms felt as numb as my legs. However, pushing myself to chase after Vinny was as unconscious an act as walking had once been. Like riding a bike, they say, though, I'd never learned.

Vinny hadn't even bothered to take Montalvo's pistol. An oversight, or he just didn't care. I was stupid to have ever thought this was the work of a carefully patterned killer. Unlike most serial killers, Vinny was a hurricane, violently tearing toward the coast, with no soul knowing whether it would shift this way or that. Chaos headed for Laura and Michelle.

I yanked Montalvo's sidearm free and raced out into the hall. Vinny's bloody footprints led right back toward the party.

The event had picked up steam while Montalvo had been busy dying. The party was in full swing, guests filling every foot of space in the lobby, sucking down and dirtying the air with laughter, bumping elbows, spinning their exaggerated tales, eyes red from bumps in the bathroom.

Down where I was, I couldn't even see Garrity's campaign banner, only a forest of legs. Vinny's footprints tracked right into the cesspool, and nobody had even noticed. Laura's detestable boss flirted with some woman half his age, hand on her shoulder, crumbs in his mustache. None of them knew that a killer was among them, stalking prey like a tiger through the tall grass.

I propped up on my palms to try and see over them but was still way too short. I felt like a kid again, jostling to watch father whip a kid who'd done bad because... that's basically all the entertainment we had. As long as it wasn't Steven on the post.

Looking down, I remembered the gun I wish I'd had that night.

I raised it, shoved my finger through the trigger guard, and prepared to pull and send everyone into a frenzy that might slow down Vinny. A *crash* beat me to the punch. I'm not sure it was a gunshot, but it was damn loud. People squealed, instinctively ducking.

Then everyone ahead of me turned and stampeded for the exits, banging into each other, stumbling. Cops and security burst inside from their posts at the doors while I pushed into the surge of people, shouting, yelling. It was no use.

Bang. Bang. Two gunshots went off, followed by Vinny yelling, "Stop moving!"

Everyone crouched in fear and I got a straight view to the mayor's table, right below his oversized banner and American flag streamers. Vinny had blown two security guards away, and now had Garrity by the throat, revolver aimed at his temple.

Chairs around his table had overturned as people tried to flee. The flower arrangement that had been in the center of the white tablecloth now laid on the floor, shattered. Chuck's duffel bag of research was nowhere to be seen. How long had I been struggling to get back into my chair that Vinny had found time to ditch it? And where?

"You'll all miss the show," Vinny said with a nervous titter, reminding me where my attention needed to be.

Police around the building fought to enter the lobby, but Vinny had his back to a corner. They couldn't accomplish much except to hop on their radios and call for reinforcements. Idiots. Didn't they have anyone up on the mezzanine level? A quick glance upward answered me. A stream of blood ran under the railing, trickling down onto Garrity's banner.

"Who the hell are you?" Garrity asked, defiant as ever.

"Oh, you know who I am," Vinny said. "I helped design this palace."

"Dad!" Laura shrieked from where she was crouched on the floor, trying to put both the table and her body between Michelle and the threat. The moment Laura laid eyes upon Vinny, though, she knew. I couldn't see her face from where I was, but I could tell by the way her muscles suddenly tensed.

Her monster had returned.

The people in front of me rose a little taller, and my view was blocked.

"Laura, stay back," I heard Garrity say, his tone betraying him and revealing his fear. Maybe he did actually care about her. A smidge, at least.

"What he said!" Vinny shouted. "Nobody move, or I paint this pretty lobby red." His gaze swept from side to side. "You know, I recognize some of you. You remember getting lunch, Jim?" he asked one of the suits to my left.

The guy stayed face down as he shook his head.

"Of course not. I was nothing to you people!" He turned his head toward Laura. "But you..." He made a perverse sucking sound that had all the hairs on the back of my neck standing on end. "My, my, have you grown up. Of all the girls I've ever been with, you were my favorite."

"Get the fuck out of my way!" I barked at the crowd.

I shoved myself forward, powered by pure fury. I ran over feet, bashed legs, all while aiming my gun. Some security hireling tried to stop me, but I yanked his leg out from under him and bashed him in the head with the weapon's grip. He went out like a light.

A woman shrieked. I grabbed her dress and used it to propel me toward the mayor's table.

"Hey shithead, pick on someone who can fight back!" I barked as I broke through the last line of people.

"There you are!" Vinny exclaimed, ducking behind the mayor to avoid my aim. "Took you long enough."

I snuck a glance at Laura. He had her petrified. Unable to move. I'd seen that look in her eyes only once before, and she was probably seeing that night over and over. She squeezed Michelle so tightly I worried she might strangle the crying child. Benjamin Aurora cowered under the table, whimpering like a frightened pup.

"Let him go," I growled.

"Sir, stand down!" an officer ordered from across the crowd to my right, his aim moving between me and Vinny.

"Stand down!" another called out from behind.

"Don't shoot!" Garrity begged. "Nobody shoot!"

Vinny chuckled, looking at me. "This is priceless. After all you did for them, they still recognize you as well as they do me. Why don't you tell them who you really are, huh?"

I stayed silent and kept my sights trained. I was never the best with guns—I didn't practice enough—but would it really matter if I hit Garrity, too? Vinny was diminutive in comparison, able to hide his entire body, so it'd be a hell of a shot. But what if I missed and he panicked and shot Laura before anyone else hit him?

My trigger finger quivered. Guns and standoffs were complicated ordeals. It was why I preferred to never barge right into a conflict like this, as I had with the Bratva by the harbor—and we know how that turned out. I longed for my shadows.

"No?" Vinny said mirthfully. He fired off another round at the ceiling, then aimed right at an officer trying to sneak through the crowd. "Not another fucking step. Guns down. On the ground. Everybody in here, don't move, or I kill him and keep shooting."

"You won't make it out," I said.

"And?"

"Listen to him!" Garrity shrieked. "Lower your damn weapons. Everyone!"

All the armed guards present listened, except for me. Guests laid down on their bellies. Covered their eyes. I bet they wished they'd supported Darrell Washington now.

Garrity urged me with his tear-filled eyes to lower my gun, but I didn't listen. I held firm, ready to blow Vinny away the moment I got an opening. Vinny seemed energized by my disobedience.

"There, just us again," he said to me.

"Vinny? Vinny Statman?" said a voice from across the room. Mr. Beaulieu—Vinny's old boss—cut in. Somehow, I hadn't spotted his golden skin earlier. In a room where everyone wore black tuxes, this asswad was still dressed in all white like Jesus. Against Vinny's demands, he stood and earned the attention of the revolver. His much younger wife grabbed at his leg as he slowly wove his way toward Vinny. "Is that you?"

"Oh, hey boss," Vinny said, offering a curt wave. "I hoped you'd be here."

His wife still crying, the man continued forward. He had his chest puffed out like he thought he was invincible.

"It can't be..." the man said softly.

"How's the firm?" Vinny asked matter-of-factly. "This place looks amazing."

"Vinny, I—"

As his hand came up, Vinny fired, plugging his old boss in the stomach. Then he gawked down at his gun, mouth agape, fake-blinking as if it were an accident.

Beaulieu toppled back like a domino. Everyone around them screamed, his wife louder than anybody. She crawled to him, holding his wound, blood gushing over her hands while others tried to pass her cloth napkins.

"Help!"

Her shriek shifted my attention from Vinny momentarily. It was a reflex, like I was a dog who'd heard 'treat.' That sound was the Roach's bat signal. My calling. The same kind that drew me to Laura in the alley.

"I told nobody to move!" Vinny barked, sweeping his aim to silence all the patrons. Even the guard hurrying to help Mr. Beaulieu halted. "He never was a good listener."

I bit back a curse and took aim again. "Garrity, I can hit him," I said.

"No!" Garrity cried, then tried to glance back at Vinny. "W-what do you want? I'll give you whatever you want. J-j-just drop the weapon and leave."

"You can't give me my life back, can you? Can you!" Vinny

pushed the gun harder against the mayor's jaw, angling his head uncomfortably. The crowd gasped in fright.

"N-n-no. But it's not too late. You're y-young, you—"

"Do you know what they did to me after you signed me away?"

Garrity swallowed the lump in his throat. His lips parted, but no words came out.

"They made me believe I'd mutilated myself, cut my own cock off," Vinny said for him. "Told me I was insane, deranged, over and over again as they pumped me numb." He nodded toward his bleeding-out boss. "I was gonna be partner, and he didn't even send me flowers. The asshole. Well, look at me now. I've come all this way, and there she is."

He pointed the gun across the table at Michelle. I shifted, hoping for an opening to arise, but unable to find one. Or I hesitated, I don't know. My mind was compromised.

"My daughter," he whispered, on the verge of choking up. "The only child I'll ever have." The people nearest enough to hear let out muted gasps. Murmuring broke out at my back.

"Who's insane now?" Vinny asked. He rammed the mayor into the table and the metal legs *screeched,* eliciting a slew of frightened sounds from the crowd. Benjamin Aurora looked like he was going to shit himself. By the smell of things, he wasn't the only one. Michelle kept crying, all I could see was her shoulders heaving. The rest of her remained pressed tight against Laura, who remained absolutely frozen.

I knew the feeling—watching your nightmares come to life, all while stuck outside the window. Weak. Helpless.

"Give our girl a spin then," Vinny said, wagging his gun at Laura. "Let me have a look at her."

"No," Laura replied, sounding broken. The powerful woman I loved, completely undone by a disgusting piece of excrement who didn't deserve to share her air.

"If you get anywhere near either of them," I said. "I'll put a bullet through both of you."

"Did you hear that, Mister Mayor?" Vinny asked. He pinched Garrity's cheeks. "Where's his loyalty?"

"Reese, stop this!" Garrity begged through whimpers, eyelids squeezed shut.

"I don't give a shit about him," I said.

"*We have the building surrounded!*" an officer shouted over a speaker horn from outside, volume as high as it could go. Red and blue lights flashed everywhere outside the glass of the lobby. Cruisers raced up, sirens blaring. SWAT would be next.

The mayor's entire army was on its way. I'm not sure what statement Vinny was trying to make, if any, but it was a pretty damn loud one. A stripper and a shopkeeper brutally slain in Harborside, he barely cracked the news. Aim a gun at a mayor? It all came crashing down.

Maybe that's what he wanted. To show how powerful he was like he used to with young women. Or maybe he was just a man put through hell, lashing out against everything and everyone in the world who had banished him. What would I know about that?

"End of the line, Vin," I said.

"Shut up!" Vinny hissed at the glass across the lobby, as if they could hear him. "This is between us."

"Y-you're right," Garrity said. "You're right. I-I-I destroyed your life, but I can make you rich."

"It's always money with you people. I don't want your money. I just wanted to meet my family." He turned with Garrity, facing Laura directly. His gaze fell toward Michelle. "Don't you want to want to meet your daddy? Mine was never there for me."

Michelle slowly peeled her face away from her mother's dress and looked back. Hair clung to the tears coating her rosy cheeks. Naivety took hold of her, just like it had with that damn SuperBall that had sent us hurtling down this path. 'Daddy' was the one thing she'd never had, and she appeared equal parts scared and curious.

"She's nothing to you!" Laura snapped, pulling Michelle's head back against her body.

"Nothing?" Vinny replied, cheeks flushing. "Nothing? I know everything, you bitch. How you stole her from me. Erased me!"

"Better than you deserved," I spat.

"She's mine!" He edged around the table toward Laura, squeezing Garrity's throat tight enough that the Mayor couldn't get clear words out. Laura's muscles seized the closer he got. Her nostrils flared. Benjamin Aurora slinked back further. Coward. A rich boy with show muscles, that's all he was.

"Just let me look into her eyes," Vinny proposed. "Let her decide."

Laura held Michelle's head tighter.

"Stop," I threatened.

He held back a snicker and regarded me. "Look at you. You think because you were there that night, she's yours, too? You do, don't you?" This time, his titter snuck through. "Chuck was right; you're crazier than I ever was."

"Not. Another. Step."

"You know what, why don't you tell them? That'll be fun. Tell everyone who you really are. Tell them why you care."

My throat went suddenly dry. I thought I could hear louder murmuring from the terrified, prostrate crowd—all of them imagining their little stories, trying to put together the pieces of this crazy showing. At least we were giving them their money's worth.

"What's wrong?" Vinny asked, sneering. "Are you scared? You are. That cop didn't just take your legs, did he? He took your manhood too. I guess we really aren't too different. I killed him for both of us."

"Get away from them," I demanded, barely above a whisper. He stood right behind Laura now. Her entire body quaked in his presence once more.

"I'm s-so sorry," Garrity croaked. "I'm so sorry."

Vinny turned the mayor to block my line of fire and extended his gun down to stroke the side of Laura's cheek. She closed her eyes, shivering in fear. Michelle tried to peek up, but Laura reeled her back in. I stared at Laura until she opened her eyes again, then drew her focus to me.

"Does the girl know?" Vinny asked. "Did surrogate daddy tell her who he really is?"

I didn't speak, just kept holding Laura's gaze. This time, I had no mask on to hide myself. Laura could see straight into my soul and I into hers. I imagined all the things I wished I could tell her, hoping that might be enough to keep her present with me. To help her find her strength again in the face of her monster. Her strength, that kept me going.

"I'll tell you what, Reese," Vinny continued. "Tell her. Tell all of them who you really are, and I'll let them go. I'll blow my own brains all over this fancy table."

I swallowed the knot in my throat, said nothing. The very thought of it made me itch everywhere. My heart was already racing a-mile-a-minute, but sweat started pouring down my back. The crowd all looked to me, judging me, wondering the truth.

Laura's melancholy eyes kept me from exploding. All those shades of green and gold. I concentrated on them, striving to dull the rest of our rotten world. To feel safe.

"What are you afraid of?" Vinny asked.

"He's the—" Garrity started before Vinny cut off his airway.

"No, he has to say it! He's the hero, isn't he? The one who saved Iron City from people like me. Who saved pretty, rich girls like her while the rest of us starved." He cackled like a maniac.

I breathed slowly. In through my nose, out through my mouth. And I kept staring at those windows into Laura's soul, just as I stared through the window of father's bedroom. God, did I want to say it. I'd already done it with Clarice. Who even cared anymore? I'd broken the seal.

With every fiber of my being, I wanted to say it. Yet, every time my lips parted, it felt like I'd swallowed a wad of cotton. The scars on my back burned and the fresh gash in my stomach stung. The pain pills may as well have never existed. Maybe they were why I was able to tell Clarice in the first place. Drug-enhanced bravery. That was cheating.

"Do it," Vinny said. "Tell them."

Laura could've urged me to do it with a nod. With a look. She didn't. She merely held me with her gaze as I held her. And in that moment, after five years, I finally felt like we understood each other. Fear has a special way of doing that. Doesn't the lion know the gazelle best as it sinks its teeth into its throat?

I'd seen Laura in her purest form of terror the night Vinny took her, but she'd never seen me unveiled. Not really. The Roach couldn't be seen. But I could, and she saw it then. And you know what?

Fuck all these people.

Fuck Father and Mother and all those bullies I grew up with who deserved the home.

Fuck a city that didn't give a shit.

Fuck fear.

I was the mother fucking Roach.

I looked at Vinny, a grin touching the corners of my lips. My pulse slowed. "You want the fucking truth?" I asked.

Vinny's eyes went wide with fear as he realized his promise was about to be put to the test.

Oh yeah, fuck him most of all.

"The truth is," I said. "I'm the fucking Roach. I'm the man who neutered you like the uncaged animal you are."

At the same time, the idiot outside shouted into the bullhorn, drowning me out so the crowd couldn't hear my words. "*I repeat, you are surrounded*! *Release the hostage and come out with your hands up*!"

Vinny grinned and whispered, "Too late."

His arm shifted, trigger-finger tensing.

I did the only I could. I fired.

He turned and the bullet hit Garrity somewhere between shoulder and neck as everyone in the lobby wailed like scared hogs.

Vinny crouched, dragging Garrity with him, and yanked hard on the campaign banner. One side of it fell, something heavy fastened to the end swinging down through the atrium. Chuck's duffel bag slammed down on the table, its bloodied contents streaming down behind it.

I couldn't risk firing again, not with Laura and Michelle in my line of fire. Scared bodies jostled me from every side as the crowd ignored Vinny's commands, fear morphing into mindless panic.

"Mommy!" I heard Michelle scream.

I rolled right, trying to clear the paper and saw Vinny trying to rip her out of Laura's arms.

"She belongs to me!" he yelled.

Laura held on like a lioness, but Vinny pistol-whipped her and pried Michelle loose. Benjamin Aurora finally grew a pair and lunged at him. He received a swift kick in the groin. Vinny chortled as the billionaire folded like a million-dollar bill, moaning.

I aimed, but where I might have risked a shot with Garrity's life hanging in the balance, I couldn't with Michelle. Vinny didn't wait to see if I had the gumption to try it, delving into the sea of party-guests.

"Mommy!" Michelle shrieked repeatedly as Vinny carried her, kicking and screaming. Her small voice was lost in the pandemonium.

Security fought to reach the mayor. "Not me!" Garrity groaned, clutching his shoulder. "Go after her! Get my granddaughter!"

"We need an ambulance at Aurora Tower," one of the guards said into his radio. "Two men have been shot, including the mayor. I repeat, the mayor has been shot."

I raced toward Laura. Benjamin Aurora sat nearby, cupping his balls with one hand, looking at us, and making only the slightest effort to reach for Laura.

"Pathetic," I said to him as I moved in front. Shame rippled across his handsome features.

I took Laura's hand even though she was already mostly up on her own and helped her the rest of the way. She spit out a glob of blood before we exchanged a look that said it all.

"You shot me. You son of a bitch," the mayor cursed, then swore in pain.

"He'll be fine," I said.

Laura nodded, kicked off her heels, and darted toward the exit before security could get to her. I spun to follow her. My wheels flattened pages of Chuck's research as I went, all laid bare for all to see. It made me hesitate. Most of it was circumstantial, but I hadn't even taken the time to look through. Chuck had Vinny's psych-ward admission papers for God's sake.

He really hadn't been a bad reporter—found out the truth about Vinny's fate while I remained ignorant even. His parents probably would've been proud.

Why did I care? He'd done this to himself with his lies. Still... uncovering one last truth was at least a noble way to go out. Dying for the truth.

And seeing the notes and photos fall across the lobby like snowflakes forced me to see the truth, myself. Cops rifling through my lair plus his research, Vinny's rampage, a pissed off mayor who I'd shot—my secret was certainly out.

The Roach was unshelled, and it didn't matter. I could have laughed. It didn't fucking matter... it couldn't have mattered less. Right now, all that mattered was having Michelle back safe. In fact, like with Clarice, the very fact it was out had me feeling lighter as I propelled my chair along. Weightless. Reese Roberts had never moved so fast.

Laura did most of the work of clearing us a path. How could I compete with the fury of a mother scorned? She shoved her boss out of the way and sent him tumbling through spilled champagne, half-ripped the dress from a society matron who got in her way. She was a wrecking ball, and I trailed in her path, yelling like an idiot.

Another gunshot rang.

Vinny had avoided the crammed exit and proved that even the glass in a building this expensive wasn't bulletproof. He glanced back at us before ducking his head and leaping through the shattered glass, probably slicing Michelle up as he squeezed her squirming body under one arm.

"*Drop the child, now*!" I heard over the bullhorn. Like telling a crazed murderer to do that has ever worked.

Laura sped farther ahead of me. I fought with all my might to keep up, popping a wheelie to get over the window frame and through jagged glass edges that at least couldn't hurt the cheap solid tires on the hospital wheelchair. She stopped outside on the sidewalk, bathed in the red and blue of police lights. If I thought it was loud in the lobby, this was exponentially worse.

Reaching Laura, I looked left with her. Vinny was down at a corner, spinning and waving his gun as he held Michelle. Her tiny feet swung this way and that, shoes flung off.

Cops were everywhere. SWAT rolled up across the street. With a child hostage, nobody could do a thing to him.

"Get back!" Vinny yelled at an officer using his cruiser for cover. "Get the fuck back!"

He aimed at the man while moving around the hood of the vehicle. The officer did as demanded, and Vinny slid into the driver's seat. Michelle beat at his chest with her fists, but she was too small. Helpless.

I knew the feeling.

Vinny peeled out in a cloud of burnt rubber and spraying water, Michelle on his lap. One officer shot at the back tire, missed, and was promptly yelled at for firing at a hostage and with so many bystanders around. Others poured back into their vehicles, ready to give chase.

I grabbed Laura's dress and directed her toward the cruiser nearest to us. An overweight cop lumbered his donut-filled body out of cover on the other side of it, but I rolled off the curb, held my chair from tipping, and skidded up to him.

"We're taking this." I aimed my gun at his chest, before noticing the tag said "Dennard." My old pal who was there the day Isaac's bullies had ratted me out and Michelle had almost been crushed by a speeding mail truck. Like some sick poetry, he was here now, just as he had been at the start of all this.

"You?" he said, incredulous. His hand fell toward his holster.

"I wouldn't," I growled.

"He took my daughter," Laura said as she rushed behind me toward the driver's seat

"Get the door," I told the poor sap.

Dennard gawked at me. No weary cop that looked like him got out of bed wanting to be caught in a high-stakes gunfight.

"You really are him?" he asked softly.

"Wanna find out?" I said.

His throat bobbed, then he stepped aside for me.

The cruiser's back door swung open, and I used the laundry hook to heave my body inside. As my ass slid along the fabric, I grabbed my wheelchair. I barely had time to pull it in let alone more than half fold it before Laura hit the gas. We lurched forward, the door whacking the poor officer on our way by. She whipped into a turn, and the door squeezed the chair against me as it slammed all on its own.

"I'm going to kill him!" Laura said through her teeth.

"We'll get him," I replied. I doubted she heard me.

More cop cars zipped by as Laura pressed the accelerator to the floor and sent us barreling down Main Avenue. I worked on freeing my arms from being crushed against a wheel while watching Laura's determined face in the rearview mirror.

It wasn't the best time to get sentimental, but... I'd never been prouder.

CHAPTER NINETEEN

Laura swerved through traffic, the wipers shedding rainwater like a dog in spring. I think our sirens blared, though it could have been all the other cops. It was like her mommy-strength transferred into the car's engine as it roared, and we sped by everyone who'd had a head-start. Or maybe it was just she took chances no one else dared.

I slid right across the backseat, smashing into the cruiser's door. Then back left, my head whacking my squished wheelchair.

"Hold it steady!" I shouted, grasping hold of the door handle to try and stay put.

"How is he alive?" Laura demanded. Her voice trembled with anger. "Dad told me he was gone for good."

"You knew who he was?"

"He promised Michelle would never have to know."

She whipped the car around a slowpoke. Our police scanner was hot with activity, all the pursuers calling out street names and unit numbers to help keep track.

I peered around the edge of the passenger seat. Vinny was far up the block, weaving around cars by using sidewalks. People dove out of the way, a man on a bicycle even flipping over his hood. A police cruiser pulled up alongside him, but Vinny stuck his gun out and fired, sending the cop swerving into a newsstand. I could only imagine Vinny's cackle at the sight of the explosion of newspapers and magazines.

"Yeah, well, honesty isn't really his thing, is it?" I said.

My stomach roiled. Cars weren't *my* thing, especially at these speeds. Or maybe my wound had torn fully open, and that was the sensation of guts spilling out of me.

"I've always been afraid," Laura said. "Every time she tells a fib or breaks something, that it's his darkness in her. That she might be capa—"

"She's not," I interrupted before she dared go there. "I know rotten kids, and Michelle's not one."

"But if he—"

"She's. Not," I said, stern. "Just keep on him, Laura. He's not taking her. He's not hurting her. All that bastard is going to do tonight is die."

Laura didn't answer, just nodded. Her fingers went corpse-white as she squeezed the steering wheel and kept on driving.

We zoomed by another cruiser. The passenger's brow knitted when he looked over and saw Laura driving. She left him in our dust, gaining ground on Vinny. In happier news, if being a lawyer didn't work out, she had a future in NASCAR. The things you learn about people in times of strife—that's the spice of life.

Vinny made a sudden right turn as we approached, and Laura cut the wheel hard. Our back tires skidded out, and our trunk bashed into a blue, public mailbox.

Laura muttered a curse I didn't know she even knew, then wrenched the wheel back and sent us swerving forward in pursuit. Two other cruisers collided, one flipping. I could hear the metal *crunch* even through our closed windows.

"He's heading toward Harborside!" Laura called back.

"Keep on him."

Vinny may have seemed like he had a plan. He didn't. He wasn't in control, I'm not even sure he had what he wanted. A guy like him? He didn't want a kid, but now he was all adrenaline. In flight mode, clinging to the last insane idea hatched in his insane mind.

More police cruisers joined the chase, shooting down every street we passed. Vinny turned this way and that, leading a labyrinthian route through the Stacks' rundown and vacant buildings, nearly flattening more than a dozen homeless men just trying to make it to the next day. A smashed fire hydrant went up like a watery mushroom cloud as he turned down Fisher Blvd. into Harborside, smashing the side of his car against a column for the city's light-rail. It helped straighten him out, sending him on a beeline toward Horton Point.

Somehow, Laura managed to keep pace. Most of the cops couldn't, though they had the benefit of a chopper according to the busy police scanner. I leaned and glanced up through the window, beyond a slew of boarded-up businesses and cracked brick, spotting the thing hovering far above.

"Hit the gas, Laura," I directed. "They can't surround him first."

I didn't bother saying why. She didn't need to hear that. A man in Vinny's state, surrounded by cops with a gun, a child, and no way out. I wished the thought hadn't crossed my mind, but the darkest ones always did. Michelle, dead on the floor alongside her father, both their heads blown open in one final act of familial solidarity.

"I'm trying," Laura answered.

"Try harder!"

She clutched the wheel even tighter and turned us into oncoming traffic as a delivery truck turned onto the street ahead of us. I winced as an old Pinto *thrummed* by. Laura knocked the side view mirror of a parked vehicle before swerving us back into our lane. We were far ahead of all the others now—the tip of the spear—only a handful of car-lengths behind Vinny.

"That work for you?" Laura asked.

"Getting there."

Recovering from my position scrunched under the handles of my overturned wheelchair thanks to her crazy—yet impressive—driving,

I pulled myself to the door. It wasn't easy to hold on without legs keeping me grounded as I rolled down the window. My left arm threatened to tear from its socket. But I got it lowered three-quarters of the way—enough to get my head and arm out and take aim. Freezing rain pelted my face and forced me to squint.

"Don't you dare shoot at her!" Laura yelled.

"I just need him to see me," I called back.

That was all. Vinny may have been Laura's monster, but I was his —well, one of them. Who knows how his father was. But for all Vinny's bluster and chaos, *I* was the one who'd turned him into the Castrated Man. Trademark pending on the name.

He stuck his arm out and blind-fired back at us. One bullet slashed through the passenger side of the windshield. Laura squealed and ducked, nearly losing control. She laid off the gas a bit.

"He's fucking shooting as us!" she shouted.

"Get me closer!" I instructed.

"Are you insane?" Laura answered. She stayed low, barely peering over the dash.

"Do it!"

She raised up a little and accelerated. I clutched the side of the car to keep steady.

"I took your advice, by the way," I said, or shouted. The sirens, gushing air, and police chatter had us yelling no matter what.

"What?"

"I talked to someone. Told them the truth."

"Oh yeah?"

Back into traffic we swerved in order to gain ground.

"You were right though. It felt... nice. She didn't run for her life."

Laura laid into the horn to scare people who were descending the stairs at a light-rail stop. Vinny wasn't so kind and nearly pulverized them.

"Reese, this isn't really the time!"

A fair point. She had us right on Vinny's tail now. I could see the back of his filthy head through his rear windshield, a mess of long hair flowing in and out of view as Michelle bumped up and down on his lap. Using my second hand, I held my wrist and braced myself to look down the sights of my pistol. Maybe I could hit a wheel.

"I'm proud of you, though," Laura added.

Words to make the heart of an old wretch like me feel full. Words I'd never heard before. Mother and Father certainly hadn't said them to anybody. I held my fire. What would hitting a wheel accomplish besides potentially sending the car flipping and break every bone in Michelle's body, if not killing her?

I had to be smart. Not rush it.

Laura was proud, and I was going to live up to that.

She drove us closer, until our front bumper bumped Vinny's fender. He fired back at us again, clipping one of the cruiser's side mirrors. This time, Laura barely flinched.

Oh, what a Team Roach I could've built. With her, and Isaac—we could've saved this city without selling our souls to outsiders like good ol' Mayor Garrity.

"The street ends in a few blocks!" Laura shouted, panicked.

I snapped back into to focus and looked ahead. We blew by my block, though I caught a glimpse of the caution tape in front of my still-standing stoop. Tinman stood on the corner, the wind blowing up his shimmering robe as he turned to watch us.

Ahead, the harbor loomed. Seeing me on his tail had Vinny pushing his ride so fast, there was no way out. We'd reach Horton Ave, running parallel to the river, and he'd have to choose left or right. The helicopter was already ahead of us hovering over the intersection. Maybe a dozen cop cars raced down the street at our backs.

I wish I could say I had a plan; some stealthy attack out of the shadows like in the good old days. I didn't. All I could do was stare into Vinny's dark green Chrysler LeBaron as Laura kept ramming him, close enough now that when he glanced back in the rearview, we made eye contact. I held his frightened eyes. Not blinking, not wavering, feeding his subconscious fear as our race toward nothing came to its inevitable conclusion.

Horton Ave arrived. He looked away and tried to turn too late. The wheels gave out, and he spun, crunching through a hotdog stand and onto Horton Point—once busy with shipments from up the great river, now a slab of concrete riddled with rusty shipping containers, abandoned factories, and a few active docks.

"Michelle!" Laura screamed as his car went into a mad spin.

I pulled myself inside the car right before she hit the brakes and caused me to nail my head on the back of the passenger seat. The gun slipped from my hands and fell forward under the passenger seat. We swerved a few times as she tried to hold us steady after bouncing over a low divider.

Rubbing my head, I noticed Vinny's car skid to a stop when the driver's side of it slammed against a shipping container, smoke pouring out from under the hood. Vinny pulled himself through the shattered windshield, squeezing up over the hood.

Michelle was slung over his shoulder like a bale of hay. The impact had probably knocked her out because she bobbed weightlessly. Vinny yanked his leg free, lost one shoe, then staggered to his knees through a puddle. He glanced back at us, then sprinted toward a derelict car factory to the east.

I couldn't think of another crime that got so much attention in Iron City. Even for the Bratva and their girls, I'd have been lucky to get a cop, maybe two called in, all while having to hope one wasn't corrupt. But this was the granddaughter of Iron City's savior. She deserved it. I'd call Superman in to help with this one if I could.

Laura was out of our car before it even came to a full stop. I shouted her name, but seeing Vinny with her daughter had her deaf from rage. She took off after them, bare, bloody feet slapping against the cracked concrete.

I punched open my door and fell out wrapped half around the wheelchair. I ignored the impact—what's one more ache?—and flipped the chair fully open. Grabbing the corners of the seat, I pushed up until my elbows locked. A twist at the shoulders and I spilled down onto it, yanking my feet up onto the footplates.

My whole shirt was stained red now. And my gun was gone.

Glancing right, I spotted it in Laura's possession. Vinny hauled Michelle through a rusty door, into the shadows of the factory. Police cars approached from Lancaster Blvd, and more raced down Horton Ave from either direction. The buffering *wump* of the helicopter's blades drowned out their sirens.

I grabbed hold of my wheels and launched my chair forward. The wind blew through my thinning hair as I zipped across the concrete. It felt like I was sprinting down tunnels and leaping across rooftops again. Well, except that one of my wheels was now misaligned, and the chair lurched with every full rotation. Damn cheap hospital chairs.

"Laura, don't!" I called out to her.

She didn't listen, following him inside. I could imagine the deafening pulse throbbing in her ears, her blood boiling over. I knew that blinding, overwhelming anger. I'd felt it on this very harbor, on a warehouse just around the corner when I'd chosen getting off on dealing justice over saving girls who'd never asked or wanted to be here.

Gunshots went off inside the factory—strobe lights in the darkness.

"Laura," I whispered.

I pushed harder across the slick concrete, heading straight for the door. Cops arriving behind me barked orders, but now I was as blind to the rest of the world as Laura. My wheels bumped the door at full speed, swinging it open and nearly throwing me out of my chair.

A big, dark, empty factory greeted me. Frozen conveyor belts crossed this way and that along with machinery untouched for years. I coughed in the cloud of dust shaken free by my entrance. When I could finally inhale, the stink of rust mixed with low tide assaulted me.

I heard Laura scream from deeper in the factory, "Let go of her!"

Then another gunshot. A *clang* of metal.

I rushed toward the sound. All I could do was grit my teeth and brush some dusty flaps aside. I rolled around the other side of an assembly line, to an open space with tall windows alongside the water. I wouldn't call it a break room, though I suppose that's where the employees used to take breaks. Even the tables hadn't been left behind. Only more dust and trash left behind by junkies and homeless.

Laura aimed at a column holding up second-floor offices. Blood was spattered on the floor. Vinny was behind it, holding Michelle with one hand over her mouth to muffle her cries. She was conscious again.

"I'll blow her fucking brains out if you come any closer!" he yelled.

Laura stood to my left, aiming the gun like a trained pro. Steady as a surgeon.

"It's over, Vinny!" I shouted, voice echoing across this metal ruin of my city's golden age.

He unleashed a shrill, bloodcurdling laugh. "There's nothing either of you can take from me now. But I can take sooo much from you."

"Yeah?" I said. "Then you look Michelle in the eyes and you do it."

"Reese!" Laura whisper-shouted at me.

I shot her a look that said, "Trust me," without waiting for confirmation before I turned back toward Vinny. I had to believe she would.

Slowly, I rolled toward him and said, "Be just like your own father when he beat the shit out of you every night after he got home drunk."

"You don't know anything about me!"

"I know everything about you."

Vinny peered around the column, moving with Michelle, and aiming his revolver at me from beside her ear. Tears poured down her cheeks, but seeing me quieted her. She stared at me with her mother's pretty, hazel eyes.

I kept rolling toward them. "We're built from the same shit, you and me," I said. "Killers. Addicts. You think I saved the people of this city because I cared? Listen, Statman, I ran out of fucks to give long before you even thought to put your little pecker inside an unwilling woman."

"Shut up!" Vinny shouted.

"I did it all for me."

Laura'd told me to talk to people, so I kept doing it. Letting the truth roll out of me, because why the hell not? It took me a lifetime to learn that, sometimes, the best plan is listening to someone else's advice.

"*Perimeter secured,*" I heard through an echoing radio. The sounds of movement from officers outside the factory spooked Vinny. But they couldn't make a move on us with Michelle still at gunpoint.

"Don't look at them," I said. "Look at me. Look at the guy who tore you to pieces in that alley because he saw himself in you and couldn't stand it."

"You think I wanted this?!" Vinny screamed at the top of his lungs. Michelle cringed and returned to crying and squirming. He tightened his grip.

"You think I did?" I stopped only a few feet away from them. In my peripheral vision, I saw more movement outside the factory. Time wasn't on my side. "But here we are, two men, tossed in the trash. *We* destroyed our lives. Not her. Not Laura. You and me."

Vinny stepped out from behind the column, toward one of the windows along the water. Laura shifted her feet, aiming higher. Police radios chattered.

"Let go of her, you piece of shit!" Laura threatened.

"I waited so long for this," Vinny said, all the former glee in his tone now absent. He peered up through the window, no doubt seeing the damn noisy chopper, forcing me to shout at him while attempting to speak from the heart.

"No," I said. "You've been waiting for somebody to take you seriously. To believe you're as powerful as you are. That's it. Anybody to show you that you deserve to live on this rock."

"What, and she does?" He gestured at Laura with the gun. My heart skipped a beat. In my concern over Michelle, I'd forgotten that he could easily shoot Laura. "In her fancy dresses and shoes? She was asking for it. They all were."

"More than us, yeah," I replied, moving slightly to be more directly in the path between them. "So, do it. You put that girl down and you put a bullet right here." I tapped my own chest.

His eyes darted from me, to Laura, and to all the shadows skulking about outside, waiting for an opening. How many of them out there wanted to be the next Lieutenant Montalvo? Desperate to take a shot and be the cop who saved Michelle Garrity, no matter the cost.

No. I couldn't have that.

"C'mon," I said, tapping hard to keep Vinny's frenetic attention. "Let's end the fucking nightmare and see what's on the other side, huh? See where monsters go."

Vinny slowly turned Michelle's head and gazed into her terrified eyes. He held her there for a few seconds that, to me, felt like an eternity, the gun against her head. I wondered what he saw in there before he looked back to me, shifting to aim at my chest as he slowly lowered her to the floor.

"There you go," I said. "Just you and me."

A sinister smile wriggled across Vinny's face as she touched down. Without releasing her completely, he said, "Goodbye, Roach.

His revolver went off. Two shots fired.

Vinny's head whipped to the side as he took a bullet to the head, disrupting his aim. I patted my unharmed chest and caught a glimpse of Laura, gun smoking.

Quite a shot, with her daughter's life hanging in the balance. And then, my weary mind reminded me of all the times she told me she was going to the gun range and I'd barely paid attention. It all clicked.

My Laura wasn't going there to relieve stress. She was going to feel powerful. To learn to face her demons.

"Mommy!" Michelle cried, running to her the moment she got free.

Police chatter amplified as they burst in from every side, swarming us. At the same time, Vinny's hand shot out, grasping Michelle by the back of her hair. He still clutched his revolver. And as much as I wanted Laura to be like me—to understand me—she was an unpolished product. She'd hit him in the ear, amputating another part of him, but not killing him.

Vinny Statman's haunting laughs filled the warehouse as he rose, a screaming Michelle right in front of him. Police everywhere demanded he drop her.

I didn't hesitate. My calloused hands were already pushing on my pushrims before I sorted out the details, and as he tried to aim at me around Michelle, I rammed into him.

Michelle fell free as he stumbled back into the oversized window, breaking what was left of the glass. My wheelchair hit the brick wall beneath it and flung me into him, pitching us both through the opening and onto a ledge where he smashed his head with a sickening crack. We rolled over the narrow ledge of the pier and into the Horton River.

The strong current heaved at me, and I lost my grip of Vinny's throat as he tumbled head over heels in the murk. Blood spiraled out from my leg where, apparently, Vinny had shot me.

I pulled down with my hands, reaching for the surface. My arm muscles were too weak without legs to help them. I was too disoriented.

So, I stopped fighting it. Let go. This was what I'd wanted, wasn't it? When I went to the edge of the harbor in the shadows of my biggest failure and prepared to roll myself in. To put a stamp on the final chapter of the legend of the Roach myself.

I'm so glad I didn't. There were still a few people in Iron City who'd needed saving...

NINE MONTHS LATER

TWENTY

"How did you get out of the river?"

I lean back in my chair and take a deep breath. "The Tinman had followed us, saw me go in. Strong current that day, deadly, but man could he swim. He had to ditch his clothes, though, and I spotted the Semper Fi tattoo on his arm. Ex-Marine Corps." I chuckle.

"What's so funny?"

"People." I sit forward. "Do you know what he said to me after he dragged me out? I was coughing and bleeding, barely able to see. Pathetic. There was so much water in me, doc, I was this close to dying, but you can't kill a Roach, can you? If I've learned anything, it's that. I bet if someone dropped a nuke right on this prison, I'd come rolling out, covered in your ashes."

Doctor Dan shifts uncomfortably in his seat. He continues staring down at his notebook, glasses on the end of his beak. He tries to remain expressionless, but I can tell when I'm under his skin. I'd gone through two court-appointed prison psychologists already, and it took Dan months to get me talking. But like Laura had thought, it felt all right. I'd learned that there were a rare few people I could stand talking to. Didn't mean I couldn't have fun with it, though.

"What did *Tinman* say?" Dan asks. He says it with a skeptical tone, like I'm some lunatic telling tall tales. Whatever.

"He asked if I was hit," I say. "For one fleeting moment, I saw the man he used to be. A young, ambitious kid, probably, who got sold a bill of goods and went off to lose his sanity in a jungle—in a war he never imagined he'd fight until he was ass deep in it."

"And how did that make you feel?"

There it was. That excruciating question all these shrinks always leaned on. Man, does it irk me that it sort of works. Nobody ever asks that out in the real world, not until it's too late to matter, at least.

"Honestly, like I wasn't alone," I say.

Dan folds his spiral notebook and steeples his hands across his lap. "Thank you for telling me that story."

I grunt.

"I just have one question. In your file, it says you fed Chuck Barnes false information to craft a conspiracy to incriminate Eugene Garrity and get revenge on him for taking credit for saving Iron City. You said you forged documents, stories, everything to convince Chuck Barnes to convince a certified lunatic to go on a rampage, even though Laura Garrity's assaulter was never caught."

"And?" I ask.

"If you're telling me the truth, that's clearly not true."

My head tilts. "Isn't it?"

He bites the corner of his lip. This is about when the last quack they assigned to me decided she didn't want to work with me anymore. Of course, the truth undermined my signed, sworn statement, but I was going to get locked up anyway after that day in Iron City. They'd found my lair, Chuck's research—heck, a room full of Iron City's wealthiest and most influential had heard Vinny basically call me out for what I was and me half-shout it over police sirens and bullhorns.

Statute of limitations doesn't count for murder, or for practicing decades of vigilantism, apparently. I made it easy and confessed, too. I had no choice. Laura was about to quit her job and dedicate herself to defending me against a new DA with a hard-on for justice. Honestly, I bet she could've gotten me off, too—spun it into some grand tale that a jury of peers with family members I'd saved would eat up.

But the truth would also incriminate her for staying silent over her father's cover-up. I couldn't drag Laura down with me. Turns out, that was all it took to erase my crippling fear of taking off my mask and everyone knowing who the Roach really was.

Saving Laura's future was my swan song. She'd have enough to deal with, raising a traumatized daughter to not turn out like me. I had faith in her.

And to the public, Vinny was called a psychopath used by a spited vigilante—not Michelle's father. Though, I knew Laura. One day, she'd tell her daughter the truth and she'd have brought Michelle up strong enough to handle it.

My only regret is that I can't talk to her anymore. After it all, she and Michelle moved out east to a bigger city, where she could be as important as she deserved to be. Some would say she ran from her demons, but not me.

I remember when she'd told me she was leaving, right at the end of the trial when my fate was sealed. I looked her in the eyes, and I could tell that, for the first time, that deep-seated fear was no longer present. She'd slain her monster, and now she was free.

"Live your life and don't worry about me. Call us even for all you've done for me. All the money, all the favors. I love you, Laura."

Of course, I didn't say any of that. Our eyes had said all that needed to be said. Then, we'd hugged and never in my six or so years of being in a wheelchair had I wished my legs worked more. So I could really embrace her. Hold her.

But that was it. No visits since, no calls. She was taking my advice to keep herself and Michelle safe. Or maybe, after everything, I'd finally gotten what I wanted and convinced her to stay away. To stop wasting her time on me.

Maybe she blamed me for a monster aiming a gun at her daughter's head. That'll change a woman for sure.

All I know is it wouldn't make sense, us remaining friendly with what I'd been charged with. She'll have to keep her distance until I get out—in three lifetimes, one for each of the three Russian girls—or until nobody cares anymore, which I suspect wouldn't be forever with how fast the world seems to move these days.

Even the prison put a new Macintosh computer into the library, fully equipped with something called Grolier's Multimedia Encyclopedia. Man, if I'd had access to this kind of information in my heyday, the Roach could have cleaned up three cities. And that's right, I've been reading in the library when I'm allowed. Learning some things. Turns out, books are worth checking out and not just keeping on a bookcase to look pretty. I'm not a fast reader, but I have plenty of time.

"I'm not your enemy, Mister Roberts," Doctor Dan says after I'm silent way too long, lost in my own head. "This can be a good thing. A way to make your time here more—"

"Meaningful," I say for him. "The last one said the same, and then, I got you."

"Well, I have no plans on giving up on you."

"Oh yeah? I must be your crown jewel." I make a flourish with my hands and pronounce, "The shrink who can crack the Roach."

He smiles. The kind of warm, pleasant smile that begs you to trust a person. Mother used to wear the same one. Each time, I so wanted to trust her, wanted to believe that when she brought us cake for Christmas that single day of the year, she wasn't merely trying to keep us quiet so she could watch her shows.

"I don't want to crack anything," Doctor Dan says. "We don't have to talk about what happened last year. We can talk about anything you want. You're the one who decided to tell me that story."

I was? I scratch my chin. I guess he's right. He sat down a few weeks ago, and I just kept spilling it to keep him from asking a million useless questions like the last ones and driving me crazy. While I'm coming clean, I suppose his predecessor didn't just leave after I told her about my false confession. I kind of got angry and threw something until guards had to restrain me.

But isn't that the point of all this? To get me to dig deep?

Doctor Dan had tricked me, though. Just let me ramble my stream of consciousness no matter how grim it got, in an almost blithe manner. No intention of checking off boxes that he'd done his job with another worthless criminal and could go home to better things.

"I've got plenty of stories," I say.

"And I look forward to sticking around to hear them all." Doctor Dan glances toward the clock and reveals how full of crap he is. "But they'll have to wait until next week. Unfortunately, our time is up, Mister Roberts."

He stands. I huff. Of course, I'm just another patient to him. He's no genius sitting back and listening, asking me how I feel. I'm a walking paycheck—an hour of entertainment, like a shitty re-run of Miami Vice.

He walks toward the door, ready to release me back to the pens, to the other murderers and crackheads who have no idea who I am up here. When I first got shipped across the state to Steeltown Penitentiary, I thought I'd have a target on my back.

None. I'm yesterday's news.

Doctor Dan stops. He turns, and something strange ripples across his features. I'm not sure if it's curiosity, or pity, or genuine compassion, but it's clear as day.

"You mentioned a young boy named Steven Dixon a handful of times," he says.

"And?" I reply. "I didn't have many other friends growing up."

"It's just... I looked up foster homes on farms that burned down around the midwest. Kind of a narrow category."

He laughs at his own joke. I'm not amused.

Clearing his throat, Doctor Dan continues. "I know you don't know what your birthday is, but I estimated. I found a home out near

Kenesaw, Nebraska. It was run by a Vince and Charlotte Miller before the entire estate burned down for unknown reasons."

I clutch the arms of my chair. My heart didn't skip a beat, no, it felt like it full-on stopped. I hadn't heard their names in decades.

"A bunch of the kids disappeared after," Dan goes on. "Most are still missing. Not surprising considering how you've told me they treated children. But the government kept track of who was placed there through the system. There's no Reese Roberts on record."

"Maybe the records burned up," I say, though I'm not sure if the words come out. I barely have enough air to breathe, let alone speak.

"The records weren't kept at the home."

Doctor Dan approaches my chair. I feel nauseous.

"There is no Reese Roberts, is there?" he says. "It's like a name stripped right out of a comic book—like the one you and Steven kept hidden under your pillow."

"What are you talking about?" I whisper. My throat is closing.

He gently lays his hand upon my shoulder. He's trying to be consoling, but I want to choke him until he breaks. Yet, I can't move. My whole body is seized up and as useless as my legs.

"I'm so sorry for what he did to you, Steven," he says. "No child deserves that."

My hand shoots out. I clutch Doctor Dan by the throat, and he calmly stares down at me. He can scream and the guards will drag me out and throw me in solitary for another month. He doesn't. And I wish I can wring his skinny neck, but I can't.

Instead, I'm crying. It's a strange experience for me, so I'm not sure at first, but yep. This is it. The real thing. I've seen enough other adults do it to know. Still, Dan doesn't panic. He takes my arm and attempts to remove my hand.

I don't let him. I pull him in close, so my face is buried in his chest and nobody can hear me weeping. That's when the bullies came out, back in my foster home. When I was alone and vulnerable at night. When I cried.

The prison guards must hear something because they burst in.

Still, Doctor Dan doesn't panic. He sticks out a hand to stop them, then leans in close until his beard is scratching against my sodden cheek.

"It's okay, Steven," he whispers in my ear. "He can't hurt you anymore."

Prison isn't so bad. Honestly. The food's decent, and I get more time outside than I used to being holed up in my house. The air out here in the country is cleaner, too. Refreshing. I can sit in the corner watching brutes lift weights or play basketball.

They all say they're innocent. That's the game, isn't it? I've always been good at reading people, and here, I can pick out who did what in no time. I suspect a few of them really are innocent. Or repentant, at least. Maybe Montalvo was right and there were a few more criminals out there I could have given a second chance.

Though, look how he turned out. I still have no answer whether or not he tipped off Chuck Barnes, but it doesn't really matter now that they're both dead. Poor Chuck. Rough way to go out, but at least he finally got the story of a lifetime. A posthumous revelation unveiling the Roach that should win him a Pulitzer. All the same papers that black-marked his career published it.

Oh, and Mayor Garrity? Wouldn't you know it, but he lost by a hair. It seemed the people of Iron City were ready for a change even before knowing the truth. I like to think Iron City is better off. I'm really not sure. And I'm almost relieved it's not my problem anymore.

I know that as long as Iron City has women like Clarice, and kids like Isaac—it'll be in better hands than when I first got there, way back when.

That's all I really ever wanted, isn't it?

"Roberts!" the prison guard calls over. "You have a visitor."

I sigh and glance up at the bit of blue sky peeking through the caged top of the exercise court. I want to say, "No." I know who it is.

All the way across the state, and they can't help but come every month, on the dot, like clockwork.

I don't deny them and follow the guard inside. I'm pretty sure the other inmates are jealous of my treatment. No matter what I say or how I curse, the guards tend to treat me like glass. Back in Iron City, I'd hated it, but here—it's kind of enjoyable. All these hardened criminals wishing they were in a wheelchair so they wouldn't get shoved quite so hard back into their cells by overzealous guards.

I roll through my detention block, past my lockup. I have a cellmate who'd baked his mind doing too many drugs. He talks to himself every night, kind of like white noise from my TV. Could be worse.

My cinderblock wall is devoid of anything except for Chuck's story about good ol' me. It wasn't a prize or a memento. Nothing like that. Someone had snapped a picture during that affair in Aurora Tower, and in the background there she was—my Laura—holding her beautiful daughter while she stared at the wheelchair-user front-and-center in the image.

Right above her, the headline, THE ROACH UNSHELLED, crops off half of Mayor Garrity's face. A year later now, he's learning what it feels like to be forgotten. To be a footnote in the history of an ever-changing city.

They're like that, cities: living, organic things, all based on the same shit but evolving in their own directions.

Who knows, maybe Garrity's vision for Iron City would come true and it'd become some tech-loving hippy haven for geniuses and creatives to nest up and breed. Or maybe, a reduced focus on safety would let all the infestations I'd burned away return to pump it with drugs and weapons. All I know is that Iron City had to evolve beyond the Roach.

"Hands," the guard addresses me as we stop outside of a metal detector. I don't fight him. I'm doing this new thing where I try to be a good role model when innocent people are around, and the visitation room is full of them.

The guards are careful as they cuff me. What do they think I'm going to do, shank a few men and escape? Roll off into the forest until —what—an oversized root blocks me?

No, I'm here to stay. And as I roll across the stained tile floor, my monthly visitors await me across a glass divider. Every time, I wish it's Laura. That she's finally ignored my wishes and says, "Fuck the stories they'll write," and travels back across the country just for an hour with me.

It's not.

She's too smart to put Michelle in any more risk. Or maybe, after everything, I finally got what I've always asked for and convinced her to stay away. To stop wasting her time on me.

When or if she ever decides to pay a visit, I'll be right here. And I'll never complain if she doesn't. Never judge her.

I'd do it all the same, over and over. I'd suffer everything I had from the day I was born to parents who'd abandoned me to the day the Castrated Man dragged me into the Horton. As long as it meant Laura and Michelle were safe, I'd change nothing.

"Reese!" Isaac exclaims. I can read his lips even before I have the receiver to my ear.

"Fifteen minutes," the guard says.

I sigh, pick up the phone. Clarice does the same, holding it so both her and Isaac can listen.

"Hey kid," I say, offering a paltry wave. My face doesn't get the message to temper my excitement, and a slight smile shines through. Isaac's mom notices it and smirks. I feel my cheeks go hot. There's a certain level of attitude in her smiles that I can't help but enjoy.

"How you doing, Reese?" she asks.

Quite a loaded question. In the moment, I feel grateful. I hate that I feel that way, but I do. I know I should tell them to stop wasting their time visiting like I used to tell Laura all the time, but I can't. One weekend a month, Clarice takes time off work to drive her son across state to come and visit a man he calls his "hero."

Despite everything made public about me, despite my own

confessions, Isaac isn't disgusted by me. I don't even have to tell him most of it isn't true—he just knows.

He sits across from me and tells me about how he handled this bully at school or that he tried out for the basketball team and made a few friends. That he wound up being a starter because he's sprouted tall over the last year.

We talk about normal things, and I'm grateful. Maybe Doctor Dan broke something in me, but presently, tears well in the corners of my eyes as I watch them get comfortable across from me.

"Are you okay?" Isaac asks.

My throat's tight, so I nod. I look around at all the visiting wives, mothers, and children—people clinging to the hope that their locked-up loved ones might be able to become decent members of society one day.

Most won't.

They're too damaged, or deranged, or greedy. But as I look around, I strangely find myself wondering which of the orange-clad inmates on my side of the glass can surprise me. Who among this sea of corruption and malfeasance is Steeltown's Tinman? Who's more than he appears?

I have my eyes on a few with potential. Though they'll probably disappoint, I've been wrong before. And if I'm not, that's okay, I'll handle them.

I'm locked in here with them. The Roach won't let them hurt anybody ever again.

...

EPILOGUE

Another visitor for me in paradise. It isn't the proper hours, so a part of me hopes its Laura pulling strings. No different from usual, really. It's been months, maybe she's attorney general or something by now. The guards bring me to a private meeting room—the kind where feds question the incarcerated.

No glass divider. Nobody else is here, just a single man sitting at a lone table set up just for us. The guards even take my cuffs off.

"Reese Roberts," he says, elbows up on the table fingers steepled. "Or should I say, The Roach."

He seems proud of the comment, as if that is common knowledge by now. And as I get closer, I realize that I know him too. Only he doesn't have a cool nickname, so we'll call him rich, cowardly, shitbag.

"Benji Aurora," I say. All I can picture is him hiding under the table while Vinny threatens Laura and Michelle. Being a pathetic waste of a man. Definitely not here to interrogate me then.

"It's good to see you again." He stands, pushing out his chair with a screech and extends his hand. I don't shake it.

"Is it?"

He frowns, returns to his seat.

"I was really impressed with everything you did that night," he says. "Seriously."

"Likewise. The way you clutched the leg of a chair, it was..." I kiss my fingers like a chef finishing up a five-star meal.

His frown darkens to a grimace.

"I know," he says. "It wasn't my finest moment. But it showed me that I can make more of a difference. You inspired me, Reese."

Well, that is unexpected. "Oh, God. Please tell me you don't want to produce a made-for-TV movie."

He shakes his head. "No."

"Silver screen? Wow. I never would have—"

He cuts me off. "Nothing like that. Though..." He scratches his chin. My glare silences him before he even asks.

"Then what do you want?" I ask.

"Your help."

"I don't—"

He raises a finger, silencing me this time. "Just listen," he says. "Some people might not see it, but you made a real difference in that city. I did my homework. Now your methods, they were... we'll just call them questionable."

I scoff. "Let's."

"But it's a solid foundation," he continued.

My brow furrows. "For what?"

"A team," he says, a perfect smile spreading across his face. "Masked heroes, like you, taking justice into their own hands. With my financial backing, it'll be the best. Top-notch training. Tech. You name it. I already have some good people interested, but I figure—we can't do this without the first."

He leans closer. His breath reeks of, well, nothing. He's perfect.

"You can teach us," he says. "Tell us all your mistakes, successes. Show us what it takes from someone who's actually done it. Heck, fight with us. I have enough money invested in robotics. We can get you up out of that chair."

I blink at him, incredulous. You know how many dreams I've had where I'm running around the city, legs fast and strong? And here he is, giving me this sales pitch. A network of vigilantes? A team? All because he's embarrassed that he pissed his pants.

"Of course, I can't promise that but why not try?" he says. "We want you on our side, Reese. What good are you locked in here? I'll pull some strings, get you—"

"Hey, Benji," I cut him off.

"Yeah?"

"Fuck off."

FROM THE PUBLISHER

Thank you for reading *THE ROACH*.

We hope you enjoyed it as much as we enjoyed bringing it to you. We just wanted to take a moment to encourage you to review the book on Amazon and Goodreads. Every review helps further the author's reach and, ultimately, helps them continue writing fantastic books for us all to enjoy.

If you liked this book, check out the rest of our catalogue at www.aethonbooks.com. To sign up to receive a FREE collection from some of our best authors as well as updates regarding all new releases, visit www.aethonbooks.com/sign-up.

JOIN THE STREET TEAM! Get advanced copies of all our books, plus other free stuff and help us put out hit after hit.

SEARCH ON FACEBOOK:
AETHON STREET TEAM

CPSIA information can be obtained
at www.ICGtesting.com
Printed in the USA
LVHW110056301220
675391LV00006B/209